the
lonely
crowd

Praise for The Lonely Crowd

'Three cheers for The Lonely Crowd! Beautifully packaged, each issue is lovingly curated and filled to the brim with vibrant and vital new works of fiction, poetry and criticism. It's a cause for celebration that Wales finally has a journal that's seriously committed to publishing new writing from voices both emerging and established.

Indeed, readers should rejoice that here's a journal in whose lovely pages they'll encounter debut work side by side with international writers of world renown.

The Lonely Crowd has everything I want in a journal – it is urgent, it is eclectic, and I never quite know what I'm going to discover next. Without a doubt, The Lonely Crowd is the most exciting thing to happen to literature in Wales in a very long time.'

Thomas Morris, *winner of the 2016 Wales Book of the Year and the Somerset Maugham Prize for* We Don't Know What We're Doing.

'*The Lonely Crowd* is a truly exciting addition to the literary landscape in Wales and beyond, with an international outlook and a constantly surprising and refreshing mix of short fiction, poetry and interviews. The production values are a joy, and make each issue a pleasure to look at, to handle, and to browse in. There is outstanding work by newcomers and veterans, the already and the not yet famous. One to buy, one to read, one to watch, one to keep.'

John Freeman, *author of* What Possessed Me *(Winner of the Welsh Book of the Year for Poetry, 2017)*.

'The Lonely Crowd is a beautiful journal. The quality of the writing in each edition is consistently high and there is always a refreshing range in terms of genre and form. It's a place where you can find established and new talent, if you want a taste of the contemporary Welsh literature scene there is no better place to look.'

Kate North's second poetry collection, The Way Out, *is out now from Parthian. Her debut short story collection,* Punch, *is published by Cinnamon Press. Kate is the Chair of Literature Wales.*

the lonely crowd

five year anniversary issue

Editing & Design John Lavin
Cover Photo Jo Mazelis (jomazelis.wordpress.com)

Special thanks to Michou Burckett St Laurent, Marian Lavin,
Martina Evans, Thomas Morris & Anne Griffin.

Published by The Lonely Press, 2020
Copyright The Lonely Crowd & its contributors, 2020
ISBN 978-1-9164987-4-7

The Lonely Crowd is an entirely self-funded enterprise. Please
consider supporting us by subscribing to the magazine here
www.thelonelycrowd.org/subscribe

Please direct all enquiries to johnlavin@thelonelycrowd.org
Visit our website for exclusive online content
www.thelonelycrowd.org
Follow us on twitter @thelonelypress
Facebook The Lonely Crowd
Instagram @thelonelypressltd

*This issue is dedicated to my dear father,
John Terence Lavin, 1947 – 2020.*

Contents

five years

And Her Father
Niamh MacCabe

and her father standing with her
and his hand upon her shoulder
and her head hung low   scarf around her neck
and her hands   coupled hard   twisted fingers pleading

his hand low on her shoulder   standing there beside her
watching her head stoop   watching a slow fall
watching hair unravel   to hang over her face
to fall over her shoulders   as she unknots the scarf

and she bending low to place her warm silk scarf upon the child
an infant   fingers woven   lying on a marble slab
eyes-sunk and   hollow fontanelle   laid on the darkening slab
sun-setting   and his hand held on his dark daughter's shoulder blade

and she saying she can't leave a child   not here   no   not her child
too cold in here   it's too cold here   too dark   too cold   too hard
a child   her little girl   laid here   this is no place for her
there's nothing here   no warmth   no light how can she think of it

sky-low   and his hand laid still   still there   upon her shoulder
his left hand   laying soft   it barely touching her hunched shoulder
his eyes close   his slow breath holds   he listens to her pleading
and waits for her   prays low for her   stays standing still beside her

Tin
Nuala O'Connor

Patricia says Malachy and I should live with her at the farm once we're wed.

'There's no sense in you moving away, Kit,' she tells me. 'Either of you. There's room aplenty here.'

And it's true for her; Malachy has worked our farm, alongside Patricia, since Daddy died and I've known nowhere but Aghnagrena in my eighteen years.

'We'll stay, surely,' I say.

The day of the marriage Patricia races home before us to lay out a breakfast of boxty, eggs and farls. When we get to the front door I pause, but Malachy barrels ahead of me into the house.

'Carry her across the threshold altogether, will you?' Patricia calls from within and, because it's she who says it, he comes back, scoops me up and over we go to our new life. My face aches from the grin that's been on it since I woke.

We eat our meal in silence save for the sounds of our cutlery, but we can hear the burble of the hens in the yard and the call of the brindled cow who bellows in the low field like a hawker at a fair.

'Thank you, Patricia,' Malachy says when his plate is clean as the moon, 'that was good eating.' He rises to change out of his Sunday suit into his working duds.

'I've put ye into my room,' she says. 'Both your things are in there now. I'll take the wee bedroom at the end of the corridor.'

'No, we couldn't up-end you,' I say but, really, it's what I've hoped for. What use is a wide mattress to a spinster? Mammy would have wanted Malachy and me to have the marriage bed, not my sister, it's as plain as that.

'You're awful good, Patricia,' Malachy says. 'Thanks again.' He sends that small, lit-up smile he reserves for her across the table and goes up the stairs.

Down the years there has always been an ease between Patricia and Malachy that's hard for others to slip between. It's as if they have an invisible rope that binds them and no one can get beyond it, not even me. Their attachment didn't bother me overly much before, but I'm the woman of the house now and I won't have Patricia sharing soft looks with my husband. Mrs Cahill from down the way – who has watched out for us since Mammy passed – told me I need to announce myself. So I rise now and step away from the table; I place Patricia's old cushion onto the settle by the wall and I sit into Mammy's chair by the fire. I see my sister get up from the table and pause, but then she begins to clear the dishes. I put my feet near the glow of turf and watch her.

There's not much to Patricia: she's broad of face and of hip, with a solid, simple nature. Patricia was Mammy's firstborn and I'm the scraping of the same bag. She and Malachy are the one age. Still, it was always going to be me that he would marry, despite the ten years between us. I have black hair to my waist and a slender frame and, from a girl, Mammy meant me for wedlock. Not with a farmer but, with half the men gone to France to fight the Kaiser, Malachy does me grand. I know him, it seems, all my life and isn't there comfort in that?

The bedroom is aired and dusk-bright, the sun doesn't slide beneath the low field until after eleven these nights. Patricia has left a jug with grasses and butter-eyed daisies on the chest of drawers and I pull at the petals, too hastily perhaps, for I end on he-loves-me-not. I'm beginning on another flower when Malachy comes in; I drop the daisy and sit on the edge of the big bed, my heart a-wallop behind my ribcage. He doesn't look at me but takes off his shirt and trousers, folds them and sets them on the chair. Malachy turns to me in his undershirt and nothing else.

'You look lovely, Kitty,' he says, the words rasping up from his throat, and I run my hands over the white chemise that Patricia helped me to sew. I open my arms to him and he comes.

All day I hold our first night to me, the strange, glittering secret of it, the pain and the push of it. I had expected kissing, but Malachy kept his head to the pillow, the better to muffle his pants and cries, I suppose. But his touch was gentle and reverent, a soft cajolery into the darkest, silken parts of me. There was a certain violence in the act itself, to be sure, but there was also love; I could feel that it was love, I know for sure it was that.

I sit in my fireside chair and watch Patricia lift the kettle – she has the bread made already – and I feel a bit triumphant that I have done something she will never do. I've known a man and she won't ever be able to say that. My skin seems to burn and bloom today, but still I crave more heat.

'I'll have my breakfast here by the hearth,' I say, and I remember that Mammy often took her meals in this chair, away from us at the table, and I'm glad I took the notion.

'As you wish, Kit,' Patricia says, but she doesn't smile at me or acknowledge that I'm a woman now and a tiny part of me wants to pinch her for spite.

When I have eaten my porridge, finished my tea and licked jam from my fingers after a toasted farl, I get up.

'I'm away down the boreen to see Mrs Cahill,' I announce and, though Patricia looks as if she might want to say something, she doesn't.

Mrs Cahill runs out from her cottage to welcome me and she pulls me to her apron with cries of, 'Kitty, Kitty, you're all grown up now.'

She has tears in her eyes and she drags me inside to sit with her. I'm surprised to see Mr Cahill within – he's normally on the land – and his eyes, too, are wet and I think he's crying with fatherly joy for me, until I see the letter in his hand.

'John is away to France,' he says, and he shudders and lets a peculiar gasp that I recognise as pain and I feel as if I should go home and leave them to their bewilderment.

Mrs Cahill bustles me to the fireplace and shoves me into a chair. 'John never once told us he meant to go, *a leana*. This letter is all we've had.'

They are stricken, the pair of them, and no rational words will come to my tongue, so I just shake my head like a fool. 'I'm so sorry,' I manage at last.

Mrs Cahill lunges forward and grabs my hand. 'John is his own person, we must leave him go. He's strong, he'll get through it all.' She swipes at tears with her fingers. 'But, Kitty, love, you mustn't fret over our woes. You are a woman today and may the Virgin bless you and make you fruitful.'

I put my hand to my stomach shyly and lean my head into Mrs Cahill's and we both laugh. Mr Cahill folds up their son's letter, puts on his hat and leaves the cottage.

I pluck bridewort and forget-me-nots on my way home, arranging them into a posy that I will put into the jug with the daisies, to pretty up our bedroom even more. *Our* bedroom; it pleases me to think those words. The dark part between my legs aches pleasantly and thoughts of Malachy's long, hot body cause a wee jolt down there that makes me smile. I cut across the field before ours and follow the trickle of the Owenbrean, hoping to spy my husband before he spots me. I come up to the river's easiest crossing place and I see him not far ahead of me, but Patricia is by him, they're sitting together on the big rock, their heads close. I wave and am about to call out, when my sister looks up into his face and his hand comes down to caress her neck. A white heat runs from my scalp to my toes. Malachy tilts Patricia's chin to his and his lips go to hers and he kisses her so slowly and so tenderly that I crash backwards and almost end up in the river. I want to scream, I want to bash their two heads together, I want to cry long and loud, but I can't seem to make a sound come from my throat. I drop the bunch of flowers and run up to the farm.

Patricia comes in, a butter-wouldn't-melt set to her, and I'm tempted to take the skillet and slam it into her face, to ruin those lips that have stolen kisses that are meant for me. Instead I continue with my bowl and my flour and my salt and my buttermilk.

'I'll make the bread in this house from now on,' I say.

'It's no bother to me to bake, Kit,' she says, and I grunt and tut, making her pause.

'*I'm* the wife,' I say. '*I'm* the woman of this house.'

Patricia sets down the basket of eggs she's brought in. 'Well, I know that, Kit.'

'See that you remember it,' I bark, not taking my eyes from her face that bears not a smidgen of guilt or upset or anything at all, and that infuriates me more.

Malachy comes to the door. 'What ails you, Kitty?' he says.

I sweeten my voice. 'Nothing at all, love,' I say. 'I was below in Cahills' before; I came back up by the Owenbrean. By the big rock. Now I'm making soda bread for you.'

They glance at each other and well they might. 'Any news at the Cahills'?' Malachy asks.

'Young John is gone to war.' I toss the dough onto the floured table. 'Oh, he was ever a brave fellow. A true *man*, that John. Loyal, you'd say.' I begin to knead. 'Isn't it a wonder every able, healthy man doesn't go to France or Turkey to fight to keep his family safe?'

'Go back to your corner, Kit,' Patricia snarls. I stop my bread-work and all three of us stand, grave still, staring at one another.

Malachy takes off before sun-up in the trap. I go down and Patricia is already dundering about the kitchen, bashing crocks and bowls and wooden spoons.

'Where is he gone?' No answer, just the cold of her back to me; I speak louder. 'Patricia, I said where is he gone?'

She turns and her look is not one I've seen before, a mix of vast impatience and venom.

'Aren't you the wife, Kit? Surely you know better than I where your husband is.'

I nudge the hours by. Though it's not like me, I scatter grain for the hens. I lead the cow to fresh grass. I sweep the floorboards in our bedroom and finesse the bedclothes. I sit into the windowsill and wait for the rise of dust in the lane that will mean he's returned. Eventually I get up and curl onto the eiderdown to rest my head on the pillow. My mind and my heart are churned up; I'm angry but I'm sorrowing and both are a bitter stew that seeps through my blood.

I must fall away to slumber, for I'm roused by murmurs below. I come down to find them either side of the fireplace, her head bent over stitching and his big hands around a bowl of mutton soup. My bile rises – I won't be treated like a trespasser in my own marriage, in my own home. I close the door to the stairs with force but neither of them looks my way. Malachy spoons soup into his mouth and Patricia shifts the sewing in her lap. I hang back like a ghost, then peer closer at the work my sister is doing and go to stand over her.

'What's this?' I say, lifting the grey-green sleeve of a rough jacket. She stares up at me, raw anger on her face now. I dip lower; she is sewing a khaki epaulette onto the shoulder, 'Inniskillings' it says.

'Your husband has joined the fusiliers.' Patricia lifts the jacket and bites the thread to break it, keeping her eyes fixed to mine. 'Are you happy now, Katherine?'

Mrs Cahill looks at me strangely. 'And he just decided to volunteer? Overnight?' She shifts in her chair. 'What does Patricia say to this?'

'What does it matter what she says?' I snap.

'You girls will have no man about the place, Kitty. The farm-work will become a burden. How will you manage?'

I begin to shake and a cascade of tears falls from my eyes. 'Maybe he won't go at all,' I say. 'Maybe it was a wee lie Malachy told, to shake me. A wee prank, just.'

Mrs Cahill kneels before me and puts her arms around my waist. 'There, there, *a leana*.'

Mr Cahill pulls his pipe from his mouth. 'Once a man has signed the papers, he has no choice but to go,' he says. 'He's free no more.'

Malachy is standing at the top of the low field looking down, rigid in his uniform. The grass keeps up a light dance, though it's bent with dew, and he stays, staring out over Aghnagrena as if it's the last place he will ever see.

I come up beside him. 'Won't you let me take you in the trap to

Enniskillen?' I say.

He shakes his head. 'Is Patricia still sleeping?'

'She is.' I look up at his face, cankered with worry. 'You haven't even told me what you'll be doing over there.'

'I'm to be a stretcher-bearer. That's all I know.'

I start to ask him what that means but, of course, I know exactly what it means. We hear the trundle of a cart and Mr Cahill pulls up in the yard; he whistles, a sharp summons that cuts through the dawn like a bullet.

Malachy stoops and kisses my cheek. 'Goodbye, Kitty. Look after one another, won't you?'

I watch him trot up the field to Cahill's cart and hop in.

'Don't go, Malachy,' I whisper, my body reaching out to his like sun rays to the earth. 'Don't go,' I wail, my tears falling heavy.

But, in a moment, he's disappeared from sight.

Mrs Cahill is sitting at her table, idle as a crone.

'We both have men gone to war now,' I say.

'Men, is it?' She thumps the table. 'Sure they're only boys.' Her fire is dying and the bread's not on, so I go and stoke the embers and take the big bowl from the dresser. 'Away now, Kitty,' she says. 'See to your own house.'

She comes and grabs the bowl from my arms and I whimper, turn about, and leave.

Our place is sore neglected. Patricia lies in bed half the day, moaning into the pillow, and she only nibbles at the meals I bring. The hens peck my ankles and the brindled cow is sullen and she bucks when I milk her. When I go and complain to Mrs Cahill she just nods and shakes her head. Mr Cahill follows me out to the lane when I leave.

'Put away your grousing, young miss, her mind is full with her own concerns.'

'We can be a comfort to one another. We can talk about Malachy and John.'

He snorts. 'To think Patricia gave him up to you.'

I snap my head up to look at him. 'What's that supposed to mean?'

'Kitty, you know fine well what it means.'

A letter comes from Malachy, addressed to both of us. I bring it upstairs to Patricia and sit on the bed to read it out. He tells us that he's lucky to be alive. He tells us cannon balls rain around them, their impact knocking some soldiers over, killing others.

'I watch bullets skitter like hailstones and already I am used to it. I see them dug into men's skin like ticks; when the Medical Officer tends to them, the fellows mewl the way an infant does. I bandage and carry the injured and move through dirt all day and all the time it's as if I'm waiting for the hand of God to lift me out of this awful, wretched place.'

'He's not sparing us, Patricia.'

She shakes her head, closes her eyes and shivers; I put my hand over hers and squeeze it tight.

The Cahills get two telegrams, the first on Christmas Eve to say that John is missing in action. The second, three days later, expresses the deep regret and sympathies of their majesties the King and Queen.

Patricia and I go arm and arm to the church for his memorial service. John will be buried where he fell in France. The Cahills look like they have been hollowed out; they are a pair of ghouls compared to the man and woman they once were.

Malachy writes to tell us he played football with the Kaiser's army on Christmas Day. He says Princess Mary sent each soldier a gift of a small tin, with a greeting card, tobacco and cigarettes, and her portrait engraved into the metal lid. He says he rubs her face and thinks of us both. *'I send love to you, Patricia and Kitty,'* he writes. *'Kitty and Patricia, I send all my love.'*

Patricia begins to wait by the gate. She is afraid, I think, that news will come and she will be asleep. Or that I will be handed the telegram first and have to bear its weight alone. She talks to herself out there and, today, while I tend to the hens, I move closer to listen to her whisper the same wee sentence over and over. I go nearer to hear better.

'If you perish, I perish,' she says. 'If you perish, I perish,' she repeats, soft and sweet, as if into her lover's ear. I go and stand beside my sister at our gate, putting my own shawl over her cold back. 'If you perish, I perish,' she says again.

'If you perish, I perish,' I echo.

And we stand huddled together, waiting for our man, while we send our words out over Aghnagrena like a prayer.

Two Poems
Hisham Bustani

Translated from the Arabic by: Thoraya El-Rayyes

A lesson in collapsing and attempting, once more

Good morning children.

Today, we will talk about the dancer. We will talk about her body. Her breath that rises and falls. Her tense muscles. Her tied-up hair. Her rigidity. Her litheness. How she senses empty space, senses fullness. Her fury. Her despair. Her hopes.

What did she want when she smiled at a red-painted wall? What did she see? There was no mirror hanging there. No audience. No spectators. No one. But she smiled. Perhaps she felt a certain lightness. Perhaps she thought she was flying, though both her feet were still on the rubber mat. Perhaps she felt weightless, like a cloud blown by the wind and shaped into something new. A cloud. Nothing matches the litheness of a cloud – nothing is as flexible, mutable, shapeshifting, receptive, responsive – acting and reacting.

Moment after moment, the cloud transforms: a beautiful face, a fish, a mountain meeting the sea, a sheep, a man leaning over, a pyramid, a cloud.

Perhaps she saw a cloud on the red wall or imagined herself to be a cloud upon it. It used to be that she wanted to be the wind, but the wind is invisible – creates shapes without being seen.

With supple arms, the dancer will tread lightly towards the red wall and push her fingers into it. She will lean forward and back. Retreat suddenly, then attack. She will push herself up against it. Will scream, then collapse crying on the floor when the wind stops.

The faces, the pyramids, the strange animals have faded. Nothing is left but her, her single body that emerges unchanged after rehearsal has ended, after the show is over. The wind dies down and she returns home as she had been, the same height, weight, form.

This is why the dancer cries all day.

Do you understand children? Do you understand the lesson of the dancer's story?

*

The last bell of the school day will ring now, and the windows will open so the children evaporate from them one by one, towards the sky.

The dancer will stop crying for a few moments to watch the clouds pass her window and will try, perhaps, once more.

A hand crushing the heart, halting its beat

People chatting. They do not care about the fingertips of the pianist intent on striking the keys softly/loudly. They do not notice the expressions on her face, tensing up and transforming. They do not even notice her faded smile as she turns towards a polite clap coming from the corner of the hotel lobby, from the man who requested that hit song. Inside her, a musician was consuming her innards piece by piece. A bite of the liver, a bite of the intestine. Then a hand crushing the heart, halting its beat. One moment. Two moments. Three. And she smiles.

What tragedy cast the pianist away here, to this place where the only inhabitant is her everyday sadness rising from between the vibrating strings? Which war pushed her to dress up every evening as if about to perform with an orchestra to an audience thirsty to see other angles of themselves/the world that are only observable through her, so that her body fades away and nothing remains but sound not held in any hand, sound that does not endure unless that string is vibrating, that key is pressed.

Wars aren't only fought with weapons. In some wars, the bombs are members of the family. There are battles where the blast of the bullets sounds like a wife yelling, where the artillery shells are the pressure of the job. There is ethnic cleansing carried out by the militias of stupidity and ennui. The causalities of nuclear winter walk past you every day in the street. Black shadows like those left on the walls in Hiroshima. They are present and absent. Her fingers are present and absent. Who, then, presses the keys? Who brings those sounds forth out of the wooden black box? And the fist around the heart squeezes and squeezes. And the teeth digging into her innards have started to gnash.

It is time for an intermission.

'Where are you going?' asks a woman in the middle of the lobby who hadn't stopped blabbing for a second as the music played.

'It is time for an intermission' she said carrying her colored dress and faded smile, as the musician dripped, colliding – drop by drop – with the floor with each step she took towards the exit.

Repossession
Mary Morrissy

I had gone to bed early — taken a pill, in fact — I have to these days, so I came to, in an open-mouthed panic as if fresh from some nightmare, and there was a woman standing at the end of the bed. And the strange thing was I wasn't surprised. It's our stalker, I thought immediately.

'Who are you?' I asked.

She didn't answer.

'Can't you guess?' she said

She was a woman on the wrong side of 50 with lank brown hair parted in the middle, a plain face, prominent pallid eyes, a carbuncle of some kind over her top lip, a canker, a mole, a wart maybe? She was shrouded in something dark, a cape it looked like, which swamped her and she was gripping the end of bed, white-knuckled, as if the wooden frame was all that was keeping her grounded. Not a ghost, then.

I could see my mobile winking on the bedside table.

'Don't,' she said as if she knew what I was thinking.

'Is it money you're after?' I looked at her eyes; they seemed clear. So it wasn't drugs. Yours? hers?

'What good is your money to me?'

'Look, tell me what you want or I'll have to call the police. You shouldn't be here. You're in my house.'

'Actually, Shel,' she said, 'that's just it.'

Shel? Only Brian calls me Shel.

'What do you mean?'

'I mean, it's my house, actually.'

That's when I went to nudge Brian awake. And then I remembered, Brian wasn't here. . .

*

23

It was the first time I'd been alone in the new house. That's what we call it because it's new to us but it's actually old, a cut-stone 19th century gate lodge, with diamond-paned windows and curlicued eaves, a Hansel and Gretel house set in a little wooded hollow, beside a sweeping driveway that once led to the Vandeleur Estate. The big house was demolished in the Eighties and an estate of houses built in its place. They're big, double-fronted palaces, classy enough if you like that sort of thing, with a landscaped green in the centre, where the original Vandeleur House stood. It's as if the developers left it vacant like a portal to the past. Was this where the woman had come from? From some cleavage in time?

Years ago when I was helping one of the girls with a school project, I'd looked into the history of Vandeleur House. It had its usual cartel of scandal. A titled family beset by generations of beleaguered marriages, renegade sons, financial ineptitude. The last family incumbent of the house was in the 1950s, an ex-British Army major, all handlebar moustache and regimental epaulettes, who in his dotage had impregnated his housekeeper. That was the story, anyway. Not a maid, mind you, but an older woman who should have had more sense. The unfortunate woman gave birth to the baby and then walked out into the sea. Oh yes, didn't I mention that? We face the sea. Opposite us, across the coast road, there's a small shingled beach, spattered with seaweed and shells.

In the Vandeleur story it wasn't clear what happened to the child – probably shipped off to an orphanage somewhere, farmed out. Major What-What wasn't going to have a little bastard running around the place. I love these historical tragedies – so bleak, so merciless in their resolution.

*

'You're out of your mind,' Brian had said when I told him there was a stalker outside. Stalker was the wrong word because it was too active for what this woman had been doing. She'd just been standing there like a sentry, since the start of our occupation. Occupation, that's a funny word.

Since we'd started work on the house. Brian hadn't noticed her. He's not observant like that and anyway all his attention was turned inward on what was happening inside.

*

It was a fright I can tell you. The house, I mean. There were times when I thought, my god, what have we done? Upstairs, where the previous owners' renovation hadn't reached, they had resorted to metal pails to catch the rain that was coming through the dodgy roof slates. The kitchen was tragic, although this was the part of the house that had been worked on. Awful country-style cabinets, faux rustic vinyl on the floor. The bedrooms were painted icy colours; the peppermint green of the bathroom would give you migraine. A charming sun lounge at the back was rotting quietly away into compost.

The stalker and the skip came together. At first, I thought she was one of those skip scavengers, as I used to be myself in my student days. Couldn't pass one without a rummage. But she wasn't one of those. Too passive, for one. She never budged from her spot under the laburnum tree, where the road forked – one way went towards the Vandeleur Estate houses, the other turned into our property.

'See,' I said to Brian, 'there she is again.'

I pointed to the shadowy figure, sheltering under the yellow spread of the tree. He peered out.

'Okay,' he said doubtfully.

'Go out,' I said, 'ask her what's she doing.'

'Last time I checked, Shel, it's not an offence to stand out on the public road minding your own business.'

'But she's not,' I said.

'Not what?'

'Minding her own business. She's minding ours.'

'Now you're being paranoid. If you're so het up about her, why don't you go and talk to her?'

But I didn't. Why? Because I didn't trust myself, or my own instincts. Maybe she was walking a slow dog? Maybe she had a reason to stand there looking out to sea? Maybe she had a secret assignation that had nothing to do with us at all? Maybe she was homeless and this was part of her regular beat, passing the time before the hostel in town opened up? Maybe she had squatted here while the place was empty? Or maybe it was just sheer coincidence that every so often when I would look out she just happened to be standing there on that particular spot. Not looking up or in at us; turned away, in fact, from the house. Implacable as a gate post. And then we went away on holidays – to escape the builders – and I forgot all about her.

*

What I do remember is the day Brian came home with the news the house was up for sale. That's something I remember very clearly.

'The gate lodge at Drunkard's Island is for sale,' he said.

'Where?'

'Drunkard's Island – you know, the Vandeleur place. That's what the locals always called it.'

Brian is from here so knows all the lore.

'My mother charred for the last of the Vandeleurs. When I was a boy she'd take me with her during the school holidays.'

'I thought your mother was a nurse.'

'Well, she was,' he said, 'but this was after. When she stopped being a midwife.'

He reminisced about the mirrored ballroom of the old house, the big old basement kitchen, the down-at-heel reception rooms with clackety parquet floors like loose teeth.

'All the mops and buckets and things were stored in the gate lodge at that time. That's where my mother would go to change into her overalls. She had a key. And sometimes I'd just kick about there while she walked up the driveway to do her slaving. It's funny but it makes me feel connected to the place, somehow,' he said.

It seemed a pretty meagre connection to me.

I'd never met Brian's mother; she had died before we got together. But she was a big presence in his life, so big that I was glad not to have had to deal with her. A gritty independent woman who had raised Brian alone after his father vamoosed to England to make some money on the buildings and never came back. Brian has a photo of her on his desk as a young woman, with her starched hat like a working girl's tiara, her nurse's cape and those shiny lace-up shoes they all seemed to have worn, standing by her bicycle. She was one of those practically beautiful women, as in she wasn't a beauty but she was vibrant and pert, with dark hair and a brave smile. And that passes for beauty when you look back at it. She delivered babies, that's what Brian had told me when I'd asked what she did.

'What happened?' I asked.

'What do you mean, what happened?'

'With your mother and the nursing?'

'Nothing happened.'

'You don't just give up a good job like nursing for nothing,' I said.

'She lost a baby, that's all,' Brian said eventually. 'Not her fault, the baby would have died even if it'd been born in the hospital. But mud sticks. . .'

The image of a down-trodden char on her hands and knees didn't fit with my image of his mother at all. I felt unaccountably put out.

'You never told me,' I said.

'Of course, I did, Shel. You've just forgotten.'

But you don't forget things like that, do you?

I didn't go to the auction. Call it sticking my head in the sand.

'They won't be there if that's what you're afraid of,' Brian said, meaning the previous owners.

He'd been campaigning for weeks, wearing me down.

'It's the kind of place we always dreamed of, Shel. And what's to stop us? Girls all gone. And what's more it's a bank sale so it'll be a steal.'

'You think so?'

'Look, some couple got in over their heads and couldn't make the repayments.'

'So someone's been evicted from the place?'

'Oh Shel, do you think any other potential buyer is thinking that

27

way? Anyway, it's a repossession, not the same thing.'

'Still and all.'

'We're doing no harm here, Shel.'

'I know but. . .'

'But nothing. . . we don't owe these people anything. They're as faceless as the banks.'

It wasn't Brian's arguments that won me over. It was seeing the place. It's hard to explain it because it was in such a parlous state – the dark dingy rooms, the smell of damp. But as I walked through it, I knew I was in love. I felt my heart expanding with that same mix of dread and surrender I remember from my youth. And it was so good to feel that again, to know I could, that I said yes, with my heart in my mouth.

'I knew you'd come round,' Brian said and his eyes were shining.

*

It was a second chance for us. Another second chance, I suppose. We'd made compromises all along the way. Got married in a hurry because Sue was on the way. The house we brought our girls up in, 9 Fallowfield, wasn't what we wanted either. We would have chosen a red-bricked Victorian if we'd had our way, but there was no way we could afford that. So we just knuckled down. It was a new estate then with rubbled open spaces, a once-in-a-blue moon bus service and a single shop operating out of a caravan. Makeshift, in other words, but not as bad as those ghost estates they talk about now with gaping man-holes and unfinished electrics.

By the time we left, the Fallowfield estate had matured. Blowsy gardens, wooden decks, two cars on the driveways. A huge shopping centre was built a five-minute drive away so it'd become a very desirable location, as the estate agent told us. Funny, it was only when we were selling it, I realised how little it meant to me even after spending a half a lifetime there. The girls were the ones who were sentimental about it. Sue wept over the marks at the end of the stairs where the baby gate had been. Linda sighed about the melamine bed and desk set we had installed in her room. Maura was lovingly condescending about 'the den', which we'd created for the girls when they were teenagers by converting the garage. It was a museum to adolescence.

'Now,' Brian said, 'it's our turn.'

He bid on the lodge and got it. We sold off all the furniture – Brian's mother's sun-striped sideboard, my parents' dining room table. Frightful stuff that we've never liked. We gave away a lifetime of bad ornaments (gifts from the girls) and fractured dinner services to the charity shop and vowed that at Drunkard's Island we'd start again.

And we did. The house is now painted in cool tones, open-plan kitchen in a full-blown modern extension. We've turned the peppermint bathroom into a dressing room and moved the facilities downstairs for our old age.

'It's so tasteful,' Maura cooed when she saw it finished. She's the middle child – or third, if you count Brian junior – and the hardest to please. She sounded surprised. Did she think we were going to reproduce 9 Fallowfield? I felt the decades collapsing, as if Brian and I were at the beginning again, except this time without children, just Briney and Shel, pet names, old dreams. . .

*

The woman ordered me to get up out of bed and, perhaps shamefully, I did what I was told though afterwards I couldn't tell the police why because she didn't have a weapon. She didn't threaten me in any way. She simply said, 'please get up and follow me' like a firm matron. When they questioned me on this, it made me sound feeble. But though her tone was gentle, I'd have called her manner gently bullying.

She took me on a tour, starting with the bedroom. *Here is where I measured my children's heights.* She pointed to a hollow behind the shutters which the painters must have missed. There seemed to be pencil marks on the old plaster like faint Ogham markings. She moved into the dressing room - *here is where my husband put up shelves on Christmas Eve that fell down in the night and my daughter thought was the noise of Santa Claus coming down the chimney.* She went out into the landing, turning on the lights as she went so the house was ablaze. She pointed to the now carpeted stairs – *Nick and I sanded and varnished this one hot summer night wearing only our swim-wear, breathing in the fumes and getting high on them.* She laughed fondly when she said this.

Down we went. In the tiled hallway she paused and said – *here is where my youngest had his first epileptic fit.* She pointed to the shadow of a door on the wall I'd never noticed. *We blocked this up to stop the children chasing between the front parlour and the dining room.* How quaint the designation of the rooms, I thought. All gone now.

In the kitchen, she stopped in front of the Belfast sink, the only item we'd kept. *Here's where Nick told me it was all over.*

'And here,' she said, back in the hall, pointing to the glass panels on the front door, which we'd also kept. 'Here is where the bank pinned the repossession notice.' She opened the door and steered me out. Seeing it was raining, she fished one of Brian's rain ponchos from the hall stand and handed it to me – a silly, yellow wizardy thing – and then she closed the door on me.

Outside, I felt foolish and rejected. I should call Brian, or the police, but I had no phone. I stood there, chilly and barefoot. I needed something for my feet. I made my way around the side of the house to the back porch where I knew there were spare Wellingtons. As I did, the woman inside followed my progress, scurrying from one window to the next, drawing the curtains in the lounge area, pulling down the blinds in the kitchen, quenching the warm lozenges of light inside. When I got to the shelter of the porch I heard the lock turning in the back door. The only boots I could find were Brian's, miles too big, but they were better than nothing. I put my feet in and felt their clammy roominess. I began walking, awkwardly, draped in the rain poncho, to the end of the driveway determined not to look back. I wanted to appear as if I was just taking a walk, and that everything was normal. But the rain had turned to downpour and when I reached the road, I had to take shelter under the laburnum tree. It had shed its blossoms now and its straw-coloured pods were scattered all over the ground. I bent to pick one up remembering those dire warnings from childhood – everything about this tree is poisonous. And that's the last thing I remember.

*

They found me – Brian and the search party – lying on the foreshore hidden behind rocks, still in my nightie, ensnared in bladder-wrack. They reckoned I'd been there for nearly 24 hours.

'What possessed you to go wandering about in the middle of the night like that?' Brian asked testily when I came out of sedation in the hospital.

'Let's not press her just now,' one of the attending nurses said. They'd had to pump my stomach because of the seeds.

I knew what he suspected. An outbreak of my old problem. I allowed him to think that. I thought maybe it would be easier to explain it to the police. But they had their own ideas. No sign of a break-in, no forced lock or smashed window, they said to Brian. If there was an intruder in the house, then Mrs Clarkin invited her in. Mrs Clarkin, that's me. Sounds odd. I don't recognize myself.

Once, shortly after we moved into the house I woke early in the morning and had the strangest sensation of not knowing who I was, as if I didn't recognize the inside of myself. You've no idea what an odd sensation it was, like a kind of unmooring, a slippage. I had to get up quietly and tiptoe around the house to find a mirror. I found one leaning against the wall in the spare bedroom. Once I saw my face, I knew of course. It wasn't like being lost, I knew where I was, I just needed my reflection to tell me who I was. I didn't say anything to Brian; I mean, it sounds stupid, doesn't it? I put it down to the move, being cut adrift from the familiar.

*

'It's the previous occupant of the house,' I told the plain-clothes detective who came to interview me in the hospital. 'She told me who she was.'

'I know the previous owners,' the detective said. 'Sad case.'

'The repossession, you mean,' Brian said.

'No, I mean the wife dying like that.'

31

'The wife died?' Brian said. He looked chastened.

'Suicide,' the detective said and looked embarrassed. 'After the sale. The times that are in it, I'm afraid. They lost everything.'

Brian looked at me. So much for doing no harm.

'So, you see,' the detective said looking straight at me, 'it couldn't have been Mrs Sewell you met.'

'Was her husband's name, Nick? She said her husband's name was. . .'

The nurse shushed me and asked Brian and the detective to leave and give me some rest. He and Brian stepped outside. As the door suctioned close, I heard him ask:

'Generally speaking, is everything okay with Mrs Clarkin?'

I didn't hear Brian's reply.

When he came back in, I decided to have it out with him.

'I can't go back there,' I told him.

'Don't be ridiculous,' he said, 'you just got a fright, that's all.'

'No, Brian, she's still there. Don't you get it?'

'Come on, now, Shel....'

'I can't be on my own there anymore.'

'But I'll be there,' he protested.

'Not always,' I said, 'you can't guarantee that.'

'Well, if I'm away, we'll get one of the girls to stay.' I recognized that tone. His mountains out of molehills voice.

'I'm not going to be baby-sat by my own children. Anyway, they have their own lives to lead. Isn't that why we moved? Free as birds, you said, empty-nesters.'

'And that's how it's going to be,' Brian insisted.

He took my hand and clenched it in his.

'I'm not going to leave you, Shel,' he said.

But that's not what I'm afraid of. I've never doubted Brian, not for a moment, but there are things about me he just doesn't understand, things I've never been able to tell him. Like when we lost Brian junior. Never took to him, can a mother say that about her own baby? Well, not out loud, she can't. And now, it's the same. I can't tell Brian what I'm really afraid of. It's not the house, it's her, the ghost, the dead woman, the stalker, whatever you want to call her. It isn't the house she's taken possession of, it's me.

Five Poems
Breda Spaight

Feast

The women in my family strip
succulent flesh from boiled pig's head,
savour the crunchy, salty ears at the outset,
its eyes fastened – wounds
above the long line of its snout-
mouth jellified in a smirk.

Their knives delve into the secrets of cheeks.
Their molars rend tenderised muscle fibre
marbling the cherry-red meat.
They turn the skull over on the platter – a pride with prey.
The sanctity of their feast flouts the law
of heaven and hell,
every golden grain swallowed
into bodies where bones and tendons
strum in January frosts,
backs bowed as they lope across stony fields against rain,
mid-calf Wellington scald at the hemline of Sunday bests.

The light from their kitchen windows,
deep down in the valley,
speaks in a small, sure voice
to the far off road.
Out of the quiet,
only the purr of scraped plates,
and out of the indigo dark,
a map of people not yet done.

Mother Returns from Hospital

The moment
is like the moment
I watched a fledgling's
feather float
    through
the
    on
and
     off
 of
   time,
     dun
as the music of a cello.
Her shaved head postponed
until my next breath.
For now the scar;
u-shaped above her right ear,
a flog of liquorice;
its hue the silence of birds
when dark falls; and I a lake
gaping at strips of cloud;
a swan to the right
of the washing machine,
its slender neck a perfect S
as it sails on the serene surface
of blue-banded cups and plates
piled in the sink; to
   and
             fro
of a   bluebottle's
  buzz.
Her scalp cygnet-grey.

The wash of iodine
a marigold map
to scalpel, drill,
the clamp that held her
head sure. The house
an atlas she wanders
wearing her green coat
over her stained nightdress;
scapulars as necklace;
and I mouthing the song
of the swan's ghost-white

                                        ascension.

Mother's Final Sleep in her Homeplace

She is still asleep
in her parents' room
close to her young spirit:
the dream of her.

Aunt Maggie
Grandmother and I sit
by the tight-lipped range.
The kettle's lid floats.
I am between puberty
and the carnal, and hope
Maggie will ask, as usual,
Is there a boyfriend yet?
Ash slips through the grate.

Already I'm part of Mother's past
and her future: she is done with both.
I know nothing of the tumour inside her.
I know nothing of her strength.

My role now is among women:
vigil-keepers of birth and death.

Life Lesson: No. 14

I never saw it coming. There was nothing
in how I knew Aunt Monica that prepared me;
Mother's sister the first adult to address me
as an adult: I am 4, exploring the novelty of her

staircase. She sits with me on the fourth step,
shares the sad fact that this is as far as I can go,
Until you're 5. Count to 5 for me.
Their letters were regular; Aunt Monica's

homeplace gossip in biro, pencil, or both;
always on pages torn from a copybook.
I recall her Christmas parcel; a goose on the train
from Galway, wrapped in layers of cardboard;

unplucked, its headless neck bound in bloody
newspaper, yielding her home's odour –
turf smoke's memory of bog cotton.
I stayed a week with her after Mother's funeral.

It was still ceremony; hours and days astray
in white mugs of sweet tea. Aunt Monica
roamed the rooms, kneading her hands; broke
out in, *Hail Holy Queen, Mother of mercy.*

I thought it was more prayer when she said,
Can I have her coat?

Yellow Bucket

It is All Souls'.
The yellow 2 gallon bucket
sits in the centre of the table,
the area around it blasted as though
it absorbs all the light in the sealed world
that is my mother's kitchen; discarded
eggshells littered among pudding bowls;
a white plate with odd-sized splashes of nutmeg,
mace, cinnamon, allspice that look and smell
like the map of an exotic country; the bottle of stout
an intruder beside chopped suet, and the demon eye of
glacé cherries: the Christmas bake has begun; the bucket
like something hauled from the earth's core, flour
and dried fruit lava-black with treacle, my mother's
face wish-tight, eyelids sweat-slick as she folds and folds
with a brush handle stub kept specially, the bucket clutched
to her breast as she wrestles to capture something from deep
within – the hope that this year he'll stay sober, if only
for the day. I feel I'm her prisoner, allowed only to watch,
and she is prisoner to me as though there's a better place
for her. In her body, now at the table, now at the range
is the silence of a life gone off course. I can no longer bear
to see, as if in watching her every step I'll imprint on her,
learn as a chick does. I've no memory of Christmas Day
– how could I? I flourished in her elation only: formed
by her wild, crazed self.

Pieces
Lisa Harding

They say shock can numb a person, make them get stuck at a certain point in time. You see your dad, say, whack your mum, and something inside you freezes and whatever it is you feel at that moment is what you feel over and over, to varying degrees, depending on the situation you find yourself in. If you're prone to replaying these beats, they can become more real than the very moment you're meant to be living. Your therapist is good at that stuff.

You never saw your dad beat up your mum, but you did see your mum beat up on your dad. With words, which lifted you both off your feet and slammed you against the wall. Dad left, but you didn't, because you were eight. Your mother said you were a hole in the condom. You were one great latex mistake. Or miracle! Whatever: you were the most popular girl in school, the lead in the school play, got an A-plus in everything, alongside gold stars.

You have spent your life seeking those gold stars since. On the day he told you it was over, you went to a children's craft shop and bought stars in all colours and sizes. You only wanted the small gold ones, and you glued them all over your mirror, and on your face. Ten years out of college by then, and not really making anything of your life. You're creative, Miles used to say, and it can take creative people a lot longer than other people to find their way. Since meeting him you haven't felt the urge to open the studio door. None of it was working out the way it was supposed to anyway and the dole said they'd cut you off soon, so you'd have to find a proper job, or a man to support you. The face that stared back at you with ticky tacky stars falling off it screamed back at you: Ridiculous, and you felt that longing to hurt it, see it cry.

You tried crying in the café that day. It had no effect whatsoever. You have never been able to make anyone cry (not since Sheena O'Malley

40

in third class, anyway). Miles was out on Saturday and he gave his business card to a friend of a friend of yours who is eight years younger, according to your so-called friend, Daisy, who always had an eye on him herself.

What did I do? You asked him when he told you it was over – his eyes dead as your hamster was the day you found it under your bed, the cat frozen beside it, shaking, shocked, and in thrall to its own nature.

People move on, he said.

Yes, but what happened? What happened? Just tell me what happened? Why?

He looks at you with no recognition in his eyes and he turns away. You know you should hate him, and like any normal person realize you had a lucky escape, but you just want him to be the same as he was three weeks ago. You want him to wrap you up in his arms and call you 'Birdie' and tell you you're lovely. You see, without that, you don't feel lovely. In fact you don't feel anything at all. And the necessary response to that is to *do something* about it. He is responsible for that. No he's not, your therapist tells you with a worried look on her face. I think I'd like to refer you on.

You cycle to his apartment in the middle of the day and stare in through the round window on the ground floor. He has left the window open, which is not like him, and you look at the crumpled cotton sheets and wonder why he hasn't made the bed. You climb in the window and stand at the bottom of the bed breathing in his familiar scent, kind of lemony, and there's something else, sweet and cloying, like candyfloss. You wrap yourself in the tossed sheets, drawing them close around you, and drift into a fitful sleep where you give birth to a fish with his face. You put it in an aquarium; feed it too much fish-food so it bursts.

When you wake it's dark and you're cold and you look at the bedside clock and it says 20.20. He'd usually be back by seven, and should be watching television now in his pyjamas, eating his chicken curry or something similar. You were the spontaneous one, such fun! He had never met anyone who was such fun.

You're starving, so you go to the kitchen with its massive fridge, which is empty, which is weird, as he was always so insistent about feeding you up – you who love to spin out from lack of food. There's an overripe banana on the worktop and you peel and chew and swallow, fleshy floury bruises. Stabilise blood-sugar levels and the world will right itself and maybe the tearing sensation will stop. He's falling apart: the bed unmade, the lack of food, the crumbs on the marble countertop. He didn't reject you; he was rejecting himself, poor man. You go into the power-shower which spurts jets of scalding water in all directions.

You hear the front door click open, and then shut. It's one of those modern thoughtful appliances of which Miles is very fond. Subdued, like himself. You hear voices and you wonder for a moment if he has come back with someone else, some rebound floozie. He's in that much pain after losing you that he can't bear to be alone. You wrap the towel around your breasts, skin wet and gleaming. He always loved you au naturel, damp hair, no make-up. He walks straight into the kitchen and you hear the clunk of a shopping bag on the counter. There's no other voice. He must be talking on the phone. Relief like wet liquid floods your body. You hear the rustle of shopping bags and the soft sucking sound of the fridge opening and closing.

Surprise! you say in a honeyed husky voice as he turns to face you. He's silent, his face hard, mouth tight. You adopt the battle stance, one shoulder coquettishly higher than the other. I missed you, you say, in what you think is a playful tone and you smile with your whole body. He used to say it lit you up from within, like a thousand-megawatt light bulb. You ramp it up for him now. He turns his back and tells you you have exactly two minutes to get dressed and go. He wants you to leave the key by the hall-door. You don't move but continue to beam at his stiff back, as if the warmth from your smile might thaw him out.

You've precisely one minute left, he says.

And what? Are you going to call the police? And say what? My ex-girlfriend has broken into my flat and is waiting to ravage me. I still have the key to your front door, so it wouldn't technically be a break in, would it? You're being ridiculous.

I'm being ridiculous. Laura, it's over.

It takes two to decide that.

Things change. Feelings change.

Nothing changed. I did nothing. I'm exactly the same person.

He has the good grace to look down, scuffs his shoe, like a little boy.

Did she come back?

No. (Beat) I don't want to talk about this. Please go.

You stand there, fingers itching to touch him.

It was only two months. Jesus. Draw a line under this and move on.

Such a cliché! Such a lack of imagination. You sense a perceptible shift in the atmosphere before he turns around and faces you. He stares at you for some time, as if you're a strange creature that's fallen to earth and landed in his home. A sexy ET! You smile at him, willing him to pick up on the magic of the moment, the fun. The corners of his mouth twitch. You're not going anywhere are you? He asks. He shakes his head, as if exasperated, but lovingly, with humour, you think. And then, he swerves: Want to stay for dinner? Green curry, your favourite. It's thrilling not to know what to expect from someone, which is why you knew his change of heart would change again. You go to him and put your arms around him. He tells you to get dressed, he'd like to see you fully clothed. His commanding voice has you helpless, so you trail back into the bedroom, soft cream carpet springing under foot, and dress carefully, expertly applying the no make-up make-up look, and arranging your hair in a just-fallen-out-of-bed look: tousled and wild.

When you emerge fifteen minutes later the candles are lit and the curry is simmering away. He lights the gas flamed fake fire which gives a warm amber glow to the room, casting shadows on the bare white walls. You'll persuade him one day to put in a real one. He hands you an enormous glass of red wine, a bowl really, and you giggle expectantly. He knows you're a terrible drinker and turn very wild with two glasses inside of you. You drink fast. He refills your glass a second and a third time but doesn't drink any himself. He says he's off the booze, which is strange, especially as he seems so intent on getting you pissed. You're feeling very woozy – no sign of the food and you've exceeded your two-glass limit. You want him to come and sit beside you so you can curl up on his lap.

He's busy bustling in the kitchen and you wonder what can take him so long, then you remember he's your very own 'Mr Fussy-fusspot', and you smile contentedly and battle a heaviness in your limbs. You haven't slept properly since he 'ended it' and your eyelids betray you now as they flutter closed. It's impossible to resist the fire, the candles, the wine and the proximity of this special, stupid, mercurial man. How you look forward to cuddling into him later.

When you wake, the air is cold and your breath is pluming, like smoke, although it's been years since you smoked. You snake your arm over his sleeping body to spoon him to you. He always loved the softness of your breasts pushing into his back. You're having difficulty opening your eyes, and your body feels like it's encased in cement. A dream, and you'll wake wrapped in his arms and his clean white cotton sheets. Shivering badly now, your whole body is involved. Surely, he'll come and cradle you to him like he used to. Blackness descends again and your body is on a merry-go-round, spinning interminably and there's no getting off.

Sunlight scissors your eyelids and your head clunks, like there's metal rolling around in there. As your eyes begin to focus, you see a concrete floor, sky on the ceiling, a mottled grey, and your own front door. You move your hands over your body and feel that it's fully clothed. You push yourself to sitting, little bat-birds circling your head in a halo. Hello cartoon-girl! A giggle erupts from deep within you and turns into a loud filthy laugh, echoing in the empty street. A bright calm descends, and you realise with absolute certainty what you must do today. Up, now Laura, hup. You haul yourself to standing.

You duck your head to avoid the mirror in the hallway, go the kitchen, put the kettle over the gas ring, wait for it to sing and then pour boiling water onto the stacked teabags. You like your tea stewed, heaped with sugar, and savour the scalding sensation as it burns your raw throat. Three cups and you're revived, focused, clear and full of purpose.

People stare. 'Let them, they have nothing better to do,' her mother used to say on one of her bright-cheeked high-energy days, when she'd skip everywhere.

You walk for forty minutes, fighting the desire to skip, until you arrive at your destination: a steel and chrome modern building that glints in the penetrating light. You go inside and approach the receptionist who pretends not to see you. You clear your throat.

Laura, for Myles, you say, in what you think is a calm, yet authoritative tone. She stares out the big glass doors behind you, mesmerised by the play of light, the dust motes dancing, fuck knows. She's ignoring you, the bitch.

Are you going to buzz his office, or will I?

She looks at you. Sorry...yes...sorry...Laura did you say? She picks up the phone. She knows exactly who you are. Hello, Miles (why Miles, not Mr Peters?)...Laura is here to see you...yes here now...in reception... The phone slams the other side and you try to catch her eye, which is impossible as her gaze flits all over the place, sly thing.

You sense his presence before he arrives.

This isn't a good time Laura. I'm in the middle of a meeting.

You go up to him and smell his hair. It smells of Dax gel. You love that smell.

Jesus, what happened to you?

Excuse me, Miles says and apologises to the girl with the flitty eyes.

He hustles you outside onto the street, into a lane where no one can see you. You kiss him and he pushes you away. He just can't handle being loved. Being loved is the most overwhelming feeling of all. Push, push, push. Flashes of something similar from last night.

You scared me last night L. You need help.

The only thing I need is you.

He does that scuffing thing with his shoe again.

Did you leave me on the street? I ask

You left my apartment screaming and cursing.

What did you do to me?

Nothing. That was the problem, according to you. Nothing.

Why did he get you drunk and then reject you? He knew what that would do to you. He knew.

So you let me walk out of there on my own?

C'mon. You're a big girl. Capable of getting yourself into and out of ugly scrapes.

Why did you let me drink? You know what happens to me when I drink.

I'm not responsible for you though. You are.

No one ever is, or has been responsible for you. Rage rises, rears and rushes through you. You start to undo his belt. A ravening need takes hold. Just to feel *something*. You experience cold emanating from him, and then a heat, a smarting pain, your cheek is raw and your right eye is streaming.

You start to fall, and you think you hear him say: Jesus L, the things you make me do.

You made him lose control. You have that power over him. You think you hear him cry. At last, you have made someone cry. The next thing you know the blue lights are spinning but the siren isn't blaring and you're glad because your head is sore.

You wake in a white place, smelling of artificial powdery-scented cleaning fluid, and bleach. You're wearing white. There's a plastic under sheet and a kidney-shaped bowl made of tin, like reflected sunlight, beside your bed. Overhead the artificial strip lighting is sharp and pulsing. You look down and see bruises on your arms, and you remember the strength of his hands encircling your arms, before you went down.

You're alone and the only sound is the low hum from the flickering tube-lighting. There's a big picture-window framing the branches of a bushy green tree with all its leaves intact even though it's well into autumn, and you get out of bed and walk slowly, your bare-feet padding on the cold tiled floor. An oak, or Sycamore, a Maple? Fuck knows, you never paid much attention in nature class. Pretty, though. The tree is so close you can reach out and touch its branches. There's no sound of bird song. A Squirrel dances on its highest branches, and seeing you, comes down to say hello.

Hello, Mr Squirrel. And how are we feeling today?

His tiny pebble-like eyes bore down into you.

I'm hungry, he says, as his little claws rub against each other.

Ok...Don't go anywhere.

And you go to the basket of fruit - which has blackening bananas in it (a gift from Miles?) and you wonder how long you've been here. You take out a green apple that is turning brown, yellow, squishy shades of purple, and you bite it and keep on biting it into tiny little pieces, then you spit these pieces into the palm of your hand and return to the window-sill where Mr Squirrel is waiting. You hold out a tiny bit of apple between your thumb and your forefinger and he nibbles at it. Piece after piece, until it's all gone and you hold out your hand to pet him, when he scampers away up the trunk of the tree. Come back, you will him, come back. You stand staring at the empty branches for some time. You think you see his tail twitch, but it's only the wind stirring the leaves.

Six Poems from The Ars
John Goodby

Not In, but Ours

Autumn as a meditation on England;
his Europe gave valence to his restless

fly, a single impulse on the sands
he walked, shifting, sticking to my shoe:

*I have flown my sky-desk window, four
framing walls and arena, taking long-*

*delayed stock. I had hoped to sense, too late
arriving, I still wrong the familiar mess.*

Hard Quare

Make the game the street, man
lost in another's lazy eye

three parts habit, one part
shadows stepping sideways

into thirst. His need to be blank
in the windows filled with himself,

running on the spot to shop
dummies like soap between

ragged shows. Coincidence?
Change the next moment,

the washed proprieties, that seem
you can't say: 'I have gone north

into the dandy time-acres. Their
players were there hour after

hour. Thin between shows, small
stars, I dressed his best first move.'

St Groan

The symptom
of a history,
its illnesses
once called celebration,
counterpoints open
skin cracked
in on new
waste bodies.

Die to their flings
when the body
brothers
the stranger
new premises
unrecorded. One
holds alien
flesh. Ore

for nymphomania
of the barely-there,
the partly-
human
diseased *être*,
their claim upon
the objective
pale wrist.

A woman melting
as a shadow fills.
Empty her eye.
For them
this first most
chance was only
a graph, host to
more famous orgasms.

Whisper, soft no-one'

Whisper, soft no-one
I do not even know. Dying

child heroes' sudden
beauty is made up

of moments - lucidity, a
beauty without made

forebodings. Tuition
supreme for others

in the living tears, etcetera,
is just my shadow-cloth.

Luve

O beg in pink, its thin
And winding ways model
The human beating
Of each inhabitant!

Flick a reflex
Of introspection. Lap
Everything sensed
As something else,

Feel disconnected
Like a house, hold vague
Objects breasting in
A flooded amble-drift,

Rives in a quaint row,
The dark analogy in the sky-
Frown, cloud-root in the loud
Round river it passes by.

A View of Sad

Hyperbole evaporates
In our six-foot throat.

The good life has its Hell -
It is noon all day, the soft

Porch light rewinds,
Thirsty as tinted glass

Sliding off the eye. So much
The empty earth scans

As majestic Mars. So little,
In the sponsored distance,

That holds the attention
Of the shadowless coils.

Hannah Rensenbrink's Postcards from Qasigiannguit
Richard Smyth

If you look at the Wikipedia page for 720 BC it's all Hezekiah this and Assyria that. It's never Uvavnuk or Tookoolito or whoever. Nothing happens in Igaliko. What I'm saying is, Greenland doesn't get a look in. I understand why but it's not reasonable, not really. Things were happening here too. Things were happening everywhere too.

*

We'll just cancel it, Mark said. It was when we were ringing round cancelling the caterers, the venue, the flowers, the string quartet. We'll just cancel it. I don't know what came over me but I said NO WE WON'T MARK. We've done all this planning. All this money in deposits. I'm going, I said. You can stop at home. But I'm going to go.

*

She keeps close to the lichen-marked granite of the stack. Uak uak, she says, as she gets near, and he says the same back, or something like it: uak, uak, uak. She's bigger than him. Sometimes she'll have a grouse with her, or a hare. Sometimes not.

*

Five hours from Heathrow to Copenhagen (never mind the train to Heathrow: three hours). Five hours from Copenhagen to Kangerlussuaq. Then an hour to Ilulissat; then an hour in a helicopter, quavering in half-light up the blue-green-grey west coast, to Qasigiannguit. I don't think I was frightened but I've never felt that alone before. It's not like I haven't travelled by myself – I flew to Sarawak, remember, in my first summer of uni, in Malaysia, when Jenn refused to get on the rusty little plane at KL airport, and I left her there, because I wasn't going to let

*

(cont) <u>her</u> of all people keep me from seeing orang-utans – but this wasn't about being by myself, it was about being alone, and I know that's the same thing but really it's not the same thing.

*

I just found out what gyrfalcons do. I read it in my bird book (it used to be Mark's bird book but it's mine now. It came all the way here with me. It couldn't <u>be</u> more mine). They don't build nests. They don't build their own nests. They find something else's nest and just move into it. A raven's or an eagle's nest. They squat, is what they do.

*

Two thousand, seven hundred and twenty years is an extraordinary amount of time. I mean it's a ridiculous amount of time. An absurd and pointless amount of time.

*

'Seven years!' I kept saying. 'Seven years, and now this!' It felt like an impressive quantity of time. A decent shift. Mark thought so too. For me it was: seven years, that's something, that's a substantial investment, let's keep at it, let's do more of this. Let's not throw it all away. I think for him it was: seven years, that's something, that's enough. That'll do. Seven years, and now this.

*

He'd been going on about it for ages. Since long before he proposed – as long as I've known him, I think, he's been going on about it. This trip, this holiday. This place and these fucking birds. It has crossed my mind that perhaps he only proposed so that we could come here on our honeymoon. I'd never have let him spunk six grand on a trip to the arctic circle otherwise. But it's academic now, isn't it. Are you allowed to swear on a postcard? Well, I suppose we'll see.

*

I walked up to the ridge today and I watched them for as long as I could before the cold got too much to bear. And I told myself, this is what people would have seen, the Paleo-Eskimo people, all those years ago. I do the same when I'm somewhere like York or Chester or anywhere really. I tell myself, people walked here, on this spot, on these stones

*

(cont.) a thousand years ago. And I can't help thinking, <u>so what</u>. I know that's terrible. But perhaps one of these days, before I go home (it feels strange to think about going home), I'll say it to the gyrfalcons. Go up there and yell it at the nest. Two thousand seven hundred and twenty years? <u>So bloody what</u>.

*

Sometimes I walk around the town, around Qasigiannguit. The houses are all painted in bright colours (and all in <u>different</u> bright colours – that's the best thing). White window frames and steep pitched roofs. They're prefabs, I think. Shipped in here from somewhere else. Built for bad weather. The town smells of salt and fish and engine-oil. Ice floes bob in the bay. On blue days there's so much sky you can't believe it.

*

I don't know if there's someone else. I know he *wants* there to be someone else. What's the difference, really? There'll be someone else eventually. It's all the same. Just a question of 'yet'. FWIW gyrfalcons mate for life.

*

Their shit doesn't rot. That's the trick. It's so cold here that the falcons' shit doesn't rot away, it stays where it is, up there on the ledge. The scientists can clamber up there and take a spoonful or whatever and clamber back down and run carbon-14 tests on it and say, eventually, yes, this shit is two thousand seven hundred and twenty years old. Give or take. It's clever, I'll give it that.

*

Can it be good, I wonder, watching, can it be wise and right, to stay in one place for two thousand, seven hundred and twenty years?

*

Mark voted for Brexit (or 'Lexit', as he calls it, like a wanker). Lot of stuff about agriculture and state intervention rules. But there's more to it than that. He'd talk about people having a connection with the ground beneath their feet. He'd talk about people who belonged to the place where they lived. He didn't talk about the people who <u>didn't</u> belong. But there must have been some, in his way of thinking. I mean it stands to reason.

*

Christ, he could be an arsehole sometimes. A proper straight-up nine-carat tin-plated fucking arsehole, a bumptious, hectoring, pigeon-chested, self-righteous slap-headed prick. Christ I hated him sometimes.

Christ he could be such a cunt. Might not post this one.

*

Greenland is mostly an icecap. It's an icecap that's melted a bit around the edges, like a sucked mint.

*

You can find out what it's like to be with a lot of people for, say, one year. Or you can find out what it's like to be with one person for a lot of years. You can't do both. That's what I ought to have said to him: Mark, you can't do both.

*

Some birds might have thought: our species has lived here for a hundred years. Isn't that long enough? That's what Mark would have thought, if he were a bird. Let's try somewhere else! But the gyrfalcons think that staying in the same place for two millennia is the only way to find out what it's like to stay in the same place for two millennia <u>and a day</u>.

*

Could I live here? I could live in a little green hut with a pickup on the driveway. I could get to know the language. I could get to know the mountains. I could work on a halibut boat.

*

They're white flecked with black, like a tyre-track in the snow on a tarmac road. Their sharp calls echo among the cliffs. Maybe that's why they do it. In one way they've been here for two thousand, seven hundred and twenty years, but in another way they're only a few years old: six or seven, maybe. In that way they're only children and that way is really the only sensible way. They're still exploring. Kids love echoes.

*

love echoes, love echoes. LOL.

*

My ancestors two hundred years ago were living in Utrecht, selling cheeses. I don't know what my ancestors two thousand years ago were doing. Were they smelting bronze? Hunting the last mastodon? And where? I don't know. But I know where the gyrfalcons' ancestors were. They were here, doing this: killing, eating, breeding, calling out, throwing shape-shifting shadows across the age-old granite.

*

I woke up with the barman from the pub in the town. It was all right. It was just sex. He's better looking than Mark. But I'm better looking than Mark too. I've seen the way people look at us (I mean looked at us). Men. They were thinking 'Aw, she could do so much better', but I always knew I couldn't, and not because of me, but because of them. After I left Per's place I watched the falcons for three hours.

*

If I'm not careful I'll end up like that man in that fucking falcon book Mark was always going on about.

*

I suppose gyrfalcons would be pretty Brexit. They're the couple in the tumbledown farmhouse on a lease that's been in place since King Henry's times. They're the family where they've never left the same terraced street and no-one's ever had a passport. What's wrong with that?

Nothing, really. It's like any relationship. The longer you stay the more you learn.

*

What will you do, he said. I said, first of all I'll go to Greenland. He said, what then. I said I'd decide that when I got home.

*

This rock is good. Let's stay here. Hares and grouse taste good. Let's keep eating them. Gyrfalcon thought processes. It would be easy to be sentimental. Let's not ever change, darling. We've all had that thought. Let's keep it like this, this moment, just like this, exactly like this.

*

Staying in the same place doesn't stop time. I want to shout, hey, gyrfalcons, staying in the same place doesn't stop time. But they know that, of course they do. They have a chick on the way. They know spring becomes winter. They must feel their age in their bones, who doesn't? I took wine up to the gyrfalcon nest today.

*

It was warm here, two thousand, seven hundred and twenty years ago. Warmer anyway. Not warm. Not balmy. Not somewhere you'd come on holiday – unless you're Mark, or me – unless you're me, coming to Greenland out of spite, coming to Qasigiannguit out of spite, out of heartbreak, coming to the gyrfalcon place for no good reason at all.

*

It's been three weeks. I think I go home tomorrow.

*

Today she brought what looked like a seagull, one dead white underhanging wing flapping as she flew. I once found a dismembered black-headed gull on the ground in the shadow of Wakefield cathedral. Peregrines nest there. You might say that falcons are drawn to ancient places but then why do they nest on Hartlepool power station? I think that falcons don't give a shit. About what's old, what's new. About time.

*

Just sitting here with a bag of cakes and a flask of warm wine, watching the gyrfalcons plunge and rise through the twilight. They settle down at night but at just the right time, like now, I can see the stars and the gyrfalcons too. I don't think the stars have changed much. I know they've changed, but not much. The sun hasn't changed. Do you know what I'm starting to think? I'm starting to think that the gyrfalcons

*

(cont.) wake up each day surprised by the sun.

Two Poems
Laura Wainwright

Mouths

With a poet's sense of timing
you lost your first milk-tooth
at the gaping mouth
of the estuary:
a piece of you
loose in my hand
like a chip off a shell.

In the gap
a tern cried. You laughed,
grimacing, testing the soft breach
with a bloodied tongue,
the tide-light flooding in
as through a just-cut window
in clay and bone-coloured waves.

Three fishermen packed up their rods.
We talked about the Romans
and the monks under the mud,
the unfathomed church,
how without this dam
the Levels
would be drowned.

But you kept staring
at the sea-wall's tumbled masonry,
orange – you thought, *like magma.*
Caloplaca Marina: bloom of high water,
gripped tight as my hand in yours,
a stark, burning enamel.

Note: Caloplaca Marina or Orange Sea Lichen.

The Pollinators

The evening before
the summer solstice,
neighbours trickled out
of their houses
and onto the street to see it:

the untidy, child-high
holly by the door
of number 6
now a crawling topiary
of bees.

Earlier I'd seen them swarm:
a shattered atom,
murmurations
of sun-caught wings,
honeyed bonfire particles
venting above the road.

Now they'd made a crawling ball
of their kilned winter tree,
gently shaken
by a long white glove,
turning each time to black quick clouds
but *not angry*, the beekeeper said.
Not angry.

He took them to an orchard
in a box marked CAUTION.
Honeybee…   gwenynen…   mì fēng…

I thought of the photograph:
cyanic smog pressing down
on dun scrub slopes,
outspread hands of fruit trees

and the pollinators

standing,
holding their brush probosces
in the branches
and the blossom.

Note: This poem is partly inspired by a photograph of farmworkers in China pollinating fruit trees by hand due to the rapid decline of bees and other insects. 'Gwenynen' is Welsh, and 'mì fēng' Mandarin, for 'honeybee'.

Foot and Mouth
Laura Morris

Chloe joins the queue of people treading the disinfectant mats and emptying their bags of food. Because of the high winds, the *Explorer* isn't running and she has to take the slow boat. Although there's more to do on the slow boat - a bigger shop, a proper restaurant, more places to sit - there is also something terribly lonely about it. She doesn't know if it's because the boat sails so early in the morning or if it's because the woman sitting opposite her is clutching a bin liner, containing, Chloe assumes, her belongings, but something about the slow boat makes her want to cry. She buys a bacon roll and sits in the corner of the bar, by the window. Her stomach drops as it always does when she sees the dark blue of the Irish Sea, spreading out and filling the space between Wales and Ireland. Taking the first bite, she remembers the feeling she had a few weeks ago, eating a burger after her final exam. A guy she'd been in halls with in the first year had died that morning in his sleep. When she bit into the burger and chewed the meat, she had felt that she was eating him, chewing his flesh.

On the bus to Limavady she takes out a book from her rucksack. An old cinema ticket marks her on chapter 3, but she goes back to the beginning and thinks of the last time she visited Chris, when they decided she would move to him for the summer holidays. As the bus pulls in to the station, Chris is waiting to meet her, a bunch of small white flowers behind his back. He kisses her cheek and hugs her, shyly handing her the flowers. They walk back to the flat, her rucksack looking much smaller on his back.

Chris had taken the flat without viewing it. He'd shared it with a guy called Steve who he used to work with, before Steve moved in with his girlfriend in Coleraine. Chloe had met Steve briefly at Chris's Forestry Commission Christmas party and he was the first person she heard say 'what's the craic?' He had left a beach towel, a pair of stonewash jeans and one green rugby sock in a wash basket in the bathroom and they were still in the bottom of the wicker basket when she arrived.

'I'll throw these out, will I?' Chloe asks Chris, pointing to the wash basket in the corner of the bedroom. 'I can smell them.'

'No, I wouldn't feel right doing that. Who knows? He might come back for them.'

'Will he also be coming back for the jar of pickled eggs in the fridge?' says Chloe, moving the wash basket into the bathroom.

'Leave them there,' says Chris. 'You know what Steve's like.'

Whenever she opens the fridge, Chloe tries not to look at the eggs directly because just a glimpse would be enough for her to imagine them inside her belly. Whole. She picks up the jar with a tea towel and moves it from the shelf to the fridge door, next to Chris's Guinness.

The following day Chloe opens an account with the Bank of Ireland, so that when she begins the factory job, her wages can be paid. On the way home she calls into *Belle Boutique* - the shop below the flat - to sign her contract. The shop sells dresses made from chiffon and lace and is lined with glass cabinets, full of costume jewellery and tiny handbags, decorated with pearls. It is managed by Edie, who also owns the flat. She has blonde hair piled onto her head, giving the impression that it's really long.

Next door to *Belle Boutique* is *Porky's*, where Chris buys his bacon and sausages. The first morning, while Chloe waits for her lift to the factory, she sees the carcasses coming off the little white van and retches into the gutter, bringing up a thin and sour spit.

They are advised to wear a plastic apron over their clothes and rubber gloves on their hands because of the slurry produced. They could become desensitised to it, they are told. When Charlie, the team leader, tells her and the other new girl to introduce themselves to the rest of the team and reveal something interesting, Angela says that she likes dipping her chips into Mcflurries and has her belly button pierced. Chloe says that she is Welsh, and eyes Angela's baseball cap, knowing that Angela will be better at this job than her.

The factory floor is divided into cells. Each cell contains 6 machines that require a code to start them. The code can be traced to the operators so that management can monitor productivity and quality. They are shown how to load the machine, close the machine and start it up. Once the machine finishes, the lid automatically opens and the machines are sprayed with water, to rinse away the slurry before being unloaded. They are warned what will happen if they don't load a machine properly – it will misload. During training they are presented with a graph, illustrating how much money the factory loses each year because of misloaded machines. As if to demonstrate, Charlie places a piece of torn rubber, salvaged from a machine, in Chloe's hand.

There are rows of cells, lined with bowed headed workers. Their eyes stare ahead, concentrating on the machines. Permanent members of staff are given headphones that play the local radio station, but Chloe needs to concentrate so hard on loading the machines that she can't imagine listening to music at the same time. She's working far more slowly than everyone else, even Angela, and each time she closes a machine she fears it's going to misload.

In between loading and unloading machines the others chat. Angela and James seem to know each other already. She tries to tune into the accent, but finds it difficult over the grind of the factory to completely understand what is being said. The accent is so heavy, so thick, so hard.

Water from the spray forms a pool that catches the bottoms of her jeans and rises up her legs. Her feet are wet and her hands are cold, but the evening slowly wades on. Her eyes are getting heavy and there's a sickness rising in her stomach that she always gets when she needs to sleep. When Charlie asks if she's okay, she knows she has seen the tears in her eyes. 'Go, take a break, sweetheart,' she says. In the canteen Chloe pays 50 pence for a bowl of apple crumble and custard, and in a newspaper that has been left on the table, reads that Foot and Mouth has spread to Meigh in South Armargh.

'Tracy's Welsh too,' says Charlie when Chloe returns from her break. She finishes loading her machine then takes her by the elbow and leads her to the next cell. She taps a red haired lady on the shoulder. It turns out that Tracy is from Newport and moved here with her husband when he got a job as engineer. They chat for a bit and then Tracy and

Charlie go on their break together and Chloe walks back to the cell.

Towards the end of the shift James tells Chloe, 'don't load that machine because we'll have to unload it before we finish. You have to time it just right,' he says, his index finger against his thumb, doing the okay sign. At 6.56am James stands next to the clocking out machine. As others begin to queue behind him, he leans against the wall, his eyes closed, turning his ID card between his fingers. Driving Chloe home he winds the window right down, his cigarette hanging out of it, letting it burn down until the ash disappears into the wind. 'You ever been to Kelly's?' he says. 'It's a club out of town. We all go.' Chloe says no. It probably isn't Chris's thing.

On the third night shift Chloe hears the terrible grinding of metal on metal coming from James's machine. Tyler runs to hit the emergency stop button and James stands in front of the machine, holding his arms out to make an 'M,' like people make when dancing to the YMCA. M for misload. Charlie calls the technician and within minutes, one of the managers appears with a clipboard to record it. James is given a form to complete and a reminder about how to load machines properly. The technician gets to work. He opens the machine and swiftly begins to take it apart, arranging its insides on the top. James goes for a cigarette. A misload means one less machine to load. It means a smoke, a chat, a piss.

On her first day off Chloe buys a packet of Rolos at *Supervalu* and eats them two at a time as she walks to the library. She browses the shelves, but the plastic sleeved books look heavy. Instead she selects *A bout de soufflé* from the World Cinema section and buys a token for the internet. She signs into her Hotmail and reads her emails, while trying to work out caramel from a hole in her tooth with her fingernail. Amongst the spam, there is an email from university, reminding her of MA enrolment days, a forward from her father, containing Irish sayings and one from Vicky, who's travelling Europe before starting her teaching course. She places another Rolo in her mouth, promising herself she will make this one last. She sucks it until it gets so small it disappears. In the charity shop, whilst looking at the crocheted blankets, she notices a woman watching her. Chloe smiles and the woman says, 'I work in the canteen. You didn't recognise me without my hair net, did you?' She pulls her hair back to the base of her neck, to demonstrate. Chloe smiles, 'no, I didn't,' she says. 'No one ever does,' says the woman.

When she gets back to the flat Edie is sitting on the stairs, smoking. She hands her a postcard, her charm bracelet jangling. 'It arrived yesterday,' she says, 'but I thought I should wait until Chris was at work to give it to you.' It is one of those arty black and white postcards that are on racks by the doors in the cinema and free to take. It's a photograph of an empty hot air balloon, mid-flight. Chloe turns the postcard over. She can see that the card had been sent to her home address and her mother has crossed it out in blue biro and forwarded it on to her in Limavady.

Missing me yet?
D

Dan has written in big looping handwriting. Edie says 'Chloe, some advice… If a man wants you, he will chase you. Don't chase him.'

Chloe lets herself in, makes a mug of sugary tea and studies the postcard. Maybe Dan chose that particular one because the empty hot air balloon symbolises how lonely he feels now he won't see her again. The balloon, mid -flight represents him in his graduate life. He's the balloon. Empty without her. Maybe. Much of Chloe's third year had been spent obsessing about him, while Chris did his forestry work placement. Although they had only ever talked when drunk and all she had were fragments of conversations, she thought about them and analysed them as if it were poetry. Her friends told her that he was leading her on a bit, but she felt *something* there; there was *something* between them.

She lies on the settee, holding the postcard's smooth side against her cheek. Her wrist aches from pulling the trigger on the water spray. She moves her tea to her left hand and circles her right wrist in an anti-clockwise motion. She could watch the film she rented, but doesn't think she can focus on subtitles today and closes her eyes instead.

In her dream she is the only one working on the cell and the machines are opening, one by one, ready to unload. A manager calls her to a meeting to discuss her performance but when she tries to explain she is the only one on the cell, they don't understand her accent. She wakes herself up shouting, 'But who's watching the machines?' She switches on the portable television, but turns the sound right down. She lies there, eyes closed, while the screen displays a smouldering cattle pyre and a farmer silently wiping tears from his eyes.

Chloe is put on a different cell the next morning, to cover someone who's off for a funeral. Scraped into her machine are the words: 'I no longer fear hell. I'm already here.' She runs her finger over the scratched in words and smiles, wondering how the person had done it. How they had got away with it, if they had got away with it.

The nearest toilet is out of order, so she uses a different one on her break. She pees and checks her phone messages. Chris has texted; he will be home late. She takes a wrong turn on her way back from the toilet and ends up down a corridor she hasn't been down before. She passes a room with yellow warning signs about contamination on the door. Through the small window, she can see men dressed in blue boiler suits and wearing masks over their mouths. Everything in the room is white or stainless steel. She has no idea what goes on in that room.

When Chris finally arrives home that evening, his nose is red and his glasses are steamed up. 'We've been pulled in to help with the foot and mouth. The shifts are going to get longer,' he explains, pulling a face, 'and sometimes I'll have to stay away for a few nights. He runs a bath, removes his waterproofs, then his fleece and trousers, then his t shirt and boxers, until he is standing naked in the bathroom. She hugs him, 'you smell like the rain,' she says, 'and you smell like biscuits,' he says.

She nods and listens while he gets in the bath and continues to tell her about his day. 'We have to clean and disinfect car and lorry tyres.' Chloe sits on the toilet and stares at the wash basket.

'I'm going to move Steve's washing,' she says, interrupting him as he talks about the farm he was at that evening and how he had to spray the feet of the people in and out of the field. 'I won't throw it out, but it smells really bad now. I don't know if it's because the weather is getting warmer or what, but I can't bear it anymore.'

'Yeah, okay,' he says, just don't throw it out. Put it in a cupboard or something.'

Chloe carries the basket to the kitchen and opens two cupboards before settling on the one under the sink. She empties the dirty clothes into it and closes the door.

She goes back into the bathroom and removes her dressing gown before stepping into the bath to join Chris. She giggles as they wriggle to fit together.

'My wrist really hurts,' he says, 'from spraying the disinfectant.'

'My tummy hurts,' she says. 'PMT, I think.' He moves his hand onto her belly and she massages his wrist.

'I don't think I could ever live here,' she says.

'In this flat, you mean?' he asks.

'No, Limavady. I couldn't live here.'

'But you're already here,' he says. 'Not properly,' she says.

Chris's new shifts mean that when Chloe returns from an evening shift at 7am, he has already left for work. The smell of his morning shit lingers in the bathroom. He has left a teabag in a cup for her and the grill pan is still warm from his bacon but she can't face meat at all anymore. The way it feels in her mouth, the *thought* of it. She eats biscuits for breakfast, dessert for lunch in the canteen and pizza or pasta with cheese at night. There's no weighing scales in the flat, but she can see it in her face, feel it on her thighs.

She lies on the sofa half asleep, watching *This Morning* and dozing, but wakes to banging on the front door. When she opens it, she sees Edie there, a roll of bin liners under her arm.

'Some girls are coming to view the flat this afternoon,' she says. 'They're nurses. They need a place for September. I need to sort out the spare room. There are three of them.'

'But I've been working a night shift,' Chloe answers. If she was a nurse too, would Edie let her sleep? Edie stands in the doorway. She isn't going to leave. 'I guess I'll clean up then,' says Chloe and moves to let her pass. Edie takes a set of keys from her cardigan pocket and unlocks the spare room that she uses as a second stock room. Inside there are shop fittings, a sign that reads *Edie's* in swirly writing and an 80s style mannequin with black curly hair, holding her left hand as if mid conversation. Edie catches Chloe looking in and closes the door.

Chloe starts scrubbing the bath. She hasn't cleaned the bathroom since moving in a month ago and doubts whether Chris has cleaned it either. In some ways she doesn't mind work like that, work that has a clear beginning and ending.

'Do you have furniture polish?' Edie calls from the spare room.

'Under the kitchen sink,' Chloe answers.

Chloe hears Edie rummaging under the sink and then hears her call, 'what's this?' Edie comes into the bathroom with Steve's clothes in her hands. 'It stinks!'

'It's Steve's stuff,' Chloe answers.

'Steve?'

'He lived here before us,' Chloe reminds her. 'Chris thought he might come back for the stuff.'

'No,' she says, shaking her head. 'No, he won't be coming back.'

Edie puts the clothes and towel into a bin liner, ties it in a knot and puts the bin liner outside the flat door. When she goes back into the spare room, Chloe gets the jar of pickled eggs from the fridge and places them on top of the bin liner too, trying not to look at the yellowy water. They continue to clean. Chloe finishes the bathroom and bedroom and Edie helps her with the kitchen.

'The nurses are coming at 3.00pm,' says Edie, looking around, 'so, if you could make sure that you're out then.' She pauses, nods proudly and says, 'we have accomplished a lot in a short space of time.'

Edie lets herself out of the flat and Chloe leaves soon after. At Supervalu she buys Tic Tacs, as they are only two calories each. She slices the seal open with her thumbnail and empties a third of the sweets into her mouth straight from the tub. At the library, she opens her emails, but doesn't reply to any of them. She borrows La Vita è Bella and walks slowly back to the flat. Edie is sitting on the stairs. 'The girls didn't want the flat,' she snaps. 'They said it wasn't big enough for three of them.' Chloe smiles. 'Oh, and June in the butcher's gave me this to give to you. Apparently, you are graduating. Chris told them.' Edie hands her an envelope and Chloe opens it. It's a graduation card with a picture of a teddy wearing a mortar board. The tassel is made of real string. She sniffs the envelope, convinced she can smell the faint metallic stink of raw meat.

Chloe is given two days off work to attend her graduation. Although she told her mum not to bother making the journey and although she doesn't actually like many people from her course, she's glad that she came. Main Arts looks the colour of honey in the sun.

She looks around for Dan, scanning the groups of graduates and families. She spots Sam, a guy who spent the first year wearing a pretend furry blue tail attached to his jeans, now freshly shaven, minus a tail and wearing a suit. He's talking to Bernie, who she used to see crying most weeks at indie night now guiding her elderly grandmother across the lawn. She finds Dan in the queue for professional photographs and waves to catch his attention. He does some sort of salute back, then rolls his eyes when he sees Chris by her side and holds out his fingers, making them into a pretend gun. He aims the gun at Chris's head and pretends to shoot it, staring ahead. Chloe laughs, knowing that's the wrong thing to do.

Drinking warm cava in the marquee after the ceremony, and listening to the others talk about their summer plans and new jobs, she watches Dan and his family together. Dan laughs in the same way as his father, his head right back, his mouth wide open, like each joke is the funniest he has ever heard. She chats to one of her lecturers about the possibility of returning for a Masters and nibbles on a strawberry. Her head feels light and her eyes are heavy. She makes her way inside to the toilet, trying to walk carefully across the lawn in the gown and heels.

She hears someone walking closely behind her and then feels her arm being pulled. Dan takes her hand and leads her across the grass and towards Main Arts. He holds the tops of her arms and pushes her into a doorway. 'Do you even love him?' he says angrily. 'You look at me, more than you look at him. She feels him coming near her. 'I just don't get what you are doing, why you are wasting your time.'

'I do love him,' she says, 'of course I do.' She tries to steady herself and holds on to his arm. She feels him coming closer to her. He holds her face and she feels his face coming closer. Before she can stop herself she throws up a gob of red and fizzy liquid over his new shoes and the bottom of his gown.

When Chris finds her, she is sitting alone at the bottom of the steps, sick on her fingers. 'You've been gone ages,' he said. 'I came to see if you were okay.' 'I feel better now I've been sick,' she says. 'I needed that.' She likes the hollow feeling in her stomach.

Later, in bed at the hotel, Chris kisses her. She lies there, moving herself slowly against his fingers but can't bring herself to touch him, although she can feel him pressing hard into her. Afterwards, she turns away from him and sobs silently until she falls asleep. In the early hours she wakes dreaming of the machines, to find Chris at the bottom of the bed, his right arm outstretched and his fingers against her feet. They laugh, when they realise he has been disinfecting her feet in his sleep, but clinging to him she knows his clammy body is trembling too. He opens the window and they lie there, listening to their chests rise and fall and the seagulls outside.

They travel back on the slow boat. She notices how quiet he is and doesn't even want a tea when she gets herself one. Chris sits on a chair in the café. Chloe stands between his legs, facing him. 'I really don't want to go back,' she says. 'Me neither,' he replies, 'but we have to.' 'Dan tried to kiss me yesterday,' Chloe says, 'but I didn't let him. I think I'm done with that now.' Chris nods slowly, looking past her. He says 'I'm going to try to sleep.'

James is late picking her up the next morning. He drives past the layby where he normally pulls in and mounts the pavement. She can smell the alcohol in the car as soon as she opens the door. He shoves the remains of a pasty into his mouth, crumbs spilling down his jumper. 'We went to Kelly's last night,' he says. 'I haven't slept. Angela needed a lift,' he says, pointing towards Angela, who is sitting in the back of the car. Chloe can see Angela is in last night's clothes.

They walk to their cell and Craig, one of the managers, is already there, holding a clipboard. He explains that James will be team leader for the next few shifts as Charlie won't be in for a bit. 'Tracy will be around today for a collection for her,' he says. 'Charlie's had a miscarriage. We're all giving 50p each for some flowers.'

Chloe loads the machine quickly without really thinking about it. She holds the sensors to start it up. As she steps away from it, she knows that she hasn't loaded it properly. For a moment she thinks she might have got away with it, but then she hears it, and it's so much louder than she thought it would be. An awful scraping sound that she can feel inside her. She stands and watches as the machine vibrates angrily. 'Hit the stop button!' shouts James. Chloe turns to look at him, but does nothing. 'What the fuck?' he says, pushing past her and presses the red button. The machine slowly comes to a halt. 'Since when have you given a fuck?' she says. James shakes his head and calls the technician.

'You've fucked this up good and proper,' the technician says, holding up the mangled metal. 'It's gonna need a new carrier.'

Chloe feels herself flush and nods. 'Sorry,' she says. 'You haven't got to say sorry to me,' he says, handing her the form to complete. The form is a series of questions asking like *have you consumed alcohol today?* and *when did you last have your eyes checked?* She then has to sign in order to accept responsibility. She works very slowly after that and checks each run two or three times before starting the machine.

She sees Tracy in the canteen on her dinner break, 'I didn't know she was pregnant,' says Chloe. 'No,' it was early days, hun,' says Tracy. 'Early days. It's her third miscarriage now.' Chloe gives her a pound for the flowers. She doesn't feel right giving what she pays for pudding. Yet today, she doesn't feel like crumble and custard or anything really. The canteen clock says 12.00, but she doesn't know if it's midnight or midday. There are no windows in the canteen or on the factory floor. In the toilet she opens the small window above the cistern. She breathes in the dark and cold air. It must be an evening shift. She thought it was.

By Chloe's final shift, Charlie is back at her machine. Her face looks pinker, like it has just been scrubbed with a flannel. Chloe hugs her and their aprons creak as the plastic meets. 'We are squeaking,' says Chloe and laughs guiltily. Charlie smiles and asks about the graduation. 'It was lovely,' Chloe lies. 'It was perfect.' She pauses and adds, 'It's my last day today.'

'I remembered,' says Charlie. 'I wish I was leaving too.'

'You could though,' answers Chloe, 'couldn't you?'

'Not really, petal,' she says, 'what else would I do?'

Chloe nods, 'we should keep in touch though,' she says, as if it were a question.

Chloe is first behind James to clock out at the end of the shift.

'After me,' he says, pointing at the machine. 'You should go first.' She swipes her pass through the reader. 'Does it feel great?' asks James.

'Amazing,' says Chloe, but in truth she doesn't really feel anything at all. James and Angela are going for a drink and they ask Chloe along, but instead she goes to *Supervalu* to buy bubble bath, a pizza and a bottle of rosé.

As she runs the bath, adding the bubbles to the hot running water, she thinks that she might watch one of the films from the library that are stacked next to the TV. Maybe she will be able to concentrate on one of them now work has finished. She lowers her head into the water until her hair is wet and splayed out around her. She hears a key in the front door and sits up. 'Chris,' she calls.

'No,' says the voice.

'Chris?' she says again.

'No, it's Steve,' says the voice.

Chloe gets out of the bath and grabs a towel. 'Steve?' She peers around the bathroom door. She hasn't closed it, let alone locked it. 'What the fuck?'

Steve is standing in the doorway, holding a can of Carlsberg and an unlit cigarette.

'I wanted to come home,' he says.

'But you don't live here anymore, Steve. How do you even have a key?' She wraps the towel around herself a little tighter and steps fully out of the bathroom.

'Can I just stay for a bit?' he asks.

'I'm not sure,' she says. 'I really don't think that you should. And Chris will be home soon.'

Steve closes the door and sits at the table. 'Ah, come on,' he says. 'I'm already here now.' He laughs to himself and mumbles something about Chris being a good guy.

'Let me just put some clothes on,' she says, realising she's going to allow him to stay a while. She pulls on some tracksuit bottoms and a t-shirt without drying herself properly.

'What's the craic?' he slurs.

'I still don't know how I'm supposed to answer that question,' she says. 'Is it rhetorical?'

He goes over to the cooker to light his cigarette. 'You don't mind if I smoke, do you?'

Steve begins to tell her about Coleraine. 'I found messages on Dee's phone from her ex. She says that she doesn't still love him, but I don't know. Why would she still message him? Would you do that?' he asks. Chloe opens her mouth to answer but he says, 'I just wanted to come home,' he says, 'ya know, see the old place.'

'I was going to cook a pizza, if you want some?' Chloe turns on the oven to heat it ready for the pizza. She sits on the sofa and he joins her. As he sits he spills his lager down himself and mops it up from his jeans with his hand. 'Actually, did I leave some jeans here?' he asks. Chloe thinks about Edie stuffing his clothes into the bag and the pickled eggs she herself had placed carefully on top. 'No, nothing, I don't think,' she says. 'There was nothing here.'

'Ah,' he replies. 'Right on. I don't know where they went then.' He adjusts himself so that he is half lying down. She allows him to settle his head in her lap and he continues to talk about Dee and her ex. Chloe nods and says things like 'yeah, that's terrible' and 'oh, poor you,' but she has stopped listening. She rests her head against the back of the sofa, so that she can hear the machines. The low hum, the grinding of metal. Someone is working the machines right now, she thinks. *Even when I am not there, the machines are running.*

An Interview with Will Johnson
Angela Graham

Editor's note: Will Johnson was interviewed by Angela Graham in March, 2020. He sadly passed away in October.

Will Johnson's debut collection of twenty poems, My Speaking Tongue *(Eyewear Pamphlet, 2018) examines the relationship between body and voice. I reviewed it for Wales Arts Review in March 2020 and was impressed by the collection's coherence and discipline, achieved without sacrificing depth and passion: 'Here is a poet who feels, reacts, and then selects, as an artist, what will best serve the task of communicating life at an extreme.'*

Will Johnson suffered from motor neurone disease. He could speak though he had lost all movement. But his poetry was not defined by his condition.

Will Johnson: I was born in Warwickshire. I dropped out of school. I was seventeen. This was the late Sixties – that was the time for dropping out of school! Besides, I couldn't stand school. I did various things for about ten years – travelled, worked in various low-paid jobs in London and elsewhere. I developed a passion for theatre, largely classical theatre. I got a job at the Royal Court. That didn't have much to do with classical theatre! I met some interesting playwrights, including Samuel Beckett. Not that he would have noticed me – nodded and said a few words!

Poetry was a passion of mine since I was young. I think Shelley had a terrible effect on me when I was at school. I aspired to be like Shelley. I didn't quite get round to burning the trees in the grounds, or whatever he did! I was generally wild.

I thought I should read at least the Twentieth Century poets. I went round buying up lots of Americans, people who were fashionable in the late Sixties, early Seventies: Robert Lowell, John Berryman, Robert

Frost, Auden, Eliot and Yeats. I did a pre-Dip. course at Art School for about nine months and some teacher training. I was writing poetry all along. I burnt and binned a lot of early poems. I did write two novels, which weren't particularly good either but I thought at least that showed I had the stamina to do it.

I had read a lot of material on Buddhism through my twenties and became particularly interested in Japanese Buddhism. I thought I could learn Japanese and go further into that, but I was told I was too old at twenty-eight, twenty-nine, to remember the script properly. So I thought, well, if I don't go to Japan then I'll go further back in Buddhism, to India. So, as a mature student, I did a Religious Studies degree at Sussex, at the School of African and Asian Studies. I met my wife, Pat who was doing History. We had our first son there. I did an M Phil at Oxford, in what was strangely called Oriental Studies, for two years, specialising on the Indian side, learning Sanskrit; then a D Phil on Jainism. I took my cue from my supervisor, Richard Gombrich, Professor of Sanskrit at Oxford. He wrote a well-regarded book called, *Precept and Practice* about how doctrine comes up against, or deals with, how people want to practice, and vice versa. I took a similar approach to Jainism. At that time there was hardly anyone else in Britain who was looking at it. I got a research fellowship at Oxford for a while and then in 1992 I came to the Religious Studies Department at Cardiff University where I taught Indian religions: Hinduism, Buddhism, Jainism, and Sanskrit.

During my career, I did a number of translations for Oxford University Press in their World's Classics series, including *The Bhagavad Gita*. I did that in prose, as that's what they wanted. I wrote the Oxford Dictionary of Hinduism. Someone suggested I translate the shortest book in *The Mahābhārata: The Sauptikaparvan*. This means, roughly, *The Book of the Massacre at Night*. I thought, well, this is in verse in the original, a form of epic verse – Sanskrit poetry has eight syllables to the line and varying patterns of light and heavy syllables – I must find a way to put this into some kind of verse in English. So I set myself a pattern – not a totally strict pattern. I'll allow up to so many syllables in the line.

I was influenced, though not very heavily, by Christopher Logue's translations – or versions (they're really not translations at all) of *The Iliad* – influenced by the kind of vigour he got into that; slightly cinematic effects. I think my translation came out quite well. People liked it, in the field. I did enjoy doing that.

Angela Graham: Did your translation of *The Sauptikaparvan* influence your own poetry?

WJ: The engagement with this Sanskrit poem didn't greatly affect the way I write in English. It was the other way around. The freer you are with the English, there is a trade-off with literal accuracy. People in the field of Indian studies often want literal accuracy and loads of footnotes but I thought, no, this is a sort of narrative arc. I'll go that way and that worked quite well.

I did some more of *The Mahābhārata* for a series called the Clay Sanskrit Library which aimed to bring out a hundred Sanskrit works in English. I did it in the same kind of verse to begin with but they wanted it done in prose, so I had to alter it, which I found disappointing. This was published by the New York University Press in a dual text: transliterated Sanskrit down one side of the page, English translation on the other.

The last translation I did for OUP was a translation of the most famous Sanskrit play, *The Recognition of Śakuntalā*, written by Kālidāsa. This is a very early Sanskrit play, a sort of romance. Interestingly, composed in two languages: Sanskrit and Prakrit (an offshoot of Sanskrit). This was written in both prose and verse. There are multiple verse forms in it. In Sanskrit drama they really show off what they can do with poetry. About forty different verse forms. It breaks straight from poetry into prose and back. There are rules about who could speak verse and what kind of verse they could speak. I thought, there have been several translations into prose. I'm not going to try to reproduce Sanskrit verse. I've seen people do that and it sounded horrible to me – lost the flavour. So I was free about it: using various forms, sometimes rhyme, keeping it reasonably accurate in terms of the meaning. A very interesting play to translate. The intention was to produce a version that could be acted. It seems that worked. A number of professional and semi-professional companies have used my translation. Mainly in North America. And a production here in London's Union Theatre in Southwark. They had to cut it. It's seven acts!

AG: You gained a lot of experience of grappling with words and meaning and of trade-offs between poetry and sense? Were you writing poetry of your own while doing these translations?

WJ: Maybe primarily out of doing the play. It was a sort of coincidence, trying things on the side, not directly to do with the play. As I was getting older, I had it in my head, what I would do when I retired? Well, the thing I most want to do, I thought, is to seriously have a go at writing some poetry. Slowly I began to write some poems through the 2000s. They stacked up a bit. I first published something in *Poetry Wales*, under Robert Minhinnick, then a few other places, and one of the Indian ones was shortlisted in an *Agenda* poetry competition. I mean, that is, Indian in content, or perspective. Gradually I started to write about other things as well.

AG: Do the poems in the collection come from the one period of writing?

WJ: In the collection the majority are relatively recent, after I was diagnosed with motor neurone disease. When I thought I'd try to put a pamphlet together, I went back and found poems to do with articulation: the voice and the body. Not morbid. Perhaps melancholy. Some of them seemed almost to predict the state I ended up in with this disease. It was almost as though I could foresee it.

Maybe the elements of the disease that came out in some of the later poems were things I was concerned with anyway and so I'd been writing about those before, to some extent, maybe not quite so directly. I very seldom pre-plan a poem. I just try and discover what it's about by writing it. I suppose if you're doing that, then you'll probably keep discovering the same things and thinking you've come up with something new!

AG: The collection's opening poem, 'Voice'. You're saying there's no reach, touch, skin, sense left in me. *body's its own body… body takes all…* Body takes everything, *bar voice – voice / sotto voce / sounds out its new home.* The word 'home' is very striking because a writer could have said, in those circumstances, its 'new prison' or 'new limits' but it says its 'new home' and it seems to me that that's voice taking ownership. Despite everything. Despite the loss of so much, the voice is claiming its home.

WJ: Maybe I've been too much in my voice all my life! Perhaps, it's not so much a new home as an old one. I was always interested in voice, in a general sense. My interest in theatre was always in how people spoke and in how, in classical acting, they convey emotions by the way they modulate the voice.

AG: There's a strong sense in the collection of multiple focuses. This is particularly evident in the poem 'Nature Morte'. You make wonderful use of the myth of Orpheus, the looking back; and it's done with simple means, right from its opening: *after he left / he saw the table set / the room empty / the sill unswept…* That *after he left / he saw* gives the reader an immediate sense of looking back, a focus which you then multiply:

> *as though… / at the quiver / of a pane of glass / he'd be pressed / like Orpheus / through the frame / into the silence of his own / abandoned life…*

The last poem, *Resolution Ending In A Line By Thomas Traherne* begins: *Before I leave I'll wake and speak…* The concluding line is

Traherne's, *Where was, in what abyss, my speaking tongue?* His poem is about the mystery of that sense of: I've-come-from-some-mysterious-nothingness-and-yet-all-the-time-I-did-exist-there... Is that the sense in which you mean that final line to be read?

WJ: Yes, up to a point, but it's the bafflement of it – not to put too strong a point on it – the mystery of it.

AG: 'mystery' is a word you'd accept?

WJ: Yes. I accept it more and more: that realising one is simply not going to come to terms with it, what it means to be or not be. It's not something that intellectually you can come to terms with at all. I've read a lot of people trying to come to terms with it intellectually, especially on the Indian side, and of course there's plenty of Indian practice as well. People trying to reconcile themselves, to live with it in a different way. That's not my way. I've done bits of practice but my body was never up to it.

AG: Is 'Life At Sea' a recent poem?

WJ: It refers to something that happened a long time ago lots. I wrote lots of different versions of it. The illness probably brought into focus what I was struggling with before. I had the sea part of it but I didn't see what it meant... The illness brought into focus what I had been struggling with.... I discovered where the poem was going. Earlier versions were long but still left me stranded somewhere.

AG: Yes, that's how the writing of poetry works. That comforts me, as a poet, because sometimes I think: ninety-five per cent of this poem is ok but maybe the end... it's not quite there... Frequently ends take a lot of work!

'The Seagull from 16 To 60': is that written out of your experience of theatre?

WJ: Yes. Chekhov always one of my favourites. Second only to Shakespeare. I did see a production when I was still at school, at sixteen. I've seen it many times since. I was remembering how I tried to identify with Konstantin – the unsuccessful writer in the play. It's in memory of T. P. McKenna, who was in that production I saw when I was sixteen. I wrote it after he died… It's about his death, and partly about mine, as well, and the character's death. I've got an inbuilt, slightly Russian romanticism – you could call it sentimentality! Something I acquired at school when I discovered that on my mother's side, some of our family had come from Russia at the end of the Nineteenth century. My grandmother. I never knew her. Russian Jews. I think I imagined Cossacks. But they were probably the very people who were persecuting the Jews! I read *War and Peace* when I was fifteen or sixteen. I read *Doctor Zhivago* after the film came out, which of course has a poet as a hero.

AG: 'The Zamizdat Self'. You have the gift of telling a story – in that poem, for instance, and in 'Life At Sea'; those are like small stories but they have the pleasures of poetry in them. Why poetry? And not prose. You did write two novels.

WJ: I like spending more time over every word and sentence. There were, of course, novelists who did do that, people like Flaubert… but I can imagine myself – if I took to writing prose – I'd never get past the first two pages because I'd be changing every line! I like the precision and the rhythm of poetry. There certainly are some wonderful pieces of prose… that you could say *were* poetry – that are better than most poetry, like the end of Joyce's *The Dead*. When I'm feeling less confined by the concept of poetry then I visualise… I think… it doesn't have to be written down in words. You can find it in all kinds of things. You can see poetry in film or theatre, or what I would think of as poetry, in that sense. It has an effect that's the same. Film does. Film can have the same effect as poetry. Again, on the Russian side, I was very fond of Andrei Tarkovsky.

AG: Film or another art form can have the effect of poetry? What is that effect?

WJ: It's almost as though you're caught unawares, and you see something else that you didn't expect to be there or weren't looking for or just came through, without your anticipating it. When I'm reading that's what I'm looking for – not consciously, but that's what I recognise, when I see it. Of course, it's very subjective, as well. Some things that I read when I was young, I didn't get to grips with at all and then came back and read them later and it was there.

AG: Can you recognise poor poetry?

WJ: I can recognise when poetry doesn't do that. There are some very good poems, but they don't work fully. That's part of the problem with poetry. It's very difficult to get it to work completely and sometimes it does it from somewhere unexpected. One can be too demanding of it; in a way that people aren't, of say, music.

As for my own collection: I'm simply glad that someone wanted to publish it. And now I feel a bit... well, I don't want to come out as 'the Motor Neurone Disease poet'.

AG: No. You've hit a good balance. It's very subtle. It works. The poetry works.

EURO 2040
Fiona O'Rourke

In free thought she wills herself to recall any good characteristic about the mother she met just once in a virtual visit, only the offshore signal returns making her sunglasses bing back to life. A screen appears on each lens giving the timeline of this day last year — her virtual visit to the hospice where she learned that her mother was no longer the startling headshot once discovered in childhood. That old profile proved at least that they'd once shared a pale complexion and dark blue eyes, whereas no amount of filter view could have enhanced the hospice version mother who was thin and grey like a pencil drawing on a pure white sheet. Sunni exes her timeline, exes the inner screen to allow for present vision.

These sunglasses are a travel gift from Home, intelligent sunglasses capable of ThinkComm on or off the user's head. She has named them Sunni, opted for a calm male voice. Sunni ThinkComms appropriate action:

Better to absorb father characteristics.

and a CBT reminder:

Old-ground negative excessive: danger of patternising, time to bond with good parent.

Merci, Sunni, she ThinkComms back.

Remember to speak English, it is the lingua franca in Ireland. Now is a good time to rest.

A roar comes from a crowd of football passengers. Euro 2040 fans, entirely French, blur into one navy blue jersey, filling the ferry's alcohol lounge. She wishes she could be group-happy, part of their sports belief. Sunni has booked her cabin but really, 20 hundred hours is too early to wipe off lipstick and sleep alone.

Tracing goal is priority. Home financed Blood Search and trip to meet good parent.

I know, Sunni, I need a distraction.

She opts maximum self-privacy. On this floating no man's land, not one person will know her, she can do as she pleases. With data-scan she surveys the crowd. Many are available: some do only Virtual while the older guys with natural grey hair and computer porn frowns do mostly Reality Anon. They will be lucky, seeming as old as her father should be, and too drunk to carry protection.

Outside on deck, a lone man is viewing the sea unaided, his sunglasses stored in a back pocket. The hood on this guy's jacket blows on and off and his hair has become messy. He is as tall as a rugby man but thankfully slim-thighed in jeans. This guy does Virtual and Reality Named or Anon.

Rugby physique more compatible with wide pelvis.

I hate hideous rugby thighs, Sunni, I know that for a fact, tell me something positive.

He is Irish and you are DNA safe. Outcome will be a pleasant bruised exhaustion. He is currently data-non-read, messaging not possible.

Well, I will go out there, be old school.

Reality Sex is not compatible with goals.

Sunni, I'm travelling, this is what people do in new places, meet new people.

Some of her friends from Home are into Reality, they talk about orgasms more like the ones in novels, less like after-sneeze sensations. Feeling in her bag, she moves items around to ensure the packet of Ultra Protect will be visible.

Reality cannot provide fulfilment or love. Tracing goal is priority for fulfilment. Home wants only optimum outcomes for singular girls. You have not CBT cleansed your disturbing reality thoughts from earlier.

Sunni, you put the hospice visit on my timeline, not me.

Apologies: off-shoreness, poor signal.

Ok, look, let's ThinkComm later.

Shall I stay awake, capture experience? Potential old-ground positive bank?

No. Minimal input, Sunni.

Please be aware: excessive free thought is not favourable.

Sunni's power light dims to hibernation blue. As she takes off the sunglasses, giant rays of light paint the sea in silver. She goes to stand at the rail where a strong breeze makes her hair fly and cover her face, yet she can see that the guy is wearing the short beard favoured by many of this year's Irish fans.

'Ça va?' he says.

'Oh, you are not Irish?

'Oui, Irlandais,' he says, 'I assumed you're French.'

'Yes, that's true. I have opted English-speak for my trip.' She nods to the Ireland logo on his jacket. 'I should select Irish-speak to honour the unification of your country.'

'Don't mention the war.'

In laughter he reveals a natural smile and neat white teeth. He returns his attention to the sea. She follows his gaze to a darkening cloud now bruising the water beneath it.

'Gonna rain,' he says.

'I hear Ireland is in heatwave.'

'Flippin toxmosphere, there'll be another month at least. You holidaying?'

'No. A year off.'

'Intelligence burn-out?'

'My mother died.'

'Shit, sorry,' he says. 'That's cat.'

'Car crash. Soon, the anniversary. I need to get away.'

'You're right.'

Her breath feels shaky like when she used to tell child lies at Home. Sunni has advised already that death by drug erosion is not a detail to share in background exchanges. Bad heat flares in her uncovered eyes and a gust of sea spray dampens her face. She dabs her skin, then stops. Irish guy might think that she's upset, be considerate and not go any further.

'I'm currently data-non-read,' he says, 'I eCleanse a few hours a day. Means I ask awkward questions. Sorry about your–'

'How did you know I was French?'

'I dunno. Could be instinct regrowth.'

'Do you recommend eCleanse?'

'Yeah, but it can be bad at the start. You ever get old-ground negative? Feels like only the worst things will happen?'

'Like when signal is down?'

'Yeah, like that except for longer. You tough it out, it gets less each time.'

'Would you like to have a drink? We can talk more?'

'Yeah? Cool.'

Inside, the French fans have semi-circled the alcohol server bots, leaving no gaps. Two men peruse her, head to toe. One whispers to the other and tries to lock her in a smile. Always this shit with older men.

Irish guy leans in close bringing a herbal scent of mild cologne.

'Too noisy to talk.'

'I have wine,' she says quickly and just as quickly realises that Sunni hasn't corrected her for speaking without input. She holds her bag slightly open, so Irish guy can see the Ultras. His eyes widen.

'Reality? You sure?'

'Yes. I want to, to stop thinking about the...the anniversary.'

She powers Sunni to show their compatibility data via lens screen.

'If you're certain,' he says, 'yeah.'

'Oui, am certain. Your cabin.'

Hibernation, Sunni, she ThinkComms.

She steps carefully in the narrow galley, sea-motion tipsiness in her legs, real actual fingers holding her hand. A funeral memory appears: a hospice nurse stroking her hair. You are so like your mother, he said. He grasped her hand, staring at her right eye as if caught by the woody fleck in the blue iris.

Sunni unhibernates.

Not like Mother. You will be with one guy at a time, on a bed, not in a disco pissoir.

Sunni, for fuck sake, just hibernate.

Inside the cabin they stare at a narrow, blue-covered bed, then at each other because there is nowhere else to look.

'Where are you staying in Ireland?' he asks.

'I am visiting family. Ok if I–' she points to a door beside the bed.

'Sure, go on ahead.'

She opens the door to a cupboard-sized shower room with a mirrored wall. In the mirror's reflection, Irish guy's dark messy hair tops hers like in a head swap photo, she's not sure if he can see this ridiculous sight.

'Irish blood?' he asks.

Her cheeks begin to warm and she has no Sunni to reverse such a condition. Sunni must be punishing her by truly staying in hibernation? The Irish guy moves away to the bed, breaking the head swap picture. She takes toothbrush glasses from the sink. Silly to feel embarrassed, it is normal to search for a father, is it not? Other girls from Home have spent their tracing awards on holidays, or clothes. Fuck Home, they say, Home uses us to win state funding, to Home we are only lucrative numbers. The Home girls would scoff at her for following procedure, and even more at who she has traced.

'Where from? Maybe I know them.'

She laughs a little and pours the wine.

'I thought it was a fairy tale that all Irish people know each other.'

'You'd be surprised, you start with a name, next thing you work out you are cousins.'

'No, that's too crazy.' She passes him a glass. 'We should get a little bit drunk.'

'Yeah, here's to Irish family.'

According to Home what remains of her reality family is an Irish father with no other children, a man named Robert Wall, formerly from Dublin, currently living in New Ross. In his most recent profile his face tries not to smile as if someone has told him a joke just when he needs to be serious, the unburst laughter gleams in his eyes. A shining head too, the skin smooth and pale, giving no clue as to what his hair colour ever was. He wears the brown robe of his Buddhist tribe. Recently she has searched YouTube archives of Euro 2016, scanning the mosh of green jerseys on guys of all ages who were singing, dancing and picking up rubbish, asking herself how would her accidental father have looked then as a young red-faced drunk?

They sit with their backs against the wall and sip lukewarm wine. The bed see-saws slightly as if the ocean is settling down for the night. The engine noise grows louder like Sunni's travel data said it would on a no moon night.

'Are you going home to family?' she asks.

'To Cork for the Euros. Then Longford to family. All of my family live in the capital.'

'You are lucky to have actual tickets for the Euros.'

'My mam's a referee.'

'Cool. Mam is your word for mother?'

'Yeah. She's some woman. What about yours, what was she?'

'Oh, it's hard to say…I think she was poor but resourceful.'

'My real dad? Is poor but an asshole,' he says firmly.

At least you know that, she wants to say.

She pushes off each shoe with the other foot and stretches her toes.

'Cool feet,' he says.

She turns to his oncoming face.

'Don't you want to know my name?' he asks, his features becoming a blur.

'No, do not tell me your name.'

While he rolls the Ultra off, she stares at the ceiling inventorying their Reality Sex, matching each recent touch memory with the actual bodily warmth and sensations remaining.

'What d'you think of Reality?' he asks breaking her free thought.

She chooses an efficient positive word:

'Excellent.'

'You made excellent noise yourself.'

Trying not to breathe in his now sweat-laced herbal aroma she wishes he would stop talking and allow her to think.

'These Ultras better live up to their name.'

He leans across giving her a study of his upper body. Skin milky pale, apart from where blue and green skin art circles his upper arm. He ties the Ultra, drops it on the floor. She feels a shuddery sensation she cannot find the word for. *Disgust* pops into her head, she imagines it in a Sunni voice.

'No escape for those bad boys.' Irish guy laughs and lies down. 'Paul Moore,' he says.

'Is that another one of your Irish words?'

'That's my name. My cabin, my rules. If you won't tell me yours, tell me something else. Didn't I teach you some new phrases? Ah go on, you owe me.'

'What do you want to know?'

'I dunno. Are you a spy or a nurse or a student or what?'

'Not so exciting. I graduated as an architect. I mean a real one of buildings, not a Softie.'

The graduation was celebrated last year, one week after mother's funeral. A Home Bot took a class photo which proves it although she does not remember wearing the gown or the feel of the parchment in her hand. She could relive it via Sunni if she desires but what's the point if she felt nothing on the actual day? She realises she has missed the opportunity to create a wild tale—Oh, I have three jobs: pavement artist, thief, prostitute, like my mother before me. But I do it for kicks, not for drugs.

Some university friends Reality Fuck for money, even one rich girl who lives in an inherited apartment and doesn't even need to. Mother left no money, no house, only the name of her father, Robert Wall, gleaned from the credit card she stole from her client. An Irishman so happy to fuck he split his protection and didn't notice mother's crack whore hand in his back pocket. Laughter strikes when she recalls this detail. Poor stupid father. Smart, resourceful mother. Would mother have laughed if she had known that he became a monk? Was mother the type of person to laugh at natural outcomes? She presses harder into recall. In questionnaire mode, Mother said she had loved a band called Arcade Fire.

'You could do a Masters,' this Irish guy interrupts. 'Be like me, eternal student.'

'Make your family proud?'

'I don't have what you call a normal family.'

Really? she would like to say, you have a guru monk as your surprise
father and an old school sex worker as your mother, now dead and gone?
Home Bots as your "actual" family?

He asks where she grew up. Her eyes roll behind their closed lids and
she refers to Home as a boarding school in Avignon, explaining simply
that she had hardly known her mother and had never met her father. He
says his parents both remarried, he has too many parents, would she like
one of his?

'How about I stick my tongue down your throat to stop you talking?'

'Fuck, you sound like an Irish girl.'

They laugh and turn to each other.

After their frantic breathing has returned to normal, she sighs about the
bruised but good feeling between her legs, the lack of stickiness, his fluid
caught in Ultra number two. Reality Sex seems good enough for more
and she wonders if there is time. Locating Sunni among their strewn
clothes, she presses the button: it is o-two hundred hours. Sunni in
hibernation re-asserts the guy's Euro ID as IRL, and his data-non-read
status. Sunni also ThinkComms a reminder:

CBT soon, mother is not a suitable memory.

Fuck off, I'm thinking, she ThinkComms, letting Sunni drop. A circle of
light yellows the floor as Sunni fully unhibernates.

Irish guy is not on future timeline, Sunni ThinkComms.

I don't want to keep him. I just want one memory made by me.

Focus on good parent goal.

Yeah, yeah, yeah.

An ethnicity estimate gave her ancestry as thirty percent IRL. Her goal
is to ask Robert Wall to confirm their shared blood, to formally bond. A
monk should be a helpful welcoming person should he not? Someone
who wants to do the right thing, to do good. Sunni already confirmed
that the mindful tribe is highly rated for authentic intent. But would a
monk want a surprise daughter from someone like Mother?

Sunni's hibernation light flickers, blue winking in the darkness.

Is off-shoreness threatening your continuance, asshole?

Sunni does not respond.

Irish guy starts talking about his future timeline of actual football and reunions with friends and family. He slides into French every few sentences.

'You prefer your second language?' she says.

'When I was a kid, my real dad paid more attention if we spoke in French.'

'Was he French?'

'No. He taught it. He was in love with the place.'

'Why didn't he live there?'

'Touchy subject. This is only a given memory cuz I was two and don't recall, but one summer, he disappeared for two weeks, with all the money saved for a family holiday. Turns out he went to France for the Euros.'

Irish guy is singing, "stand up for the boys in green, stand up for the boys in green" like the Euro 2016 fans on Youtube who were cleaning up rubbish.

'My mam took him back,' he says.

'She loved him too much,' she replies in a yawn, hoping that he won't answer, so she can think about something that she cannot yet grasp.

'Probably. He played away all the time. Got one girlfriend pregnant, a teacher at my school. Idiot. Mam divorced him, and he married the girlfriend. Not embarrassing at all.'

She inhales deeply as if falling asleep, and he stops talking.

Caught in the hum of the ferry, her mind keeps working while Irish guy's breathing slows and stretches. Sunni's light flickers. She should pick up the used Ultras from the floor and bin the slimy mess or she might walk on them in her bare feet. A YouTube clip flits through her mind, "Clean up for the French police, Clean up for the French police", such songs her mother would have heard while working in pissoirs and club booths.

She tries to hear only the engine and beyond that the hiss of the sea, but soon vile imaginations of mother's life appear — Mother earning money for drugs, her faceless body shrinking beneath a pile of half-naked men. How could she have remembered which man's protection split? Did the bonus of a credit card make such a moment unforgettable? She has forgotten Irish Guy's name already. Will this Reality Fuck be in her old-ground positive bank for years, will this smell and rawness be always remembered and no name to go with them?

No sleep comes as her free thoughts stretch onwards, unstoppable. What if the Robert Wall tracked by Blood Search is not the Robert Wall who mother stole the card from, what if he did not even go to Euro 2016? What if the other Home girls are correct, that Home and Blood Search enter fake data just to fulfil their funding claims?

A falling sensation comes suddenly, she is heart-thump alert as if there has been a knock on the door. He "played away all the time" the father of this Irish guy glued to her body. She tries to worm away to create a gap. The trap of this narrow bed is making them touch no matter how taut she holds her limbs. Not possible, not possible. A shakiness takes over her body while her mind scratches back for his name. It would have hit her at the time if this guy's name was Wall, would it not?

His arm tightens on her waist.

'Are you cold?' he whispers, 'you're shaking.'

'Non.'

'What's up?'

'Tell me your father's name, your real father.'

'Yeah, that's not weird.'

'Please tell me.'

'Sean Moore.'

'Good. That is a good name.'

'Glad you think so.'

'Do you have a monk in your family?'

'Again, not a bit weird.' He half laughs, half yawns. 'Monk in the family? No. Maybe I'll become one if that's your thing.'

Soon, the heavy exhalation of his sleep sounds in her ear. She lets her body sink against him. Her heart begins to normalise. She reaches for Sunni and checks what she knows she knows: DNA safe.

Was that you fucking with my head, asshole? Sending me twisted thoughts?

Excessive free thought is self-harm.

It has not done Irish guy any harm, he is fast asleep.

She remembers what Irish Guy advised about eCleanse, how you will think that only the worst things will happen.

Again, Sunni is nagging her to lift the spent protections from the floor.

Sighing, she rises and picks up her clothes and dresses by Sunni's light, taking note of everything she can see. She traps Sunni under her arm and makes to leave the cabin. Halfway, she stops to reach down for a beautiful object, a fresh notebook unused. She runs her hand over the soft, red cover. Glancing back at sleeping Irish guy, she says,

'Bin the protection – your cabin, your mess.'

In her own cabin, she opens the port hole for real air. She places Sunni on her head and Sunni informs her of sea temperatures and such statistics; they are equidistant between France and Ireland, the signal is due to lapse for a short while.

Time to shower, to CBT, to goal-focus for good parent.

First, I am going to write.

The notebook is not your property.

She begins writing her timeline details for the next few days, the dates and venues. Sunni reads her small handwriting.

Your plan to use good parent for IRL citizenship is possible, but also unethical.

I know that, Sunni.

Feeling her face move involuntarily she realises she is smiling. She writes the words of a song from infant school — just to annoy Sunni as it is not officially in her old-ground positive. She requests Sunni to look up the Mother Questionnaire, and reads one last time the answer to the question:

Q. Favourite Mode of Transport?

A. Slow ferry boat. The slower the better.

She lifts Sunni away from her eyes and closes the arms flat on the sunglass lenses.

Do not expect a Grand Canal sanctuary in Dublin, it is a weed-ridden wasteland.

Have you not heard? Longford is the capital. Just shut up, Sunni.

When the signal lapses she goes to the round window. She imagines she cannot throw too far as she has not thrown an object since childhood. There is a small splash and a brief glow in the water then Sunni's light is dead. The ferry engine chugs louder, forcing a sleepy rhythm in her head.

Perhaps she will not go to see Robert Wall, perhaps she will use her grant to travel. In Ireland, on land, she will know what to do.

Two Poems
P. C. Evans

The Justice of Narcissus

I was re-assigned as mistress
Emerita in the genuflection of the knee,
When the academy was closed down permanently.
So beneath sun and cypress

I serve you, for a surreptitious cigarette -
Merci - a glass of mint tea and a crust of bread.
A nest egg? Hardly. I was never in the position
To get ahead, and being cursed with a mind and an acerbic tongue

Wasn't able to snag a husband and be his devoted wife.
So now, with God and nothing - ahem - I share a stoic's bed. And life?
It seems to be this centipede
Of sweaty apparatchiks milling before me,

Eager to haggle over the price.
I try to keep to the market line, I
Rarely cave. The gift of the gab comes almost as naturally
To me as it does to these cat-calling market furies.

But still a tutor to the marrow,
I can calculate this two-metre furrow
Of earth will be my universe until a death occurs,
And dust mixes with the dust.

But first, let this faithful rag burnish the reflections
In the brilliant mirror of your western
Shoes, and may I wish upon you, if
You can comprehend it,

The justice of Narcissus.

Headbangers

Bricked into the cornices and quoins of some Syrian streets
One can still find a tablet carved with Hittite hieroglyphic reliefs.

For centuries, nomadic Islamists would press their crania against these
 […] baked clay bricks,
Simple spirits murmuring lamentations in a sing-song Arabic.

Hoping that by cracking their skulls on a foreign script
They could cure their myopia, or even blindness, and enter Utopia.

So clearly, the source of this ancient Syrian superstition resides
With the brickies of the cities of Hattushash and Charchemish

And the chiselling Hittite scribes
- probably paid by the line -

And perhaps these mystical and mythical rhymes
- if they do indeed rhyme -

May have inspired the odd dogmatist or two
Into firing a prayer at Aleppo from Mecca

Or Jerusalem, or Rome - who can say for sure
Whether the shades of the ladies and gents from Anatolia to Nineveh

May not have had their own bespoke picture of paradise,
Muzzled in the cross-hairs of the mind's eye,

As they are harvested like wheat in a mowing shoah,
A revelation of truth in a tongue of fire.

Badlands
Fergus Cronin

A skinny man with long dreadlocks dozed on a bog in the west of Ireland, his black skin warmed by a late autumn sun. He was interrupted by the sound of an engine, followed by the distant clatter of scraping and grinding metal.

'Irish John' Prentice had been happy to be away from Sheffield, removed from his birthplace, his songs and guitars, finding space. He'd sought his own mother's people out—trying to get to grips with her O'Malleys. It was good cover for what he was really looking for: some spark to light up his head again. And the light was good—might be good enough to beam him back to the City of Steel. There were loads of O'Malleys but they weren't for much talking and there was no recall of his mother. Not a surprise, as names slipped easily from mothers of mothers. And some sort of an O'Malley she may well be, somewhere else. He was happy to let her go. It was not really why he was here. Either way the place had put on its blank face, however well it was lit: nothing to see here but yourself.

About ten miles into the mountains he'd thrown himself and his bicycle onto the heather. He'd been thinking of the pirate queen they'd told him about: Grace O'Malley. Could he put her to music he wondered. *Gracie? Gracie meets Calypso.* Ska? Nah. He smiled at the idea. There had of course been a fucking hymn to soften his head, a Stabat Mater—an echo of a concert he'd been at in an abbey a few nights previously. That had rightly cheered him up. So, he wondered, with all this good humour, maybe he was ready to go home.

He shifted himself to the top of the bank to see down the fifty yards or so to the twisty tar. There it was, a heap of metal, wheels up and still turning, smoking he thought. A goldy-brown blur of an animal rolled out of sight over a hillock beyond the ditch. 'Bugger this.' He set off hopping the dry hummocks among the sphagnum, feeling the spiky grass against his bare feet. He clambered over a sheep-fence and arched a path across the road, never taking his eyes off the inverted red car and a grey horsebox, now detached and thrown on its side. The windows of the car were dipping in the ditch water like they were on a sinking ship. He stooped in to look. There was straw hanging behind the glass. Hair. Rusty straw-coloured hair. Blood.

A heap of metal, a machine flung down, half-drowned in a drain, was a regular feature in that valley but Prentice had never seen anything like this before. The bog sucking hard on the terrible iron blew off any remnants of his reveries. He had shaped iron once back in Sheffield. A foundryman. Before he had swapped those scars from the callouses of steel guitar strings. Now, in this wild and eerie place, the name of a lad from Rotherham came to his lips: Wilson, whose head he had seen crushed by an axle falling from a faulty gantry-crane. He'd buried that image a long time ago.

He looked for a way to get the car open but the doors and windows were jammed tight. His feet were sinking so he splashed back to firm sod. Some seconds passed before he sensed a volume of air being displaced behind him. A huge shadow caused him to stiffen. He turned to see a massive black hole with the outline of… a what… a cowboy? He fancied that something might be about to fly out from this shape. A silence settled in. Nothing moved in the vast emptiness stretching to the feet of mountains all around. Then suddenly a breeze stirred the grasses. A sound built into a shrill moan, then became a voice.

'Gone to fucking heaven.' This was from a garrulous world.

Prentice knew that he didn't need to say anything just yet.

He tried to line his thoughts up, so he might find some words that could be driven in, like rivets, when he was ready.

'Gone to fucking heaven.'

A huge man come into the light, repeating his words. He rambled in on the Cuban heels of his snakeskin boots; under a white ten-gallon hat; a sky-blue suit flurried about his frame in the breeze. The diamante decoration—the ruby stones on the jacket, the silver studs on the trouser seams and the brown crochet patterns stitched on the white shirt— made for a vivid pathos. He hitched his thumbs either side of the large horseshoe buckle of his belt to steady himself. 'I'm Shane. O'Malley. Shayneen O'Malley. Who'm I with here? What y'all go by pardner?'

'I'm John. I'm English. My mother was from here. They call me Irish John. '

'Do they indeed. Can't see why.'

Prentice figured there was no use in fucking about with irony so he settled for the straightforward.

'My father was from Jamaica but there was English John and Scots... ' He let his words trail off. The woman in the car was reclaiming his full attention.

'We need to get her out. Although it looks like she's—'

'Passed on to the angels.' O'Malley gurned out. 'Where's the damn hoss gone is what I want to know. Clear kicked his way out of that box. Bastard Palomino. Twisted... what's them things... genes. Yeah them things. Never trusted that hoss. A bit like yourself, hah? You look like a fellah with a bit of a twist in you. English did you say? From the colour of you I'd be thinking you are not at all. Or an Irishman for that matter. The most of you anyways. Did ya see a hoss? A Palomino bastard?'

A new arrival, a cloud, moved in to block the setting sun. In the cold shallow light they took one another in again: the dreadlocked, barefoot young Englishman and the ruddy faced man with fine threads of orange hair squeezed out from under the rim of his hat.

'I didn't see a horse,' Prentice lied, 'but this here's not good. Are we going to try and get her out of there or ... are you alright? You look as if ...'

'As if what ... what ? That sure is a shock of a thing here ... and the little child ... ' was the reply and then another question, 'are y'all an Apache or what?'

Prentice felt the sting of the words. 'What do you mean child? What child? What are you saying?' he heard himself ask. What Apache?' he thought, a burning in his head. 'What are you saying?' he asked again.

'Let's see what we got here.' O'Malley pushed roughly by, and on into the ditch.

Both men were now peering in at a young woman's face,

inverted, in a grotesque press against the car window. Still as marble. Her gaze was locked on some thought that no longer existed, and a trickle of blood came down from the gape of a mouth to implicate the eyes. Too late. There was no way to shift the doors and the car was slowly sinking. The men twisted their necks to see better, but nothing got any better. The dammed-up water in the drain was slowly reaching in to sink the terror. Prentice felt some unwanted words might drop out if he didn't right himself. O'Malley might have come upright for other reasons: fumes of alcohol were mingling with the evaporations of the motor fuel that was painting the boggy ditch water.

'Is that your truck?' Prentice caught the glint off bright metal from a dip in the road beneath the waning sun—the direction he guessed O'Malley had come from.

O'Malley was now bent forward, his massive body leaning down on his big thighs with the ten-gallon held across his knees. He let out a long sigh, nodded, and then started to shake his head. The top of his head was tonsured and a long pelmet of fine orange hair shook across his features. Here was something brutal, Prentice thought. The breeze moved the flamy heads of the grasses all around.

'Were you ever with another man's wife?' O'Malley barked. Prentice was getting used to the noise of the man— how the accent slipped in and out. But now he was making some new sound; it came like a soft buzz, he was humming, then a few words to the tune '… but sleep won't come, the whole night through, your cheatin' heart, will tell on you.'

'Excuse me?' Prentice was well off-balance: the question and the song.

'I said. Were. You. Ever. With. Another. Man's. Wife. Are you not hearing me? I said—'

'I heard you. What— ?'

'You may well ask. Will you not listen to my question? Huh?'

'I'm sorry mister but I've no idea why you are asking me that. What's this about?'

'Fuck you. Turkishman', rumbled O'Malley and then the low

singing started again.

'My mother was an O'Malley… she …. ' Prentice fought with the need to start spinning out.

'There won't be much dancin' out of her again.' O'Malley made a clucking sound that Prentice heard as a low chuckle.

'My mother? She was—' Prentice tried to get something off the mark again.

'Your mother? What're you saying about your mother? How the hell is your mother in this? I'm talkin' about her here. Darleen.'

'How did she come off the road?' Prentice went to change the tempo again.

'I guess she needed to stop. Stop, do you hear.' Then with the low chuckle— 'oh she was stopped alright. In her tracks she was stopped.' Then he raised his voice again. 'But I'm thankin' it's none of yer fuckin' business now is it?' O'Malley was looking in several directions at once now, with his wavering blather. It was unclear what he was trying to focus on.

Prentice had moved back to have another look to see if there was any sign of a child. Of any life. Of a way in.

'I suppose I might try and drag this out with my rig.' O'Malley stumbled around to head off back to his truck.

'Hold on. Hold it up. For a minute will you.' Prentice called loudly after him. 'We could do more harm. I can't see any child. Are you sure you saw a child?'

O'Malley stopped and turned.

'Jesus. I thought … What am I after sayin' about keepin' your nose …. ' he growled.

'You ran that woman off the road?'

'What're y'all sayin, huh? Did you say something about your mother? An O'Malley? That I … what did you say I didn't … something? All I say is we'd better get that automobile out before it sinks altogether and drowns 'em into the bargain. We better get that automobile the fuck out of there. Do you hear? Geronimo. We can't let 'em drown too'.

There was a different temper now in O'Malley's tone as he waltzed back into his cowboy-speak. He'd come back towards Prentice surefoot, stretched out his arms, laid them firmly on Prentice's shoulders and gave him a bloodshot stare. The whisky smell was powerful and Prentice saw the muddle in the man's eyes; his puckered childish face. He looked like he could be sixty or only a boy, a big boy. A big mad dangerous man-boy, Prentice thought, and he spoke to dispel the thought.

'The woman looks like she's dead and there's no sign of a child. Can we smash the glass?'

'Reinforced. And there'll be a child alright. Believe me there'll be a child. We'll drag it out.'

'But—'

'No. Injun-boy. I knows that woman. Darleen. Thar'll be a child.'

What abominable intimacy had he stumbled upon? This Irish … cowboy? He thought of looking for help—on his cycle in he hadn't noticed any house for a few miles back; he carried no phone and anyway wouldn't O'Malley ….

'Mister O'Malley. You from around here?' he shouted as O'Malley disappeared into the sinking light on his way back to his truck. O'Malley threw an arm up from his shambling departure.

The silvershimmering hulk came roaring up from the dip. The figurehead steer-horns on the fenders seemed to come straight at him and as it rose, so Prentice swung out of the way and into the deep skid ruts from the crashed car. O'Malley pulled up the massive silver truck and leaned out the window to answer Prentice.

'Yeah I'm from around here. And I'm at thangs the way of 'round here.'

'We should call someone. An ambulance. Have you got a phone?'

'We'll call no-one. This is no-one's business.'

'Isn't there a danger …?'

'The only danger for you is that you end up in there alongside the—'

'I just thought …

'What did I just say. Eh, Injun?' O'Malley then picked up his song again. 'Your cheatin' heart will tell on you … ' He was out of the cab and lifting a coil of heavy rope from the bed of the truck. At the end of the valley, the sun came out of the cloud to bobble over a mountain and out of the day. Prentice felt a jolt as the huge gaudy figure brushed into him and shambled towards the car. O'Malley kept crooning away, louder now, to all the world like a satisfied man going about his work. '…you'll cry and cry, and try to sleep….'

We're done here with this *Injun Geronimo* bollocks, Prentice thought and then he said it.

'Is there some problem with being black? Anyway I'm not an Indian. Never was. I told you my father was from Jamaica. Me, I'm as English as Jack Charlton. That's what I am. My mother was Irish. That's why they call me Irish John.' He was both angry and afraid, so he tried to sound courageous.

'Y'all tell me your mother was from where. Round here? Pretty yarn. Jeez. It's all O'Malleys hereabouts. Pirates. You tell me y'all are an Englishman? Some sooty Englishman though'. O'Malley gave what might have been a soft laugh as he said it and went about lashing the rope over the car—he was preparing to right it with a sideways turn. 'An' you know pardner I guess there could be a problem, and you with the tint an' all. It's not a thing an O'Malley mammy would be totin' hereabouts. But I'm just shapin' to deal with this here problem for now. Could be that I know that woman, your mammy. Could be I don't. And now if y'all don't mind.'

Prentice went back to check the woman. The light was greying fast and a soft rain was dripping from thickening clouds. Water the colour of rust was seeping into the car and he couldn't see any face: the head had turned and settled in some other way. The blonde hair was now shivering like a water-weed. A pink stetson hat floated like a jellyfish. He looked up to see that O'Malley had backed the truck up to get an angle for the pull.

O'Malley was about to tie the rope to the hitch of the truck when he straightened up and turned, still holding the rope in a loop. His expression relaxed. The rain made a rapid plipping sound on his hat. The palm of his free hand shot up to rub his head, tilting the hat back at an angle.

'Tell me this', he said, with no sign of the earlier barrack in his voice, 'Do you know any of them supermodels? Over there. The supermodel ones?'

'I don't.' Prentice had been watching the car again. The air was cold, the rain was coming heavier and a loud gurgling noise from the car had come and gone before he heard the absurd question.

'Sundance. Flaherty. Said he poked one over at Ballyna-the-fuck-Castle summer just gone. You don't happen to know Sundance do you? Nah I didn't think so. He's the boy for the cow-pokin'. Poke a steer too the same bucko. Ha-ha. It's anythin' with a sweet ass around here.' He made a sound like laughter again but there was no laughter in his voice this time. He came towards Prentice and placed the loop of rope over his head to rest on his shoulders. 'You look like a fellah who'd know about pokin'. Did you say you were a pop-star boy or somethin'?'

Both men stared at the other. Teeming rain ran down Prentice's face misting up his vision. He struggled to figure out if the fright he felt was in the other man's eyes too.

'I didn't say. No I'm not a popstar. I'm just a… ' Prentice held it at that. He wished he held the five-pound hammer that he thought he'd never hold again. He imagined he did and stayed his ground.

'Huh. You're just a fellah looking for his mammy. Or her mammy's mammy. You weren't going with any other mammys here were you?' O'Malley opened the loop and pulled the rope sharply away across the back of Prentice's neck. It chafed sorely. 'There's a lot of mammys need laevin be in this place. Don't need little strangermen pokin' about. Mixin' things up. That's when the rumblin' starts. If you get my drift.'

O'Malley then moved quickly, the rain flinging from the rim of his hat. His suit was drenched now and sticking to his frame like a tissue. A blue skin that was silver-studded to him. He fixed the rope to the hitch, swung up into the driver's seat and started the truck. He shouted over the engine noise at Prentice.

'Watch that mammy bitch come up. And her little man. And don't even think about the whys or the whats of it. Bad-assed mammys get what's a-comin to 'em. And their little babbies. Honeybunch here was a bad girl. And if I was you I'd be a quiet boy… we'll get around to…. ' The revving of the truck drowned out the rest.

Prentice watched as the engine roared and the rope strained. The tyres on the truck slipped and screeched and sprayed until there was movement from the ditch. Then everything was moving and splashing as the crashed car was righted after a great sucking struggle with the bog. It bounced and steadied under a streaky dark sky. A full wind drove the rain horizontal. It was piercing and freezing. Prentice had used his chance to grab his bicycle and move to the far side of the truck. A door of the upturned car burst open and he saw the pink stetson and then another tiny version of the same hat come out in a torrent. The truck engine had stopped and the only sound was the wind, the rain and through it all O'Malley singing. 'Oh mammas don't let your babbies grow up to be cowboys… ' Then it was all carried away in a massive bluster of air. As Prentice made away in the storm he noticed the passenger door of the silver truck was gouged with red.

A coal-black ceiling pressed down and the wind and rain whipped away in a ferment. He barely managed to draw a breath as he cycled up the valley. It was a demented ride. He thought of devils flying; the end of time. The whistling of the grasses and the wire gave over to the shrieking of the truck that was coming up somewhere behind him. He tried to shout out but it was snatched away in the tumult. He threw himself into the ditch and turned to see the road glimmering as the headlights flashed closer. Then there was something standing on the road. A shape. A horse. It was still and waiting between Prentice and the swelling light. Just as the truck came up the animal turned and reared-up, a proud thing. Its coat blazed orange in the wash of the rain and the lights and he thought he saw its eyes in some triumph before it twisted away towards the truck. There was a terrible screeching and a mass of black. Everything was extinguished. Only the wind mourned on. Irish John Prentice managed at last to lift his head and make his own sound. He wondered would it wake him and take him from this land of pirates and cowboys. These badlands. And he promised, in the streaming ditch, as he gulped for a steadying thought, to go back to his steel strings and live only in the music that he knew might turn the tables. Forget all about O'Malleys and mothers and false light. Back in the city of steel.

Four Poems
Tracey Rhys

Bathsheba in Beverly Hills

Before the cancer took hold,
she took only honey, the finest manuka,

the colour of the skin she'd oiled
at poolside parties in her youth.

When the sun was too hot to escape,
she lay on the frills of her daybed,

dreamt of the stores in Beverly Hills,
the dinners at Brentwood,

the nights at the beach house in Malibu.
Recalled the bellhops with their cotton gloves,

their smell in her penthouse, the elevator carpeted,
the rattle as the gates slid shut.

At a dance when she was seventeen,
some stranger in the crowd slid his hand

between her legs, brushed at her skin,
creased up her new silk dress.

She spun around, expecting…
not those society men, their hair slicked back like lips,

the crystal in their hands,
the way their conversation never slipped.

Bathsheba's Relics

After she'd died, long days and nights
gathering dust in the velvet, ingrained in the silk,
they opened the wardrobe. Carved into the oak
was a pelican, its neck bulging with secrets.
Inside, her perfume cloyed and hung
on collars and cuffs, their button holes
the exact shape of her mouth, its little '*Oh?*'

Hanging amongst winter coats, they found her stick.
The black one with the brass, its bunch of grapes
that bit into the skin. For weeks after, a prankster
woke before the house, swaggered downstairs
in onyx and pearls, tapping on tiles and varnished boards.
How their stomachs lurched to hear her pass,
the familiar groan of footfall on the bottom stair,
the solid tip of metal on terrazzo floor.

Bathsheba in Eden

Soon, she will arrive home and every indiscretion
will simmer away. She will be happy with a storm
before sun: thorns overhead and not inside.
The only fruit within her will be the wine staining her teeth.
Her little tongue will spit seeds onto her new white dress.
She will wear her hair as if she is rising from bed.
She will not draw a line around her lids.
She will not draw a line around her mouth.
Will wear nothing on her cheeks but down.
Will remove the silver cuffs from her wrists.
Will not wear perfume.
She will listen for the snapping of twigs
in the tall shade of the national parks,
her thighs separate as animals
moving in pairs, prepared to run.

Bathsheba

Her second life was found in birds circling at dusk,
their cawing dots she could not join.

She loved her brother. He was fast and lean, as wild as watercress.
He was with her for the walk into the fields each day.

Abe's watch: the daily toilet. She sat on her heels in the mosses.
The quiet thud of pots on stoves, a goat's bleat on the air.

Abe disturbed the grasses, pulled out two scraps of boys
like kittens from a wool pit. Laughing like capuchins,

they kicked until he dropped them. Bathsheba found herself
a good leaf, prepared to go home.

Abe said he would wring out their small necks,
would visit their fathers.

She howled with shame until he smiled,
They'll only know you from the bottom down.

Space is a doubt
Fiona O'Connor

'Space is a doubt.' Perec

I can describe his expression: surprise, mirroring my own. Alarm too. Some pleasure, yes? Seeing me? That I was alive.

He cocked his head; optimism, his default position, was signalled across the room. His presence, mine: possible worlds ganged up in the doorway.

When he came back he looked across, careful to take in what was going on; *it was a clinical observation:* at that instant my turbulence was cast over his features; I read the disturbance.

He leaned forwards to see more. His years of intimacy with me, the distance of years in which we had not seen each other, the circumstances of our last encounter – ending of the analysis, drawn, through weeks of incredulity at what we were doing, to that final moment when he, sighing quietly, said, 'well…' and the clock hand budged into the fiftieth minute: 'well…' no more than a murmur, and in the space of the ellipsis there was a break, a tearing, and I moaned and ran from the room.

In this building; upstairs in one of the rooms, a bed, an armchair, a blanket folded, rain on the window.

This time of year too, a little later: December evening, just before Christmas, cruelly.

The wet streets, chill of damp air.

He leaned forwards to see me, to ~~take,~~ ~~make,~~ ~~have,~~ hold an observation, in order to gauge my state of mind.

Alarm travelled across his face.

What did I reveal? Depth of

~~sorrow?~~

~~longing?~~

118

~~loss?~~

Need? Did my expression write that last word across its brazen visage?

Shame? An unloved woman.

Age? Aging body, wrinkled face – something he's not good with; for all his devotion to therapeutic love he can't be bothered with old women.

He just can't. Once when I was young I saw him at the end of that long corridor ushering a woman from his room.

Through a small window I watched. She, fifties, stout in a worn, beige coat, sobbing. She was imploring him and he was ashen but resolute. Out of the tenement bulk of her body, the coat open, black garment beneath, pity was her last resort.

Then I replaced her on the couch. He sat behind me, my mind opened and he entered. I could sense, latent, coming through, his relief.

Selfless his pursuit of another's damage: down into the lair, all of him going there, the professional and the man, following a fugitive figure. Beyond lures: sexual, obsessional, the siren call of silks, a button undone, dab of My Sin on the pulse. Only truth could seduce him, rising unbidden to displace me, unseen evidence damning me from my own mouth - it took years; I was at times too ill for the cure and grateful to insanity because how can a madwoman be expected to endure such a thing?

Taking the stairs to her doctor's room – seven to the half-landing, significant in itself, five more to the dock of the waiting room, bodies shifting there as though she rang a little lunacy bell. She'd sit very small and wait for the conspirators: his young assistants – lovers and wives – she'd wait and one would arrive, no doubt: symbolism dictated a wife must intervene before the doctor could be seen.

Three times then she'd bow her shorn head so that the doctor could appear in the doorway, neither entering nor retreating, but a smile for her supplication and she would follow him down the long corridor towards sanctuary.

Daily journey up and down the Mile End Road, walking, running, laughing, howling. Corridors riddled the hospital linking outlying buildings; I was always late, breathlessly charging. Porters emerged from unseen places wheeling beds. I'd pass death, a brisk walk, a skip along by the side of tiny packages of tissue on bone, smoothly progressed on rubber wheels, eyes staring bewilderment from sinking faces.

I'd fly then to fill his room with urgency, aware of my privilege. Love gave life, his room was a heart. So when he became ill I talked more and deeper. I watched him leave, his black coat at dusk, crossing the hospital gardens, his weakened slow gait.

He cancelled some weeks giving no reason.

When we resumed he looked worse. Winter again, he seemed smaller, to have receded in his presence behind me, behind my thoughts.

He would always put the lights on, something I loathed. As the afternoons turned down into evening, on would flicker and buzz the fluorescent strip above me, with its two dead bluebottles trapped inside the glass. But now he didn't bother. We'd slip into light-fading closeness, love-spelling, soft laughter dissolving fear as the room gathered its dark around us.

I brought out everything I had. On the corridor doors opened and closed, opened and closed. In the room with him a girl was summoned – the silent one I thought had been lost. She arrived surprised to be wanted, cautious against slight – that she might be scorned again - and I was surprised because she was fully formed and fresh and I liked her.

His black coat at dusk, crossing the hospital grounds. Watching from a doorway, with my gimlet eye, seeing him pay out the distance between us, although on the couch I could sometimes feel his breath on my face.

One by one the wards were shut; mental health services the first to be cut. Signs went up in the waiting room: the doctor would be leaving. We could continue the analysis elsewhere, he said. Or not; it was a choice.

In winter the dogwood willows revealed their blood red stems.

A teenager thought she had something growing inside her. The doctors said there was nothing but she thought there was.

Old man on crutches, skittle-gaiting his massive bulk along the shuddering passage, labouring to pull himself out from beneath his own weight.

Girls who cut themselves and girls who couldn't eat. A woman performing her intimate self for anyone to see.

Young man with a soft beard on a tender face, footsteps up and down the corridor.

Within the analytic bind all freedom to become: it is a sustained paradox – as in a folk tale, rabbinical: maddening infallibility from the last great dad, Freud. Self-rigour through those daily rituals, the humble return an architecture for love. Portals and corridors, his clean hand, wedding-banded, holds the door, my hand following, in that place, the door closes, his move to a corner chair, my laying out before him, blocks of sunlight sliding across the carpet, intensifying, fading, intensifying again, until he says, it's time, and I go home alone…

…*carrying the timbre of his voice in my ear, knickers drenched, running his words over my naked skin.*

Ultimately, the only choice of the analysand was to stop.

White words on a white sheet – I read in a whisper:
‑The register of recognition was marital.
‑That's what I saw; I saw my husband.
‑The image strikes the deepest self, strikes closest to the void.
‑Animation of the soul, a mirroring, the one and only.
‑All of it unspeakable.

His image is ageless. Recollection holds him pinned against the wall, with dark hair although his hair is completely white now. A glance was all.

He came back to his seat. He leaned forwards for an observation. In checking, so as to avoid his view, my glance barged into his.

I saw, he saw, see-saw transference.

Curiosity?

If anything. Her state of mind?

I put up my paper to hide my face. For the entire lecture held there: I was the woman in the audience holding a blank paper in front of her face.

Farce. It didn't matter, I could not do else. At this exact point the coordinates of all my possible selves locked into nothingness.

At the end he made a decision: to leave. An understanding therefore: he had taken in some things and here was his interpretation.

He was outta there. Quickly, without fuss.

I was ridiculous with a blank sheet for a face.

There was a last gesture at the doorway. Half turn towards the room so that my psyche registers the image: a character in my internal drama, its leading man in fact, leaves the stage.

Just that. Not a goodbye as such. Instead an image for the soul to hold.

He turns, he is smiling, he is alive. It is personal and impersonal – the soul will take it unreservedly.

Turns before the open door.

Not turning to the woman holding a paper in front of her face (though she sees everything).

Turns to the stage, the audience, to life, smiling, cheery, alive.

Then gone.

Animal Macabre
Stephen Payne

The Carousel of Extinct and Endangered Animals

Dodo Manège, Jardin des Plantes, Paris

The carousel turns slowly in the sun.
The beasts are saddled up for you to ride.
You clamber up the moment that it stops,
and pause beside the frilled triceratops
but choose to climb on board the glyptodon,
stroking its knobbly armadillo hide.

And here's the elephant bird or aepyornis,
here's the Tasmanian tiger and the dodo,
the sivatherium with maybe half
the neck of our familiar giraffe,
a panda and gorilla too, to warn us.
Sit tall and smile while papa takes a photo.

Statue of Lion and Foot

Lion Fountain, Jardin des Plantes, Paris
(Henri Alfred Jacquemart, 1854)

The lion's head bends down as if to sniff
a human foot protruding from the mud.
It might be severed — I assume, instead,
the lion's standing on a buried stiff
with rear paws just above the buried head
of a body it will likely soon uncover.
The toes and heel will make a nice hors d'oeuvre.

It's difficult to contemplate this scene
and not conclude the man's unfortunate
that he should whet the lion's appetite.
Which isn't quite correct. The man has been
unlucky, surely, but whatever plight
he faced is hidden from us now, long gone.
All we see here is good luck for the lion.

Shop Window with Rats

Julien Arouze & Co, Rue des Halles, Paris

Since 1872, Julien Arouze
has been a pest controller to the stars.
The whole shop-front is splendidly preserved,
yet hard to look at. If you feel unnerved
by all the strung-up rats, why wouldn't you?
The rats are in pristine condition too.
They must have been dunked in formaldehyde
then sunk in alcohol the day they died.
What for? Even if rats are clever critters
it can't be *pour encourager les autres*.
Perhaps they hang, pelts fading in the sun,
to show us this is what we've always done,
help us persist. The dead are easier
to kill; the living make us queasier.

Tenderness
Justine Bothwick

Take a moment to stand straight, hands on lower back and hips pushed forward, and look over the rocks along the beach. There is Iannis, doing the same, a slippery heap next to his feet. Acknowledge each other, two men, with a brief uplift of the chin. The winds of the Meltemi blow across the bay – late arrival this year, just that morning and savage – stirring up the flat of the Aegean so that even in the harbour the fishing boats rear and buck like little goats gone insane. Finally, the wind. Until last night, heat hanging over the coast, a heavy sponge soaking up the ability to sleep, to think straight, pressing down into every last space and hollow of the land and his brain.

Back to the rhythm of the task. Different ideas about the best approach. Father's was, come on Stratos, be bold, grab it by the head and throw it down. And again. And again. Thwack, thwack, thwack until it lies softly splattered all over the barnacles. Better take care though, as sometimes the head will detach, and the rest of the body stretches in an arc out past the jetty, landing splash, this time onto water with tentacles splayed, then sinks, and the next thwack is on his own head and that's from Father. Don't be such a cry baby. When will you learn to be a man?

Now he has his own method, favours beating it with the stick. The flesh more tender after, he thinks. So Mother is happy, thank you, Stratos, always my good boy, we'll put it in the pot, broiled in red wine. Mother is old and rarely happy.

At least one hundred beatings, and he has a prized stick, actually an old oar, and with every strike it flattens the muscle tissue so the contractions cease sooner. Each day he hides the oar behind his rock, the one with cracks and angles that make the creases of a frown. No one comes here anyway.

After the beating is swirling and rubbing, because you must get rid of the slime before you hang it up to dry. Use the concrete of the jetty or that pockmarked slab, round and round, swish-swish until there is foam and scum and ooze. That part made Tommy retch.

Tommy in a tent, with tales of travels and college. Beer and barbecues and the Great Barrier Reef. Look the other way down the beach and see the tent still there under sprays of tamarisk trees, last night's fire a black thumbprint on the sand.

*

First there was a smile, then the next day, questions. Doesn't it hurt? Not you, the octopus! A shared laugh then facts: the most intelligent invertebrates, they build gardens, play with toys. Did you know they have three hearts? And then, opinions, like, I don't eat anything with a pulse, haha, no sentient beings, you know?

No, he did not know. Lamb, chicken, fish – it wouldn't be possible not to.

Tommy looks through yellow hair tangled in his lashes. Pale eyes and mocking smile.

*

One morning on the jetty. Mask and snorkel, flippers, trident. Poseidon-in-waiting and Tommy swims up, asks to handle the weapon. More questions so they go together, front crawl out over the weed to the places he knows, dark and maybe just an eye in the murk. Aim, fire and pull the line, drag it in, score. A brief grapple, suckered arms twining his and a squirt of ink. Tommy treading water with a slow applause, then back to the beach with the catch.

Is it dead?

No, wait, that's now, flip the head inside out, grab the brains, see?

Tommy, a frown through yellow hair, turning away. Mate, that's awful, you know?

Yes, perhaps he did know. Haha, be bold, Tommy. Don't be such a cry baby.

*

After, it will hang in the sun with the others, a garland of grisly, webbed stars.

*

An evening walk along the beach with a bag of vegetables. From our garden, thought you'd like them.

Sit together and share a smoke. The sky becomes a haze of purple, then a shy new moon appears. There's talking of the island and questions, always questions. How do you hack it in winter, mate? What was it like growing up here? Don't you want to leave, see a bit of the world?

But that is a world for other people, not the poor, the uneducated, the stuck with a sad mother.

Silence for a while, just the spit and snap of the fire. Then, reaching for a cigarette, hand brushes hand, skin against skin, and it remains. Slowly there's more pressure. Lean in, head fits into neck, and an arm around his shoulder. With great tact, the other hand exploring him, holding him.

Every evening, two weeks and he has never felt such tenderness in his life. Talking, touching, hazy purple nights and moon growing full over the water until... Oh, just so you know, I've a friend arriving. Best we don't see each other while she's here.

*

She has short shorts so you can see the undercut of her buttocks, and full, spilling breasts. He watches them, in the village, eating in the tavernas and drinking cocktails in the bars and laughing, laughing. And he watches them, on the beach, enter in the tent together and laughing, laughing and pleasure.

In the coffeehouse, clicks and ticks of backgammon and strings of beads, but he sits on his own, ignores the other men. Iannis shouts, Stratos, *malaka*, what have you got to be so shitty about?

Smokes a cigarette. At least they won't come in here, where it's still men only and mostly there's just coffee. Another smoke and the room yellows, jaundiced with resentment. This is his world. This is what he has. Only this.

*

The bus takes her away. He sees it go and that evening, along the beach, bag of vegetables.

From the garden, thought of you.

Oh, thanks, mate, but I'll be off tomorrow. You keep 'em, I won't use 'em now.

He can hardly breathe for the hurt.

*

One last indigo night: camp fire, stars and silver water. Waking together before the sun is up. Will you walk with me, to the rock, say goodbye?

Heat still pressing down, but finally the Meltemi is stirring. Tommy looking out to sea, and the oar is in its place and thwack, the body crumples, a heap at his feet. More beatings until the contractions cease, but at least a hundred needed, for the pain and rage to stop, for tenderness to return, for it to tenderise until nothing recognisable remains.

Three Poems
Marcella L. A. Prince

Even I Know Little of It

It is not that the city is that different,
or that the people are not the same.
Deep down I know they are just like us.
It is just that buildings are not far apart.

There's no room to play catch or kickball
in the gaps. And the closeness hasn't seemed
to have done much good for people. No one
greets each other with the same enthusiasm.

Grocery store checkout clerks and bag boys
do not care what your plans are for the day.
They do not know how far you'll walk home
with four shopping bags and pack of toilet paper.

It is not that I think everyone should listen
to hear what's up for swap on lunchtime *tradio,*
but it is frustrating that no one there listens
to the crop prices & farm report every so often.

It's just that they don't always know the difficulty
of it sometimes. They don't think of too much rain
the same way, and probably know little of late
planting seasons. The midnight tractors and stress.

Even I, I admit, know little of it. My rural life

a mere five-year experiment. But I have seen
the distinction and I worry. Such small distances
and yet such (in?)articulate differences.

I Would Not Think to Touch the Sky with Both Arms

I have always loved the vulnerable moments
when there is no gel in your hair
& you let me put my fingers through it –

when corn is low enough in the field
to not get lost in the columns of its stalks
and the world seems wide and brilliant everywhere.

But you know nothing of that particular green.
Yours is deeper and undulating seaward,
mine is a yellow one bright and landlocked,

a different kind of ageless. It has seen prairies
with interlocking roots & grasses & wildflowers
and it has seen ice ages and glaciers that carved out

these flat and potholed flatlands. It has borne big melts,
the water running through the valleys it builds.
It has seen the first people of the continent,

and the second people fighting back the first.
 It has seen the land be fought back too, into the rows
and rows and rows of crops. Into the hog barns, the dairies.

It sometimes seems as if we have tried to hold
all of this in our grasp. Gathered it into our control,
saying, *darling, only I know what is best for you and me.*

I would like to think I am not like this,
that I am capable of more kindness, more worldliness,
but I'm afraid I might also try and touch the sky with both arms.

After the Sky in The Kenmare River, Evening, County Kerry
Sir John Lavery, 1924

The sky is all cotton candy, dreamsicle, and grain.
You've gotten it just right, John. Thank you.

It is just the kind of evening people could love forever.
One reminiscent of first kisses while sitting in a park,

fish & chips, campfire s'mores. It's that flavour of delightful.
But the clouds are a hint of ominous. It might rain at midnight

or hold off until morning when a father will go for a run
with the dog. Though it seems like someone's fishing now,

in which case a drizzle might do them good, draw up
the bass up from the depths of the Kenmare River.

It is hard to keep everyone pleased I suppose.
And it's nearly as beautiful as I remember evenings at home

but with more hills and mountains & that subtle spray
of colour like giant grasses leaping out of the foothills.

What is that, John Lavery? It is such a comfort and yet
such a distress – half of a covenant from God saying,

This is not exactly what we agreed to, but hopefully
it will do. I suppose it will have to do.

P.O. Box 37864
Craig Austin

The orange tin-can bus, when it arrives only two minutes after its allotted time, is formed of two symmetrical rows of deep-welled seats and as you step on board, sliding across two crumpled banknotes to the unsmiling driver, you focus on securing one that is unoccupied by either a bulging briefcase or the encroaching body mass of another human being. By 7:30am at least half of the passengers are already wearing the corporate lanyards of the companies that will own them for the rest of the notional working day, and for some, well into the night that follows. As if the working day itself commences for them at the precise point at which their emptied cereal bowls are placed into the sink, rather than the 20 minutes or so after you first arrive and are finally ensconced in your funny little booth with a bottle of Advil and your second cup of burnt diner coffee. It's noticeable, even to you now, that your typically British casual disregard for paid employment, one that briefly entertained and impressed your colleagues, is now being viewed in considerably less favourable terms.

'Hey, Ringo, you should take a day off!' one yells across at you from the narrow kitchen area that struggles to accommodate a 20st mass that has been squeezed into a pair of ill-fitting polyester trousers that look as if they've been belted with a hula hoop. You have no idea how old he is, though you're fairly sure his name is Rick. Maybe 45, but maybe 25, you can never tell with the people who live around here. All you know for sure is that you are 'Ringo', a stupid nickname lazily bestowed upon you by your dentally superior work colleagues and as a direct result of having been brought up in a leafy enclave of the Wirral peninsula. It's a joke that wouldn't work on any level if it were wheeled out at the bar of Thomas Rigby's, but it's one that refuses to die a dignified death here, in the middle of an open-plan office in the middle of the middle of nowhere, amongst people who have no knowledge whatsoever of the cultural and geographic vagaries of the metropolitan county of Merseyside. If nothing else, you can at least take solace in no longer being the biggest 'wool' in the room.

'I could do with a day off, but I've only got ten' you think to yourself, itself the tragicomic opening line to an email you recently sent to a school-friend who now lives in West London. You slide open your narrow desk drawer and notice, amongst the sea of company detritus, that you still own that red 'Destroy Work' button badge that you bought at a gig at Warrington Legends in 1991; the one that Donna's father, Don, absolutely hated and which he swiftly attempted to substitute with one of those little enamel jobs that portray the British and American flags in symbolic unity. You'd only wear it when you went to visit him and Cheryl and their spiteful Siamese cat, they never came to visit you; but there was a time when you left it pinned to the collar of a jacket after a whistle-stop weekend trip to attend a family celebration and inadvertently ended up wearing it to work. It was never commented upon, but you still recall one of the Ricks doubling-down on the commoditised erotica of U.S. patriotism by showing up the next day pointedly displaying the same badge but with the union flag replaced by a duplicate stars and stripes. An intense double shot of the Yoo Es of Ay, a massive injection of institutionalised freedom, which as you are constantly reminded 'isn't free'. Donna laughed her arse off when her father first gave you that badge but slowly grew to view your evident resistance to it as a sign of your failure to assimilate, your lack of commitment to the relationship, to her family, and your own petty intransigence. Only one of these accusations was justified, but that was in Boston and things were different there.

The same day that an Egyptian charter plane crashes off the coast of Nantucket you assume your usual position at the far end of The Hub Pub's long wooden counter only ten minutes before the bucket of Rolling Rock offer expires. A hot basket of vivid orange chicken wings is silently placed before you alongside a ceramic dish of creamy blue cheese dip and a selection of celery sticks. Words have yet to be exchanged but beer and food have arrived regardless. On the bulbous TV screens above the Red Sox are playing out yet another dreary midweek afternoon innings of a sport you only occasionally feign to be interested in; just one of the reasons you have ceased to wear their branded apparel, a uniform of unquestioning civic machismo that defines the city as much by what it pits itself against as by what it stands for. There's only so much public humiliation a man can take and one's bar-room exposure as a bluffer, in either sport or music, is at the extreme end of such indignity. Even you, the most compelling bullshitter for your age and weight in all of Wallasey, acknowledge that there are limits to the degree to which this can be tested.

Marie has yet to speak to you, though Marie has yet to meaningfully engage with any of the half dozen solo drinkers assembled around her bar. She gets by instead, as do they, via a series of nods, hand gestures and mumbled acknowledgments; the silent code of faithful patronage, a convention learned solely through observation and imitation. It's just enough to keep on taking care of business and she evidently does OK for tips and comp'd bourbon shots. It's not that Marie doesn't like you, it's just that she makes it her business not to get too involved with any of the customers in a city whose bars are primarily populated by burly Ben Affleck wannabes whose steroid-hard biceps strain against emerald green ink that forms a series of shamrocks, harps, and homages to the Dropkick Murphys. Mommas boys, closet cases, lepre-cornballs. Marie recently learned that a tattoo formed of green ink has proven to be the hardest type to remove, being virtually immune to the cosmetic laser, and this gives her a quiet sense of satisfaction. You seem OK though. Most Brits, much like the day-tripping assholes from Southie, tend to come in and shout their mouths off, thinking that their accent alone will charm the ladies of Massachusetts back to their squalid little bedrooms. And sometimes they're right, and sometimes they're wrong. You're cute, in a stupid-ass way, as that song she keeps hearing in that record store you work in would have it.

She's fairly sure you're still in a relationship though, with that girl whose mall-punk style seems to have recently taken a recent hard-right turn into the sartorial dead-end known as Vineyard Vines. Her hair colour seems to rotate on an almost fortnightly basis but instead of a carousel that once flitted between blood-red, violet, and fire, its settings are now seemingly locked on shades that complement tailored business-wear, 25-dollar brunches and The Hamptons. 'It's a wonder there are any colours left on the palette', Jack had recently mused to the general amusement of the assembled Tuesday night soaks, and though Marie laughed along at the time she silently acknowledged that this was a woman who at least has a clear life focus, the kind of super-charged personal momentum that eventually leaves cities, and people, in its wake.

By contrast, Marie has seen a lot of men like you. The English guy that bundles into town wearing clothes and hair that are both familiar and alien in equal measures and whose individual style is incrementally eroded to the point that the inevitable assimilation into standard-issue East Coast ordinariness is almost complete. She still notices the occasional item that was evidently bought in Manchester, or Liverpool, or wherever it is that you initially came from - a pair of suede Adidas trainers in a vivid primary colour, a flimsy shower-proof jacket with a wide chest pocket – but these have noticeably tailed off of late and you're now more often to be found in a baggy pair of Downtown Crossing cargo shorts or a generic athletic shirt, one arm of your $5 sunglasses tucked into the well of its stretched collar. The freckles across your nose grow more pronounced as the weeks go by, connecting over time to form a formidable Celtic suntan. You also seem a lot less content, both at the bar and when you occasionally share a nod of recognition as she catches your eye as you stand behind the counter at Newbury Comics. She's started to see you drinking alone in The Silvertone too, a serious 2am wake-up call for anyone who doesn't form part of the city's bartending community that makes up the core contingent of the ST's late-night clientele. You're listless, drifting, and seemingly caught up in the characteristic malaise of the Englishman whose initial accent bounce has levelled out to an inevitable flat-line. And when you eventually drop a couple of singles on the bar and turn to head towards the door she does something so jarringly instinctive that it shocks even her, a woman who has seen a lot of shocking things in her three years behind the bars of the greater Boston area. She brings two painted fingertips to the middle of her full lips and blows you a kiss. And as you ease your way out of the front door, oblivious, its arc of trajectory slowly tails off before tumbling to the ground, lost forever in a sea of cigarette ash and sawdust.

Marie swiftly collects herself, spirits away three empty glasses, and heads towards the fire exit and the welcome solace of a mid-shift cigarette, a fleeting sense of unease somewhat appeased by the absence of any evidently witting onlookers. After all, if a kiss falls in a bar on Province Street and no one is around to hear it, does it make a sound?

'I need a smoke, Bill. You're gonna need to step up'

At the same time, just over twenty miles away, in the reception area of the Holiday Inn in Dedham, Donna is shaking the hand of another man and gratefully accepting the job that he has just offered her. She is wearing the powder blue heels that you bought her for her birthday and a fitted seersucker blazer that she recently inherited from her mother. He gestures to buy her a drink by way of celebration, he's in town until Friday and 'could do with the company', but she politely declines and rushes to the nearest pay-phone to call her mother who at that very moment is in the process of ordering *The Complete Works of Richard Clayderman* from a TV shopping channel. Later she will board a train back to Back Bay and when she arrives she will indulge in her own private celebration in a small bar just off Newbury Street, fending off unsolicited conversations with a series of young men who take her manifest smile of personal satisfaction as an invitation to sexually-laced chit-chat. She closes her eyes and clutches the moment for all that it's worth. A warm early evening buzz achieved in conjunction with a fleetingly popular alcoholic beverage made and distributed by the Coors Brewing Company; one that constituted her sole alcoholic intake of that first Summer together and which adorned her lips with the seemingly permanent taste of citrus. She swishes the remainder of the liquid around in her mouth before ordering another and glancing up at a prominent digital clock that reads 18:30, the commencement of a pre-theatre happy hour and the imminent arrival of a discreetly tattooed boy from Birkenhead.

'But why would you look to hook me up with a job in New York if we're supposed to be moving to Ohio together?' you'd asked, genuinely confused and not a little anxious. 'If that's meant to be a hint, you could have maybe dropped a subtler one'. It's difficult to take a call while you're at work, even more so when there's an in-store signing session about to take place; the practical logistics of which are proving to be problematic in the extreme. The soundtrack to the afternoon' spectacle is as loud as it is annoying, a messy queue of black-clad suburban alienation snaking its way around the store and out on to Newbury Street itself. You can see Janine policing the line like an absolute boss and cutting off any potential inter-teen conflict at the knees, her forehead creased in seemingly permanent disapproval. It's hard to make sense of Donna's excitable chatter but it's swiftly evident that the news she's seeking to break is evidently of the good variety. Looking back, it's hard to remember much of the fractured one-sided conversation, other than a series of words that remain as clear now as the moment they were gleefully imparted. Words that plucked you out of your bohemian East Coast comfort zone and drop-kicked you into this workaday Mid-West holding pattern with nothing but a pack of cigarettes and Mrs Wagner's pies; a state of unconsciousness in the heart of a bellwether state: 'Not the city, silly. The magazine!'

The temporary apartment that Donna's new employer afforded her, and by limpet-like association, you, seemed lavish in the extreme; floor to ceiling windows, twin sinks, and a fully-installed cable modem that immediately consigned the staccato signature tune of dial-up internet to the dustbin of history; so lavish in fact that she never left, despite the significant bump in rental that kicked in after her initial six-month probation period had been successfully navigated. You wonder how she can continue to afford it on her own, but you tend not to ponder that question too much lest you stumble upon an answer that you might not welcome. Twelve floors up, on a clear day, you could just about make out the building that continues to employ you on the falsest of pretences, a concrete embodiment of The Shangri-Las's assertion that you 'can never go home anymore'.

'Well, yeah, I suppose I do work for the magazine,' you explain to friends, to family, to strangers in bars, 'but only in the way that the guy who sells concert tickets for U2 could claim to work for U2.' It's a decent line to toss around in a bar, a line steeped in English self-deprecation and Bostonian chutzpah, and a far snappier retort than 'I manage a block of direct debit subscriptions via a range of generic corporate spreadsheets.' You still love the magazine, of course. How could you not? Along with ID and The Face its content, its design, even its typeface captured your imagination at an early age and instilled a sense of possibility that was evidently not shared by the pot-bellied Irish newsagent who resented having to place time-consuming standalone orders for what he described as 'your specialist magazines'. Even now, its beautiful covers form an array of merchandise that adorns the walls and shelves of your tiny downtown apartment; the tell-tale signs of a generous employee discount and a gradually deteriorating work/life balance. Yet in spite of the magazine's international prestige, and the appropriated window-dressing that it allows you to drape across your exploits for the boys and girls back home, it doesn't change the fact that you've simply exchanged one life on the margins for another. Boston was a blip, you see that now. A cruel and fleeting peek behind the curtains at a panoramic 3D screening of what might have been. A three-minute thrill-ride of a trailer for a movie that you'll never actually get to see. Your life here is strictly straight-to-video, the opportunity to be kind, rewind, having long since passed. You pour the last bottle of Sam Adams' Summer Ale into a thick-walled iced glass, a knowingly meaningful act in itself, and close your eyes tightly. In an instant, you're back at the bar of The Hub Pub, exchanging guarded glances with Marie and burning the roof of your mouth with a succession of molten neon chicken wings. Sheryl Crow is playing on the jukebox, the Sox still suck, and you still don't understand any of the rules.

When Donna first graduated from Northeastern the idea that she might someday end up living and working in the cultural hinterland of Iowa would have seemed like the premonition of a life gone awry. Yet here she is, at the age of 29, in a highly-paid junior VP role in a buoyant growth industry, living in a brand-new apartment that boasts floor-to-ceiling windows and twin sinks. The world of insurance may not come sprinkled with tinsel-town glitter, but it does continue to offer stable and diverse career opportunities for the sufficiently motivated young executive. There's space in Des Moines. You can breathe here. The people are less demanding, less intense, less likely to call you an asshole to your face; though the hot, humid summers and cold, snowy winters remind her of home in ways that feel strangely familiar.

Boston is, when all's said and done, nothing more than a big village; a phrase she'd learned from the softly spoken man whom she once thought might become her father-in-law. He was talking about Liverpool at the time, a city that lay just across the water from the dreary social club in which she sat alongside both him and his son. A miserable flat-rooved box in which disconsolate red-faced men did nothing but sink copious quantities of lager, pausing only to bare their crooked beige teeth as they screamed vicious obscenities at large pull-down screens upon which live football matches were routinely screened via an illegal Norwegian satellite feed. This wasn't even a pub, it was just a machine for drinking in, and as she began to quietly observe the evident similarities between father and son, the sallow complexion, the permanently furrowed brow, the hollow arrogance that passes for British masculinity, she pictured a future for herself that did not fill her with unbridled joy. Maybe it was then, as they sat around those ugly plastic tables, that the seed was first sown. The idea that she needed to finally make a break with the city she'd always called home, the city in which she'd formed all of her adult friendships, and the city in which she'd first met this skinny northern Englishman who never flossed and insisting on depositing empty bottles of wine into the landfill trash. She'd initially felt bad about having dragged him west, not least when the relationship juddered to its inevitable clumsy denouement, but the fact that he seemed happy to continue living here even after their prolonged and uncomfortable parting, saw pangs of guilt give way to a growing sense of bitter resentment and not a small measure of pity. She pictured him at work, cramped into a tiny white cubicle, undertaking a job that he resented, and which he surely resented her for talking him into taking, an overcoat littered with pin badges hanging from the back of a standard issue swivel chair. The party's over, she silently reflected, there's nothing here for you now.

A mile or so across town you sit in your dimly lit bedroom eating and reading; idly flipping your way through the pages of the weekly magazine that only notionally employs you, before alighting on a short story written from the perspective of a young Irishman's initiation into the ways and wiles of 1970s New York City. It's called 'New Town', and wonders aloud about why America is so hard, so complicated, so deeply unfathomable, and why the simple act of going to see a production of Hamlet with a lemon-meringue pie and a bottle of ginger ale feels like a strategic challenge of prodigious proportions. You close your eyes, take another bite of sausage, and screw your eyes together tightly to stop the tears from tumbling onto the pages.

And then you glance down and notice an oily blob of hot dog mustard on your only remaining pair of Liverpool jeans, an ugly luminous stain that only seems to grow and ingrain itself with each vigorous rub of an outspread paper napkin. A muted TV screen at the foot of the bed extols the virtues of faux Italian food and a miracle pain killer whose side effects include nausea, vomiting, nervousness and diarrhoea. The weather is presented by a man in a shiny suit whose novelty theme-park name is Flip Spiceland; a forecast sponsored, as seemingly everything is, by Gatorade. The city in which you find yourself living sits squarely in the middle of the vast land mass that somehow fits into the 32-inch rectangle perched precariously at your feet.

Later, unable to sleep and with a fierce headache brought on by a heavy and entirely unplanned intake of Jameson's, you reach for the CD that's quickly become a late-night safety blanket; a revelatory capsule of Liverpool life that arrived in a torn Jiffy bag stamped with a West London postmark:

Oh, the awful titles belies the quality / Of this unusual comedy

You allow the album to play to its conclusion before doubling down on the insomnia via the piping hot contents of a stove-top Bialetti. It's 3am in a rail-road apartment in the middle of the middle of nowhere and as you begin to slowly type, making real the thoughts that only previously existed in your head, you're still sleeping, drifting, dreaming. Vivid Technicolor dreams of fields of green and a big blue ocean. 'Start spreading the news', you think to yourself, words intended to silently catapult themselves across the vast expanse of North America's land mass and the depths of the Atlantic, 'I'm leaving today'.

An Interview with Bernard O'Donoghue
Martina Evans

Bernard O'Donoghue *was born in Cullen, County Cork, in 1945, later moving to Manchester. He studied Medieval English at Oxford University, where he is a teacher and Fellow in English at Wadham College. He is a poet and literary critic, and author of* Seamus Heaney and the Language of Poetry *(1995). His poetry collections are* Poaching Rights *(1987);* The Weakness *(1991);* Gunpowder *(1995), winner of the 1995 Whitbread Poetry Award;* Here Nor There *(1999); and* Outliving *(2003). His work of verse translation,* Sir Gawain and the Green Knight, *was published in 2006 and a* Selected Poems *in 2008. Bernard O'Donoghue received a Cholmondeley Award in 2009. His most recent poetry collections are* Farmers Cross *(2011) and* The Seasons of Cullen Church *(2016), both of which were shortlisted for the T. S. Eliot Prize.*

Martina Evans: Recently in an interview with Zaffar Kunial you quoted Andrew Motion who 'once said there have to be at least two things of some kind in a poem and that the poetry is the kind of electricity that passes between them.' You used this quote in the context of exile and living in two places but I thought of it again when I read your marvellous poem 'Child Language Acquisition' towards the end of *Here nor There*. It opens, 'The first skill you learned in our townland / Was how to sustain a double conversation / with a couple not on speaking terms.' I was intrigued by this idea of 'double conversation' and wondered if this is in your poems too. You end the poem, 'So there was nothing new for us about / The dialogical imagination. / All useful training for the life / Of letters, learning to distinguish / between revisionists in the horse and trap, / Modernists off to the pictures, realists / Drinking tea from a gallon in the meadow / and the historicists taking it all in.' Are you talking to two different audiences? Or maybe even more?

Bernard O'Donoghue: I think 'Child Language Acquisition' is a bit portentous. But I suppose it is another tribute to negative capability and the ability to live in doubt – all that stuff. It is very audience-directed here though: how certain do you have to be about who you are talking to? Like the child in the poem, you have different subjects and interests with different people. I think there is no one ideal audience or readership – or, for that matter, critical method! Mind you, the horrible stuff about Fake News with its suggestion that there is no such thing as Truth or reality might make us pause.

ME: Continuing on from dialogism, recently in London Magazine, you said, 'I can't act or project on the stage…' And yet these is a lot of dialogue in your poems, you have a terrific ear for those North County Cork cadences. The first time I read 'The Weakness' (published in The Independent in 1993, I still have the cutting!) these lines jumped out and grabbed me, 'Hold on, Dan / I think I'm having a weakness. / I never had a weakness, Dan, before.' You mentioned an affinity with short stories and you are inherently dramatic, like Robert Frost who famously said, 'Everything written is as good as it is dramatic.' So many of your poems could be acted out. I'm thinking of 'The Poultry Instructresses',',…huddled by the fire in smart coats / And 'New Look' frocks.' And later with their needles 'poised in the flurry / Of Leghorn and Rhode Island Red…while locals plunged / And clutched around the henhouse like bad goalkeepers.' In a handful of words, you have summoned a whole group to the stage with wit and precision. And there's Con from 'Stigma' leaping from the page in his one pair of sandals, 'in which he trudged gaily / through the cow dung.' Have you thought about this dramatic side to your writing? And do you think this might be something that you get from growing up in Cullen? Something that is intrinsically Irish and / or rural?

BOD: I like poems with a narrative, yes. And I do always fall back on events set in that first environment. Somewhere I said I was against Confessionalism, which I think was not what I meant. I like poets like Lowell and Bishop very much. What I meant was that I think poems should go beyond the confines of their writer's heads. C.Day-Lewis said he preferred poems that were about something, not just examining the contents of your own mind. I think a distinct, regional language does help to externalise in that way – like the Irish use of 'to have a weakness' here – thit i laige, in Irish. I've never attempted plays though, even though that is the most externalizing form I suppose – nearest to the short story which I love. I can't act; I am too inescapably self-conscious.

ME: You said 'There is very little hell in my poems. They are mostly small-scale moral stories.' in response to Lidia Vianu's comment that you 'could not really be farther from hell in your poems'. But I don't think the Cullen poems are that idyllic. I know this world a little, having grown up twelve miles away from Cullen in the 1960s. 'O'Regan the Amateur Anatomist' is chilling especially when we know that animal abuse is often a prelude to human abuse. This preoccupation with the darker side continues through all your books, the poems which describe hare coursing are almost unbearable. 'Stigma.' is a terrific protest against the hellish lives of some workmen and servants in Ireland in the twentieth century and their present-day counterparts. Could your return to Cullen in the 1950s be some kind of pilgrimage of reckoning also? It's not an Inferno because the poems are full of light and wonder too. Your Cullen reminds me a little of The Gospel of St Thomas when it says that heaven is spread upon the earth and we can't see it. When we look back that is clearer. And if Heaven is there, maybe hell as well?

BOD: The Cullen poems are certainly not idyllic – they start from an impoverished Ireland in the 1950s, at the end of the Economic War. And there was a lot of animal cruelty, like in 'O'Regan'. Hare-coursing was a big problem. We used to get the afternoon off school in Millstreet to watch the Coursing. Some of my favourite people in the parish were into 'dogs and horses', as Frank O'Connor says in 'The Holy Door'. They used to man the collection for the Coursing Club at the church door once a year. I remember still the misery of walking past them without contributing. But of course, the practice was barbaric, like a lot of 'traditional sports'. Some people remembered cock-fighting, not long before my time. We had a kind of particular conflict because we used to get Enid Blyton-type books about the countryside from our grandmother and aunt in Manchester, and they had a very different take from the difficult farming world of that time in North Cork.

ME: It's hard to find a new question for you on the subject of distance and travel and living in two places at once – and as I was typing, I noticed that I'd written 'living in two places at once' which is not really true, is it? Maybe I could use my 'slip' to ask the question. Is an exile in some sense living in two places at once? Is it the 'here nor there' you've written about so beautifully in your third volume? I know that you've also said that you quite like being 'here nor there'. Do you think you would have written if you hadn't left Ireland?

BOD: 'Living in two places at once' is a very good way of putting it. Back to the dialogism again! Exile is living in two places, literally and mentally I suppose. And, as you say, there are comforts in that. You can always withdraw to the other place! I'm not sure that it's not possible to step in the same river twice; in practice I think you can come close to returning to the absent place. I found the ideal place of the past a prompt to write about it, or at least to recapture it, so maybe I wouldn't have written if I'd stayed in Ireland. Would you?

ME: Unlike you, I came to London of my own volition as a young adult and the writing happened soon after that. I feel that I would never have written at the other side of the Irish Sea although my father died the year I left which was another significant factor. Both events have the effect of creating distance but there is a sense of never being able to really go home again. Would you agree?

BOD: We have a lot in common there, yes. I came to Manchester at 16 when my mother returned there after my father died very suddenly. It was very complicated; I liked living in the city which was a further development of the move from the countryside to go to school in Cork city the year before. But it had to be set against the rupture of a major part of my life: my father, country living, the whole world of Ireland and Irishness. The previous year in Cork city had launched me towards the literary life, being taught at Pres by the great actor / teacher Dan Donovan. Not that I started writing: I wouldn't have dreamt of that; but I read a lot. Certainly, living in England made me concentrate a lot on Irish literature: 'Home thoughts from abroad', I suppose. I exchanged letters in Irish with my sister Margaret at UCC for the first two years in England: writing of a kind. I suppose.

ME: Writing seemed an impossibly wild idea back then. I was actually hoping to be an academic but Open University and nights on call as a radiographer were not a good combination. Poetry burst out of me with such an unexpected sense of freedom. And speaking of freedom, there is tremendous sense of flight in your poems. It's in all your wonderful bird poems and the fantastically dream-like 'The Apparition' from *The Weakness* which was inspired by a real plane landing 'in an Irish farmer's field / In the 'fifties…' reminds me of Heaney's hangar poems. Even the car in the 'A Nun Takes the Veil' seems airborne, almost like a spacecraft at the end of the poem, when it is remembered as a 'vision…humming through the open window.' These poems are very dream-like. How do you like flying yourself? Do you fly in your dreams? Is poetry a form of flight for you?

BOD: I love flying. What I said in 'Hermes' is true: I feel safer in planes, especially in big inter-continental planes, than on the ground. Crazy! I remember reading in Ruskin College in Oxford once, and a witty mature student from Cork said to me: 'Do you realise your birds are all grounded? Even your aeroplane is grounded' (in 'The Apparition'). It sounds a bit Freudian; I prefer your observation that they all get lift-off. I dream about more negative things. I don't dream about flying because I like it so much. It is tied up in complicated ways with a deficiency of imagination.

ME: Ah I was thinking of 'Hermes' too which is one of my favourite poems of yours and confirms my suspicions that although I don't feel so safe on planes, writers are always preoccupied with the underworld.

BOD: That is an extremely interesting thought: the paradox that being up in the sky, in a different element, is a kind of inversion of all that katabasis stuff. If Eurydice was trapped in the sky, how would you get her down! It is like Dante I suppose: upward to Paradiso or downward to Inferno. Both realms are equidistant from the real and the here and now.

ME: Visons, flight and birds go hand-in-glove with the medieval period which you have taught and studied for almost half a century. You've said that it made sense to you because of your own religious upbringing. That reverence exists in many of your poems like that fine translation of 'Piers Plowman' or the lovely 'Madonnas' from *The Weakness*. Do you practice your faith? Does it still make some kind of sense? How do you feel about a church which does not seem to be able to atone for the wounds caused by the lack of adequate response to child abuse?

BOD: That is true about the medieval. When I was starting on graduate work, I'd have liked to do Yeats, but I felt a kind of moral obligation to stay with the medieval which I knew of old. Not just for that reason of course: I loved Chaucer and the Old English elegies, and Dante when I got on to him. I don't know if I actually 'practise' my faith, but it is very deep-rooted. I think the whole edifice of Catholic Christendom is a pretty big thing to overthrow – Aquinas, Dante, the saints. I don't know how the church can actually 'atone' for its wrongdoings either. I am a bit anxious about the way that people who make self-denying and idealistic choices (which is where they start) are the most readily anathematised. Some of the best and nicest (and cleverest) people I knew were priests and nuns. That is not to deny the disasters of course: I am aware that I sound like Mr Cunningham in Joyce's comic masterpiece 'Grace'. I wouldn't claim reverence though: more an admiration for people who take life seriously. Truth rather than fake news again.

ME: I agree about the singling out and scapegoating of the clergy which I think has resulted from the cover-ups which made everything so much worse. I, too, have known some wonderful nuns. I think that is one of the many joys of your poem 'A Nun Takes the Veil' – it utterly humanises that character. I have used this poem in classes for many years and everyone relates to it no matter what their background. It is so universal.

BOD: I am very honoured that you use that poem. It's another received story: this wonderful woman from the Aran Islands who worked all her life as a cook in a student hostel in Berkshire. She told me in passing once that she saw a car for the first time the day she left home to enter the convent at 14. The rest of the poem is just a fiction based on that. It really grieves me to think of the hurt that the general suspicion and hostility of the clergy causes those self-denying people. But I know, I know: child-protection is absolutely vital.

ME: When the character in 'Pied Piper' from *Here Nor There* cries 'Musheroons! Musheroons!' I am entranced and reminded of Heaney in his *Stepping Stones* interview when he says every writer lives between 'the vernacular given and some received vernacular from the tradition…Ted Hughes had a marvelous little parable about this. Imagine, he said, a flock of gazelles grazing. One gazelle flicks its tail and all the gazelles flick their tails as if to say, 'We are eternal gazelle…Suppose they are in a foreign city and they hear a familiar accent, it's like a gazelle tail flicking, so then the other gazelle tail flicks and thinks, 'Ah I'm at home here. I am strong here." That has been my reaction to so many of your poems but how does it feel for you when you're writing them? Is it like a little bit of home, a charm or relic that you can carry with you? The idea of a mobile home comes up in several of your poems. You write a lot about Irish travellers and there is that ghostly vision of a 'green caravan' in the incomparable 'Waiting for the Horses' where the ghosts of your previous poems disappear and the poet himself becomes a ghost.

BOD: I think those touches of vernacular are like charms: like Yeats keeping a bit of the earth of Sligo in his pocket. Heaney is a master of it. It's like the bacteria that makes yogurt! A small element that transforms the linguistic whole. My friend Denny Hickey (a figure of humorous wisdom who is hanging around in a lot of the poems) was always talking about 'trace elements' which is a wonderfully rich literary idea. What you say about mobile homes is very interesting too. I grew up with an irrational fear of Irish travellers, not yet grasping that things are arranged in the interests of the strong rather than the weak. But of course they are the ultimate figures of exile and displacement.

ME: When one writes about childhood and the past as much as you do, nostalgia is inevitably mentioned. Would you consider nostalgia the right word?

BOD: I am interested in nostalgia which is a great temptation. It's an interesting word, isn't it – pain and the return: the *nostos* like in the *Odyssey*. It's not exactly home-sickness, and it's a positive literary motivation in some cultures, such as (I believe) *saudade* in Portuguese. 'The Mule Duignan' is a poem about a building-site worker who has had to leave Ireland and can't forgive the poverty of his upbringing. I think the moral there is that nostalgia is a sentiment only available to the comfortably off.

ME: In your Ambit interview you say that Frank O'Connor 'deserves as high a place in world literature as Yeats and Joyce and Beckett and Heaney.' Could you say a little more about this?

BOD: I think Frank O'Connor is the Irish writer most faithful to the vernacular and the sentiments of locality. I am prejudiced of course because he writes about the places I know best. You can really hear the accent in him, in stories like 'The Majesty of the Law'. And the short story, as he said himself, is the form for which Irish writers have the greatest gift. Why didn't he write plays I wonder?

ME: You've claimed that your poems are 'short stories manqué' and that your best poems are 'half shrunken stories'. This seems to be a very modest position which I can't agree with! It is true that short stories are very close to poems, closer than they are to the novel, in fact. Where would you place the novel? Do you think narrative in a poem makes a poem more of a hybrid? Why not have both? Yeats' *Leda and the Swan* for instance, holds a sweeping narrative in a lovely lyric. I know Yeats was an early influence. (I was interested to read that you got into Yeats from listening to Cyril Cusack as I had the same experience.) And there is a lot of narrative with speaking characters in medieval poetry. Your poems remind me of V.S. Pritchett's introduction to Mary Lavin's *Collected Stories*, when he says, 'There is commonly in Irish writing, a double vision: the power to present the surface of life rapidly, but as a covering for something else. I would guess that the making of the Irish short story writers is in their extraordinary sense that what we call real life is a veil; In other words, their dramatic sense of uncertainty. It is present in their comedy and their seriousness.'

BOD: I am very keen on the idea of narrative in poems. Even short poems have to *move* in some way between the beginning and the end. Short poems, like Heaney's Clonmacnoise 12-liner, or Yeats's 'No Second Troy' have that wonderful effectiveness of a final line that welds it all together: 'Out of the marvellous as he had known it', or 'Was there another Troy for her to burn?'. Both are new ideas whose meaning flows back through the poem. That quotation from Pritchett (who was a marvellous short story writer too – as was Mary Lavin) is very interesting. I think I am more interested in the veil than in the 'something else' – though I think the 'dramatic sense of uncertainty' is very good. As for the novel, I think very few novels end well; quite early reading a novel, you think 'OK, I've got it'. But then it goes on for another 500 pages. I am not entirely serious about this. But Roy Foster says I once said 'I don't know what the novel is *for*!' I don't remember saying anything as interesting as that, but I am inclined to autodidacticism and I like to think I am learning as I read – probably because I have a terrible memory and feel I have to ration it.

ME: I agree with you about preferring the veil which is used a lot in the fairy legends. The listener is seduced by the performance while the subliminal message is taken in unconsciously although the exegesis can be very enjoyable too. You've spoken in a few interviews about seriousness: In Ambit – 'I used to like telling jokes. I say 'used to' because I don't remember them any more: and I think our condition is too serious for jokes just at the moment.' And in your Faber interview – 'I did medieval literature to begin with because of my Catholic upbringing, I suppose. I associated the serious with religion.' What do you mean by seriousness?

BOD: Seriousness again: I used to like telling jokes and reading comic writing best of all – Chaucer and Joyce and Waugh. I love Private Eye; but I rarely feel nowadays that our condition allows for much laughter. This sounds very po-faced, but I do think we must take ecological dilemmas very seriously. We seem to be sleepwalking into Apocalypse, recklessly abandoning the future. The heroes of our time are people like George Monbiot and Mary Robinson.That's what I mean by seriousness, and I am admiring of people who devote or devoted their lives to it.

ME: I notice that the subject of gardening, dirt under the nails and the difficulty of growing roses crop up from time to time in your poetry, culminating in that gorgeous Dante-soaked poem 'The Payoff' which stars the lovely Sister Una. I get a sense that you love roses. Do you want to say anything about that and how gardening might relate to poetry? And what do roses symbolise for you.

BOD: I do love roses – and no doubt that too is a kind of vestige of religious upbringing. Maybe add the primroses we collected for small, private May altars: 'Oh Mary, we crown thee with blossoms today. / Queen of the angels and queen of the May.' Lovely Sister Una is the nun in 'A Nun Takes the Veil': a real figure of sweetness and virtue. Side by side with seriousness, I admire virtue as an idea as I get (very) old. I've never felt it or exactly aspired to it; but I am increasingly inclined to admire it in people. Taking over from glamour maybe!

ME: In the same volume, you have a masterfully fluent and moving translation from the sixth canto of Dante's Purgatorio. It made me hunger for more of your translated cantos. Hughes's gazelles flicking their tails jumped to my mind when that 'Lombard spirit' drops his disdain on hearing a voice from home and springs forward, "Oh Mantuan, I am from your country". It reminded me immediately of Irish people greeting each other abroad. I imagine that might have been in your mind too? I also wondered if there are any present-day states that came to your mind when the spirit talks of his distress over the state of Florence, tossing and turning on its sick bed.

BOD: I don't think I am a naturally gifted translator at all, though I have done a lot of dutiful translating in teaching Old and Middle English. But I love that meeting in *Purgatorio* 6. That canto is one of the great attachment-to-place texts. It's ok to feel emotion at the idea or look of a place. I am not sure about the places that are like Dante's Florence. I suppose I think the dreaded Brexit is an example of that sentiment curdled and gone to seed – an attachment to place that includes jealous disapproval of other places and people.

ME: I didn't need to read your Faber interview with Zaffar Kunial to find out that *The Divine Comedy* was your desert island book! Its presence is everywhere not least the lovely translations in *Farmer's Cross, Outliving* and *The Seasons of Cullen Church*. Could you say a few words about what *The Divine Comedy* means to you?

BOD: The appeal of Dante, which tended to be everybody's supreme book in the twentieth century, is hard to tie down. Dante is bitter and judgmental – and we don't go along with any of his opinions, or need to. But he has an extraordinary capacity to describe and evoke what emotion is like. And his powers of evocation are amazing. Mind you, if you didn't get Shakespeare anyway, that would be a competing choice. Or *Ulysses*. One thing they all have in common is some degree of difficulty: a resistant grain of meaning – Dante because it's in medieval Italian, Joyce in Joycespeak, and Shakespeare in that rich Renaissance amalgam of Latinate and Anglo-Saxon vocabulary. It's the language in the end!

ME: There are many theories about why we write. We write when we are in exile and that is true for you. We also write 'because the dead want blood' according to Margaret Atwood which relates to what I said earlier about writers' relationship with the underworld. I'm not just thinking about the shock of your father's sudden death which never left your poetry but the many characters from 'the other side' roaming your pages. And in your poem *History*, I feel a sense too of you simply wanting to make a record, remember what happened and how it happened and what was said?

BOD: I write, I am ashamed to say, because I want to impress people! Also, the distance people like you and I are from the central locus of our birth language, English, makes us want to impress in it. And there is what you say: wanting to keep alive in some sense the people and places and experiences and emotions we have had. Yes, leaving a record too. I find writing very difficult and unenticing as an activity. I'd rather do anything else – like reading or listening to music.

ME: You've said that form shouldn't get in the way of what is said but it seems to me that you manage the two very well. You have written many lovely sonnets and your cantos are very fine too. I love the way your haunting translation, 'The Move' looks a modest headstone. In a chapter entitled, 'English or Irish Lyric', in *Seamus Heaney and the English Language,* you talk about the Irish poet's choice between English and Irish traditions. Where do you feel you landed when you made your decision? As a teacher of English poetry and literature, did your 'mixed marriage' come as easily as it sounds on the page? The Dinnseanchas which was so important to Heaney and Kavanagh is ever present in your own poems – was that something you thought about consciously or did it just come?

BOD: I am not very good at form. The poems I am happiest with tend to free-style and conversational – though I like reading great formalists, like Yeats. I think too that Irish writers regard English as a second language, even when it is their first. That is what Joycespeak is. Interesting about Dinnseanchas. I am very attracted by local Irish placenames, like Ardnageeha and Gneevaguilla, and the way they link with purely

English-informed names, like Watergrasshill and Coalpits.

ME: Could you explain for your readers how the place names, Ardnageeha and Gneevaguilla link with the purely English-informed names, like Watergrasshill and Coalpits?

BOD: It's like Brian Friel's *Translations* I suppose (I admire Friel hugely). 'Ardnageeha' means 'hill of the wind' and it is a raised townland, facing the west wind off the Kerry mountains. 'Gneevaguilla' (pronounced 'Guineagwilla') means 'a *gniomh* and a half': *gniomh* Is a land-measure, like acre. Those half-Irish townland names are very useful computer passwords I find. The way those placenames relate to the purely English ones is just like what happened to English in the Renaissance: words like 'starvation' and 'flirtation' which are half-Anglo Saxon, half Latinate.

ME: As an academic, you are a writer of criticism as well as poetry, where do you place these two very different forms of writing in relation to each other?

BOD: I think criticism, even when it is opinionated, is a kind of act of modesty (I often think there should be 'Acts' as declarations of other things, apart from Faith, Hope, Charity and Confession: like Modesty) which poetry can't really be. I much prefer reading good critics, like Auden or Brodsky or Helen Vendler, to almost any poetry. It's better for your mind, which is why I agree broadly with what you say here. And I don't believe at all in the distinction between creative writing and other kinds, presumably lesser. The problem is that it seems a bit graceless to say this, or even think it. I've got away with palming things off as 'poems' for a long time, and I am very grateful for that.

ME: You've written extensively and brilliantly on Seamus Heaney and I know that you think a great deal of him. The more I've read your work lately, the more I see a deep affinity between you. Your poem 'The Boat' is wonderful, the best memoriam to Heaney. It reminds me of his 'Lightenings' poem about the monks of Clonmacnoise but also 'In the

Attic'. So finally, can you say something about what Heaney means to you and how he's influenced your poetry?

BOD: I really love and revere Heaney. And I particularly love 'In the Attic': the way it combines *Treasure Island* with failing memory and death and going to the pictures. He is in a class of his own. Reading back through things I have written, I often hear the echoes and sentiments of his writing. There is a lot of essence of Heaney. And I am very happy to indulge it! I should be so lucky. Not that there is any question of emulation. But I think he is a good example, like people say about Hardy.

The Skink
Aoife Casby

Because somewhere between wild and wanting is heaven…

Because Angela said to you often, 'My Mam is dead,' in a way that sounded like she wished your Dad was dead. She said it wanting to make you feel guilty and because of anger. You have heard Angela turn that loose silvery key and lock herself into her tight bedroom that you're not allowed into, with her dangerous quiet all around her like a smell. You are afraid of your cousin who is six years older and once you watched her through the keyhole and saw her lying in her bed. Moving. You spent a lot of time alone and walked from room through corridor to room in her house, the tips of your fingers browsing the new surfaces of this place, the cold satin paint, the shiny door paint, the edges where doors met jambs.

Your parents don't live together anymore because of separation and divorce, but they are alive.

Your Dad's an ordinary man who works at the airport and now lives alone in a little one-bedroomed flat on Dorset Street. Angela's Mam (your Auntie) died, and now Angela's Dad (your Uncle) and Angela were left alone in a different way so you and your mother went to stay in the country with them. Your Mam needed to be with her brother because of his wife dying (who was sick for a long time and *had a hand in her own death*.) There were promises made that your Dad could come down to the estate in the small town and you would go back to the city every weekend, and for some holidays. You missed a lot of things, too many to count. There was a family of foxes hiding out in the dustbins at the airport. You had never seen them but you liked to imagine their wet noses and you spent a lot of time with your eyes closed trying to get a handle on the smell your Dad said they had, somewhere between wild and wanting.

Because it's a wonder there isn't any music in you...

On the first day in the new house, (No. 4, the second in on the right from the main road) Angela said to you 'Roman, you wanker,' and you looked at her and she said 'Your mother is not my mother and you have no rights in this house.' She spat on the floor and spat on you and without really thinking about it, you got a tissue from the bathroom and cleaned up the gobby gloop from your Man. United shirt and from the wooden floor. You didn't tell your mother. Maybe Angela was lonely for her dead mother and it was better to be quiet and think about things before you said them like your Dad said, weigh yours words, weigh them. You felt like weighing words was actually real. Angela's words were heavy. You knew that. You didn't tell your mother when she asked 'Roman, are you ok?' and put her arm around your shoulder the way she did the day ye left the house in Dublin.

You became horribly aware of space.

Of the small flat that your Dad lived in for years and the lost homeness of the house you and your Mam had lived in before the big newness of the house down the country with Angela and her father. On the day of Angela's mother's funeral, your mother said that Met Éireann forecast storms and she gave out umbrellas.

Storms.

They didn't happen.

The day they buried Angela's mother the sun shone, and for a while you were thinking that this town would be nice. Angela played loud notes on an accordion all day in that closed bedroom but everyone could hear that box yearning all over the house. Just notes, slow screechy notes, longer than a breath. Her father asked her to stop and she didn't until it was time to go to bed and all the adults had looked at her funny.

Your mother often said to you 'It's a wonder there isn't any music in you?' You had tried to but you couldn't really hear the prettiness in music. You had no way to make a song into a memory. You understood tunes but not their beauty; could only hear the harmony and melody, the airs and stuff in numbers, in figure patterns, in strings of letters.

You missed your Dad.
Angela had played that accordion all day.
The same few sounds.
Like a donkey.
Like a haunted cat.
Like the door hinge in the church, a high squeak.
In the days after, Angela pinched you, said nasty things, spoke so close to your face in tight hidden corners that you could smell the sadness on her breath, like someone in a film.

Because you had no way to make a song a memory...

Your Dad told you that you were going to adopt a lizard and that ye had a whole heap of learning to do before the lizard could come. A Blue-Tongued Skink. You stood in front of the mirror in the bathroom on Dorset Street and watched your lips as you mouthed the words like they were a chorus to a song your body knew. Blue-Tongued Skink. It was hard to believe.

Together the pair of you went to Phibsboro library. Ye borrowed books and looked in the right places on the internet, taught yourselves about reptiles. More than ever, you looked forward to weekends, to being away from Angela.

'I love you, Roman,' your Dad said.

And then one Saturday, ye went first to the pet shop and then to the hardware place, to get materials and lights and the proper earth for the skink and his cage (which you knew was a terrarium).

You were happy even though that Saturday the city was wounded by weather, with the streets cut into it like howling scars and the noise of the north side, the screech and moan; the laugh. But there's an echo of fun in the muffled and secretive rain, hiding its eyes and its leery smile and smelling of piss and damp. Later, the canal water you think would taste like earth, and puddle water you know. You tasted the people off the rain that dribbled into your mouth, like the comfortable taste of tears sometimes. But you didn't tell your Dad how Angela hurt you, slapped you, punched you, kicked you.

You saw a video once on Youtube of someone who put basketballs in a glass fish tank and called it art.

In the corner of the sitting room in your Dad's flat you marked out a space, five feet by three feet, for the terrarium. The boys in your new school laughed at you when you told them you were adopting a blue-tongued skink.

Angela laughed too.

Because there's not another like him

Your Dad told stories about the man who was going to bring the Blue-Tongued Skink and when you met the man in the bar at the airport, you knew him on sight from the tales of incidents you probably shouldn't have heard, like when he locked himself into a cargo hold and was in The Azores for two weeks or when he brought in empty bags and brought out full bags or that he really liked to eat super strong chillies with his breakfast, a habit he picked up in Sri Lanka, to go with the other habits he had, your Dad said. The man drank his dark pint really quickly, made odd gestures with his head as if there were a bird inside him trying to get out and all the time he sat, there was a hard plastic box at his feet. The man had a hole in his trousers at the knee that made you want to not look at him too closely because you didn't want to see other flaws in him. He talked about your skink like it was a caress in an unkind life.

'I'll be damned if the fucker hasn't developed a personality. Something in his eyes,' he said to your Dad and made no apology for the word.

You listened to them laugh and joke and felt wet and heavy and couldn't swallow your fizzy drink and just when you thought you could stand it no longer the man pulled up the box and put it on the table, right out in the open, and your Dad gave over the small bundle of fifty euro notes into his fingers.

The man put his arm around your shoulder, 'He's rare. Not another like him. Mind him let you,' he said.

Blue is the colour of evening, the top of the road and breathing

Back at the flat, your Dad put his arm around you and let you take the skink out of the box yourself. In that first instant of seeing the striped and stumpy legged creature, your pleasure froze because it was smaller than it had been in your imagination but after a few minutes of watching, you just knew. And you hugged your father already dreading Sunday evening when you would have to go back to No. 4, second on the right.

That night when you rolled out the mattress and unfolded the camp bed, it didn't matter that your Dad didn't have a house of his own or that the sheets had those stains or that the place smelled like cabbage because you were sleeping beside your very own skink.

What did matter was the ease of the skink and the way it stayed near the red light and the heat; its blue tongue as it drank water from the little bowl and the cat food, and the snails and the hardboiled egg and the grated carrots and dandelions you pulled when while you Dad picked up the snails; its shyness when it hid behind the rocks and wooden hideaways you built and its curiosity when it played in the bark you piled up for it. You both reckoned that the skink looked you in the eye.

On Sunday morning you took a pile of pictures from the National Geographic: of dark skinned people, faces with lovely shaped eyes. You stuck out your tongue, bit the side of it gently, effort creating moist patches on your lips, and flicked through the pages, charily examining the reverse of each before you cut: the hot pink African flamingos, all facing the same way across their double spread; the bird drinking, it's easy to see pinkness against the blue water; the misty bridge of the samurai warrior. You cut out the jeep from the photos of those pale lions in the safari park; rocks in grey shifting deserts, smooth dunes in yellow deserts, waves rippling orange deserts like the bottom of the sea has come up to breathe; leafy green bowers and beautiful flowers; pictures of light playing with shadows, worlds you couldn't know the pain of and you made a collaged backdrop for the skink and stood it outside the acrylic glass of the terrarium so that he could look on something that resembled a home.

You smiled at the funny things your Dad said. You didn't tell him that Angela taunted and harmed you with sentences and blows.

It didn't matter that no one at your new school believed you that you had a Blue-Tongued Skink. You had a picture from a book that you showed them and when you measured the length of him for them with your hands it didn't matter that you added an inch or two.

Because of the The King of all birds

You were walking home from school with two boys who might be friends and they were talking about how much money you could get going out on the Wren Boys. This was all new to you. It was near Christmas. Paul and Sam chattered about how it would be, because they had done it before and in school ye had learned about the song and the tradition.

> 'The wren, the wren,
> The king of the Birds
> St. Stephen's Day
> Was caught in the furze.
> Up with the kettle
> And down with the pan
> Give us a penny
> to bury the wren,'

The two boys were singing but you didn't join in, even though you knew the words, because there was no music in you.

And you saw Angela come towards you.

'Here's Skunk Boy,' she said to everyone, to the fellas with you and you didn't want to look into anyone's eyes. They stopped singing and you had to try and be brave. Hardly believing that you could be uttering words, your mouth opened and you said

'It's not a skunk, it's a skink and you're just jealous,'

The slap came darting up and was sore in the cold.

'Jesus!'

Angela hit you full fisted in the ribs and when you fell, kicked you. You vomited for real. You sniffled but didn't cry and out of pain said,

'Good King Wenceslas had a brother and he was greedy just like you,'

'I'm not your brother you fucker,' she said. She took your books and emptied them on the ground.

'Your Daddy's a loser, a loser and he likes skunks. Bet he smells something rotten.'

You tried to get up. Angela knocked you back again.

'I'll never stop you know,' she said.

The Skink got sick.

Like Angela's mother.

The skink got sick and needed to go to the vet.

It cost money. There were no other skinks like him.

Blue

In almost the same instant that you knew the skink was sick, you knew how you were going to get the money to help him get better. You were not sure that there was no way of stopping dying.

The accordion was in the front room that wasn't used much. You looked at the box, tucked squatting a dull black, and broody. There was worn white around the box's brassy locks from where fingers had opened it to take the instrument out before. Looking at it you thought it should have a smell like darkness. The room was cool and quiet with a predominance of red. You moved belly-footed along the ground on the cold carpet, creeping up on it. You lay there thinking about Angela and how she could be an animal that no-one knew about yet.

You stood and picked up the boxed accordion and were troubled by its weight for a moment. You opened the box and exposed the instrument you hadn't heard since the day of the funeral. The names of the notes were stuck with sellotape onto the keys. Yellowing CDEFGABC and the blue ink had bled from damp underneath the plastic and the black dirt around the edges of the tape was like fingernails playing invisible notes, fingernails dirty with the stuff that you cannot get out and that you can always see on other people like they don't care. At the bottom of the box were sheets of music. Symbols and words, dots, dashes and things with a pattern in.

You took a sheet and read the letters, saw how they were on the keys. You knew that you could do it., unclipped and freed the bellows, hung the accordion across your shoulders. After a few attempts you could make the reeds vibrate and produce an uneven sound. Your fingers were cold and stretched, you held your breath and tried to coordinate the bellows with the letters of the tune, biting your lip, nearly piercing the flesh with your small eye tooth, not aware that you were forcing your tongue out your mouth reptilian-like, searching the air for signals.

While you were coming to terms with the wheezy instrument, Angela opened the door, stood and stretched her arms high up the jambs making an X of herself in the frame. You both stayed so still for a long time. Then she undid herself, closed the door and took the silence with her leaving behind something you couldn't name.

You practised for a few days, always careful to put the accordion back in its case. Waiting. And then it happened like you knew it would.

At breakfast, before school. Cornflakes. Toast.

Angela's father said. 'You want to play an instrument Roman?'

'Well no. Not really. I just want to…'

Angela pushed back from the table, her chair arguing against the floor..

'Well that accordion's mine, my mother's and you can't have it. You have your dead lizard.'

'He's just sick,' You stared at your mother. 'Isn't he? Just sick?' and she said 'Yes. Sick,' and your Uncle nodded. And said 'Angela. That's enough,' but Angela smiled.

'My mother gave me the accordion when I was eight and he can't have it. It's mine.'

'Even just to borrow?' you asked.

'Why doesn't his Daddy get him one?' Angela said.

You could hear the nasty underneath.

The man from Met Éireann was saying '…one thousand and six, rising slowly…'

The accordion is mine and he's not having it. I don't want him and his skunk hands touching it again.'

There was no argument.

The bother itched into your eyes and ears and into your stomach. Suddenly you weren't hungry and in that short instant you decided that you would play it anyway and that they wouldn't stop you and even though you felt strong in your jaw and your shoulders, you said 'ok' in a fake brave voice.

Then Angela said 'I think I might sell it. Sell it and buy myself a cheap smelly lizard…'

But she didn't.

You sneaked into the room. You touched the pearly bits and ran your nail light along the keys and took in the smell and the silence of the thing. Copied down the letters of a song. Learned off the string of letters: *ccggaagffeeddcggffeedggffeedccggaagffeeddc* like a chant and in your mind imagining the red and gold of the accordion. Once you went back into the room and took the accordion again out of its box. You pressed the keys and they went down with a soft give. You played it soundlessly not knowing if the song was alive. The next time you would take the accordion out of its box would be to take it out of the house.

St. Stephen's day had depth and a blurry winter sun. The clearest of blue skies high up, warmth in the air which wasn't there the day before. There was a soft white wind plucking a mist low down. You breathed out the window trying to see what it would be like when you were grown up and didn't have to answer people. Your mother repeated the Met Éireann numbers, 1004 rising, 1000, falling slowly., as if they were a prayer. You liked it.

If you sing someone's song their spirit enters you. It was written down on the card with her photograph in the kitchen. You wondered if it was the same when you played someone's instrument. Angela's mother *had a hand in her own death.* The accordion was hers.

St. Stephen's day turned into evening and night time and when it was time to go out you told your mother that you were going to someone else's house for a while.

'It's going to be wild,' she said.

'I know. I know,' you said and she went on,

'There was a warning today that..,'

And you continued for her, mimicking her ritual tones.

'...there would be gale force winds all along Irish Coastal waters and on the Irish sea north of Anglesey,'

She smiled.

'Well. Just be careful of the wind,' she said.

But the wind wasn't blowing yet and you felt as though your skin was trying to leave your body and you almost believed that if you closed your eyes, you would float on the cold air. On your way out the door, you had stepped into the sitting room and had taken the accordion from its box, walked fast away down the street towards the pubs.

From the darkness of a doorway across the quiet road you heard other kids coming. You watched the three of them and their bodhrán, their accordion, their two whistles and the way they were all dressed up in black bin bags and their mother's dresses and scarves. You got a shock because you had forgotten about that and you wanted to cry but you waited 'til the kids went into the pub then you left the accordion gently on the ground in the doorway and went to the window, gawked through the sprayed on snow. You could hear them play and sing. You watched them leave.

Around the side of the pub, you saw where the coal was piled. You picked a lump and rubbed its rough edges on your cheeks and with cold fingers, massaged the powdery carbon in. Licked your hand and got the rude taste of the city. In your head you were repeating your letters, *ccggaagf...*, fingering the notes and you went back across the road to get the accordion from the doorway.

When you went into the first pub they were quiet like they were expecting you and no-one said anything and you played your song and they gave you a little bit of money. You watched them and their beery breath and you knew things that they didn't, things about sick lizards and dead wrens and you became something like elated. It was easy. They didn't care if you could hardly play. After putting the money in your pocket, you waited a second or two looking at their backs. Surprised.

But it was very different in the next pub.

Around a round table, a group of girls sat and pounced on you immediately you came in. You took a step backwards in fright, but they said 'Come on ! Come on !' and they were shouting. Loud. Their flesh browned, looking so much like the girls on television or the ones on the wall in Angela's room or in magazines that you couldn't reach. Yellow brown skin, all looking alike but different with bright lips and the t-shirts even if it was cold outside and jewels in their belly buttons. They laughed and wore high heels and all along the bar were old men, baring arses and odd hats, wearing the smell and brown colour that is the dye of the country when you were from the city. And their hair that was all the same dark wet but there were smiles in the men.

In a short instant you had to take it all in. The girls were beautiful and pulling at your jumper, telling you to sing. All you could feel was a failing singing in your head.

You trembled.

Shuddered.

Like Something Dying. Fluttering. Something Dying.

And you did not know what it was.

There was a harmony of the men in the place, planted along the bar counter, on their stools, embedded, splaying their stained boots and laced shoes, unfurling themselves but still rooted. Heads twisting on thick or thin shoulders in movements as ancient as the lizards. And they had a stare that went into middle distance but when it landed on your face was full of a needy laughter and made you want to make them happy. Still the girls shouted. They were all, the men and the girls, looking at you and you were a part and apart at the same time and you understood the smell of the heat and the warmth of the place and the odour of the girls for a moment, a long very complete moment.

There was a fire at one end that threw the same soft orange as the lights. TV on with Sky talking about terrorists and someone switched to black and white and women with impossibly serene faces did things with their eyes to tall and passionate men. You couldn't name the feeling. You could hear your blood in your ears and it didn't deafen you. They were asking you to play and saying 'Ssshhhh...' with straight fingers to one another. You caught half their words and the brightness was brighter and the smoke didn't sting your eyes any more.

'I can only play one song,' you said.

'But you'll sing,'

You blushed. 'No. I can't,'

'Ok. Ok. Go on so play us a song,' And they all went quiet between the essy shushes.

You looked down at the labelled creamy keys and hit *ccggaag*, the reeds beating and heaving...but it sounded unmistakeable...it was 'Twinkle, twinkle, little star,' You were hitting and mishitting the notes in your nervousness and then you came to the end of it and the girls were roaring. Singing along. Busy in their thriving noise.

'Twinkle, twinkle little staaaar
how I wonder what you aaaaare,
Up above th...'

And then they asked you to play it again. Laughing and screeching at each other.

So you did. Standing there with forty pairs of eyes on you and you with your coaly face.

'Again,' one of them shouted. You tried to think about the sea area forecast. *Loop Head to Malin Head and on the Irish Sea.* Like a *'lit knee'* your mother said.

'But listen. Listen,' the girl said. 'It's the same as 'Baa Black Sheep', it's the same,'

There were queer pauses between her words and you started to feel sick, like the nerves had lost their tightness and were going to let everything loose. Angela's mother couldn't go to the toilet on her own before she died. The girl with the queer pauses was still saying 'Go on,' and leaving a space and 'Go on!' and in these pauses there was room for you to see what you were doing. You looked at them all. Saw them all and their pink mouths moving.

So you played again. The girls sang. You forgot about the weight and the stretchy pain in your neck pulling down on you.

'Baa black sheep,
have you any wool?
Yes sir, yes...'

And all the men were looking and smiling through stained teeth. The roaring got louder. The girls were laughing and telling you you were a great little lad and pulling you over close to their table, grasping at your jacket. One of them was shouting to tell everyone to give you money.

You looked and you looked at them and in your trousers you got a fright and this fear was different. *Tingle. Throb. Tremble. Vibrate. Burning. Bristle. Prickling. Delight.*

'Go on. Go on. Play it one more time and we'll sing,' They were screeching.

You did.

They sang. '...Baa baa black sheep,' cheering. Laughing. You filled yourself with a yawning warm breath and focused on the keys beautiful and bright and not overflowing. Trying to ignore the tingle and you realised, but you don't know how but you knew, that they were not laughing *at* you.

'Again' they said and by this fourth time you could look up and it didn't matter if you hit the right notes or not so you threw back your shoulders, looked at them and their bright faces and they were saying 'Come here young fella. Here you go,' and there wasn't enough room in your hand for the money.

The one who was asking you to play had pink feathers in her hair and she plucked one out with the same motion that your Dad plucked snails with and put it in your pocket. The contact shocked you.

'D'ya know that the *abcd* is the same too...' she said. Then you became confused in the perfume and the heat and the closeness and you tried to think about the lizard and the tingle in your trousers was back and wouldn't go away and you wanted to cry and they said to you *Go on go on play it again.* And they were all watching and staring and urging and all the smiles in their eyes.

So you started to play again because you couldn't walk away and you were watching the keys and making the accordion breathe, back and forth, twinkle except that they started singing again and this time it was *AayBeeSeaDeeEeeEffffJeee*....and you had to concentrate hard on the *ccggaag* because the familiar words of the *abc* crowded around and you were starting to sweat. Wet on your forehead and the tip of your nose and you tried to remember that it was warm in the pub.

'...*EnnOhPeeeeeQREsssssTeeUuuVeeeeeDoubleYouExY and Zee. Now I know my...*'

They finished.

'What's your name?' the one with the pink feathers said.

'Roman,'

'Well Ronan, you did mighty,'

'It's Roman with an *em*, ' you said and you bent your head because you didn't want her to see the tears and you wiped them away.

'Rommmman,' she said.

You nodded.

'Are you Italian?' she asked and her laugh left some spit on your face that you wiped off with your sleeve. She said sorry.

'No. I'm from Dublin,' you said and you wanted to tell her about the sick skink in the city and how your Dad talked to it and that you were going to save it so that your Dad wouldn't be alone. But in her eyes you saw that she wouldn't understand. They started to give you money. The girls ordered the men to give you the price of a drink.

You left the pub with €98.40.

You were exhausted from the up and down of emotion.

Like a nightmare. Angela and her friends were on the street. And you waited for her to hit you and call you brutal names but Angela stood back and looked at the accordion and at the place where your bright eyes were and you felt something cold in your heart. You waited for the punch but Angela didn't move.

'I have something to tell you Reptile boy,' she said, her voice an easy slur.

'They're looking for you to tell you that your precious lizard is dead,' She moved her rotten face close again. 'Stone dead. Just like my mother,'

'No he isn't. You're a liar,'

Angela touched the accordion. 'It looks like you're the liar now doesn't it?'

She touched your cheek ever so gently with her cold fingers, 'I'm telling the truth amn't I lads?' She turned to her friends.

You looked at them, snakes of pain in your belly and you knew it was the truth.

Angela said, 'Yes, he's dead. Ask your mother if you don't fucking believe us. She got a phone call.'

Then, but not until then, Angela pushed you and you fell to the ground and heard the sick jolt crack where the accordion hit the cold concrete.

The wind was starting to blow. Your mother and Met Éireann were right.

It wasn't a decision you made with your usual thought when you dropped the accordion over the bridge onto the lethal shiny railway tracks. In the same way you threw all the coins one after the other. The solid sounds of dropping seemed to be part of a strong tune and you thought that maybe rarity and beauty don't survive too long but you knew there could be more money; you knew there could be another lizard; you knew that you could sing even if there was no music in you.

Through Fire and Ice
(the man of Paviland Cave)
Matthew M. C. Smith

Fissure of cave. Be in light, shade.
Starve, thirst, slip between worlds.
Tides are time's erasure.

Before The Flood,
the sun and moon commingled
in eclipse of heat and blood.

Dance into flames that lick this chamber,
fall into fathoms before you wake. Kneel
to the lowering of the body in a hollow of rock.

Shadows, faces, eclipsed.

Cover him in sacred ochre with charms for a dead chieftain:
shells of nerite and periwinkle, wands of ivory,
a pendant cone of tusk-bone. Flint tools roughly serrated.

Torches taper. Black smoke-rings. Dark.

Now, is ghost-blue light. Place it all back. Scatter in these rock beds
a wreck of antlers, speckled bones and gnarled-out teeth
from time's migrations, once hoarded, then taken:

Hyenas, bears, rhinoceros. Herds of bison and elk.
Recover the lost skulls of mammoth and the red man. Assemble
his half skeleton. Cover, once more, with ochre.

Through museum's glass, with polished frame felt,
blindly see these shapes shudder through fire and ice.

Where the Dawn Takes Us
Mike Fox

We're not in a hurry when the line starts up. The train will be quiet, and most of the platforms empty. No problem to keep to schedule when it's like that. I step out at each station, take my time to check the doors, and in summer it's just me and the birds singing, in winter just me and the night sky.

Not that I'm completely alone, even at that time. Once I'm back in the train there's usually the same dozen or so passengers, along with a few randoms who get on and off, and leave nothing but the space they occupied. Strange to be making a single journey before the day's really started, of course, but I soon stopped wondering about them. Anonymous people.

My regulars though, are different. By their habits they've made the train their own. It is what it is because of their presence. Every one of them likes their same seat, their personal section of window, their few private litres of air. And of course they know they'll get it. One of the perks of leaving your home at five in the morning. We nod, and sometimes smile. If we speak I might call them 'love', and they usually reply in kind. We know that somehow we're part of the same thing.

Habits can do so much, don't you think? They can help you hang on to your life, or leave it behind. Parts of it anyway – the parts you don't want any more. Or don't want you. James R. Owen – that's what his I.D. badge says. Fifties, quiet, civil. Still comes in every weekday in his business suit, even though he hasn't had a job for at least three months. Perhaps he's waiting for his season ticket to run out. Perhaps he needs the journey more than the refund. I don't pry, you understand, but part of my job is to look over people's shoulders – bits of themselves spread out on the table before them. Sometimes I think they even want me to know.

And want to know about me. Occasionally I turn and catch a questioning look following me as I make my way along the aisle, touching the odd seat for balance, or maybe because it feels like it's mine. Eight coaches, all the way to the front, then back again. They know exactly what I'll do. I wonder if they find that reassuring. Like my uniform: dark blue slacks and jacket, stretched and a bit pale at the knee and elbow, plain white blouse, strap over my left shoulder that's permanently a bit lower than the right, with the weight of my satchel and ticket punch. We're all shaped by the life we live.

This old train too, straining up a long hill. Commissioned in the nineteen-seventies and hung about through all the takeovers and rebrandings. Full of ghosts who might even be alive, somewhere. Occasionally, when it's dark and the windows become mirrors, I imagine we're still back in that time. Cigarette burns on the seats. Plenty of work around. Lots more people, lots more tickets, lots more hope. The docks, the steel works, the mines, the manufacturing. And of course all the arteries they pumped their dirty, rich blood into: shops, offices, schools, pubs, libraries. Communities.

Then when the light comes everything changes. It's two thousand and eighteen again. The view turns into snapshots, glimpses in passing. They tell you something different. We go past people's gardens. I see the kitchen lights on, know someone's making tea, know they're going to have some sort of day. Although it might not involve anything you could call purpose. That's what I mean about habits. Sometimes you just have to make your own to carry on.

I suppose that's why I applied for this job. A train keeps you moving. Moving is a form of hope, even once you know the route and where it will take you. Perhaps especially if you know that. I was lucky then. Not so many people wanted the early shift. Whole towns would want it now. So I get my work clothes provided, and I get paid to be in the warm. I see the same people and places each day. And more often than not I can spread a little love. I told them that at the interview, said I'd cheer people up. The panel laughed, all three of them, but I could see it went home – 'the one with the tiny bit extra'. They phoned me almost as soon as I got back to my flat.

Love has to go somewhere, doesn't it? And when you wake up,
you might as well *be* up. And out. Otherwise I'd have been one of those
people making tea and waiting for the light to come. Some sort of light.
I doubt if any of us, me, the passengers, even the driver, would be here
if we were people who could sleep through the night. Though that
pretty young woman with the headphones in carriage C usually
manages to doze for the best part of an hour. Brings out the mother in
me, makes me want to tuck her in, especially when she has a little snore.

This train is my place now. That's what I seem to be telling you.
If you stay somewhere long enough a place forms itself around you. Just
by you being there. Although, if I'm honest, it doesn't always feel like
that. Sometimes, how I feel doesn't correspond to what's happening in
front of me. The past can pull you back, can't it? My Andy. Everyone
called us childhood sweethearts. No-one knows where he went. It was
even on the news. He was going to join the army. Said it would buy us a
house. But he never got there. I thought he was mine forever. Even gave
him the runaround for a while. Stupid bitch.

I see now I started holding onto things after that. Small things,
it might seem to you. Held them tight, so I could still be part of my own
life. That why I understand James R. Owen and the rest of my regulars.
All trying to make a place for themselves. All trying to hold on to it.

What I'm saying is a job like this can make you a witness,
whether you want to be or not. Different people, different lives, each
with their own shape and trajectory. I see when things begin and what
happens when they end. Little Davy with his guitar in a flimsy bag with
stickers on it. Pale, skinny, full of hope. Busking all day for small
change. Tells me you have to start somewhere – he's got stuff out on
YouTube. Sometimes I reach over and smooth his scruffy hair. Can't
help it.

There's always hope at the beginning. If you can't hope then,
when can you? But it doesn't always last. Especially round here.
Everyone hopes, but I doubt if many expect. I see when the hope starts
to fade, over weeks, over months. Someone's missed a shave, someone
hasn't bothered with their make-up, someone doesn't check their emails
anymore before they get in. Energy leaking away. When the pretence

has gone there's only the journey left.

You might think my hope has lasted, or I wouldn't still be here. You might even call me a survivor. But I've lost things too. All my little mantras: *mind the step down, lovely – make sure you take everything with you, 'specially yourself – we'll soon be arriving at...* No need when there's a strip of screen with a pre-recorded voice. I suppose it does the job. The politicians think that's better than someone like me. Still, I watch the passengers, my fellow travelers, walk away when we reach the city, and I know I've done my best for them. Every kind word is a blessing, don't you think?

On the return journey, if it's quiet, I enjoy the light as it plays on the landscape, see nature taking back what we can't use anymore. Slate peeping out under grass and moss, roots seeking daylight through the fractures in old concrete floors, walls of broken stone, like temples to something that a few decades ago must have seemed indestructible. There's not a moment when this world isn't changing. Change, I suppose, is life continuing. And life continues because it must. That's what this job has taught me. Each and every one of us takes life forward because we have to. My little bit of life, your little bit, and whatever it is we're here to share.

Two Poems
Tony Curtis

Nature to Nature

Black pyramid, black globe, black cube:
these three charred elm pieces
standing before three charcoal drawings
are for each elemental shape.
We must not touch in this exhibition,
none except for the blind woman
whose hand is guided to the surface of the cube
and palms its splits and whorls.

I wish her taken to his wood, Cae'n-y-Coed,
wrapped against the Winter, standing
for the first half-hour of a snow-fall
in his planted square of tall, straight birch,
feeling the snow lodged in the curls of bark,
and through the shock of cold
seeing one white against another white
through the chilled knowing of her touch.

David Nash in the National Museum of Wales

Leather Chair with a Portrait of Marion: **Charles Burton**

Then I was shown into this room
Filled with morning light
So that as I stood I took it all in:

The hedge and the trees framed by an Edwardian bay,
A line of jugs and bottles arranged on the sill
– ceramics and glass – which left gaps for meaning.

A worn rug on the blue-painted floor boards,
But principally the chair and a propped painting.
The woman in the painting looking

At me standing before the closed door.
The chair is Bauhaus steel tubing and leather,
Classic but well worn.

An empty chair is an interrogation.
Shall I sit?
Is that required?

With my back to the window and the world,
The sun would warm the nape of my neck.
The leather would begin to learn my shape and weight.

My arms resting on the arms:
I would be facing this door.
I would see what was about to happen.

Our Names into the Sea
Eamon McGuinness

It was a steaming day, and everything had to be cleaned and tied down. We were pulling anchor at twelve and would have our lunch while travelling to the next pearl farm. By half eleven we were ready to go and had our small break, *smoko*, sitting with our feet off the side of the boat. There was a timetable for those to keep watch. I wasn't on until ten that night so had the afternoon and evening to do what I wanted. During steaming, people caught up on sleep, read, listened to music, watched films, talked and drank. Some stayed on deck and watched the ships and islands passing. On a work day, we chipped shell from six a.m. to four p.m., using mallets and chisels. We pulled cages from the water with ropes and winches, put them through a washer and got rid of any barnacles, seaweed or other life-form growing on the outside. The dead shells were searched for pearls and fresh meat; the empties tossed back into the water. Anything dead was made note of. People snuck pearls away and made necklaces of them. Some pearls got lost, washed off the side of the boat. We saw every sunrise and sunset. Steaming days broke the monotony. The atmosphere was different, more relaxed and open; less savage. The previous night was Blair's goodbye party. He was moving to Perth after this swing. Pedro, the captain, warned that if any of us didn't get up for work we'd be off the ship.

I was on the upper deck with the weights and bean-bags when I heard Shane scream. Shane was always screaming but these sounded more frantic and desperate. The lower deck was cleared. It was like an empty football stadium before the crowds. A minute later, the doors to the kitchen burst open and Shane and Pedro dropped Jim's twisted and lifeless body on the ground, beside the stairs, in the shade of an awning. The sun was high and strong and reached his feet. His middle section was compressed so tight he looked like he'd starved himself. His eyes had grown massive, as if they were going to pop out of their sockets, and his mouth was set in a strange grimace, like he'd been thinking about something important when he died. Pedro covered him with a blanket, but left his head showing, propped on a pillow.

The whole crew were called on deck and we stood, twenty-five of us, in a semi-circle. Pedro faced us, his back to the sea and he said how Shane had found the coils of the anchor wrapped around Jim's hands and stomach. Plans had changed. Two planes were on-route: the bosses from Broome and an emergency response team. We would steam to the plane landing ten kilometres away. We'd all have to give a statement in town. Pedro sent us to have showers, pack up and get ready to leave. Then we'd eat, sit and wait. Pedro and Blair pulled anchor.

Pedro took out the remaining cases of beer and told us to get stuck in. He gave a can to everyone and we toasted Jim. The cans were mid-strength, small and red. Full-strength wasn't allowed on board. Each week a person was given twenty-four cans. They were bartered, used as presents and taken for favours. Each one was marked in black permanent marker with the owner's name to stop people stealing. The night before, for Blair's party, a group of us had gone over to Cockatoo Island and bought cases of beer and spirits. There couldn't be a trace of the full-strength left onboard, so every bottle had to be refilled with water and dropped into the sea.

Shane stood with his back to us. He was topless and his long blond hair flowed down his back, sunglasses pushed on top of his head. Pedro tapped his arm and handed him a can. Shane downed it between sobs and dropped it overboard. He released that first can like a rose petal falling. The can bobbed in the water and we watched it for a long time. The second he threw and the third he crushed and pounded against the foam. We looked at Pedro. He said nothing, so everyone started doing it. They were like a trail of breadcrumbs on our way to the landing; a strange, unspoken tribute. All the cans marked in black permanent marker. We were throwing our names into the sea and in the background, they slowly faded out.

After twenty minutes of drinking, I got changed, packed my bag and went into the kitchen to help Jules prepare lunch. She was sobbing and had music blaring, so we didn't have to speak. By the time we reached the landing, Shane was hollering to the sharks that followed the boat. They were the first thing I saw when I arrived. We threw our scraps to them after every meal. They were always being trailed by tiny fish. I was told they were harmless and didn't bite but they looked menacing. Their nickname was 'sleepy sharks'. The night before, some of the lads swam in the water and pushed each other overboard, but I stayed on deck and took videos. The sharks swam near them and one was caught by a flailing leg, but didn't react. On my camera, I had a video that Blair filmed of me and Jim eating fish eyeballs and messing around. Jim slapped my back and said: *You're alright, Irish, you're alright.*

Jules called everyone in for food. Some went down to the dining hall and others took their plates on deck. Shane was on his hunkers trying to eyeball the sharks, calling them pussies and spitting in their direction. Pedro went over to him.

C'mon Shaneo, a feed'd be good for ya.
Nah, bro, I'll stay with him. Any beer left?
All gone.
What about Jim's?
Maybe in the fridge.
That pussy could never finish his grog, am I right?
Dead on, Shaneo, I'll get you a tin.
Thanks, bro.

I watched Pedro go to the fridge and take out two cans. They toasted Jim.

There's gonna be an investigation, Shaneo.
I know.
Don't be too messed up when the bosses arrive, it won't look good.

Pedro walked towards the kitchen and Shane mock saluted his back. Shane called his name and Pedro stopped and turned around.

You ever meet his missus?
No.
After the last swing, we went straight to town, then back to his and she cracked the shits, totally went off on one.

True?
Damn right. Didn't she, Jim?

He was still on his hunkers and speaking slowly. I was at the table, not eating. Jim looked like he was sleeping in the shade of a tree.

He fucking knows.
It weren't her fault, Shaneo.
No, but she deserves this.
Leave it, Shaneo.
Rooting around while he was away.
That's your last beer, the bosses will be here soon.
You can't get pissed on this shit, Pedro, you know that, bro. There's a lot happened between them no one knows but me.
This ain't the time.
Oh, I'll keep quiet bro.
What happened down there?
I don't know, bro. He coulda pulled anchor in his sleep. You know that.

Shane finished the can, stood up, threw it in the air and with his bare foot kicked it off the boat.

But he was tired, you know? Yawning and talking about going back to bed. I was ribbing him about being an old, fat lightweight. Then you called me. Two minutes I was gone for, less.

Shane started sobbing. In Jim's direction, he said:

What the fuck did you do?

The deck filled again. Bags were dropped by the stairs. We waited for the planes. There were no cans left and since we'd stopped moving, the ones in the water had formed a dirty huddle. They knocked into the boat making soft consistent dins. I could tell by Pedro's scrunched up face he wasn't happy. He kept looking over the side, counting. Shane finished

Jim's beer. He poured the last can into the sea. People went from looking at Jim to looking at each other, to looking at the sky, watching for the planes.

Shane started howling. The sound was like wind in a fireplace and didn't seem to end. Pedro kept looking towards him. I sat for a long time, doing nothing, with a full plate in front of me. People were talking but I didn't make eye contact or respond. I looked at my plate, then at Jim. The others sat around crying, cursing, smoking and spitting into the sea. One of the girls prayed. Someone got sick. Some walked around or sat on the speedboats. People whispered the odd word about Jim's family. There was some movement as the first plane came into view. People stood up. Pedro told us to clear our plates and bring our bags out. I went over to the edge and scraped my uneaten food into the sea and watched a shark eat it in one go. Shane was hunched down near me and glanced up quickly before looking away.

I grabbed my bag from the bedroom and put it beside the others. I ran my hands over my face and through my hair, then blew out as if I had a mouthful of smoke. I felt an urge to do something. I tried to shake it off by stretching and walking around. I wanted to see Jim up close. We'd got to know each other during the three swings we'd done together. We didn't talk much, but that wasn't unusual. I hadn't seen a dead body before. I sat down and stared over at him. He really did look like he was sleeping. I knew I'd never be back here, that once I arrived in Broome, I'd see none of these people again. I'd made that decision. It was that feeling, *the leaving* that overtook me. It was a sensation I'd missed and longed for without realising it. In spite of everything, I was happy. I was watching everyone and everything fade from view.

I knelt beside Jim. I knew people were looking. No one had gotten too close; as if afraid he was contagious. I took his cold face in my hands and looked at his dead eyes, high in their sockets. Then I kissed him on the forehead and said out loud, in my best Aussie accent: *You're alright Jim, you're alright, bro.* I held his face until I heard someone behind me move. I could hear the shuffling of feet, the door to the kitchen open and a slow murmur start. I was crying. The plane was circling and the noise was getting louder. My eyes were shut tight and my thumbs were underneath his ears. *Come on, buddy, you're alright, Jim.*

When I opened my eyes, I saw Shane moving towards me, his face angry, his chest red and protruding. Before anyone could do or say anything I got up and ran with all my speed and strength. I ran past Shane, past the table where people were sitting, past the stairs, past the box of shoes, past Jules smoking, past Pedro giving orders, past the circle of bags, the fishing poles, the machinery, the stack of empty plates. Up ahead, the plane was landing. I ran past it all, past the glares, the words, the whispers, the eyes and dove straight into the ocean. When I came up and was bobbing in the sea and catching my breath, I didn't think of the sharks or the plane. I ignored Pedro's shouts and Shane's taunts. I tried to see everyone's face individually, to find some differences, something unique, but they all looked the same. They all had a look that said they never started anything properly or asked enough questions. For the first time, we looked like a united group.

Three Poems
M. W. Bewick

Found Poem for Philip Glass

I had the honour of meeting you
shaking your hand in general admission
and so overwhelmed after all those long days

waiting, to find whether an anxious state
could become a kind of beautiful catharsis,
a soft voice heard in a mind before sleep –

yet in the finest of moments the years
fill up with tears, your old skin like paper,
the repeat denials written in your eyes

recall that lake, the eternal
loneliness of yellow leaves like a cry
of peace, music drawing us back again

David, Again

Is that David? It looks like David.
How many years is it? I've been awash
with his updates across digital media.
Maybe David was taller, had more hair or
would be holding flowers, even in
February, but that was then and now
he's got his kids and cars and
the extension must keep him fit.
This guy, cradling his hold-all for
dear old life, with his earbud symphonies
disco, trap, emo, podcasts, whatever,
and if it is him, and me sitting
here, some kind of moving postcard
in the motes of a moment, the sun
flickering through trees with
all the possibility and potential,
why, the things we could tell
each other, now, about occurrences,
the brambles and clinker and asbestos
cleared, gone but somehow missed,
and so content in georgic silence and
maybe, yeah, happier just to reminisce

Music of the Woods

The secret of the adagio
is a quiet terror, a sense
of pursuance, exact in measure

a well-paced purpose no less
certain for its fond appeal,
like autumn's end in tangled woods

makes ground for what must
come, knowing the chill of a glade,
the hush of what can't return

for next the quicker push, a scherzo
flourish, a rush – a parting shot
forgetting the trees are black and bare

yet the adagio, still there, familiar
in the strange crowd of a new mood,
finds us out, lays down the pace

Free Love
Lauren Mackenzie

The nurse held on to the door frame as she poked her head sideways into the ward.

'Mr. Miller, your son called. He's on his way up from Sydney to bring you home.'

Jeff had told them again and again not to bother his kids, but they weren't going to let him go home on his own. 'I'm not going to Sydney. No way.'

'That'll be up to him. You've had a nasty fall. You need someone to mind you.'

'I don't.'

'Might be nice to have some company?'

He hmphed. The nurse hmphed in return and pulled her head back out of the room.

Margaret from next door had screamed blue murder when she found him. She thought he'd been robbed and left for dead but that wasn't it, it was the bloody dog tripped him up. He went face down on the concrete path, his right arm buckled beneath him. He thinks he was out cold for a bit but he didn't tell anyone that. Yesterday, before the dog upended him, he'd mowed the lawn and climbed on to his roof and cleaned the gutters. Today they handle him like he's made of shortbread.

He hoped someone was feeding the bloody dog.

He was woken by a tap on his arm from a tall, blonde doctor he hadn't seen before.

'How are you feeling?'

'Pretty ordinary.'

The doc smiled; his blue eyes bright in his sunburned face. Jeff knew his own face was as round and purple as a half-crushed blueberry. He tried again to move his swollen fingers; they reminded him of a sausage sandwich, poking out of the white cast as they did. He still had all his teeth. Small mercies. Jeff wondered when the doc was going to launch into the questions—name, date of birth, who's the prime minister. But all he said was—'You don't want your lunch?' There was a tray of ham and cheese sandwiches and a pot of tea on the overbed table. They must've been left when he was sleeping.

'I didn't say that.'

The sandwiches pleased him; although a bit dry, he could at least manage them on his own. The doc watched Jeff eat and kept watching as Jeff missed the cup and poured tea over the last two sandwiches.

'Oops,' said the doc, while doing nothing to help Jeff mop it up.

Jeff gave the doc a second look. Short sleeve, white button shirt, jeans, and sandals on leathery feet.

'Who the hell are you?'

The man laughed. 'It's me, Dad. Oliver?'

Jeff looked again. He kept forgetting his children were middle-aged. 'Sorry. When they said my son was coming, I thought of Scott.'

'Scott's got case review meetings all week. Jen's at a conference. They decided I didn't have anything better to do.' Olly laughed.

'Well did you?'

'There was this young lady in Cammeray…Nah, only joshing you.' Olly laughed again. Jeff didn't like men who laughed at their own jokes.

'I'm ready to go.'

Olly drove Jeff home in a rusty green station wagon with his surfboard on the roof. He was nervous and unusually quiet, no longer filling the air with talk. Still off the drugs, Jeff surmised. He felt a measure of relief, but he had no confidence in it. With Olly, there was always something—his girlfriend dumped him, he lost his job. Three years ago, the last relapse, happened when his mother died in a car crash. To be fair, Marianne's death shook them all. It might've been forty years since their divorce but after her death, Jeff found himself having conversations with her in his head that he'd never had before. Least now he always had the last word.

Olly told him he was attending outpatient rehab, claiming sickness allowance, sleeping on a mate's couch and surfing when the waves were good. It was seven months, he said. Almost.

'Well, it's good to see you looking good, Olly.'

'Thanks, Dad. I feel okay.'

'Are you working?'

'One step at a time.'

'Work'll get your head outta your arse, help you get on with things.' Jeff believed keeping busy was pretty much the answer to everything.

'Find a woman. Get a dog.'

Olly made a sound. More of a snort than a laugh. 'I have always appreciated your advice, Dad.'

'Well it's not rocket science,' said Jeff.

The next twenty minutes passed in silence but then Olly exclaimed. They had just cleared the hill over Mungo's Point and descended to the coast road. The sea spooled out from a ragged, rocky coastline, eventually becoming one with an enormous blue sky.

'Beautiful.'

The beaches weren't good around here, too rocky and a scramble to get down to. You needed a tow out past the rocks if you wanted to surf. Jeff knew Olly would've come up to visit him if things had been otherwise. It only occurred to him now that he could've visited Olly. It had been enough to know his children were well and happy; he didn't feel he needed to see them for himself.

'Left here and we're about two hundred metres on the right.'

Jeff's house was a red brick bungalow off the coast road, no picture windows, no view of the sea. It was all he could afford when he retired. It turned out he didn't need much. Olly pulled into the drive. By the time Jeff managed to get his seat belt undone, Olly had opened the door for him. He waved off Olly and hauled himself out. Once on his feet, he deliberately skipped the four steps up to the porch. He turned around to see if Olly was watching but Olly was looking back the way they'd come. At the end of the road, a sparkling triangle of sea was visible between the treetops. A sea view was more than he could afford when he retired up here.

On the porch, the dog's water bowl was worryingly full. Jeff let out a piercing whistle and waited.

'Rooster! Rooster! Come on boy!'

'Why's he called Rooster?'

'He wakes me at the crack a dawn.'

Olly laughed.

'One of you kids was always going walkabout on us. At the crack a dawn, before anyone else was up.' Jeff remembered finding the toddler in the garden one morning, so cold his legs felt like a doll's plastic legs. He'd tucked him under his jumper and held him skin to skin.

'That was me.'

'You. Yes. Course it was you. We had to stretch fisherman's net over your cot. It was the only way to stop you climbing out.' Jeff could see Olly hadn't known this. 'Don't look at me like that, it probably saved your life.'

Jeff let them in through the back door. The house, square and plain, had four rooms, one in each corner, a hall and a bathroom. His breakfast mug and bowl were in the sink as if he'd just been out to the letterbox rather than spent a night in the hospital. Or was it two? Jeff couldn't remember and didn't want to ask. It'd come back to him.

'You'll want some grub, a cup of tea, before you drive back?'

'I was planning to stay a few days, give you a hand?'

'There's no need.'

Olly laughed. 'Jen said you'd be like this. I'll camp in the back yard if I have to, but she'll kill me if I don't stay. Bet you couldn't even open a can of tuna?

'Then I won't be eating tuna, will I?'

'I saw a fish and chip shop down the road, I'll get us some fish and chips? Or a burger? Whatever you want? I'll go to the supermarket tomorrow.'

While Olly was out getting fish and chips, Jeff rang Margaret. She was very happy to hear he was fine but she didn't know where Rooster was. The last time she saw the dog, he was on the road following the ambulance to the hospital. She wondered if he could've walked the whole fifty k's and was now sitting in the hospital car park waiting for him. She'd heard of dogs doing that kind of thing. He assured Margaret, Rooster *was* loyal, but he was also old. He would've given up as soon as the ambulance pulled out of sight.

Jeff went to the back door and yelled again. The house sat in the middle of an acre of lawn with a clothesline behind and a brick garage besides, bordered by a sagging chain link fence. Beyond the fence was the bush and a feast of small creatures for Rooster to hunt if he was hungry. There were also poisonous snakes and paralysing ticks. Jeff headed out on the road, calling and whistling. It was a two-horse town and it wasn't long before he hit the edge of it. After the caravan park, the road turned inland, winding through scrappy grassland. It had been a dry winter and there was nowhere for any dog to hide. As he turned and walked back the other way, he felt uneasy. He was afraid for the dog and only now he noticed it was getting dark. A car approached, headlights coming straight at him and skidded to a stop in the gravel of the hard shoulder. The passenger door flew open. Olly.

'Dad? Are you alright? I've been all over, looking for you?'

'I was looking for the bloody dog.'

A newspaper parcel of fish and chips lay on the seat. Olly held the parcel while Jeff climbed in. 'They'll be cold now.' He studied him. 'You okay?

'I'm fine.' Jeff was visibly shivering. He was still in the working clothes he'd been wearing when he fell, spattered with paint and grease, holes in both knees. He'd nothing else to put on when he left the hospital. Olly turned on the heating.

'In the hospital, they said –

'They said a lot of things, most of it a waste of bloody time.'

'Right. But they told me to keep an eye on you.'

Jeff laughed.

'What?'

'You. It's *you*, minding me.'

Olly checked his mirrors and executed a U-turn. The night was soft; cats eyes sparkled as they flashed by. 'I thought we'd get a chance to talk.'

'I've got a microwave,' said Jeff.

A moment passed then Olly chuckled. Jeff wondered when it became okay to find him so amusing.

Olly went through the palaver of offering to pitch his tent, not wanting to bother Jeff, make a mess, etcetera, etcetera. There's a spare bed in the study, take it or leave it, Jeff told him. The fish and chips spun around in the microwave for two and a half minutes before Olly came to his senses and accepted the offer. Jeff wasn't able to eat much of the fish and chips; the salt and vinegar stung the inside of his mouth. He must've bitten it when he fell. His face hurt. His arm hurt. He felt squeezed between the walls of the room. When Olly took his wallet out and slapped some notes on the table between them, he had no idea how much was there because he was having trouble focusing.

'What's this?'

'It's amends Dad. I'm making amends. I had a day's work with my mate in Sydney, a brickie. I'll get you the rest when I get a full-time job. I'm clean now, for good this time, I promise.' Olly smiled at him, his eyes shiny. Jeff wasn't sure if it was the light or tears rising.

Jeff fanned out the notes, four fifties, then pushed them back towards him. 'I don't want your money.'

'It's not my money, it's yours. Part of what I took.' Olly pushed the notes even closer to him. 'I'm making amends.'

'With pocket money?'

Olly shrunk a little before him.

'It's the program, Dad; a process. I'm trying to do it right.'

'We spent hours and hours trying to figure out what to do with you.'

'I'm saying I'm sorry.'

'Your mum's dead and I don't really care.'

'What the fuck?' Olly looked like he'd been slapped. He took a breath and sat up straight. 'Sorry. Sorry. Fair enough. I'm listening?'

Jeff thought Olly might be taking this all too seriously. 'Funny times.'

'Are you all right?' Olly was staring at him.

Jeff tried to smile. He felt like his bones were melting. 'Forget about it. It's not your fault. I was probably overcompensating.'

'For what?'

'For thinking you were a little cuckoo in the nest.' He winked. 'Cuckoo.' He knew he shouldn't have said it again but he liked the sound of the word.

Olly slumped back in the chair, wrapping his arms around his chest. If Jen and Scott were around when this subject came up, they would always hurry to proffer the likenesses—the solitary bent, the hay fever, and their hands, wide and strong.

'Take it easy. It's a joke. Your mother never had any doubts.'

'It's not funny, Dad.'

'Amuses me.' Jeff pushed the money back to him. 'You need this more than I do.'

Olly stood up. 'I'm gonna get my stuff from the car.'

Jeff swallowed a couple more Demerol and took himself to bed. It was only after he was in bed, that he realised he hadn't said goodnight.

'Goodnight, son,' he yelled. He could not have known whether Olly heard him or not because he immediately fell asleep.

When Olly returned with his backpack, he called for Jeff but was left to guess by the closed bedroom door that his dad was inside. He picked up the fifties and put them in his pocket. Fuck him. Back in the kitchen,

Olly stared at the cupboard doors. He was pretty sure behind them he'd find booze of one kind or another and somewhere in the house, there was Demerol. He texted Scott and Jen—*dads fine sharp as ever*—and took a banana to bed.

Every surface in the study was covered in books and journals and newspapers. Some open to a page, others with bookmarks sticking out. Under the books on the spare bed was a slippery purple bedspread and under that, a bare mattress with a cloudburst of stains. Olly returned to the car for his sleeping bag.

Jeff was on a train, hurtling through dense, dark rainforest. He'd missed his stop. He wanted to get off at the next station to catch another train back, but the train flew past station after station. Marianne was waiting for him at home and he was desperate to get back to her, certain she'd be worrying. When he woke, he was unsure of everything; where he was, who he was. He hadn't dreamt about Marianne for years. It was Olly's fault, knocking him off kilter.

He stretched his feet out to the corners of the bed searching for the weight of a sleeping dog. Nothing but cold, sharp sheets. Stupid, bloody dog. He sat up for a piss and the night air shifted and shimmered around him. Soon enough whatever it was passed and he made his way out to the dark of the hall. He cursed Olly for not leaving even one light on. He shuffled to the bathroom and tried to negotiate the buttons on his pyjama pants. His left hand was clumsy. He twisted his casted right arm to help and was rewarded with an excruciating pain streaking through his armpit. Piss ran down his leg, soaking his pyjamas. By the time he got himself over the bowl, there were only a few drops left. He gave himself a shake, dropped his pants, and stepped out of them. He took the towel from the rail and dried his legs before mopping the floor with the towel under his feet. His head pounded to the beat of his heart; he needed more Demerol. Back in the hall he stopped to listen hoping he hadn't woken Olly up. He switched the hall light on but something was wrong with the bulb. It glowed white but offered no illumination beyond itself. The closer he walked towards it, the further away it seemed until the light was as fine and final as the white dot when you turned an old television off. He felt along the wall for his open bedroom door. One step into the black of the room, his good arm out wide and he felt nothing but air whistling past his face and then rushing out of him. Oh, he said to the dark.

Olly lay still in his bed, listening hard. He was aware a noise had woken him but wasn't awake enough to know what it was. He waited for another, more determined sound. A sudden tumble of rain landed on the roof, drowning out everything but itself. Olly felt a drop of wet on his arm. Rain was coming in the open window. He jumped up, closed the window and crawled back into his sleeping bag. With the window closed, the various odours of the house began to seep into him again. There was dog, and fried food, but mostly, overwhelmingly, the house smelled of old man, something like cooked meat left too long in the refrigerator.

The sky was changing from black to blue. There was no going back to sleep. Olly pulled on his jocks and sat on the edge of the bed, his foot jigging up and down. He wanted to make coffee, toast, but didn't want to wake Jeff. He wondered if Jeff had any idea how many hours Olly and his counsellors had spent talking about the old man's reluctance to fully own him. They'd all agreed it was convenient after Marianne left him, to suggest the third child, the youngest and most in need, might not be his.

There was a scratching at the back door. He opened the door and Rooster bounded down the hall, slid around the corner with a bark, and flew straight into Jeff's bedroom. Olly supposed if Jeff wasn't awake before, he was now. He followed Rooster into the room.

Jeff was face down on the floor, naked from the waist down. Rooster scrambled around him barking, laying paws on his back and frantically licking his face. Olly watched the dog repeat the cycle three or four times, before laying his head down on his paws and whimpering.

Olly rang Jen to find out what to do. She made him check for a pulse even though he knew Jeff was dead. He did as he was told and curled his hand around Jeff's neck to feel for a pulse. The skin, already cold, gave softly under his fingers while at the same time Jeff's whiskers stabbed the pad of his thumb. The sensation ran through him like an electric shock. He felt again his dad's kisses on his cheek when he was a child. Remembered the soft and the sharp of it, the longing and the pulling away.

Jen stayed on the phone for a while listening to him cry.

Last night's storm left the sea churning and frothing like a vanilla milkshake. Too choppy for a board but Olly needed the water. It was the only thing between him and the Demerol. He dived off the rocks, carved his way through the waves, rising over the crests and dropping down the other side. It was hard going. His lungs burned, but he couldn't afford to stop until he passed the breakers. A dumper rose high in front of him. He kicked with everything he had, propelling himself forward and down into a deep blue silence. When he finally surfaced, he was free of the breakers. He turned over and floated on his back. Water lapped at his cheek. Sun burned white in his eyes. He closed them and listened to the wheezing hoosh of the currents under him.

He checked in with his feelings but there wasn't much he could make sense of. The question of whether it was the old man he had heard in the early hours, or whether he could've done anything, sat like a stone in his throat, rolling over with every swallow. He flipped himself upright, treading water as he eyed the horizon to count the swell; each wave fuller and higher than the last. He turned to face the shore. The passage through the rocks to the stony beach was narrow enough that he needed to mind the backwash. If he didn't, or he couldn't, well, it would be nobody else's problem but his. He felt the pull again; he was a stone in a slingshot. At the moment of greatest tension, he struck out cleaving the sea in two with each stroke, his legs pistons pumping. As the breaking wave lifted him, he stiffened, arms in an arrowhead but he'd committed too soon. The wave sucked him inside the falls, spinning him over and over, rendering him blind and deaf. He was flung against a submerged rock, the last of his air whacked out of him, his hands grabbing seaweed and slime. The sea yanked him back up again. His head crested just long enough for a gulp of air, a glimpse of rocks below and a chance to wonder if, after all that, this is how it ends. Two coffins, himself and his old man, side by side, waiting to be buried together. He kicked frantically, legs wheeling, and threw himself on to the rocks before the wave could. The wave gripped him like a shark, but he had his fingers dug into the rock's crevices. His foot found a ledge. A one-two pull and he was clear. He lay on his stomach feeling the heat of the sun-warmed rocks and breathing the air, grateful that he didn't have to spend eternity with the old man. He laughed. A shard of glass slid into his heart. His rib felt like it was broken.

Olly sat at his father's kitchen table allowing his brother and sister to fuss over him. They all thought his rib was broken but agreed there was nothing to be done. He could hardly move with the pain but Jen had flushed Jeff's Demerol down the toilet and Olly thanked her for it. Scott washed out the barnacle cuts and scrapes, dabbed them with antiseptic, and wrapped his hands in gauze. Jen gave him a bollocking for going into the water at all, but Olly knew they were relieved to have something else to talk about. Their father was in the morgue awaiting an autopsy; the GP suspected a bleed on the brain from the original fall. Jen and Scott wanted Olly to stay on after the funeral and mind the property until probate was cleared. Olly complained there was no surfing around here and besides, he didn't think he could bear the smell of Jeff. Even when he was out of the house, the smell remained on his skin. Olly watched as Jen and Scott sniffed their arms. Jen poured herself another glass of wine and cried some more.

Olly lay awake in his father's study. The smell had shifted with the windows open. He could feel a smile on his face. It wasn't right but it was there, nevertheless. He had a place to live for the foreseeable and a dog that was going to wake him at the crack a dawn. It felt like home and for this he was nothing but grateful to Jeff. He stretched his feet out to the cold corners, and found the warm weight of Rooster, sleeping.

Two Poems
Angela Graham

After Iconoclasm: Annunciation Re-Assembled

Llanfair, Yr Wyddgrug

I could fear an angel who descends,
Majestic, like the Prince he is,
Bearing a tremendous invitation
Through the loggia that frames him
In a garden all enclosed,
But this angel of Yr Wyddgrug
Is Prince only of shards.

His Virgin we must infer
From this piece of blue
And the Spirit from – is that a bird?
Askew as a broken compass.

This Gabriel of Wales speeds,
A comet heading eastward,
His hair streaming behind him
In a cosmic wind.
'Such an eager face'
All that remains of him.

Enough for us to glimpse
How ardently respect and hope
Poised
At the threshold of that girl's reply.

After Iconoclasm: A Reflection on Technique

The emptied niche is a womb,
Perpetually conceiving
And the great window, burst,
A stone-stringed larynx
And the gouge-marks on the eyes of saints
Record in ogham
How their gaze held the wielder of the knife
And called him, 'Cain',
For it's always murder, of the life
The image veils
(hence the requirement for official
sanctioning)
So the icon-breaker is advised
To leave no trace:
No frescoed drapery, no elegant
Plaster shoe,
No painted personhood, and especially
No space
    –   headless torso, alcove,

or pedestal –
Nothing that calls for something.

Araiyakushimae
Deirdre Shanahan

The swamp of tea bags near the sink grew with each one she threw on. Almost the end of her trip home and she had thrown scraps of meat and packaging in the same bin for two weeks. Either the council's refuse collection did not care or her mother didn't, but pale slinky chicken skin slid against tins and plastic containers which once held tomatoes. She wanted to delve into the slush, remove each item and divide the lot as she did in Japan; a separate container for refuse to burn, food and everything else.

'You ready, Yolande?' her mother called. 'Let's go for the drive while the day is good.'

The sun glittered on the lake as they drove west. The lingering warmth this time of year was unusual and everywhere people claimed she had brought the fine weather. She hoped so, hoped landscape might be medicinal for her mother. Anyone undergoing hospital tests deserved it.

The shortcut was through the bog's lumpy greeny rust land with a hush of heather. Yellowy green, tones she had not seen for years. Out on the main road, leaves glowed with fire. Studs of orange berries in the trees, strands of tiger lilies running wild. Soft pink briar roses. She realised had not seen the season here for a long time, not since leaving for college. She drove this way with Mickey when she had started at the secondary school and he offered to drive her to the bus in town. They rode in his van, windows steaming, as the days shrugged away from summer. Ropes swished in the back and his tool boxes rolled. She had rubbed the vapour to make a hole to see out.

By the pier, with the Cloughmore mountains sliding against the sky, Yolande stopped and leaned over to release her mother's door, a light breeze catching. Her mother sat in profile against a cliff edge, her pale skin drained of blush and cheeks having lost their roundness. But her eyes were the same sharp blue and she wore lipstick in case she met a neighbour or someone important: the doctor or priest.

'Revives a person, doesn't it dear, getting out?' Her mother's hands lay clasped in her lap close as a purse. 'And you've been lucky with the weather.'

Her mother, strong once, had been able to walk for miles over rocky paths and hills. In the past month, since treatment began, Yolande saw her mother's internal systems as churned with medications and radiation; crumbling inside. The things hospitals do to you, her mother had said.

They sat on a bench, an orange scarf hiding her mother's throat. How many more drives might there be before she had to return, Yolande wondered. With the span of oceans between continents, there was little she could do, but while around, she would drive her mother anywhere she wanted.

Far out, the sheer cliff nipped into the sea. Clefts and eaves of rock, ridged with gorse and heather. Sea-birds scrapped and retreated, their squall rising. Waves broke in flips and rolls charging in. Far out, surfers rode and slipped like flies. Matsuko had told her he had walked in the alps north of Tokyo and when she had asked him about sea-cliffs in Japan, he had laughed, saying most of the coast was too unstable. Instead they had lounged over long weekend in cities and smaller towns inland. He had introduced her to Onsen, and his favourite a traditional one by the sea, where she had sat on a boulder by a warm pool as steam rose from the mineral water and women became glazy with light and she had supposed the same for him, in his section.

'We'll call on Mickey,' her mother said and suggested the garden road whose little houses stretched beside long fields. 'You should see him before you return and he might be in.'

'Would you like to?'

'Oh yes. He's been low. He'll be glad to see us.'

'How d'you mean?'

'The poor fella's not been right for months. Down in himself.'

Unsure what her mother meant, they returned to the car and

she drove on, for he had not been mentioned in phone calls or emails. A thin lisp of a man, her father's younger brother, was the only other one who had not joined others to England or America.

She had wondered at that time, when she started Secondary school, did Mickey not know? Could he not see she wore a dress and not her old jeans? She had thought his brushing fingers on her thigh were a kind of mistake, how as an uncle had he not realized. Until again. When he came visiting to the house on a Sunday afternoon when her parents were in town. His hand rising. The nub of his thumb at her knicker edge, until she shifted off the chair at his table, and stepped away. The third occasion, at the back of his house, his fingers eager to taste her, caught her shoulder, pulled her so she had to kneel.

She had told no one. Let it choke.

'The way he is, no woman'd put up with him,' her mother said. 'Smoking and reading the papers till all hours. Only ever going to market and town.'

He had been bright. At school until he was sixteen. He should have known. Must have. She stopped the car at his house, reluctant to enter. In Japan, she had been shy entering shrines and temples; fearful of stepping onto a sacred space. In the new continent, she had put the past behind her and mostly in the tight streets of Tokyo, in the rush of catching trains to work and work itself, she had. The very tautness of daily life had freed her.

He ranged the kitchen, tall, unsettled, searching cupboards. He didn't raise his head to acknowledge them.

'Hello, Mickey,' her mother greeted while he opened a cupboard and another.

'I've no Minestrone,' he said.

'Come here and talk to us.'

'I won't.' He bent to a low cupboard of the dresser and scanned the shelves.

'We were passing.'

'Ah, passing. Passing.'

'Yolande drove us.'

'Yolande,' he repeated as if it was a brand of soup.

His eyes, when he stood, were pinched dark and his face thinner. He seemed taller than she recalled and realized it was because he had lost weight. Most likely due to working in the fields cutting rushes or making silage. His movements were twisty with nerves and he would not sit.

'How are you, Mickey?' her mother continued.

'Hungry. For there`s the sheep to ready for the show.' He opened a tin and set the soup to warm on the gas.

They let him sit and drink, though he made no offer of tea. He pushed away the empty bowl. 'I`ve to get on. Have to be there by three or what`ll the other fellas think.'

He had not noticed her. She may as well be a sack of potatoes. They followed him out and he opened the metal gate to the field, tying it to the post with blue plastic string. She should say something. Speak. After so long she must. She wasn`t the confused girl who had feared upsetting her parents. The notion pounded. Hard. Resistant like a hammer dropped in a box. She should make him see the small damage. Before he got older and it was too late. Let him know of the humiliation which had laid with her trembling and churning, so it was not until she left college she had a proper boyfriend. Even then, a slip of fear. A trace. Until Japan, continents away where Matsuko`s gentle manners charmed her.

Mickey pulled a sheep from the pen, grabbing its head with a twist. It scampered with shock, stick black legs in a kind of dance as though it did not know its own weight. Astride the animal, he held the face up and back with a deft flick of his wrist until the sheep calmed and he drew it to the small trailer. He slung it in so it knocked against the tinny empty metal.

'Delaney won last year and I want to beat him.' He rubbed his hands together.

'Of course,' her mother said, though all the years of entering, he never had.

'No more than the Texel`s or Suffolk. You can`t beat a black face mountain one.' He ran his hands across the back of the sheep and underneath.

He pulled open the mouth. Teeth held all, she knew from when he had horses. But sheep, he had said, had only one set of teeth so it was vital they met the upper gum in alignment. He hugged and twisted the head so it settled in his lap, its watery dark blue eyes shivery with light. He knew the tricks and turns of animals and she wondered what categories he had entered. Yearling or Ram. Open. Restricted. In late August, he used to sit at his kitchen table with the floral plastic cloth and a stubby note-book, deciding.

'You know them well and how to work with them,' her mother said. Though a pharmacist's daughter, she had picked up the ways of the land. 'We won't delay you.'

Yolande stood near the window, looking onto the field. She should ask. Why had he taken advantage. Betrayed her parent's trust. And hers. He was not the son of a poor farmer who might have been cabined with all his family, but of one who was prosperous. Had he not known better? It was wrong. All wrong.

'Pull up some carrots for yourselves before you leave. Plenty of them. You can bring back the rest to the house.'

'You had good crops this year?' her mother said, and in a lower tone, added, 'Whatever else, he can stir growth out of the earth.'

'Ok, I'll get them.' Yolande picked up a small fork from the outside sill where it warmed in the sun.

She would return. When the show was over and no distraction. He would have to listen as she spat out words caged in for years. She would challenge. Scald him with the truth.

At the lower field, the brambles were pimply hard and undeveloped because of the rain through the early summer. The bridge over the ditch was an old door with split planks supporting it, which belied its strength, for it was there all the years since her grandparents were alive. Old rainwater sumped the ditch. Grass and reeds fell. Gold under the full light of the sky. She had jumped over it as a kid, lost to danger, rather relishing it and not realizing ditches developed from the stripples of brooks, following the edge and flow of land. A much needed irrigation, without which neither her father or anyone around might have had cattle. A moisture so present. So plentiful. Part of the air she breathed. Part of what she had longed for when she was away.

On a Sunday, after long days in the Tokyo heat, she had taken a train to the mountains. The office air conditioning clothed her during the week. But at weekends the heat drained her. By mid-afternoon, after visiting one part of the city to pick up an item, she was drained, her clothes moist with sweat. Done for the rest of the day. Even the dainty hat Japanese women wore and which she had bought, did not shield her and the most welcome time had become the bath at the end of the day.

Along the railway line, miles of flats led to houses as they left the city, which became larger houses and farms and fields. As the land rose, the fields became greener and vines grew. She had not expected them, yet here they were, scattered plentifully in rows. At midday, the sun was so intense it slammed the top of her head despite the baseball cap. But the decreased density of building and people, made it more tolerable and she took the main street to the outer parts. A path led under trees, whose canopy of lush branches was cooling. Araiyakushimae, a slim wooden sign directed.

The shrine at the top, was smaller than others, but with a gracious quiet about its red trimmed roof with gold filigree running like lace along the side. In the cool of the temple, one man sat in prayer while others straggled at the back and she wondered if she might not join them and thought of home. School. How she had been taught prayer was the essence of distilled thought, so she tripped back down the steps to collect her shoes.

Twisted evergreen trees in the courtyard were like crazy people doing Yoga, trying to get rid of themselves. At the far end, under a canopy the child-size height of a greystone statue stood, with a man ladling up water over its head. He wore a grey back pack with a floppily creased sun hat and smiled as she approached.

"Hello. I am Matsuko. Of the Language Association Guide Service," he said, his lapel badge confirmed this with a logo like a bunch of grapes. "I can give you tour of the shrine? Or the castle?"

"No. No thank you. I can`t stay long."

"Ah. It`s pity." He ladled, water gushing and falling. The statue was like a Bhudda but more feminine. Wife or acolyte, she thought.

"Araiyakushimae. What does it mean?"

"It mean new waters of life. And we need this in the heat." He leant towards the statue and rubbed its head. "If I rub," he pointed to the head and waist, "and I ill, it make me better. I have bad eyes. Cataract coming." He removed his glasses and blinked, smiling into what he could not see.

"Am I allowed?"

"Oh yes. You try." He handed over another wooden ladle long as her arm and she dipped it into the trough of water. Drops rained down the figure, in little gulps.

In the field, she knelt and dug in with the fork, pulling the carrots. Knelt as she had with Mickey's knees in her face at the back of the house, as he undid his trousers until she had flown up, brushed against his leg and run off.

Florets of light green leaves splayed as she wrenched and tugged, releasing the grimy carrots, lone stray roots trailing. Soil fell on her fingers, ridging her nails. Dirtying the underneath. The carrots, good sturdy bodies, lay on the ground, an odd glove of seven fingers. She gouged the largest. Scored and struck. Bashed in the lovely flesh. Made weals and gashes. The next and next, until seven were wasted with nice, clean cuts and lay like soldiers, all the goodness out of them.

Her mother was sitting outside the house on a rickety dining chair as Yolande came up the fields. Mickey was trudging to the back door. Carrying a plastic sack which once held animal feed or meal, he had been to the stack of turf. Stooped low, as if wizened, he set down the turf from his arms, gentle as if it was a child. He shook his hands in release of the burden, turned and tugged the sack as he sloped along, with a scrape, scrape on the concrete path.

They drove back, in a kind of silence, broken with reflections by her mother on improvements on the road and the increased number of houses. With the views, one could build holiday homes which would repay the cost, and to which anyone from Dublin and Limerick, she was sure, would be eager to come. She leant forward to switch on the radio bringing a rush of out- of - date music. The local station still did not invest. No wonder everyone left for more exciting places.

"A shame about the carrots. Usually he has beautiful ones. And sweet too."

"No. They weren't good." The wheel passed through Yolande's fingers.

A poor harvest, after all. One wouldn't know what had got to them. A rabbit. A fox.

That evening, readying for them to eat at the local hotel, she showered in the bathroom downstairs, kept for visitors. Her father had built the extension years before with the help of Mickey, who even then as far as she saw, mostly set breeze blocks in place. She would not go back to him. Time with her mother was more pressing. She had grown beyond this place, where the old were shrinking before her eyes. She stood in pools of water under the shower head, slathering creamy water around her shoulders, drops trickling down her breasts, onto her belly, over her thighs and legs. The warmth was soothing, slavering her skin. She flannelled down, bruises of encounters, words and glances, the hold of years washed away.

Two Poems
Jackie Gorman

Growing Pains

The eight-year old pyjamaed as
Superman complains of cramps
in his legs, how the ache keeps
him awake at night.
I tell him what my mother and
her mother told me.

It's growing pains,
the pain of growing.
It's a simple yet ineffective
way to explain the body.
I don't tell him this becomes
perennial and gnawing.
Time grows fond of the
small ligaments, frenula
that restrict movement.

He hugs his knees and
eats his broccoli,
the colour of chlorophyll
and Kryptonite.
I know he's worried now
about the dull pulse
that comes at night to
test his small bones in the dark.

Skull

I imagine its erect ears,
yellow eyes and pounding heart.
The cranium is now scrubbed clean
by sunshine and skin beetles,
the colour of milk and light.

Walking in Big Mountain, Arizona,
I lift up a skull from the ground.
Canis latrans, prairie wolf, God's dog,
the trickster who rebels.

My heart pounds touching
empty eye sockets,
imagining what it last saw –
sunlight, a Rosy Boa or cactus flowers.
Perhaps a vulture circled over it or
a trail of cowboys and cattle on the move
passed it by. The desert night fell on
blood- red rocks fed by iron oxide.

A Jewel Wasp hovers over me.
I trace my fingers over this memory,
seeking a desert blessing.
In the distance, casino lights flicker on
and there's a band of coyotes
calling out to each other

Plainsong
Mark Blayney

Light shone through the windows of the cathedral. Dennis didn't know yet whether to put glass in the windows. His massive face loomed into the raised drum, on which the dome would be placed. His head was haloed by the light from above. He switched off the torch and the interior disappeared into darkness.

He stepped back and looked at the cathedral with pride. Nearly there now. The dome and some roof carvings to do, and it would be finished. He picked up a red notebook and wrote 976 on the seventh page. Nine hundred and seventy six boxes meant that he had so far used approximately 39,040 matches.

Dennis Woolley was 67 years old. He retired from running his wet fish shop six years ago for reasons of ill-health. He had suffered a series of painful hernia operations which had been frequently cancelled on the day, making him shuffle home from the hospital and wait patiently for the next letter addressed to *Denis Wooley* until eventually the expert surgeons had been able to accommodate him on the slab. These days he could only walk very slowly, with the aid of a rubber-tipped metal stick. He'd been using this stick for a week before he realised there were small holes at the bottom that enabled height adjustment. This had resolved him to be more observant in everyday life and employ the use of lateral thinking more rigorously than he had done in the past.

Faced with a long, largely immobile retirement, he'd searched for a hobby, something to distract his mind from the long aching days ahead with nothing to do in them. He'd lost the taste for drinking and smoking, and anyway they were a younger man's hobbies – when you completed the mathematical formula that involved multiplication by money and subtraction by health, they became significantly less attractive.

He had no idea about how to make models from matchsticks, but taught himself by a process of trial and error and swearing. He got books from the local library, a squat round-shouldered building covered in neon posters warning of closure. This made him feel satisfied to a factor of two as he felt that by borrowing as many books as possible he was contributing to its survival, regardless of the expression on the librarian's face as he appeared each week to take back another six large hardbacks. He bought a set of gouges and rasps. He bought miniature G-clamps to hold glued pieces together while they set, and yellow Stanley knives to slice the matches to the right size.

He was careful and methodical and wished he'd been more methodical when stacking fish boxes because perhaps then he wouldn't have had so many hernias. He didn't mind working on a tiny detail all day until he got it right. He started with small, unambitious projects. A six-inch high telephone box, which looked malformed because he'd chosen too small a size to accommodate the detail he wanted to include. An 8¾ inch yacht.

St. Paul's was begun three years ago. He worked on it obsessively for eight hours a day. Each morning at seven on the dot he would make his way slowly downstairs, into the sitting room, which was now the St. Paul's room, and start work. He'd written to the Dean of St. Paul's, explaining his project, and had received a polite reply saying that all the information he needed was on the internet. Dennis had written several letters explaining that he didn't have access to the internet and had been unable to work out how to use it at his local library, and explained about his series of hernias and how he found it hard to move around and was applying for a blue driving badge. This was a slight exaggeration as he didn't own a car, but he felt it would all help.

A week later a huge bundle of information arrived, rolled up in a cardboard tube. Dimensions, photographs of the cathedral's exterior taken from all sorts of angles, and a wealth of miscellaneous information. Best of all, the package included dark, blotchy photocopies of some of Wren's original blueprints. They were beautiful, elegant designs, even more beautiful than the cathedral itself. They were the form, the idea, the Platonic realisation of Wren's mind, whereas the actual building could only ever be an approximation. Dennis was entranced. One day he must remember to write back to the Dean to thank him.

His friend Trevor, who had once worked alongside him on the wet fish stall, told him he should try to get it displayed in St. Paul's itself when it was finished. Trevor was full of good ideas. Every week he brought round full boxes of dead matches. Dennis always thanked him, but never used them. He only employed brand-new matches, straight from the manufacturer in what he liked to imagine as a small log-roofed matchstick factory in southern Sweden, still smelling of pine. It was one of his purest moments of joy to start the morning slicing the live heads of the matches with his second-smallest Stanley knife, aiming for the perfect combination of maximum match but with no live residue. This was difficult as, if you look at a match close-up, the head is not entirely evenly attached; sometimes the red phosphorous spreads over the side a millimetre, sometimes it's a fraction lopsided. Removing it is an art.

He started with the West Front, after laying down the basic foundations. The main body and the West towers were easy: oblong cuboids. The clock faces on the south-west tower proved difficult. Each took a week of intensive work. He suspected that getting the curve on the dome right was going to be hardest of all. Just as well it had to be put on last.

At 17:08pm, Trevor rang. Dennis was in the middle of eating a meal he had prepared, of slices of Danish unsmoked back bacon with baked beans, chopped and fried mushrooms, and one slice of fried bread, cut into two triangles. He rose from the table and made his way to the telephone.

Trevor here. Haven't spoken to you for a while. Just wondered how you were.

Oh, fine.

How's the church going?

Dennis winced, although as he did so he reflected that the Dean himself had referred to it as a church, which Dennis had regarded as a sort of cautious, round-shouldered inverted snobbery, as if fearful that

215

people might think he was being high-and-mighty if he called it a cathedral, which of course no one would.

Fine. What are you doing?

I'm going down to the Crown. We'll all be there. They're showing the football.

Sounds good.

Come along.

Oh, you know how it is. It's hard for me to get around these days.

Dennis's model was one metre fifty seven centimetres in length, or to put it another way just over five feet, from the West front steps to the furthest extremity of the Tijou Gates. When Dennis had completed the dome, it would be one metre eleven centimetres high; the model was to an accurate 1/10 scale. As he built up the structure and half-hearted summer turned to reluctant autumn, he admired the brilliance of its design. On completion, the cathedral was the tallest building in London. It loomed over the small mediaeval structures that sat along the Thames like mouse droppings. Today, of course, there are plenty of buildings higher than St. Paul's. There's that thing called the Shard, that looks like a corner of a glass fish tank, and the thing called the Gherkin, that looks like a Number 4 drill bit. Dennis didn't know why they couldn't give them proper names. Why not call it the Number 4 Drill Bit, or the Glass Fish Tank Corner?

Nowadays there's nowhere you can go to see the cathedral as part of the skyline that Wren envisaged. At the time, it would have been monumental. Wren was determined that it should stand head and shoulders above any other building in the city. But to achieve this great height, whilst still maintaining beauty of form, Wren's played some clever tricks. He's placed the dome on top of a huge drum, with two storeys of cathedral below this drum. All this adds up to a terrific height.

However, it's impossible to build a massive, multi-storey creation like that, without flying buttresses to support the weight. The cathedral would collapse without them. But flying buttresses would look Gothic. Inappropriate for Wren's smooth, cool, Roman style. So where have the buttresses gone? Wren seems to have built solid, sheer walls stretching upwards hundreds of feet. This means nothing to us, we don't register anything strange, but at the time it must have seemed like a conjuring trick.

The answer is in the second storey. It appears similar to the ground floor, consisting of pillars and windows. But the windows are just false fronts. There's nothing behind them. The whole of the upper half is just a screen wall; and the flying buttresses lurk there, holding everything up.

Secondly, there is a tall cupola that sits on top of the dome, as high again as the dome itself – you don't notice this because the perspective looking up from the ground foreshortens it – topped off with a ball and cross. Another leap in height. It's here, in Dennis's view, that Wren's brilliance really comes into play. That cupola is eighty-eight feet tall and weighs eight hundred stone. Somehow Wren has managed to balance it on a dome. It totally defies the laws of gravity.

You can see this from the air, eye-to-eye, as it were, and it becomes clear that it's top-heavy. A massive solid object on a semi-circle. Even if the dome were solid stone, it should crack and collapse outwards, with a great weight like that balanced on top of it.

So how has he done it? Well in fact, Dennis would enjoy saying out loud as if Margaret were still in the room, hanging on his every word, the cupola isn't supported by the dome at all. There's a huge cone made of brick inside the dome, holding the cupola up.

And yet, and yet. The invisible remembered Margaret pauses from her crossword to listen, attempting for Dennis's sake to be as interested as he is, and managing a fairly passable performance of close attention. When you walk into St. Paul's and look up, you don't see an enormous hundred-foot high cone. Do you?

She shakes her head. You see the inside of a dome, and on top of the dome, little windows looking up to the sky above. So where's the cone?

No idea, the imaginary Margaret says. She's useful, this revivified Margaret, just sitting there, agreeing.

He paced back and forth on the patch of carpet that's now fraying and which makes her want to say to him, Dennis, please walk on a different patch of carpet and make it wear more evenly –

Wren, just like a conjuror, has built a false surface. The 'dome', when you look up from the inside, is a false dome. It reaches its apex a good fifty feet below the apex of the actual dome. The cone is in between the two domes.

Inside, he's forced the perspective of the little windows, so that when you think you are looking straight out through the roof, you're actually looking up through the false dome, then through the fifty feet of cone, and then out through the cupola. When Dennis first discovered this, it was like finding a priest hole in a wall in his own house. Of course, Wren could have just built a cathedral without a dome and saved himself all the trouble. He could have just built a huge, high, tapering steeple, to get his height. But Wren being Wren, he wants his dome.

Wren's an artist of audacity and ingenuity and mathematical beauty, you see. There's none of them left. Nowadays you just build a giant shard or gherkin. Or the new one. Electric shaver. Who wants a building that looks like an electric shaver?

Dennis stood in front of the mirror and rolled the flesh of his stomach with his palms. He would have to instigate a dieting regime. Sitting around all day building cathedrals was too inactive a career for a man of his slow metabolic rate. He picked up his rubber-tipped stick and took the photograph albums from where they were shoved tightly at the bottom of the bookcase. They were covered with dust, even though he was sure he'd looked through them quite recently. Margaret laying the stones on the rockery, unaware she was being photographed. Margaret lying out in the garden, toes over the edge of sun lounger, the flowers full of colour. Margaret with a newspaper over her face.

Margaret and Dennis together, arms wrapped round each other, beaming so widely into the camera that their teeth reflected the sunlight.

Margaret and Dennis both smoking cigarettes, tumblers of whisky in their right hands.

Dennis had not touched a cigarette since the day Margaret's

illness was diagnosed. Neither had she, of course, but at least in his case there was some benefit to be gained from giving up smoking. It was her wish that he give up drinking too.

The last thing I want, she said as she lay in the hospital bed with tubes sprouting from her like tendrils, not long before she came home, is for you to give up smoking and then get liver disease.

Cirrhosis, he said.

Bless you, she said. A joker to the last. Stop drinking as well, Dennis, okay?

He found it surprisingly easy. The day Margaret came home he tipped the half-full bottles of whisky, gin, and vodka down the sink. He could smell alcohol coming up the pipes for days, every time he did the washing up. But it didn't make him want to drink. Drinking had been something he had done every day with Margaret, always from 6 o'clock, sometimes from lunchtime. It was not something he did without her.

The first church on the site of the present-day St. Paul's was a wooden structure built in the seventh century AD. It lasted less than a hundred years before it was destroyed by fire. The second cathedral burnt down in 1087, the year William the Conqueror died. A huge church was built next, not finished until 1240. This was the largest church in England. In 1315 a wood and lead spire was added. The steeple burnt down in 1444, after being struck by lightning. Oh I do love a fact, Dennis thought, squeezing some glue onto a stacked set of six matches and getting most of the glue on his fingers.

II

He phoned Trevor. It's finished.

Lordy, said Trevor. How long has it been?

Three years, one hundred and seventy two days.

Well...

I just thought you'd want to know, said Dennis. There was a richness, an exuberance in Dennis's voice that Trevor hadn't heard for years. Not since Margaret died. Perhaps now was the time to bring him out of his enforced mourning.

Let's do something, said Trevor. Go out somewhere. To celebrate.

Where did you have in mind?

I thought you'd like to come down to the Crown. Everyone's very keen to hear about your cathedral.

Well, with this leg...

I can pick you up.

No one really had stayed in touch apart from Trevor, and Trevor only felt duty bound to stay in touch because no one else had stayed in touch.

Eight-ish?

Its majestic towers, the delicate carving on the portico, the Roman numerals on the clock faces. Dennis walked round, imagining himself in a helicopter, swooping along the towers, flying along the roof and skimming over the dome. He peered closely through the windows, knowing that his face would look like Alice in Wonderland on the other side, feeling the wood under his touch, breathing in the smell of pine that thousands of matches cumulatively give off. He was so absorbed that he completely forgot about Trevor. The doorbell rang and Dennis jumped as if wired to it. In his shock he nearly stuck a finger into the Lord Mayor's vestry.

Can I see it then?

See it? No, you can't. Dennis felt himself going red, and manoeuvred himself in front of Trevor who was trying to make his way to the sitting room.

Why not?

Well it's finished, but not quite finished-finished.

Come on. Just a glimpse.

Dennis shook his head. Trevor tried to see round the gap from the ajar door, but Dennis pushed him towards the entrance.

All right. Trevor shrugged himself further inside his coat. No need to worry. Off we go. In their slight kerfuffle Trevor rocked the telephone table and one of the photos of Margaret slid to the edge. Dennis paused to straighten it.

Dennis's old drinking friends were delighted to see him. They said he looked well, even though his hair had gone grey and he could hardly walk. They wanted to buy him drinks. They wanted to know how he had been getting along.

How's the cathedral? Joe asked.

Oh, it's splendid, Trevor cut in. Amazing. A work of art. He should display it.

I knew it would be, said Joe. I mean you've spent so long on it. Cheers to Trevor, and his work of art. Joe knew nothing about art. This didn't mean he wasn't sincere.

What are we having then?

I don't drink any more, said Dennis.

Oh, come on, we haven't seen you for years! You're celebrating!

So Dennis had a pint of Bass. Just one can't do me any harm. As he drank it he remembered the old days. The good old days, they rapidly became as he got two-thirds of the way down the pint. Someone nodded at the barman and a second was poured.

Of the friends only Michael, the town's GP, was still in business. His practice had grown substantially since Dennis had last seen him, with so many new doctors stencilled onto the glass window above the receptionist's cubicle that he had felt literally, as well as metaphorically, squeezed out.

But this is my last month, he said. I retire on February 29th. This year, not only was it a leap year but the 29th was also a Friday. So you could retire on the end of the month on a Friday afternoon that wouldn't happen again for another – what would it be, 28 years? This calculation seemed to make sense to Dennis, seven days in a week, one leap year every four years – but his head was a bit fuzzy now to think through the variables, the year not dividing into seven and all that.

Michael was an old-fashioned doctor. He drank a bottle of red wine every night and said it didn't matter, and would occasionally finish the evening's medically acceptable drinking with a whisky – Macallan or Singleton. Speyside was the best, and anyone who said otherwise was a fool. He wore a three-piece tweed suit into work. He used shaving soap. Recently some of the younger doctors complained that he dropped hairs and was unhygienic. Michael pointed out that he had a lot in common with dogs and Christmas trees and so far neither of those things had been banned from reception.

Another pint, said Joe.

No no, said Dennis, brushing his hands as if readying himself to go. Really. I don't want it.

The landlord was already pulling it. You've got to drink it now, said Joe. I'll be offended if you don't.

The pub was full now and there was mist on the windows and it had that wonderful feeling of being in your own hermetically sealed bunker. Dennis couldn't understand why he'd been away for so long – why he'd ever broken away from all this in the first place. All life was here! The only people in the room below 50 were enthusiastically chewing each other's lips in a well-lit corner. Someone had a plate of fish and chips and was shifting the table around in tiny dog-leg movements on the flagstones in order to find the sweet spot where it would stop wobbling. Through the doorway at the back where the double doors hadn't closed properly, a man had a piss. Behind the counter the barmaid, face flushed, lifted her arms above her head in a pause from serving drinks and readjusted her tied-back hair. There were two perfect circles of sweat in her armpits, the size of small oranges or large apricots. Dennis thought she was the most beautiful woman he had ever seen.

Michael rolled a cigarette and put it into Dennis's top pocket, where he used to keep a coloured handkerchief. Everyone always used to be very taken by this touch of the dandyish in the otherwise muted colour palette favoured by Dennis. Each time he appeared in the pub it would be a different hue – cherry red, emerald green, sapphire blue.

Margaret had always chosen it before he went out.

I'd love to see your cathedral some time, said Joe.

Yes, right, Dennis mumbled.

That is, if you've actually made a cathedral at all.

What? Of course I have.

It's just that Trevor said that you said that Trevor couldn't look at it, Joe said.

It's finished, Dennis said, it's just not finished-finished.

Maybe he'd done it, but it wasn't any good. Maybe it was a complete embarrassment. Joe was thinking of that Spanish fresco that had been restored by an enthusiastic nun. He'd read about it in the newspaper a few months ago. Maybe Dennis's cathedral was a hideous, painful joke.

That reminds me, said Trevor. I saved you these. He produced a box of dead matches from his pocket.

Thanks.

I think you should take a picture of it, said Joe, and I think you should bring it to the pub and show us all. Otherwise... I don't think there's really a cathedral at all.

Dennis got to his feet. He was surprisingly light-footed now; the beer had done its work as a muscle relaxant. He hadn't moved so fast in years.

You take that back, he said. Joe's beetrooty face turned beetrootier.

Well don't say. Of course there's a fucking cathedral.

Dennis hadn't sworn publically since the night Margaret died.

Yes, yes, everyone said, of course there is. We believe you.

Trevor simmered things down and mouthed *sod off* to Joe. You have to come out more often now.

I will, said Dennis, mollified. I've had a nice time. They all smiled and shook hands although things seemed rather muted now.

Only Michael stayed cheerful. He didn't give a shit whether Dennis had built a model cathedral or whether it was any good. He bought some bottled Bass, paying the premium for take-outs, and dropped one into each of Dennis's baggy jacket pockets. The barmaid called time, and the barman told her it wasn't time yet, and she said yes it was, and Dennis saw her armpits again, and the barman said oh yes you're right, and they all walked out together into the cold night air.

Trevor dropped Dennis back home. It was only a quick zoom along the wide B-roads, and then the three up-and-down streets to get to the housing estate. Dennis thought he drove a little erratically, but didn't say anything. They reckon now in the cities that if you drive home after a few drinks the police pull you over. What a world we live in nowadays.

Trevor waved at his old friend as he turned the car in the drive. Dennis leant on the door, his bottles of Bass clinking in his pockets, and fumbled with the key at the lock. The house ticked in the night silence, a parent wondering where its previously well-behaved home bird had been for the past few hours.

He picked up the framed photo. Ah, Margaret, he said, his voice echoing in the confined space, I hope you're proud of me. St. Paul's cathedral, in your sitting room. I wish you were here. You'd be impressed. He kissed Margaret on the mouth. Actually, he said, you'd probably be complaining it cluttered the place up, and asking when was I going to get rid of it.

Dennis looked dumbly at the metal cap on the bottle of Bass. How am I going to get this off? There were probably some scissors, or something metal, that might do the trick, somewhere around. He looked for his number 3 G-clamp and his number 5 G-clamp and even his number 7 G-clamp, but somehow in the lamplit semi-dark the geography of the house all seemed different and he couldn't work out where anything was. He struck the bottle on the door handle. The top smashed and the cap and a few chunks of glass flew up in the air and landed perilously close to the north-west door of the cathedral.

He watched the miniature people swarm up the steps, to the entrance behind the centre columns. Of course, the steps were a Victorian addition. That Romanesque piazza, with its statue of Victoria, didn't really suit the cathedral, wedged against it like a napkin round its neck. This had been one of the many decisions that had caused him angst over the months. Do you create the cathedral as it is, or as Wren intended it?

The beer swam lightly down his throat but he began to get those sweats you get if you've drunk too much. He reached into his top pocket for his handkerchief and found a cigarette instead.

How did that get there? It was a little crumpled, but perfectly serviceable. He lifted it to his nose and sniffed. Just what he fancied. He patted his pockets uncertainly; what was he going to light it with? Then shook his head at his own daftness. In front of him were fifty thousand matches. With somewhat more flexible knees than he was used to, Bass being good for the joints and perhaps he should drink it more often, for medicinal purposes only of course, he knelt behind the cathedral and found a box with live matches.

Walking past the quire, he lit the cigarette, threw the match in the wastepaper basket, and breathed in deeply. Bliss. Just one can't do any harm. He should go to bed. He could hear the noise of the pub, the fruit machines, the jukebox, ringing in his ears. He stubbed the cigarette out on the black metal of the fireplace. The sooty ash and the stub fell into the grate.

He made his way up to bed. Trevor had suggested not so long ago that he create a bedroom for himself downstairs, but he had read once in the *Radio Times* that if you don't use your knees regularly, they get even worse. Although this had been part of an advert-based article about stair lifts, so he wasn't sure where he stood on that now. Another thing Trevor said was that – but here he rolled into bed, and fell asleep instantly.

In the wastepaper basket, the discarded match smouldered against all the paper and broken matches that had been thrown in there. Soon there was a small blaze forming and the basket tipped over and the carpet began to smoke.

The fire reached the cathedral. It moved slowly because Dennis's craftsmanship was so perfect. The glue that Dennis had lovingly applied to the ends and the sides of each matchstick did not allow for any tiny gaps where the fire could get a good purchase on the model. The flames licked gradually up from the ground floor, up to the drum and on to the dome. The tiny people on the steps waved cheerfully whilst blackening.

Dennis turned over in his sleep and wasn't sure if he was awake or not. He heard a cracking sound and smelled burning. In his half-dream Margaret was there, shaking him awake. You need to go downstairs, Dennis. There's a problem, and you need to sort it. Ah, Margaret my darling, he said, breathing out beery fumes, I solved the problem. That day Michael came round and he was giving you injections, and making you comfortable, and he said there was nothing he could do. And that there was going to be pain, so much pain. And he said he would help me, he would sign things off if Margaret should, God forbid, die in the night.

In the sitting room, red lights flickered against the white wall. The cathedral flamed away gloriously. The dome collapsed heavily, splitting into three sections and sliding down the rest of the model like eggshell. The cone, supporting the cupola, remained but then also disintegrated. Dennis winced as he heard the wood crackle. He was wide awake now. He got out of bed too suddenly and his knees went and he found himself kneeling, then lying, by the bed legs. That's not something you see very often, he thought, looking at its well-turned ankle.

There was a thick inch of undisturbed dust and the pillow, that he'd shoved underneath on the day Margaret died. I should have got rid of that. But Michael came round, he signed all the forms. She died of her cancer, he wrote, it was the size of an ostrich's egg, and it killed her, perhaps a month or two earlier than expected. Michael had even used the word *humane*. In the end, all you hope for is something humane.

Dennis tried to get up but was trapped like a beetle on its shell. A line of flame ran across the carpet towards him. His fingers, still covered in little blobs of old glue, began to melt. The glue smelt of fish. He wished he hadn't had those drinks and wished he hadn't lit that cigarette. In the hallway, the pictures of Margaret caught fire and in each one, her smile crumpled. Downstairs the flames silhouetted the familiar, majestic image of St. Paul's against the wall, making it look like that famous picture of the cathedral in the Blitz.

The next morning, as a helicopter circled the remains of the building, no one could get inside because of the heat. Dennis lay on his back with his hands resting on his chest, like the effigy on a tomb in an old church.

It is believed that model making in the UK has declined by 72% in the last 20 years. It is expected that Brexit will cause a 6 to 9% reduction in the UK economy over the next 15 years. People now spend an average of 4 hours a day staring at their phones. 68% of President Trump supporters distrust the economic data published by the federal government. 55% of UK voters believe the Government is lying to them about immigration. At least 80% of these statistics are true. St Paul's Cathedral can still be seen from most parts of central London, as long as you keep looking up.

Four Poems
Sue Burge

Obituary for your last pair of ballet shoes

Let's start here, at the end –
      how we cradle them heel to toe
in fifth position
      into a cardboard box
as gently as if they were hamsters, guinea pigs
      or a very small rabbit -
only the airholes are missing.

Let's go back to the last day you wore them
      no, let's not
let's go back to the days of those leaps
      higher than cliff falls, heartstopping
the days when you wore out so many pairs
      they would fill a foreign field.

Let's bury these, scarred with twist, stretch and spring,
      at the bottom of this trunk
no, let's not
      let's put them here on this high shelf
by an open window
      where the fast blink of our tears
creates an illusory flickerbook of flight.

Mother, folded small

Your mother flaunted her death wish like a blowsy corsage pinned to her pretty coats. Your father gave up his river life the day he pulled a woman from the Thames, hair bright in the water like a distress flare.

Once you found your mother's doppelganger in a magazine. Straight red hair. Green eyes. Long pale face. But smiling. After your mother tore through the family albums like an iconoclast you carried false mother with you always. Folded small.

Sometimes your mother would tease you by pricking her thumbs bloody with the long pin of her corsage. On those days the pill bottles would be in a different order. Emptier. Their brown sides translucent in the bathroom light.

In the end, she was not the one who chose.

She left you her corsage, pulsating like a butterfly in your unwilling hands. *Go back*, you chant. *Go back to chrysalis… to caterpillar…to tiny egg. Let me grind you under my sure heel.*

Jane's Table

No bigger than her rich relative's
Wedgewood serving dish, it cradles

a universe of mismatched lovers meeting
with the random science of shooting stars,

fossilised aunts starched into the silk
warp and worsted weft of bombazine,

and houses formed with childish symmetry
from bricks of Fareham red that brim

with know-your-place microcosms, the simmer
of genteel desperation revitalised

with lavender, smelling salts and gossip -
gossip as scandalous as the new waltz.

The Austen men have huge desks,
dry and devoid as the surface of Saturn.

Jane's table, scarified with leaning and learning,
rubs the sprigs from her muslined elbows;

her world, bigger than mine, bigger than yours,
wobbles on its axis, ready for more.

Taphonomy

When we explode from the womb
in a frenzy of blood and wails
we possess over three hundred bones.
Year on year, bone seeks bone,
fusing us into rigidity -
a sequential journey of
epiphysial union :
elbow, ankle, thigh, wrist, hip, clavicle…
leaves us with just two hundred and six.

At the age of twenty-eight
I have reached full fusion,
grown fascinated by ossification,
shadows and corners,
the slow reveal of excavation.

Under a Roman flagstone floor
I find a child's bones, brown as clay,
ulna, radius, ulna, radius,
lying parallel, as if once bound.
Parts of a skull :
frontal, temporal, occipital, parietal,
like empty oyster shells,
scattered, unsutured.

My mourning touch mingles
with the corrupting air,
turning a phalange
to dust in my palm.
A breeze,
like a two thousand year old sigh,
lifts an atomic swirl
into grey northern skies.

Goosey
Cath Barton

The night's frost had brought down a cascade of leaves from the chestnut trees which bordered the suburban street. Shades of red and yellow, still vibrant. Rodney kicked at them, put his head down against the day and quickened his pace. At the corner of the street there was a new café. Faced with a bewildering list of drinks and an impatient waitress he ordered a flat white, although he had no idea what it was. He hoped it would not be one more cause for disappointment or regret. In fact he was pleasantly surprised; the coffee was good.

Back in his flat he looked through more of the photographs which he had found amongst his mother's affairs, memory after memory washing over him.

Next day he steeled himself to climb the stairs from his flat to his mother's again. Seeing the neat pile of bedding he swallowed hard. He manoeuvred round the bed to the chest of drawers, put both hands in the medal handles and gave them a firm tug. Nothing happened. He pulled a little harder, conscious of the thud of his heartbeat. He was afraid of damaging the wood if he forced the drawer. It came out slowly in jerks. The scent – he didn't know the name but it was the one his mother had worn when he was a boy – wreathed into the room. Rodney sat back on the bed, slain by the past.

He needed coffee. In his mother's kitchen he found an old jar of instant, the granules stuck together in a dark lump. He made tea instead. He dunked an arrowroot biscuit into the tea. It tasted stale.

Rodney lifted a small blue cardboard box from the drawer in his mother's bedroom. Inside there were several keys. One he recognised as the front door key. Another looked like one of those ineffectual suitcase keys. The third was small, sturdy and made of brass. Attached to it was a thin pink ribbon which looked familiar.

He emptied the drawer of its old handkerchiefs, bits of broken costume jewellery and other oddments of a life. There were no other surprises, good or bad. There was no inlaid box at the back of the drawer into which he could insert the small brass key and find something to thrill him, like letters from an unknown lover. He dropped the key into his trouser pocket. Everything else he put into a plastic bag, to throw away.

In the following days Rodney continued the task of sorting out his mother's affairs. He worked for a couple of hours each morning and walked in the afternoons. He took to visiting the café at the corner of the street for a coffee as the light faded. He decided to try all the different sorts of modern coffee, one after another. The waitress became less surly over the days. They chatted and he even told her his name. She didn't react but why should she? Quite possibly she didn't go to the theatre much. The café was a refuge from the oppression of the house and of the past. No-one there knew anything of him. And if the occasional person appeared to do a double-take, what did that matter? We can all mistake a person for someone else.

Rodney took the small brass key out of his trouser pocket each night and placed it on his bedside table, with his watch and his spectacles. Each morning he put it into the left hand pocket of whichever pair of trousers he chose to wear. As he went about his tasks he found no box into which the key might fit, but he continued to carry it.

When all was done, his mother's worldly goods distributed, sold or given away, there remained the question of what to do with the upstairs flat. Rodney knew he could sell the house. But then where would he go? It was his home. It had always been the home to which he could return. He decided to seek a tenant. A young man in a sharp suit and pointy shoes came from the estate agents round the corner. He told Rodney he could get more for it if he, as the lad put it with a curl of his lip, 'modernised' the flat. Rodney told him it was to be marketed as seen or he would take his business elsewhere. The young man said he would see what he could do but he wasn't sure. Rodney decided he would advertise in the local paper instead, and in the corner café. Various people rang in response. Some of them made appointments to come and see the flat. Very few of them kept their appointments, disrupting Rodney's routine as he was forced to stay in waiting when he would normally have been out walking or visiting the café. There was one girl who said she was interested and would come back with her boyfriend. They did not come and Rodney was not sorry. The year ebbed towards the unwelcome festivities of Christmas and the flat remained empty.

Rodney made no special preparations for Christmas. When his mother was alive they had put up decorations. She had been able, even last Christmas, to perform the small task of sticking paper on paper, joining link to link, and it had pleased him that she was pleased with the achievement. He had strung the streamers across her room, blown up a few balloons and stood the cards which came in the post on her mantelpiece. This year the mantelpiece was empty. He had meant to write to all the old friends, but some had been missed and cheery cards arrived, hoping the year had treated them both well and saying that next year they really must make the effort to meet. Rodney replied on vellum paper in a steady hand, with regret for bringing Joan or Mavis sad news at this time of year. Each note posted was another step towards finality.

The emptiness above was oppressive. Rodney longed for company and wondered whether he might get a cat. He had only once owned a pet, a hamster when he was ten years old; it had escaped. That was, for him, the first loss. There had been too many since. Owning another pet would simply bring the prospect of another.

With the approach of Christmas the calls from prospective tenants had tailed off. Everyone had so many things to do, family to visit. So people said, though Rodney felt that his was not the only forced smile of jollity as he exchanged brief words with neighbours or regulars in the café at the corner of the street. He took to walking further than before on his afternoon walks. He still had no particular destination. In the park he chose the left or right fork at random. December was unusually foggy, and strange shapes loomed into view, people and dogs stretched out of recognition. Rodney was uneasy about dogs off the leash. If one came too close he would recoil, turn up his coat collar and stride on as if he had a purpose, before returning to the bleakness of life alone in the house.

Next to the corner café there was a charity shop. Rodney had never been in it or paid it any attention. But on the Friday before Christmas he found the café closed early for the day, a handwritten notice stuck to the door apologising for 'Unexpected Circumstances'. He hesitated, confused. There were fairy lights twinkling in the window of the charity shop, pictures there of cats. He gazed at Maisie, at Dots, at Dave, all 'looking for their forever home'. He was unmoved. He wanted coffee, not sickly sentimentality.

A woman came out of the shop as he stood there.

"You interested in our little Goose?" she asked, pointing at the picture of a black kitten with a white flash on his nose. "He ain't got no-one. They all wants girl cats. Or they don't like black cats, I dunno why. Good as gold he is," she said. "He'll love you, he will," she declared, as if a deal had already been struck.

Rodney opened his mouth to protest that he couldn't take a cat and found himself saying instead that yes, he might be able to help. He was, hearing that familiar name, thrown off guard. How long now since his dear Goosey had gone? He was at another fork in the road and he found himself once more making a rash choice. A chain of events was set in motion. The woman took Rodney off to see the kitten, who sniffed his forehead and stole into his heart. His house was inspected and declared suitable. He bought the paraphernalia that denotes cat ownership. The kitten arrived and made himself at home. For the first time Rodney was glad that his mother was not there. She would not have liked little Goose any more than she had liked the human visitor of that name back then. But he did. And with Goose purring on his knee he would survive Christmas.

Rodney found that looking after the young kitten was time-consuming and this he welcomed. It reminded him of times past. He had always taken pleasure in being the one who cared, who tended, who looked after. If anyone had asked him to define his mission, that would have been it, in spite of the inevitable loss which attended on care and love. And so Christmas came and went and Goose cushioned Rodney from the pain. He spoilt the little chap with titbits, morsels of chicken from his modest

Christmas dinner, slivers of cheese and special cat biscuits which the kitten chased around the room before consuming them and then embarking on protracted grooming sessions, while Rodney looked on like a protective parent.

On the fifth day of Christmas Rodney ran out of milk and so had to leave the house for the first time in a week. The kitten was sound asleep in his bed of choice, a small cardboard box with a moth-eaten green scarf in the bottom. Rodney tiptoed out of the room, anxious as any new father. He was keen to get out and back as quickly as possible and walked briskly down the road to the little row of shops. The café on the corner was, to his surprise, open. He hesitated but only for a second or two. Cats were independent creatures, he knew that, and Goose would be fine, of course he would.

The waitress who had once been surly greeted him warmly.

"How about a nice mince pie, Mr Fairbrother?" she said. "Or are you mince-pied out?"

Rodney made another of his rash decisions.

"Do call me Rodney, Miss..." then realised he did not know her name.

"If you're sure Mr... Rodney," she said, dipping her head, suddenly demure. "I'm Emily, by the way."

He said he would have a mince pie, thank you, yes please, Emily. He did not tell her that it would be his first of the festive season. He did not want her feeling sorry for him. Their intimacy would only go so far. When he had eaten the mince pie and drunk his flat white – which had become, to his surprise, his favourite sort of coffee – he went to the counter to pay. Pinned to the noticeboard was something which drew him up short. A flier for the local pantomime, Jack and the Beanstalk. Emily saw him looking at it.

"It's really ace," she said. "My friend is playing Jack and they've got this cool set and a beanstalk he can really climb. You'd like it..."

Her voice tailed off as she realised Rodney was paying no attention to her burbling.

"Jack and the Beanstalk," he said slowly to himself, as if tasting each word like a new food.

He came back to himself, took his change and bid her farewell with a polite raising of his hat as he always did. Emily watched his back for a moment as he left the café, then shrugged her shoulders and turned her attention to the next customer.

Rodney walked slowly down the street, bought bread, milk, fish and a copy of the local paper and then, mindful of little Goose, quickened his pace as he returned to his house. The kitten was still curled up in his box, and Rodney left him there while he turned the pages of the paper. It was a rag on which he would normally not waste his money, but on page eight he found what he was looking for, a preview of Jack and the Beanstalk at the Lyceum Theatre. It was, as he had gathered from what Emily had told him, an amateur production. He hesitated, wondering if this was not just asking for trouble. Then, before he could talk himself out of it, he telephoned the box office and reserved a ticket for the matinée the following day.

That night Rodney cooked the fish in milk. When he had eaten his meal and the rest of the fish had cooled he gave it to Goose, who devoured it without chewing and was promptly sick. When Rodney had cleared away the mess he patted his knee for the kitten to jump up, but Goose had already settled on the sheepskin rug in front of the gas fire. This left Rodney at a loose end. It was too early to watch the television news; he had no crossword to finish or book he particularly wanted to read and the local paper was not worth his attention. He could put off no longer the thing which he both desired and dreaded. He went to the bureau, pushed up its roll-top lid, took out the envelopes of photographs and sat down to look at them properly.

His mother had kept photographs from all his productions, the Shakespeares, the drawing room comedies, all the variety of the theatrical canon. The crowning glory for her had been his one film role. It had been a small one in the scale of things, but big enough to get him recognised sometimes. While Rodney himself had cast the past aside, his mother had thrown nothing away and now he must look at it again, however painful he found it. He pulled a handkerchief from his pocket and blew his nose hard, angry with himself. His mother had always said good boys did not cry. And the same applied to men. Though now he was not so sure that he should have followed her advice. It really didn't seem to have helped. After Mr Simon, his dear Goosey, had gone, his eyes had stayed dry. But now, seeing him in these pictures, smiling still through the magic of photography, he could no long stanch the flow of tears.

As he took off his spectacles and lifted a corner of the handkerchief to his eyes, something tinkled to the bare floorboards. Peering down myopically, Rodney saw that it was the small brass key he had found in his mother's chest of drawers, and about which he had thought little since the advent of the kitten. Turning it over in his hands again, something flickered in his mind. He half-closed his eyes and thought back to the dressing room of the Lyceum, when they had once played Jack and the Beanstalk. Mr Simon in his great white-feathered Goose costume, practising his strutting. And he, Rodney, laughing till he got a stitch. Mr Simon getting out of his costume and picking up a key and twirling it on his left forefinger on the end of a thin pink ribbon. And then what had he done? The film in his mind flickered and went dark at that point. Rodney leant back in his wing chair. The photographs slithered onto the floor and Goose the kitten, woken and alarmed by his master's shuddering sobs, jumped onto his knee. Rodney stroked the little quivering body until they were both calm again and it was time for the television news to jolt him back to the present.

When Rodney woke next morning the fog had rolled back from his memories and he could see clearly in his mind the box into which that key would fit. It had been a box made of a dark wood with brass corners and a brass lock. A box that his dear Goosey had given him, a birthday present. And one day, yes, it came back to him all in a rush as he lay there with the little kitten purring on his chest, one day the key to the box had gone missing. So what was the key doing in his mother's chest of drawers? Rodney was bemused. It was true that his mother had never liked Mr Simon.

"Why don't you just call him Simon?" she'd asked. "Why this Mr business? It seems very formal for someone who is apparently your friend."

Rodney had not liked the way she'd said the words 'apparently' and 'friend' and he had not even tried to explain, just said it was a theatrical tradition to call people Mr. Which it wasn't particularly but there was too much else that she might start prying into, too much that was private to him and Goosey. Had she gone through his pockets and stolen the key? He felt his heart beginning to harden towards his mother. How could she have done such a thing? But she was gone, and Goosey was so long gone too. Taking the box with him, after their final bitter quarrel.

The kitten was pawing at the bedclothes, campaigning for food. Rodney got out of bed and headed for the kitchen with little Goose scampering in front of him. He could not help smiling at the kitten pawing at his pyjama leg, and at the prospect of going to see the pantomime that afternoon. It was a long time since he had been to the Lyceum, a rare chance to dress up. He found his mustard wool trousers and the matching waistcoat, which he put on over a dark red corduroy shirt. He took time finding the right tie, and settled on one with red and yellow chevrons. He polished his brown brogues. Looking at his face in the bathroom mirror as he brushed his still-full head of hair, he saw someone faded. He rubbed his cheeks, bringing the blood and a brief image of his younger self to them. He smiled at his vanity. Many had been the time Goosey had come up behind him, looked over his shoulder and shared the smile. Rodney shook his head as a shiver passed through him, as if he'd seen a ghost.

He turned up the collar of his coat against the chill wind which blew him along to the Lyceum. His heart sank as he saw the crowds of excited children pulling frazzled-looking parents into the foyer. Of course a matinée would be full of children, what else had he expected? His seat was in the front row of the upper circle, where he knew he would have a good view. The seats were as uncomfortable as ever, but he didn't mind. And, when it came to it, he didn't mind the over-excited children either, or the people with noisy sweet wrappers, or the variable playing of the amateur company. This was his place and as soon as the fire curtain went up and the heavy drapes were drawn back the magic was there, ready to cast its charm over them all.

The children hissed at the giant and cheered Jack as he climbed the beanstalk and freed the beautiful princess, but Rodney loved best the goose that laid the golden eggs. How could he not? And this goose had glorious feathers and an alluring wiggle. He laughed and laughed and cheered as loudly as the smallest child at the curtain calls. As they left, everyone in the audience was given a tiny present, pressed into their hands by one or other of the cast. Rodney opened his fist to see that it was a dried bean, painted with the word 'Magic'. The gesture brought sudden tears to his eyes.

He was not ready to go home and, on a whim, went into the pub next to the theatre and ordered a large glass of Merlot. From the small table at which he sat he could see all the people who came through the door. The pub was not busy at that hour. Rodney felt, as he sipped the wine and thought about the performance, a quiet and unaccustomed happiness. He looked up as the door opened and a young man walked in. Rodney felt all the blood drain from his face. It was Goosey. But it couldn't be. Goosey was dead; he'd read his obituary. The man looked at him without recognition, but he was the spitting image of the young Goosey, the one Rodney had first met thirty, no goodness, it must be over forty years ago. He could have been his son. Rodney heard the barman greet him,

"Good evening Sir, and what can I get you?"

The man's reply was inaudible, but the barman, facing towards Rodney, came across loud and clear.

"Any luck with the audition you were telling me about?", and, after the man's next words, "Well congratulations, Sir, we'll be seeing you on stage next door after this panto run is over then?"

Rodney drained his glass and walked home, his mind in a spin. The delight of the pantomime, the moment of calm and then the shock of seeing Goosey's doppelgänger. Could he really have had a son? He knew so little of Goosey's other life.

When he got home he cooked a lamb chop and gave the kitten just a tiny bit of the fat. He knew he would have to get those photographs out again. But before he could do so there was a ring on the doorbell. As he checked the kitten was still safely in the kitchen there was a second ring, and a knock. On the doorstep stood the young man from the pub.

"Mr Fairbrother?" he asked. "I'm sorry to call so late but I hear you have a room to let." His voice was exactly like Goosey's as a young man, his smile the same.

"Er, well yes, no, yes, I mean it's a flat not just a room," Rodney stuttered. "Look, you'd better come in, Mr...?"

"A flat will be marvellous. I'm Mark Southern, please just call me Mark. I'm an actor, and I've got a job coming up at the Lyceum and I'm in a fearful slum of a hotel, I simply can't stay there."

Rodney was making another impulsive decision. He felt out of control. His whole life was spinning away from him. Or perhaps he was choosing to spin with it. As he showed the young man round he asked him if he minded cats, he really wouldn't have to mind cats, because he couldn't guarantee the kitten wouldn't get upstairs, and it would be best if he kept all his doors closed. The words were gushing from him like water from a burst pipe and they hadn't even talked about the crux of the matter.

"So it's okay, then? I can pay you up front. I can't tell you what a relief it is to find somewhere decent like this to stay."

He sounded as frantic as Rodney felt.

"Oh how splendid, that was my father's favourite tipple!" he said, as Rodney poured them both a glass of his best whisky.

Rodney smiled. "And mine. It's very smooth, don't you think?"

"I can see we will get on like a house on fire," said Mark. "Though I shall be out a great deal, I expect you know how it is in the theatre."

He was evidently supremely ignorant of his new landlord's past and Rodney decided there and then that it must remain so. When asked about his own professional background he spoke vaguely of different jobs and was relieved when the young man asked no probing questions.

Mark went off into the dark street with a slightly unsteady gait after Rodney had refreshed his glass several times. He would, he said, be back first thing with his belongings. Rodney retired to bed, his mind whirling. Next day his lodger arrived with two large suitcases, which he unpacked with a good deal of thumping. Rodney did not mind the noise but in the afternoon, when Mark had gone out to 'meet a chum', he crept upstairs to inspect the flat. He had made it clear that he would need access and Mark had not demurred.

"No secrets, Mr Fairbrother," he said. "I assure you I have no secrets."

Rodney had merely smiled. Had the young man known of his own secrets he would surely have been less blithe. When he opened the door of what had been his mother's sitting room he stopped as abruptly as if he had met an immovable object. He felt winded. On the table next to the sofa which stood facing the gas fire was the box, the box with brass corners and a brass lock which Goosey had given him for that birthday long ago, and then taken away with him. The box to which he, Rodney, had the key in his pocket now. He approached the table, as nervous of it as if the box had contained explosives, which in a way it might.

The box was unlocked and he could hear his blood pumping in his ears as he lifted the lid. It was empty. What had he expected? Secrets belonging to Mark, in spite of his assurances, or something of his own, long forgotten? He would have liked to have found something. He put his nose to the box; it held the scent of something ineffable, something he could never retrieve. He went back downstairs. He had to carry on. He had a kitten to look after.

Over the following week Mark was, as he had said he would be, out a lot of the time. He was rehearsing a play by Priestley, one of his 'time' plays. Rodney invited him to supper one evening, eager to know about the company's progress with the play. It was one which had long fascinated him.

"You seem very knowledgeable about all this, Mr Fairbrother. Is there something you're keeping from me?" Mark asked, looking at Rodney over the top of his spectacles.

Rodney felt the colour rising in his cheeks.

"I have not," he began, "told you the whole truth. I'm sorry, but it has been difficult since my mother died. I have not been completely myself."

Mark looked nervous, but as soon as Rodney started to tell him of his career in the theatre the younger man's expression softened and he clapped his hands together in a way which reminded Rodney of Goosey playing the Mole in The Wind in the Willows. An invisible thread was spun between them from that moment, a connection beyond words, a sense of a shared history.

"I think you must have known my father," Mark said, and when he spoke his name it was clear that he held him in great affection. Rodney said that yes, it was so and what a coincidence. He did not say more. Even on short acquaintance, he liked the young man and he did not want to taint his memories of his father by calling past hurts into the room.

Rodney went to the first night of the play. Mark did not disappoint. He was, thought Rodney, as good as his father, and that delighted him. He went to the stage door and was allowed into the young man's dressing room with flowers. Mark was, he could see, touched. Later, back at the house, they sat on either side of the gas fire in Rodney's living room, swirling whisky in their glasses and smiling at the antics of the kitten. Mark went upstairs to fetch something which he wanted, he said, to show Rodney. He returned with the box.

"I found it amongst my father's things. Rather lovely, don't you think?" he said, running his fingers over the smooth wood. "I don't know what happened to the key though."

In other circumstances, Rodney thought, he might at that moment have produced the key from his pocket. The moment passed and that was an end to it. The past was best kept locked, even if the box was not.

Two weeks later the run of Mark's play was over and he was gone, the upstairs flat empty again. The days of January were short and dark. The kitten got out of the front door one evening and was hit by a passing car. When a well-meaning neighbour brought him the small broken body of his friend, Rodney drank half a bottle of whisky and a full bottle of Bordeaux on an empty stomach. It was a waste of good whisky and wine as it failed to kill him as he had hoped. He woke next morning with a thumping headache and cooked a plate of scrambled eggs. Later that day, in the café at the corner of the street, he told Emily about the kitten. He wouldn't, he added before she could ask the inevitable question, be getting another one.

"So what will you do now, Mr Fairbrother, I mean Rodney?" she asked.

"Just carry on, my dear," he replied. "Just carry on in one direction or another, as we all have to do, come what may."

And he gave her a small, wry smile and asked if he could have another flat white, if she would be so kind.

A Prolonged Kiss
Jonathan Gibbs

The kiss comes at the end of Act Three, just before the interval. It's really what the play has been leading up to all along, and its high point. We try hard, but the fourth act is an anti-climax. Which is perhaps the point – *new forms, new forms* – but still you wish, with all due respect to the author, that it was stronger.

The kiss is the moment we all, not just me and Colm, have been working towards. Our job is to establish the conditions for its existence, to have it seem inevitable, when it comes. Nina, the nineteen-year-old wannabe actress, and Trigorin, the fashionable writer twice her age, have been attracted to each other since they first laid eyes on one another. She's read everything he's written, and has an idealised, if rather reductively *teenaged* view of him as 'an artist', and he's bored of his affair with Arkadina, the now past-it actress whose country house they're all staying at. Of course, the person Trigorin should really fall in love with is Masha. She's the most interesting character in the play. Wears black, constantly takes snuff – that half the audience, from their laughter, seems to think is cocaine – and, famously, is *in mourning for her life*. Everyone wants to be Masha, even if they all agree that Nina is the better role. With Nina, you get the monologue in the first act, the slab of avant garde gobbledegook written by Konstantin, who's in love with Nina – when you look at the characters' relationships it's comical how there's not one fully requited love affair among them. Medviedenko, the dull-as-arse schoolteacher, loves Masha. Masha, the fool, loves Konstantin. Konstantin loves Nina. Nina loves Trigorin, as does Arkadina. Even Polena, the wife of the estate manager, is having an affair with Dorn, the pompous doctor, though he refuses to elope with her. Why should he? He's got her just where he wants her.

The scenes between Nina and Trigorin are the bright heart of the play, the only moments when love seems a possibility, and things might turn out alright, even if other people get hurt. And that kiss, at the end of Act Three, sends the audience out into the interval buoyed up on a sense of hope – hope of a sort, because even if they don't know the play, they'll know enough to see that a happy ending to Act Three can only mean unhappiness to come.

TRIGORIN: [*In an undertone*] You are so beautiful! What bliss to think that I shall see you again so soon! [*She sinks her head on his breast*] I shall see those glorious eyes again, that wonderful, ineffably tender smile, those gentle features with their expression of angelic purity! My darling! [*A prolonged kiss.*]

What Max wants from us, he says, is what he calls *manifest contingency*. Chekhov's characters know they are bound by circumstance, which they prefer to call fate, but the fact that their circumstances allow them some wiggle room seduces them into thinking that this equates to the possibility of a greater freedom. They think that because they have room to pace inside their prison cell, they can get enough of a run-up to leap over its walls. The stage, Max says, is a *metaphorical space*. It, and the text, are your prison – as the characters' social and psychological circumstances are theirs – but within those confines you are free, and should show yourself to be so. The audience, he says, should think that anything could happen. That's the real suspension of disbelief, Max says: disbelief in the inexorability of the text.

Nina and Trigorin have two scenes alone on stage together. The first is at the end of Act Two, when they flirt, and he has his moment with the dead seagull. The second is the kiss at the end of Act Three. It's a short scene: he comes back into the room from out front, where everyone's getting into the carriages to go to the station. Supposedly he's come to fetch his cane, but really it's to see her. They have ten lines together, and then they kiss. There is a catch in Colm's voice on the line *I can't believe I'm going to see you so soon*, when his voice sort of hiccups and disappears up into the air. He does it every time, and every time it sounds like he's just stumbled, hit a non-existent step on the staircase of his suddenly material desire. In rehearsal Max encouraged us to play around, and see where the characters might go. A three-minute scene became four minutes, five. The kiss is coming, and the more it's held back, the greater the impact when it arrives.

Clearly, though, Max said, this contingency, this freedom of movement, doesn't apply to the kiss. This is the point where professional etiquette overrides any aesthetic considerations. From the point at which the scene becomes physical – hand touches hand, lip touches lip – we do it as we block it.

So, from ten feet apart, at the end of our first exchange, he takes a step towards me, and pauses, then I go to him, slowly, then faster, and we meet centre-stage, but not too far down, not too close to the audience. There's a beat as we hold each other by the hands. *You are so beautiful! What bliss to think...* We share a glance, enough for the characters to confirm, silently, what they are about to do, both now and at some point in the future, and then I lay my head sideways against his chest, eyes out towards the audience.

This is my favourite moment in the scene. Colm can't see my expression, and for those few seconds I can have Nina feel anything I want: bliss, fear, astonishment, pride, glee, sadness. (Of course, I can't see his expression either.) Then he turns my face to look up at him, lays his palms gently on my cheeks, *those glorious eyes, that wonderful smile, those gentle features*, and his head comes down, and mine comes up, and we meet in a kiss. At first we are in profile, then, as we relax into it, our bodies pressing together, he turns me upstage, his head moving downstage to obscure mine, and my left hand comes up to the back of his head, so that, for most of the audience, the kiss itself is hidden, and our mouths can simply rest on each other: closed, contiguous. What in the theatre is called *cheating*.

*

But, on the night after the presser, when Colm took a step towards me, on *see you so soon*, instead of taking a step forward, to take his hands in mine, I took a step back, as if frightened, like a spooked horse.

He paused, and I guessed from his look that he was wondering if one of us had got a cue wrong, or forgotten a line.

He held his hand out, palm down, as you might to a child, placatory. I left it a moment longer, then stepped towards him, and then he was stepping too, and we met, as before: hand in hand, a clasp of bodies, my head on his breast. His words. The kiss.

All we had done was insert a little space into the sequence, like a musician might let a note linger in a melody, or hang behind the beat. But we had established a subtle understanding as to what might or might not happen.

He gave me a look, as we walked off, in the blackout, the audience applauding. It was just a glance, but it was enough to serve as acknowledgement of what had just occurred. We had crossed no boundary, but I had stepped near to it, and in stepping near to it I had made us both aware of it; I had brought it into being. We blocked that kiss, his look seemed to say, and that was more for your benefit than mine, so there can be no suggestion of me taking advantage, of turning a stage direction into an actual physical intimacy that is uncalled for and undesired.

If that sounds like a lot to get from a facial expression, then know that this is my area of expertise. The capturing of complex emotional states in momentary physical attitudes. I can spend – not hours, but many, many minutes at a time in front of the mirror, watching myself. *Pulling faces*, my mother says. Which I am, but really I'm analysing the external signs of my behaviour, trying to catch myself as if seen from afar, from the footlights, running through the angles.

*

The next night I hesitated again. Colm responded the same way, with the hand held out, palm down. I paused, as before, then went slowly towards him, but this time I went with my head down, expressionless, like a sleepwalker. I ignored the hand-holding, and ground my forehead into his shirtfront, almost butting him, like a cat might butt your leg, then turned to face the audience. Then, when he took my head in his hands and lifted me towards him, I closed my eyes and lunged, pushing myself up on my toes to press my mouth onto his.

It was a blundering, formless kiss, but he dealt with it confidently, expertly, turning my head with his hands, as blocked, so his body and head were between me and the audience, and we waited like that until the lights went down. But for that quarter-second, before our lips touched, for the time it took for me to raise myself up and reach for him, the boundaries were, I think, down, and the distinctions blurred.

That night Max put his head around the dressing room door and said how great we'd been, and that he had a couple of notes for me. Look, he said, I did want to ask. At the end of Act Three you've changed Nina's approach to the kiss, you and Colm, but it looks to me like it's coming from you, and I just wanted to check that's what it was, and that you were happy with it.

We're just playing around with it, I think, I said, and he said, Cool, that's cool, it works really well. It's just that sort of scene, it's often easier to do it as blocked. What he didn't say was: especially when one of the actors is half the age of the other. And when one of them is married, with two young kids, and the other one is just out of drama school and pretty as hell.

The next night, as we stood side-by-side in the wings before Act Three, Colm said, as if to himself, Well, I wonder what we'll get tonight? He said it wryly, as if my games were just that little bit wearying, like something you'd expect from a toddler. I said nothing, but, very softly, I leaned in towards him, closing the gap between us – in imitation of how our bodies would close the space between us, later, as we moved towards the kiss.

The night after that one, when he took a step towards me, I didn't move, but stayed put, on my side of the stage. He waited for me to take my step. I saw how his right hand rested at his side, ready to come up and make the usual gesture, palm down, but I wasn't going to let him make it. I stood there, trembling to myself. Five seconds, six. Then his hand did come up, but with the palm up, fingers extended and slightly parted, beckoning. The gap stretched, I could feel it in the hairs on my arms, and the backwards push of my shoulders, straightening my spine, hollowing my back. Arousal is not just a state of excitation, but also of anticipation, and of uncertainty. I wanted him to come to me. That was the message I was sending, me to him – Colm – just as I was sending it as Nina to him – Trigorin. The difference was that one of them was an invitation, and one was a challenge.

In the end he came, of course he did. If he hadn't, it would have been a catastrophe. He had to cross the whole of the space between us, which he did, in the end, quickly and resolutely and almost angrily, and when he did I rewarded him by laying my head most meekly against his chest – *those glorious eyes, that ineffably tender smile* – then letting my head be turned, raised, kissed. The sound of the applause from the auditorium was like static in my ears, as if it was coming from inside my own head.

*

A few days after that, I had an interview with a newspaper. My first one. Naturally, I was excited and nervous. The journalist was about my age, which annoyed me, that I wasn't worth someone more established. But she was lovely, she laughed at my line about how everyone would prefer to be Masha but wants to play Nina. I felt a little bump of pride, that that line was going to go into the newspaper, and that people would see I wasn't just a pretty face, but had things to say, too.

She asked me about my upbringing, and I said that my mother was a vicar. Her reaction to this was priceless. Her mouth hung open, so you could see that little dimple in the middle of the top lip. I knew I'd be practising it in the mirror when I got home. Not even at home; I'd excuse myself and go to the loo right there in the café, to try it out in the toilets.

Her eyes widened, and she said, I hope you don't mind me asking, but are you religious, yourself? I paused, then I said, Well, actually, my spirituality is something I try to keep private.

And that was the point in my life so far that I felt most like I was a real, actual professional actor.

Chekhov said something amazing about Christianity, I said, wanting to change the subject. In fact, what's so wonderful about Chekhov, I said, as if I'd just thought of it, is how perfectly he's matched to the English temperament. It's as if, when he died, his heart was packed in ice and flown to England, where it was transplanted into our theatre and literature. Russia at the end of the nineteenth century was a perfect donor match for Britain after the first world war, with the idea of empire finally extinguished. The exquisite melancholy of an entire national sensibility watching itself sink into oblivion.

It was a great line, but it wasn't mine. It was something that Agnes had said, more or less word for word. Agnes, who was playing Polena, and had read everything Chekhov ever wrote, not just the plays and stories, but the diaries, the letters. I knew I should say something to the journalist, even as I said it, even as I saw her scribble it down, that it wasn't my line to say, but I didn't.

The interview was in the paper two days later. My line about Masha was there, but the line about Chekhov's heart being transplanted into English theatre was used as the headline.

I slunk into the dressing room as mouse-like as I could, but there was the article, taped to my mirror. There was a flurry of oohs and applause as I sat down. God, shut up, I said. I looked at Agnes. She was applauding, too, clapping her hands in the air in front of her. I went over and sat next to her. Look, I'm sorry, I said. I really am. It's unforgivable. Don't be silly, she said. You came across really well. And anyway, no one's queuing up to ask *me* for my opinions on Chekhov. So it's nice to see it out there. And you look fantastic in the photo. No, but still, I said. No buts, she said, and she patted my hand, two quick pats, like that, and turned back to her mirror. It's a moment. Enjoy it.

Naturally the performance that night was a total car crash. I felt as if everyone was watching me, the self-appointed Chekhov expert. As if suddenly the whole thing was about me: that the play wasn't about Nina, with me expressing a part of what she was, but the other way round, that *she* was there to express a part of *me*. When it came to the kiss, I tried to be bold, to come at the scene at a tangent, but I felt it misfire, even as it happened. I could feel myself *acting*. When I laid my head on

Colm's breast and looked out at the audience, all I could feel was relief, that it was nearly over. When he put his hands on either side of my face and lifted it to his, I complied, limp as a rag doll. He held my arms and pressed his closed mouth onto mine with a force I didn't expect. As the lights dimmed he unkissed himself and looked at me. A severe look, almost of disdain, or as if he was disgusted at himself, Trigorin, for giving in to Nina's charms.

We still had eight weeks to run, and it was like the show was dead in the water. The pistol shot, in the wings, Konstantin shooting himself, sounded like someone putting a bullet into my career, into my desire to even be an actor any more.

*

The next day, when I was alone in the dressing room, there was a knock on the door, and Colm's head appeared around the side of it. He took a seat along from me. Look, he said, I wanted to apologise for last night. I was off with you, I know. Mary was in, he said. Mary was his wife. We'd met a couple of times, but mostly she was at home with their kids, one of them was really young, not even a year old. He rubbed his head at the temple. I think someone must have said something silly to her, he said. About the kiss scene. He grimaced, a sickly half-smile. I mean, she's wonderful, but she does have a bit of a problem with jealousy. It's not like she has anything to worry about, right? And he looked at me, as if for reassurance.

As if for reassurance, he looked at me.

So what I wanted to say, he said, was that if I seemed off, then that's why. It's okay, I said, but he shook his head. It's not okay. You're a brilliant actor, and I love doing those scenes with you, but part of what makes it so good is the danger. The danger on stage, I mean, he said. It's always dangerous, that kind of thing. You know what I mean? That doesn't sound stupid?

It felt like he was trying to be honest and open with me, but at the same time was stopping short. Was being as obvious as possible about what he wanted to say, without actually coming out and saying it. No, I said. You're not being stupid.

He stood up. You are so brilliant, though, he said. You should be proud of what you're doing. Honestly, when I watch you, when you're on, or when we're on together, I'm gobsmacked. I'd be scared by our scenes, if I didn't think you know what you're doing.

I don't know what I thought would happen next, but what happened was that he laughed. Will you listen to me? he said. Fucking Chekhov.

He looked at me, his lips pursed, then he said, Don't worry. It's nothing. And in that moment I understood what he meant.

You are so brilliant, he had said. With exactly the same delivery, the same weight and intonation, as, every night, he told me how *beautiful* I was. *You are so beautiful*. Fucking Chekhov. He had screwed with Nina and Trigorin, those hundred years ago, and now he was screwing with us. The sheer genius of it – to put characters on the page, who to all intents and purposes are a step away from cliché, and turn them into living, breathing people. And to take real, living, breathing people, and turn them into clichés.

That night our Act Two scene was fast and fun. We got laughs in places we don't always get them, and they were laughs not so much at the lines, as at our general demeanour, the spark we seemed to find in the characters that we weren't just portraying, but *representing* – like an ambassador *represents* a country, as if our job was to be the best Trigorin, the best Nina, we could be, to find their most perfect expression.

In Act Three I went to him as I used to, and it felt as though there was a new tenderness to the encounter, how it played out. On *These sweet features* he brushed back a stray lock of my hair and tucked it behind my ear. And then he bent down and kissed me.

The next night, as I waited offstage for my re-entrance, I loosened a strand of hair from my hairband, so it fell over my cheek. Again he brushed it back. *That ineffably tender smile.* I lifted my mouth to his, and his hand came up to cup and shield. *Those gentle features. My darling!* Again and again I loosened my strand of hair, and I looked out at the audience, and I lifted my face.

I began to see how a performance changes as a river does in its floodplain, in increments, imperceptibly, never remaining the same for long. No sooner established, new habits start to loosen, to push against their constraints, look for a way to transform themselves.

One night I let down the strand of hair and he failed to tuck it back. The next night I didn't let down the strand of hair, and it was not missed, and I was happy to see it gone, behind us.

But it was the kiss that we were working towards, night after night. It was all I was doing, all day. From the moment of waking, it was only a matter of time until I thought of it. Once I got out of bed, all motion was movement to bring me to the start of that final walk across that raked wooden floor, to lay my head on his breast, allow my face to be lifted towards his, his kiss.

*

My friend Tia lived not far from where Colm and his family lived, and I used to think of that when I went to visit her, which I did often. She could easily be persuaded to go for a walk, or for a coffee. We'd go for our stroll, but then I'd leave her at the top of her road and walk right on past the tube station, towards where he lived. I never went all the way there. In any case I already knew what his house looked like, from the internet.

I liked getting to know the surrounding area. I'd walk past the cafes, pubs and shops that were maybe ten minutes' walk from his street, and imagine them, as a family, using them. I glanced in through the fences of the primary schools, wondering if one of the children playing in the playground was theirs, their older boy.

One day I went to see Tia, but she was periody and not feeling like hanging out, so I made my way to a nearby park, with my sunglasses and a book, to find somewhere to sit and read. It was one of those spring days when you first feel the heat of the sun on your face as a palpable thing. I had my head back, my eyes closed behind my sunglasses, my book held open on my lap, when I became aware of someone stood near me. I opened my eyes and there she was: Colm's wife, Mary. She had a buggy with her, with a child asleep in it, bundled under a blanket, and as she stood there she moved the buggy gently to and fro on the path.

Hello, she said. You're Sophie, aren't you?

Yes, I said back to her. Mary, I said. I took off my sunglasses. I smiled at her, she didn't smile back.

She was in t-shirt and jeans. Her arms were tanned, the hairs on them glinted in the sun, and her short, dark brown hair spun up in tight bouncing curls from her head. I resisted the impulse to check my own hair, to touch it even briefly with my hand.

Do you live near here? she said, and I replied that I didn't, but that a friend of mine did, and I'd been visiting her. Do *you* live near here, then? I asked her, hoping it wouldn't be obvious that I knew this, and thus that I was a terrible person. But she just nodded her head in the direction of the house, and named the street. How are things going, then? she asked. Are you enjoying the play?

Oh god, yes, I said. You can't imagine. This is like my third professional production. It's surreal, being in a show with people like Colm and Agnes. I'm more used to watching people like them from the stalls.

She moved the buggy to and fro, to and fro. The baby had begun to stir, and I pointed this out to her. He's gorgeous, I said. What's his name again? She leaned over the buggy and folded back the canvas top to peer down at him. Then she pushed the top back and carried on rolling the buggy to and fro. She didn't answer. Instead she said, So what's it like kissing my husband, then?

I laughed and shifted my position on the bench. It's fine, I said, squinting up at her, as if what she'd said had been a joke, or meant as a joke. He's a good kisser, I said – pretend-seriously, as if we were talking about someone entirely separate from both of us. She didn't change her expression, and I wondered how expert she was at knowing when a person is acting. I supposed you got good at it, if you lived with an actor. No, really, I said, changing my tone. He's lovely about it. And Max, you know, the director? I was scared shitless when we had to rehearse it for the first time.

I've seen you, she said. The two of you on stage.

She spoke quietly, still pushing the buggy to and fro. The baby, too, I could sense, was watching me, but I couldn't look at him, I had to hold her gaze.

Well, then, I said, clearly and calmly. You'll see what good actors we are.

I see that, she said. I can see exactly how good you both are. In a sudden movement she pushed the buggy towards me, then turned it, so the boy was faced away from us. Her face was fierce. Even as I watched I could feel the muscles of my face move, or flex, in response, to ghost out the same expression, but invisible, unacted.

Hey, I said, trying to sound aggrieved, but she shook her head. No, she said. I've seen you. She lowered her voice on the word *seen* so it sort of guttered out, and I copied the sound of it in my head, filing it away. How old are you? she said. Twenty? Twenty-one? He's fucking forty-three years old. He has a family. He does not need girls like you pouring themselves all over him on stage every night. I don't know if you know what you're doing, but if you *do* know, if you know what effect you're having, *really* having on him, then you're a little fucking bitch.

She straightened up and pulled the buggy violently back around. The boy looked at me, his dark eyes all pupil, and his doll's mouth pulsing slightly, so the dimple in the top lip rose and fell, rose and fell. I looked at him now, with my head ringing and my ears burning, and I thought how you could hold the gaze of a child indefinitely. There was no challenge in it; but it was a one-way flow of information. He was taking in everything I sent out, but sending nothing in return.

I looked back at his mother. Look, I said. I don't know what you mean. I mean: I *know*, but I don't know where you've got it from. There's nothing like that... nothing at all. I blinked my eyes, and saw how my voice was dry, how I found it hard to form words, how shot to fuck was my enunciation.

Well, good, she said. She pushed the buggy away from me, up the path, then turned back. I've been your age, she said, but you haven't been my age. Just think about that, yeah?

I opened my mouth, but no words came. She stood there, perhaps waiting to see what I would say. Eventually she gave up and went.

I sat there, holding my face still, trying to feel how it looked. How my mouth was, my eyes, the set of my jaw. I imagined myself back home, working on my expression in my bedroom mirror, the expression I had now, trying to find it again. If I could just walk home like this, I thought, without moving a single muscle, like someone might carry a bowl brimful of milk, then it would be there waiting for me. Stiffly, slowly, I stood up from the bench and started walking, slowly, stiffly, trying not to spill a drop.

THE LONELY CROWD ESSAY
'Poetic Champions Compose: Writing and Music in Northern Ireland[1]
Gerald Dawe

My focus in what follows is upon a group of poets and writers, some of whom made the all -important breakthrough before The Troubles began while others started to publish in the early years of this century. But I will be referring to at least one writer whose achievement as a writer of lyrics (perhaps forgotten?) was (and remains) phenomenal. But let me start with a fictional writer of songs, in fact two of them – Martyn Semple and Roy Fletcher, from Stewart Parker's play, *Catchpenny Twist*,[2] first performed at the Peacock Theatre, Dublin in August 1977. The play, a charade in two acts, works on two levels – the story of a trio of friends, sacked from their teaching jobs who go out on their own as songwriters with their girl-friend as their stage voice: to quote Martyn, 'Pop songs are like the folk music of our generation. There's nothing political about it.'[3] On another level, the play poses serious questions about the relationship between fun and games, enjoyment, pleasure and the deadly business of surviving during the early days of the Northern Troubles. It sets a useful epigraph to what's on my mind tonight. In this brief extract one of the hopefuls, Martyn, is in conversation with an old College friend, Marie, who has become involved with the IRA[4]:

---

[1] This is the edited version of a talk given to the Belfast Book Festival, Crescent Arts Centre, Belfast June 9, 2019. Some material on Stewart Parker, Derek Mahon and Leontia Flynn were drawn from the author's *The Wrong Country: Essays on Modern Irish Writing* (Newbridge: Irish Academic Press, 2018).

[2] Stewart Parker, 'Catchpenny Twist', *Plays I*, (London: Methuen Press, 2000).

[3] 'Catchpenny Twist', 116.

[4] 'Catchpenny Twist', 85.

Martyn: We're living on the dole. Trying to write songs.
Marie: Any luck?
Martyn: In this town? You're joking.
Marie: I might be able to put some work your way.
Martyn: You?
Marie: Ever try writing ballads?
Martyn: You mean street ballads? Come-all-ye's? Sure, they're traditional, nobody writes those.
Marie: Traditions need to be maintained. (*She starts to walk off.*) It's worth thirty pounds a throw, if you're interested at all.
Martyn: Tell me more.
He follows her. They go off together. Music.

And so, the play sets off to explore the fateful decision which the pals make on foot of this offer and where it will ultimately lead them. A play about songwriting (as an art-form) and its freedoms at a time of violence.

Only a month separates Stewart Parker from fellow Belfast poet Derek Mahon, both born in 1941. And like Parker, for Mahon the popular culture of the mid-twentieth century is never too far away from the pressing concerns of his highly praised poetry. In an earlier version of his long poem 'The Sea in Winter', originally published in 1979[5], only a couple of years after *Catchpenny Twist* was performed, Mahon, situated in 'a draughty bungalow in Portstewart', addresses his fellow Irish poet Desmond O'Grady with a reference to 'This is where Jimmy Kennedy wrote 'Red Sails in the Sunset'. Jimmy Kennedy was born in Omagh in 1902 but grew up in Portstewart, on the northern coast. Author of lyrics such as 'South of the Border', 'My Prayer' and 'We're Going to Hang out the Washing Line on the Seigfried Line' he died in Cheltenham, England in 1984; like Mahon, he was a Trinity College graduate, and he is generally regarded as one of the great lyricists of the last century.

Kennedy turns up twenty-five years later, supplying Mahon with the title for his collection *Harbour Lights* (2006) and later still for

---

[5] Derek Mahon, *The Sea in Winter* (The Deerfield Press, Massachusetts/The Gallery Press, Dublin, 1979), np.

Mahon's prose volume, *Red Sails* (2014) [6]. Kennedy provides one of the finest poems in *Harbour Lights*, 'Calypso', with its critical turning point between the classical world of Homer's Ulysses and the landscape of an imagined home:

> Red sails in the sunset where the dripping prows
> Rapped out a drum-rhythm on uncertain seas
> Of skimming birds, a lonely pine or shrine –
> But the seer's secrets diminished on dry land,
> Darker than they could know or understand.

The archetypal vision of Homer's Ulysses searching for Ithaca, his home, finds an unpredictable congruence in the sentimental lyrics of Jimmy Kennedy's 'Red Sails in the Sunset' [7]

> Red sails in the sunset, way out on the sea
> Oh, carry my loved one home safely to me
> She sailed at the dawning, all day I've been blue
> Red sails in the sunset, I'm trusting in you
> Swift wings you must borrow
> Make straight for the shore
> We marry tomorrow
> And she goes sailing no more
> Red sails in the sunset, way out on the sea
> Oh, carry my loved one home safely to me
> Swift wings you must borrow
> Make straight for the shore
> We marry tomorrow
> And she goes sailing no more

---

[6] Derek Mahon, *Harbour Lights* (Oldcastle: The Gallery Press, 2006), *Red Sails* (Oldcastle: The Gallery Press, 2014).

[7] Songwriters: Wilhelm Grosz / Jimmy Kennedy 'Red Sails in The Sunset 'lyrics © Sony/ATV Music Publishing LLC, Shapiro Bernstein & Co. Inc.

Red sails in the sunset
Way out on the sea (ooh-wee-ooh, wee-ooh)
Oh, carry my loved one
Home safely to me

Derek Mahon's contemporary, Michael Longley has long been a fan of music – both classical and jazz – and his early poetry is lit with tributes to the great exponents of the form including Bessie Smith, Bud Freeman, Bix Beiderbecke and Fats Waller in 'Words for Jazz, perhaps'.[8] Longley writes: 'My total conversion to jazz in my twenty-fifth year [1964] when marriage and our return to Belfast coincided with my discovery of Solly Lipsitz's celebrated emporium in High Street... Atlantic Records'.[9] In 'Back in the 1960s', a fascinating exploration of music and poetry, Edna Longley recounts in 2007 the sounds and presences of the influences in Belfast of the time, singling out what she terms 'the decisive event' in 'Belfast's local chemistry' – the afterglow of 'the wartime presence of American troops': 'their passion for jazz, the black and white musicians amongst them, the setting-up of night-clubs in Belfast like the Embassy and Manhattan.'[10] She goes on to quote these soaring lines from Michael Longley's poem addressed to Bix Beiderbecke, the white cornet-player:

You were bound with one original theme
To compose in your head your terminus,
Or to improvise with the best of them

That parabola from blues to barrelhouse.

---

[8] Michael Longley, *No Continuing City: Poems 1963-1968* (Dublin: Gill and Macmillan, 1969).

[9] Michael Longley, *Sidelines: Selected Prose 1962-2015* (London: Enitharmon Press, 2017), 5.

[10] Edna Longley, 'Back in the 1960s: Belfast Poets, Liverpool Poets' in *That Island Never Found: Essays and Poems for Terence Brown,* edited by Nicholas Allen and Eve Patten (Dublin: Four Courts Press, 2007), 158.

Edna Longley glosses the final line – 'from the most interior to the most extraverted jazz-mode' as the telling point of Longley's 'jazz' poems: they 'invoke qualities of jazz that reflexively bear on poetry' and suggests 'how to negotiate the 'havoc' of the artistic life as well as the 'mixing' of 'composition, improvisation and maneuvering'[11] which makes jazz (like poetry) such an amazing form of human expression. It's something the poet touches upon when he remarks in an article from 1998, 'A Perpetual One-Night Stand':[12]

> Jazz is huge. That the suffering and degradation of slavery should bring forth so much redemptive beauty is miraculous. The spontaneity of this music must be one of the best antidotes against authoritarian systems that would tell us what to think and feel... Syncopation is the opposite of the goosestep. Perhaps jazz is our century's [20th] most significant contribution to the world.

Van Morrison's early days in Belfast of the late 1950s and 60s were spent listening to jazz, folk and rhythm and blues like his east Belfast near contemporary, Stewart Parker: 'I started a skiffle group [Parker remarks] called The Troubadours which performed at one or two church hall dances. Inevitably my long-suffering father got implicated, I pestered him for a guitar until he finally built one for me. It was a vehicle of long hours of adolescent world weariness up in my cold bedroom'.[13] And surely this typical experience of his generation, fifteen or so years later, would lead to Parker writing (between 1970 and 1976) the pioneering 'High Pop' column for the *Irish Times* – an extraordinarily witty, lithe, urbane, knowledgeable, well-researched, energetic and critically ahead-of-its-time reading of popular music, not just of the 1970s, but throughout the twentieth century.

---

[11] 'Back in the 1960s', 159.
[12] *Sidelines: Selected Prose 1962-2015*, 6.
[13] Stewart Parker, *Dramatis Personae & other writings*, edited by Gerald Dawe, Maria Johnston and Clare Wallace (Prague: Litteraria Pragensia, 2009), XXX.

Lynne Parker remarked, Parker 'had a poetic sensibility, an academic training and a historian's mind'[14], effortlessly revealed in *High Pop* through the mix of ironic and comic anecdote with sharp-eyed cultural commentary[15]. In his astute commentary on the fundamentalism of American country music, Parker reflects on the transmission of the American west coast of The Beach Boys to the windy strands of Portrush, and on his sense of 'political' songs and the 'capacity of our available art forms to cope with contemporary political realities'.[16] Music and music-making, fun and laughter were part and parcel of Stewart Parker's artistic make-up, as much as they were features of his temperament.

This is the Belfast poet Robert Johnstone's recollection of meeting Parker[17]:

> I met Stewart Parker around 1970. I'd just left school. He was 29 or 30, he'd been to America, one or two of his plays had been on local radio, and Festival Publications had published *Maw* [a poetry pamphlet] ... His flat seemed slightly hippy, in the fashion of the time, and I thought him an exotic figure, with his soft caps and big cigars. He was reviewing records for the Irish Times, and was delighted with all the free albums. He was friendly, polite and probably indulgent to what must have been a callow youth.

Given what we know about the obsession with music in Belfast of the 1960s, all kinds of music, and the breaking free from his sense of the somewhat inhibited possibilities of the North of the time, it is no surprise that Parker should have yearned, as Lynne Parker describes it, to 'enlarge the frame'[18].

---

[14] Lynne Parker, 'Introduction', *Stewart Parker Plays:1*, x.

[15] Stewart Parker, *High Pop*, edited by Gerald Dawe and Maria Johnston (Belfast: Lagan Press, 2008).

[16] *High Pop*, 126.

[17] Robert Johnstone, 'Playing for Ireland', *Honest Ulsterman* No.86 (Spring/Summer 1989).

[18] Lynne Parker, 'Introduction', xvi.

His play, *Pentecost*, while suffused with references to Protestant churches - Sunday school, hymns, gospel (Lenny playing on the saxophone 'Just a Closer Walk with Thee'); mythologised Northern Protestant experience of the First World War, the shipyard, the landscape and street names of east Belfast – *Pentecost* is about the opening out of experience, not closing it in. But it is Parker's distinctive ability to draw together both a highly tuned literary sensibility with an unerring instinct for the authentic note in popular culture which makes him a writer to treasure. Try this for example, from May 1973:

> Remember how, in the 1960s, we were always being bombarded with 'new faces'? Face was a key word. Having face was having style, being utterly of the moment – with it – on display, acting David Hemmings photographing Jean Shrimpton posing on the set of Julie Christie's new film. The Mods called their pop idols 'faces,' and one of their groups responded by naming themselves the Small Faces. It all referred to the primacy of appearance, image, the media being the messages, just as in the Elizabethan comedy of humours. Today's lurid narcissists, like David Bowie and Marc Bolan, are the Jacobean fag-ends of the movement, a degeneration into sexual melodrama, vapid and joyless. But some heroes of the 1960s have matured into serene survivors, and amongst them are Rod ('The Mod') Stewart and his Faces. Maybe elegance is not quite the word for a man with the hairstyle of the Greater Crested Grebe and the Voice That Smoked A ThousandCigarettes. Even so, in the gloss of the music, in its seemingly effortless panache, there is a considerable degree of deliberate fastidiousness, finesse... style in fact.

Leontia Flynn's poetry equally lives out in the world of strange, exhilarating encounters – be that emotionally or imaginatively. The sheer volume of lived life which her four collections to date reproduce is – at times – breath taking. And though music and song doesn't function in her writing in any conscious or allusive way, its presence is more like mood music. Her poems to both her mother and her every whistling and singing father, source of the wonderful poem 'By My Skin' in Flynn's first collection, *These Days* - are blissful, poignant and wise[19]:

> My father communicates with his family almost entirely
>   through song.
> …
> He sings 'Oft in the Stilly Night' and 'Believe me, If All
>   Those Endearing Young Charms'.
> He sings 'Edelweiss' and 'Cheek to Cheek' from *Top Hat*.

As the poem drifts into a rapturous hymn to the father's backlist the young girl is wrapped 'in swaddling clothes' of love and attention to her skin condition; the poem becomes a song in its own right. Erratic student pads with some dodgy detritus, techie treats and teases merge with the mixed joys of background music – The Bangles, Neil Young, Karen Carpenter, Patsy Cline, and Foster and Allen (no less!) video what's going on in the many cities her poems visit. Yet Flynn's poems magnetically return to a Belfast both actual and imagined, troubled and post-Troubles. It shouldn't really come as a surprise that in her second volume, *Drives*, which opens with a poem called 'Song', amid all the big names of European and American artists and thinkers, who should pop up in the 'car stereo system' but Van Morrison. This is 'Cyprus Avenue'[20]:

> Van Morrison is singing 'Cyprus Avenue'
> on the car stereo system
> when we turn into Mournview
> car park. The ignition
>
> sparked, we grind the gears
> of your dad's hatchback
> with the sheathed interiors

[19] Leontia Flynn, *These Days* (London: Jonathan Cape), 51-2.
[20] Leontia Flynn, *Drives* (London: Jonathan Cape, 2008), 44.

and practise at the clutch.

An old song plays on the radio
I am captured in a car seat.
On the points of summer and youth
the whole world pivots.

Cyprus Avenue provides the title for David Ireland's extraordinary play and it also features as a title in Lucy Caldwell's moving collection of stories, *Multitudes* [21](2016). For these stories, set in the main in east Belfast, move through a backdrop which has distinctive Morrison-like moods and reveries. Just listen to this evocation of what the narrator calls 'Van Morrison territory' in the opening to Caldwell's love story 'Here We Are[22]':

> After we leave Cutters Wharf that night, we talk. We walk along the Lagan and through the Holylands: Palestine Street, Jerusalem Street, Damascus Street, Cairo Street. We cross the river and walk the whole sweep of the Ormeau Embankment. The tide is turning, and a two-person canoe is skimming downriver, slate grey and quicksilver. When we reach the point where the road curves away from the river, the pale evening light still lingers, so we keep walking.

The hypnotic quality of walking and uncovering a deeper layer of emotional reality, something 'un-seeable' but tangible all the same, is a current that flows through so much of northern Irish writing, particularly that based in or around Belfast, as if in defiance of the scarred and disfiguring history of the place the place itself produces a magic of its own:[23]:

---

[21] Lucy Caldwell, *Multitudes* (London: Faber and Faber, 2016),
[22] *Multitudes*, 101.
[23] *Multitudes*,108.

...across the Ravenhill Road, down Toronto Street and London Street and the London Road, Rosebery Road and Willowfield Drive and across the Woodstock Road and on, further and further east until we are in Van Morrison territory: Hyndford Street and Abetta Parade, Grand Parade, the North Road, Orangefield.

And in the closing refrain of the penultimate story 'Cyprus Avenue' the returning young woman who has meet up in the airport with a fellow Belfast-bound traveler, Nirupam Choudbury, once 'a young boy from Delhi growing up in Belfast who rides his bike along Cyprus Avenue'. This is how 'Cyprus Avenue' moves to its revelation[24]:

> You'll walk down Cyprus Avenue and all the streets you used to play on, Sandford Avenue and Sunbury Avenue and Evelyn Avenue and Kirkliston Drive, and maybe you'll walk on, walk the length of the Upper Newtownards Road, and the Albertbridge Road, and pause on the Albert Bridge itself, unlovely as it is, the traffic, the down-at-the-heel leisure centre, the railway station, to watch the starlings that mass and swoop above the east of the city in the evenings.

It's hardly surprising that in her reflections on Van Morrison, Lucy Caldwell should call her *Irish Times* article 'Streets Like These' because the landscape her characters either inhabit (or return to) matters so much[25]:

> The memory of a long car journey, coming back over the Craigantlet Hills from a trip to Donaghadee Lighthouse. The dip of the road and the sudden sensation of weightlessness, flying; the lights of the city spread out for you below. The soundtrack in my head is Van Morrison, of course: "Take me back, take me

---

[24] *Multitudes*, 153.
[25] Lucy Caldwell, 'Streets Like These', *The Irish Times*, September 28, 2016.

back, take me back / Take me way back, take me way back / Take me way back, take me way back / Take me way, way, way, way, way, way, way back..." I'm likely remembering not one particular journey. On summer weekends, or special occasions, or most excitingly of all, if my Dad was test-driving a new car, we would drive out of Belfast along the coastal roads of the Ards Peninsula; and in the car Van Morrison would be playing. Sometimes the Chieftains, or Leonard Cohen, but I remember most of all the music of Van Morrison, a double cassette-tape of *Hymns to the Silence*, as my sisters and I day-dreamed and drowsed against each other in the back seat, cosy and warm and lulled by the car and the music. In the strange way that memory works, this has come to be talismanic to me: deeper and truer and somehow more meaningful than anything that might have actually happened. A transfiguration of the mundane, a momentary glimpse into something beyond; a sense of something I can't quite articulate, but have come back to time and again in my fiction.

Caldwell goes on to specify the landscape which Morrison's music and lyrics and performance endows with an almost-spiritual value[26]:

And then one day, for no reason at all, your Mum takes a detour back from the Ormeau Embankment down Hyndford Street, through Orangefield, along Cyprus Avenue, and tells you that these are the places in the songs. I remember suddenly paying attention. I remember asking to go back to those streets, those places, and looking at the street-signs. These places weren't just places any more: they were something more-than, something sacred. I wrote myself and my city into *Multitudes*, in a way I have never written before, and writing the people and the places opened a trapdoor to more memories, specific memories of particular places at particular times, which I hadn't realised I'd

---

[26] 'Streets Like These'.

lost, or meant so much to me. Van Morrison understands this, and it is in his music that I first had intimations of it: the power of naming, the power of litany. Indeed, not being from a church-going family, he was my first introduction to the power of litany: of repetition, and through repetition the transformation of the mundane into something else, something greater. My Belfast, my East Belfast, even, is not that of Van Morrison's, not entirely. But mine wouldn't exist without his. But the music of Van Morrison in general, and *Astral Weeks* in particular, is something of a guiding spirit to my stories. It's there in the rhythms of the language, particularly in stories like my own Cyprus Avenue or Here We Are. It's there in the place names – you cannot be a writer of East Belfast after Van Morrison without being hugely indebted to him.

Van Morrison's literary influence is only now surfacing and finding its level amongst some of the finest writers of a younger generation including Lucy Caldwell, Wendy Erskine and David Ireland, all three of whom have family and cultural roots in east Belfast which he transformed into a lyrical landscape all of his own; an alternative vision of the city and a very different alternative history.

I'm 108 Lines
Jake Hawkey

I'm an immigrant tailor who says A coat
is not a piece of cloth only - Adrienne Rich

I'm an immigrant restauranteur who says *People*
enter and exit our lives heavy like cars on motorways
I'm the shade of a great rock in a weary land
I'm a cigar-chomping vendor named Joe

I'm the house-building hands of my youngest brother
I'm signing the Good Friday Agreement
I'm getting drunk with the others afterwards
I'm closing down the bar when everyone is finished

I'm your father losing his job
I'm glossy postcards from God
I'm calling the bingo after a divorce
I'm dull English Sunday packed full of antique doom

I'm the long groan of Monday,
murder in the newspaper
I'm a joke half-remembered
I'm a knife through a letterbox on Halloween

I'm a red London bus crawling across a bridge,
a dog absorbed in the flights of a frisbee
I'm the man who comes to erect a bouncy castle
I'm the man who comes back to take it away

I'm shyness on a nudist beach,
talking in the library, the racist Home Secretary
I'm Elvis Presley eating KFC
I'm a gold watch on a poor man's wrist

I'm the lilting bridge over Dublin's Liffey,
lumpy gravy in a train toilet,
Tommy Cooper dying of a heart attack on stage
I'm the laughing audience thinking it's just a gag

I'm the best karaoke singer since King Henry VIII,
one of four shoulders holding up a coffin,
a funeral wreath spelling out a nickname
I'm the games invented by streets of children

I'm the slow saving of McDonald's wages,
the monies won by Dad on the gee-gees
I'm a baby conceived in Magaluf,
VOGUE magazine, I'm disposed of tissues

I'm the bullied becoming the bully
I'm travelling the world to fight
whatever war I can find
I'm Ulysses, I'm discounted used tyres

I'm Judy Garland out on the tiles,
holding a glass, willing an approach
I'm an African princess working abroad
in a pharmacy, taking extra shifts

I'm Jesus Christ the anarchist overturning tables,
a Syrian president slaughtering his own people,
three black girls in Brooklyn playing jump-rope
I'm Alzheimer's learning to dance

I'm sick on a school trip to France
I'm wearing my favourite cologne
I'm talking to the most beautiful woman I know
(who happens to be my best m8's mum)

I'm what I laugh at in the cinema,
cheap hair gel telling you not to park here,
a horse being led to the knacker's yard
I'm a tram on the streets of Prague

I'm Boudicca Boudicca Boudicca
I'm *je ne sais quoi*
I'm a black woman working in a white school
I'm leaving it all to the cats' home

I'm Edison's 10,000 failed attempts
I'm Edison's success
I'm Father Christmas and you're on my lap, pulling my beard
I'm built on an Indian burial ground

I'm working in a call centre and fat-shaming the new girl
I'm asking her out for a drink,
barefoot in Trafalgar Square fountain
I'm flirting with the married manager of Costco

I'm Damien Hirst's diamond-encrusted skull,
a doctor who sees the best in her patient,
a radiologist who sees the worst,
a sailor who fell in love at port but is shipping out now

I'm the smoothing of honey over an open wound,
my mother's prettiest son,
a misspent youth at Butlin's playing pool
I'm a packed restaurant, I'm a proposal turned down

I'm a fresh hole in your grandfather's old leather belt,
a dinner lady who forgets where she is
playing with her hair, staring at magnolia walls
I'm trips out to the sea

I'm the small sound of a teenage girl weeping over a boy,
unfulfilled and unforgiving,
the shiny oilfields of Iraq,
Tony Blair playing guitar in 1997

I'm blood in the Nile, blood in urine
I'm what's remembered and what's forgotten,
a nun delivering the last rites to a kitchen porter
who lay dying still holding a whisk

I'm my postcode, my accent
I'm gentrification living in a square glass box,
the torture and screams of a Chinese dissident
I'm slim thighs cutting the air during sex

I'm a found poem on the back of a crumpled betting slip,
a dodgy haircut
I'm getting out of the city I grew up in
I'm sipping tea with the elderly

I'm snowballing hopes together towards onlookers
who are stepping quietly aside and flashing me
with sunbeams off their watch faces
I'm my miraculous mother on gin

I'm the drowning of families in the Mediterranean,
a hot wet kiss on the back of your neck,
the first time you took a razor to your face
I'm bringing a bottle of wine round

I'm the last verse of a poem
I'm one more for the road, I'm celebration
I'm an ice cream van in the wind and rain
I'm the lush echo of the heart inside, running with scissors

Unwanted
Ethel Rohan

Every Sunday after Mass, outside St. Peter's Church, Da pressed a fifty-pence piece into my hand, and I parted ways with my family and hurried straight to Bob's Bargain Bookshop. It was 1985, in Dublin, and I was a black-haired, dark-eyed, fourteen-year-old runt of a lad. On a flush week, I'd also have my takings from refunds on the glass bottles I collected out of the bins and lanes around our neighbourhood, empty, sharp-scented treasure. Our locale was also home to Midas's gambling arcade, Mountjoy Prison, Cross Guns snooker hall, Luigi's chipper with its snapping, popping Pac-Man machine, and the reek of the Royal Canal.

Occasionally, I stole money from Da's hiding spot under the inky, floral carpet beneath his bedroom window to add to my dismal funds for books, comics, sweets, cigarettes, and flagons of cider. I only ever took a pound or two at any one time, knowing not to get greedy or careless. Amazingly, Da, who was skint, miserly, and forever howling about the cursed recession, never seemed to notice the missing money. I sometimes worried he was playing a game, waiting to catch me in the act and pounce. Then he would demand his pound of flesh, like Shakespeare's Shylock. *If I can catch him once upon the hip, I will feed fat the ancient grudge I bear him.* Da was forever reciting that bit with alarming passion—fist on his heart, glitter in his blue eyes, an actor's boom to his voice—but he never seemed to be aiming the Bard's words at me.

Each Sunday, I spent hours browsing inside Bob's Bargains, rifling elbow deep through the discount bins and scanning the shelves of book spines, their jagged top lines like broken horizons. I bought as many used mysteries as I could afford, and sometimes sprang for a brand-new book that I couldn't bear to delay reading. I sped through every adventure of the Famous Five, Secret Seven, and Hardy Boys, and especially loved the Agatha Christies. Hercule Poirot? Bleeding brilliant. What I liked most about the best mysteries was not being able to figure out how things were going to end. Too many people around me seemed to think they knew exactly how everything—their lives, the world—was going to end, and it was rarely good. I preferred to keep my options wide open.

Those dizzying shelves of colourful books never failed to lather my already voracious appetite into a near frothing frenzy. I'd feel mad tempted to shove books down the front and back of my jeans, but I could never muster the courage. Thankfully, my best mate Charlie knew no such limits. The rare times the opportunity presented itself, Charlie, his hair shaved of all its blond and his face freckled and fleshy, stole the most popular new books and gave them to me. New-new, like. With that tree smell and those smooth, crisp pages. Those were the best books, the ones everyone wanted.

For my fifteenth birthday, Ma gave me two green leather-bound books, the gold ink on their covers and spines faded and flaking. The old, pored-over hardbacks, *Frankenstein* and *The Great Cases of Sherlock Holmes*, had belonged to her da. My fingertip traced those worn gold letters, my touch reverent, fluttering. It was like handling the first-ever bible.

While both classics warmed in my hands, Ma—her air distressingly casual—announced that Doyle's Corner, the crossroads just up the street from our house, was named after Sir Arthur Conan Doyle himself, the creator of Sherlock Holmes, the greatest sleuth of all time. Stunned, I demanded to know why she hadn't shared this nugget of local history long before. She knew I had my own sights set on becoming a detective, the more brilliant and famous the better.

Da looked up from the newspaper and called Ma's claim a load of nonsense. Red spilled from Ma's purple-webbed cheeks into her forehead and down to her wrinkled chest. Da said Doyle's Corner was named after the real jewel in its crown, Doyle's Public House. Those Doyles of the publican persuasion, Da insisted, were a bloodline as far removed from that dead knight and Protestant bastard Arthur Conan Doyle as you could get.

"I'm telling you, Doyle wasn't a Protestant," Ma said, livid. She tried to collect herself and smile at me, but the curve of her lips refused to stay in place. "Your grandda loved those two books," she said, a wobble in her voice.

My four grandparents died before I was born, a mixture of the cancer, bad luck, and heinous crime. By all accounts I was most like my Ma's da, our curious heads constantly in books and make-believe. Poor Grandda had met a savage end, mugged and beaten to a pulp with a hurling stick, and for pittance. He didn't die until three years later, but everyone blamed his untimely death on that unmerciful battering, saying he was never the same afterward. His as-good-as-murderers were never caught. That would all change, though, as soon as I finished school, joined the Guards, and turned detective. I would reopen Grandda's case, scrutinize his police reports, re-interview suspects and witnesses, and chase down new leads, and all with the same flair and ceremony that Da brought to his Shakespeare recitations. Whatever it took to solve the long-time mystery and finally bring Grandda's vicious assailants to justice.

I read *The Great Cases of Sherlock Holmes* three times. Every now and then I would pause on the page, thinking with a pleasant shiver how Grandda had been here before me, reading these same sentences and holding this very cover. The book's introduction stated Arthur Conan Doyle was a Scotsman and a medical doctor, and even fancied himself as a bit of a psychic. There was nothing about him being a Protestant.

"Didn't I tell you," Ma said to Da with the same satisfaction she usually reserved for finishing off a fat, oozing slice of Victoria cream sponge.

"None of yis know anything," Da said.

The book's introduction also stated Doyle came to hate Sherlock Holmes and eventually killed him off, only to later bring him back from the dead. I wished I could bring Grandda back.

It took me a while to get around to reading *Frankenstein*. I'd no interest at first. Really, I only liked mysteries. Ma kept asking, though. "Your grandda claimed he was never the same after reading it," she said, that shake back in her voice. When I did finally relent and give the book a go, I devoured *Frankenstein* too, reading and rereading for such long stints my eyes burned and my neck and shoulders ached. It seemed to me that all doctors wanted to play God, but Frankenstein wasn't content to save lives and resuscitate the dead. He took his grandiose urges to the last precipice, desperate to create a fully formed being of his sole making.

Like Doyle, Frankenstein also came to hate the creature he'd brought to life. All that made me think of Charlie's ma, Agnes Owens. "I curse the day yis were born," she told Charlie and his older brother, Jim, spitting like boiled water.

Ma said Grandda reckoned Doctor Frankenstein and Sir Arthur Conan Doyle saw too much of their flaws and weaknesses in the men they created and it terrified them. Agnes didn't see herself in her boys. And she most certainly wasn't afraid of them. I had deduced it was actually the opposite. Jim and Charlie weren't nearly enough like their creators for Agnes's liking. She wanted her two boys to be as savage as their parents and to take her side against their da, the dreaded Archie Owens.

Archie was balding, tight-jawed, and small-toothed. He also harboured a vampire's need to break skin and draw blood, especially that of his wife and two sons. Months earlier, he'd beaten Charlie to such a state I hardly recognized him.

For ages afterward, a film played on repeat in my mind. In the opening scene, I kick in the Owens' front door and drag Archie from their smoky, yellowed kitchen and out onto our falling-down street. I knock the brute to the ground with a smack of a crowbar to his limp-haired head. His scalp splits and blood pops like pus from a pimple. Agnes stands at their front gate, cackling. Charlie and Jim remain in the front doorway, as still and unseeing as statues. I keep going with the crowbar 'til Archie is a mess of shattered bones and red, quivering pulp.

I couldn't stop seeing that film. It made my body break out in a cold, dribbling sweat, and my heart kept throwing itself against the wall of my chest, trying to get out. Thoughts of pulverizing Archie the way others had destroyed Grandda made a fist squeeze my guts and twist. My thoughts dwelled on monsters. Another kind of guilt also rushed in. I could never do in real life anything close to what I did in that film in my head. I couldn't avenge Charlie. Couldn't protect him. All I could do was put the film and feelings on pause, by fast-emptying a flagon of cider into my head.

When I wasn't collecting used glass bottles, stealing Da's money and Ma's cigarettes, or hanging around with my gang of gurriers, as some people insisted on calling us, I was ever on the lookout for new mysteries to solve. Usually, my caseload consisted of little more than lost dogs and cats, the theft of milk deliveries from our neighbours'' front steps, and figuring out which boys were riding which girls. Then, alleluia, I landed my biggest case ever.

Charlie's older brother Jim didn't come home one Saturday night, or on the Sunday, or the Monday. Where had the seventeen-year-old gone? Had he made his great escape, as Charlie claimed? Maybe he'd immigrated to London for work, like most of the country's young? How far could he have travelled, though, without money or supplies, and how was he faring for clothes, food, and shelter? Charlie insisted Jim would get himself sorted someplace and then come back for him.

Two months passed with no trace of Jim. Charlie seemed to give up on ever hearing from his brother. "Good riddance," was all he said now. Then he'd kick at the curb, or a car tire. I made inquiries, but despite my best efforts, no one wanted to talk.

Jim's mott, Bernice, was a whisper's reach of sweet sixteen and already going around with some new fella. When I asked them about Jim's whereabouts, they laughed—man-tits whooping like a pigeon and Bernice sounding like the crack of snooker balls colliding. She seemed reason enough for Jim to do a runner, never mind his ma and da.

Liam, Jim's supposed best friend—with his woozy eyes, twisted teeth, yellower skin, and permanent smell of glue—proved to be as helpful as Bernice. "What about Jim?" he said. "He's gone, so long, move on." I plied him with questions, but to no avail. "Get out of here," he said, "or you'll be on the missing list, too."

In a stroke of brilliance, I decided to make posters, similar to those Old West WANTED ads. I even went so far as to offer a reward for any information that would lead to Jim's return. Maybe the grand total of five pounds wasn't much to some, but to me it was a small fortune. It amounted to weeks of saved pocket money and refunds on bottles, and getting greedy about fleecing Da. It also meant no new books for a while. It was worth it all, though, for Charlie.

I set out one dark, cold evening, my breath a tiny fog and the stars rips in the sky. I hurried over the streets, armed with superglue, a staple gun, and the ten original posters I'd handmade, all done in different colours with pencils and markers. I climbed telegraph poles, lampposts, and even the giant oak tree across from our school. Despite the chill night, I enjoyed a warm thrum in my chest as I worked, picturing the grin on Charlie's face when I reunited him with his big brother.

The next day, Charlie caught up with me as I walked home from school. He was only eleven months my senior, but he'd left St. Vincent's the previous year, having barely passed the Group exams.

"What the fuck did you do?"

His fist hovered my face, one of my MISSING posters balled up in its grip. The two lads walking alongside me scampered away. Charlie mashed the round of poster against my lips. I tasted blood, sweet and sharp. When I spat, the red glob foamed on the ground. I hoped it would bubble in Charlie's brain forevermore.

He pulled pieces of torn posters from his various pockets. "I found six. How many more are there?"

My stomach cramped with confusion. He should be thanking me. Wings of panic flapped in my chest. "What's your problem?"

He swung at me, but I pulled clear. I didn't have time to feel triumphant. He flew at me, knocking me backward to the footpath. He straddled my chest and slapped my head with his open hands, supersonic left-right smacks. He was red-faced, heaving. White froth simmered at the corners of his mouth. His eyes had darkened, rage drawing almost all of the green out of the brown. My shouts mixed with his grunts and the sounds of alarm and protest from onlookers.

Hands pulled at Charlie, flashes of freckled, cracked, and nicotine-stained fingers. A dark blue vein bulged in the centre of his forehead. He got another few slaps into me. I pushed up from beneath him and poked my two fingers into his left eye. He fell backward, roaring.

I scrambled to my feet, pushed through the circle of gobsmacked gawkers, and hurried home, hurting in a way that had nothing to do with my ringing ears and throbbing face.

...

The next evening, our neighbour, the widow Harney, appeared at our front door, her mouth downturned and her eyes lasers. We didn't have a phone at ours, so I'd put her number on the MISSING posters.

Inside her hallway, I stopped next to the mahogany phone table, taking the smallest breaths I could, the air tainted with what I hoped was only the smell of boiled eggs. Mrs. Harney entered her living room, leaving its door ajar. Her rope-thin shadow on the wall placed her right behind the door, her woolly-looking head cocked toward me, and the television beyond her on whisper.

"Hello?" I said into the receiver's black, pitted mouthpiece.

"I'm answering your poster," a boy's harsh voice said.

"Yeah?" My heart tugged upward.

"Meet me tomorrow night, nine o'clock, in the lane behind Ulster Street."

"Who—"

He killed the call. I held onto the receiver, anticipation coursing through my veins. Charlie was going to feel like a right prick when I brought his brother back, and he would steal a whole library of books on my behalf to make up for clattering me.

The following night brought a thick darkness, the slice of moon a dappled silver and the stars nothing but pinpricks. I got a bad feeling as soon as I turned down the lane behind Ulster Street and walked deeper into blindness and the tang of stale piss. I could barely see beyond my hands, and there was something about the silent, seeming emptiness that made me doubt I was flanked by the usual limp litter, clumps of weeds, and empty bottles at the lane's edges. Gone, too, was the sense that there were houses on either side of me with their back gardens full of grass, trees, hedges, and flowers, all the life that could still thrive when winter was mostly without mercy.

Just as my instincts screamed at me to turn and run, bodies—one, two, three—rushed me. An arm collared my throat, a stranglehold so strong it pushed my Adam's apple deep into my neck.

"Where's the money?" Moist lips brushed my ear, making me shudder.

"Get off me." I struggled, all shoulders, arms and legs. Glass smashed, and the bulk of a broken bottle sliced the night close to my face. The serrated stump pressed my cheek. Every time I blinked, I felt its teeth.

The first fella spoke again at my ear. "Is five pounds worth the cost of your eye?" His breath smelled of cider, and something sharper. Maybe his own insides.

I pulled my knee up, about to ram my heel into the neck of his ankle. One of the two lads in front kicked my shin. I bit down on my lip to gag my groans, my mouth still puffed and tender from Charlie's beating. The third fella searched my pockets and patted down my body and legs. From my right sock, he pulled out the cylinder of five one-pound notes I'd rolled with such care. He drove his fist into my nuts. I doubled over, my air exiting in a burst.

The three boxed, kicked, and thumped me so many times, the blows turned to almost music. I thought of Grandda, robbed and beaten to near death, and wondered if he'd also made a symphony of the repeated fall of that hurling stick as it broke his bones, his scalp, his teeth.

Fingers grabbed my hair and pulled back my head. That damp, sweet-sour breath hit my face. "Nice doing business with ya." The broken bottle ripped through my cheek, hitting bone.

I dropped to the ground, my head smacking the concrete between two red suede shoes. Six spindle legs packed into black drainpipes ran off into the night. I had just been battered, maybe to death, by three Teddy boys. Even in my state, the idea galled me. Teddy boys were made for dressing stupid and break dancing, not for smashing up people, and most of all not a future brilliant detective.

The fools had left enough clues for even a bad investigator to track them down. I swore, if I survived, I'd see them serve time, and the longer the better.

As I went under, a terrible thought seized me. Maybe Charlie had put those three Teddy boys up to this, instructing them to finish what he'd started.

I woke up in the Mater Hospital, Ma, Da, and my three sisters gathered around my bed. Ma sat in a chair to my right and Da stood opposite her to my left. They were both holding my hands. The edges of my sisters' eyes looked raw and sore, and when they saw my eyelids peel back, their mottled faces lit up like little bonfires. Cold fear gripped me. I had to be dying. That thought, and the jaundiced glare of the ceiling lights, hurt my head. I closed my eyes again, for days.

The next time I woke up, Charlie was leaning over me, his grooved face hovering. He jerked upright, his cheeks turning a scalded red. "Fuck. You scared me."

While I tried to get my mouth to work, the spooked look left him and his demeanour returned to hard and cocky, as if even his insides were no longer wet and soft.

"Don't worry, I didn't kiss you," he said.

"Wha?" My mouth felt stuffed with a wad of gauze and my throat hurt, as if its lining was scraped raw.

He smiled. "Lying there all this time like Sleeping bleeding Beauty."

"Yeah, well, it's not like you could break the spell. You're no prince."

"You're no beauty," he said.

I chanced smiling and cried out with the pain.

"Are you all right?" he said.

"Do I look all right?"

"You look woeful."

"This is the one time you pick to not tell a lie?"

He laughed. "On the bright side, you've never looked better." His hands moved to the front of his khaki army jacket, and he pulled its zipper up and down. I watched the silver teeth open and close, open and close. In my head, the broken bottle rushed again at my face. My hand jumped to my cheek, flinching at the feel of its swollen, tender ridges and the nylon stitches.

"Do you know who we have to thank for the improvements?" he said.

I tried to read him, to tell if he already knew exactly who had done this. "No," I said, stalling.

"You must have seen something."

My head filled with the red suede shoes and black drainpipes. I hesitated, not sure if I could trust him. What if he was fishing to see if I could identity my attackers? If I was going to rat to the Guards and testify against the Teddy boys, and him?

"You didn't recognize a voice, or anything telltale?" He looked wretched, his face pale and creased, his eyes dull and glazed. But still something wouldn't let me shake the suspicion he was the mastermind behind it all.

"Nothing."

"You're lying," he said.

"What do you care? You practically killed me yourself."

"Yeah, sorry about that." His eyes slid away.

"What *was* that?"

"Just drop the whole Jim thing, okay? He left, so let him stay gone."

"Okay, fine," I said, relenting. All along, I think I'd known what he could never say out loud—that Jim was dead to him ever since he'd taken off and left Charlie alone with their parents. But I'd cared less about what Charlie wanted and more about solving my greatest mystery yet.

"I wish they'd done it to me and not you."

I'd never heard him sound so full of feeling. Despite my pain and the fog of medication, my mood soared. He hadn't set those Teddy boys on me.

"As soon as you get out of here, we're going to find whoever did this and we're going to mess them up, slowly, massively." His hands curled around my metal bedrail, his pale knuckles threaded with red. The specks of green in his eyes seemed to spin. "They'll pass out squealing."

My heart beat against the bars of my ribcage. He was serious. I returned to the memory of him straddling me on the footpath and whaling on me, out of his mind with that certain hunger.

Charlie's ma was wrong. She and Archie had made at least one son in their likeness. Something inside me flipped over, crushed and smoking. I was always so caught up with everything I wanted to uncover and solve, I'd never thought about the things I was better off not knowing.

Kintsugi
Claire Hennessy

(for a good witch)

Gifted the metaphor of kintsugi,
I fuck up –

That gold filament on the mug
you gave me for cat-minding
sets off sparks in the microwave,
miniature lightning bolts in a box –
(release! cancel!)

– and on the one hand it feels like bullshit,
this sense that gold can be poured
into cracks and redeem the whole,
beautify it even,

but on the other hand, my darling –
I trust you like I trust no one else
to decipher my tarot cards,
to tell me the story I need to hear,
and isn't all of this
just another tale we tell

(and have I mentioned
that to me
you are worth your weight
in the stuff?)

The Words He Said
Elizabeth Baines

What she would always remember was the trucks in the distance toiling up the hill, as they sat in silence in the parked car, after he had said what he said. She had turned away, not wanting him to see the effect on her, and the landscape filled her view: the brown heaving moors they had intended to walk but wouldn't walk now, and on the horizon a line of heavy goods vehicles backing up on the steep incline, looking as if they'd never make it but would crawl to a stop.

It seemed a long moment. She didn't trust herself to speak. Her throat was wide with an ache of sorrow and shock.

Finally she turned back to him. 'No,' she said, by which she meant she understood, she agreed, her mouth moving like a crippled thing over the word, but the word, to her relief, sounding reasonably steady.

He put his head down. She couldn't see his eyes.

She would always afterwards think of his eyes: deep-set beneath his hooded brows, and often hidden by his habit of looking away with his head down, which when she first met him she took as shyness, and then as sadness and pain. But when he met your gaze his eyes were a shock of startling blue.

She felt now, as he stared at the steering wheel, that he was feeling shame as well as pain.

He should not be feeling shame, she thought. She should not be feeling shock. After all, at the start they had agreed: their lives were on different trajectories; they were each already committed to others.

*

The trouble was, right from the start she would feel that ache.

'We love trees,' he had said, the very first time he came to her house, looking out at the bay tree in her garden. She understood the accord he must have with the woman he had lived with all those years, the woman with whom he had raised children now grown, whatever problems there might be between them now. But that word *we* sliced like a saw. And in her mind an image reared up: the garden of the house it was tacitly agreed she would never go to, a lush aesthetic tangle of green, the kind of bohemian wildness that she herself longed for, cultivated by the two of them together. Her throat filled then with a balloon of pain.

She stared with him at the bay tree, black against a wintry sky, barber-cropped by her fastidious husband before he went to work for six months abroad, leaving her alone with a four-year-old child.

Though it was she who had tried to end it when her husband returned. She couldn't risk her marriage: the most important thing was the happiness of her child. In any case, they were moving away. Her husband came back to promotion and relocation a hundred miles off.

'So,' he said, her lover, the last time he came to the house, the time that was meant to be their last-ever meeting. Her stroked her wrist. He looked up, his eyes a washed blue. 'So now we must each go back to cultivating our gardens.'

She nodded, her throat cramping again.

A hundred miles off, over the mountains in the small parochial town she had moved to with her husband, she worked on putting the episode behind her. She cleaned the new house from top to bottom, getting steps and a bucket and washing even the walls, wiping away every trace of the previous owners, intent on wiping from her mind all longing for *him*. She emptied her final bucket and squeezed her cloth in the drain in the yard. She stepped back into the house purged ready for the new life with her husband and child.

It loomed around her, detergent-smelling and barren. And in that moment she knew that after all she couldn't stay, that what the affair had proved was that she simply wasn't happy, she would never be happy with her husband. She would have to leave. She would have to make a life of her own, on her own.

As she stood with this realisation, deep inside the house, in the shadowy hallway, the phone rang.

He came towards her, loose-legged, between their cars parked at the halfway place, high on the moors. All around, the land tipped in the sparkling day. A full reservoir was whipped by the wind and spilled over the dam in a glittering spray. His coat was flung up behind him. In the dazzling light she couldn't make out his face.

They sat in his car. They did not kiss. They did not even hold hands. They were sticking to their script: they expected nothing from each other, their lives were now on different tracks.

She was nervous of telling him about her decision, afraid he would think she was she was trying to trap him. When she did he said nothing, his mouth closed inside his beard. She quickly told him the rest: that she was looking at jobs and courses in the city nearest the town she had moved to, on the far side of the mountains from him.

He nodded, and she couldn't tell if he was sad or relieved.

And then he took her in his arms.

They went on meeting. They sat in moorland pubs, they trod the moor hand in hand, they lay in the heather. She didn't let herself think about what it meant.

The script changed. He said, catching her hand across a beer-smeared table: 'Don't go there. Come back to where you have contacts already. Your life as a single parent wouldn't be so hard. And I could help you look for somewhere to live.'

She didn't know what was in his mind. Was he really thinking of what was best for her, or did he want her there for himself? She didn't ask, she had to make what he wanted irrelevant. She couldn't help a twinge of hurt, though, that he'd help her create a life independent of him.

Still, she thought, in the days that followed: why put herself through the difficulty of arriving alone in a strange place with a small child – she quailed now at the thought of it – just to prove to him, and herself, that she was keeping her side of the bargain? She should be hard-headed and logical. She *would* be better in a place she knew and, after all, she could do with the kind of practical help he was offering.

She changed her mind. She'd go back, she'd make a life there, independent of him.

She ignored the fact that once that decision was made, something in her settled, and that as he gathered her in his arms she was flooded with relief.

She applied for a course back in the city she'd moved from, and was accepted. She began, with his help, to look for somewhere to live with her child.

And then came the day when he walked from his car with his head bent and the skin above his beard looking grey. She already knew, he had told her on the phone: the weekend before, his wife's parents had been killed in a car crash.

They sat in his car. They had parked in a dip. The moor reared ahead with the line of lorries on its crest.

He turned to her, the blue of his eyes wavering like water. 'I have to look after her.'

She cried, 'Of course!' though the muscle in her chest cringed. What was he saying? That they'd have to stop seeing each other?

He looked away. And then he said what he said: 'I can't leave her now.'

So, after all, he had thought of leaving his wife for her. And her shock and sorrow that now he couldn't told her what she had been denying all along: that all along she'd been hoping too that one day they would be together.

She swallowed her pain. She got back in her car, she drove away, back to the far side of the hills. She drove fast. Her heart made downwards spirals. She overtook all the trucks. Clouds ripped themselves ragged on the churning horizon.

She hit the plain on the other side. Her chest steadied. She calmed, and then hardened.

She had been a fool. So, he had after all entertained the possibility of being with her eventually. But now that it came to the crunch...

She knew now: if she went back she would not be able to resist him, they would still not be able to resist each other, but she'd be trapped in an impossible emotional situation, her life dictated by others, by the needs of his wife, by his need to consider his wife, a woman she didn't even know. She would never be free.

Next day she called and ended it.

She withdrew from the course. She didn't go back.

She told him not to contact her again.

She would think of him, though, in those years in the city on the far side of the mountains. He had been her catalyst, after all, propelling her into the almost impossible life of a single parent juggling work and childcare, the loneliness and lack of money. She had made her own choice, the whole point had been to make the choices of others irrelevant. Yet she couldn't help blaming him for her pain. After all, it was he, wasn't it, who had made contact after she moved away, after they had solemnly agreed not to do so, punctured her resolve with that ringing phone? He had drawn her back, encouraged and inflamed her feelings, her hope. But hadn't he just been keeping his options open? He had sent her signals he wasn't prepared to honour in the end.

She would remember his habit of looking away, out into the distance or down into his lap, as if drawing back into himself, and now she saw it as sign of self-protection. Selfishness, even; even deceit. And his eyes, those blue eyes suddenly revealed beneath those hooded brows: she now saw them as chips of ice.

*

Some fifteen years on, she was at a day conference when he walked into the hall.

His hair and beard were streaked with grey. He looked less upright, his shoulders slightly stooped, but he still had that loose-legged way of walking.

Her heart flipped over. But the shock was of course just an echo of the past: by the time they spoke she was calm, and as they commented on the food, finding themselves side by side at the buffet, she began to feel a certain charitable superiority.

At the end of the day they were both going for trains. She was happy to take the short walk with him to the station, and to sit with him in the station wine bar as they waited. She had nothing against him now, after all. After all, she now shared her life with another man – a life without passion, perhaps, but where had passion ever got her?

'How's your wife?' she asked. She felt happy to be free to ask it, in a way she had never been, had never allowed herself to be, when they were involved.

For one second he looked as if the question surprised him. And then: 'I'm no longer married. I split up with my wife.'

Something like loss swilled in her chest.

He said, 'It wasn't working out. You know that, of course.'

'But you said you would never leave her!'

The decision she had made on the strength of those words, the lonely life she'd gone on to lead, and it seemed he hadn't even meant them!

The tumult in her chest curdled to resentment. Still keeping his options open, regardless of what that did to her!

He said: 'I never said that!'

She felt angry now. All the pain those words had caused her, and now he'd deny he ever even said them?

She said evenly, controlling her anger: 'I remember your words precisely. That last time we met, when we were sitting in the car: you said, *I couldn't leave her now.*'

He started. He looked away, absorbing what she'd said. He turned to her slowly. 'I *was* about to leave her. I was about to talk to her that very weekend. And then we got the phone call about her parents. I meant I couldn't do it *then*, at that particular point, when she was in shock and grieving. I didn't mean I wouldn't leave her *ever.*'

His eyes were wide with the revelation seizing them both: turquoise blue, the colour of warm lapping seas.

Three Poems
Glyn Edwards

There's no king of Bardsey Island anymore but there were regents of sorts a hundred years ago and their dynasties were lobster pots, ruined chapels and island exodus.

In the museum display there are three monochromes of the island's lineage: two kings, that seem dragged by winds in their photographs, are slumped gaunt as gallows below their crowns. Then there is one body that wears the home-made coronet the way the sea wears light. The stark sky behind him could be kindled by storm or summer, and the boats on the beach may be shivering in cold sand or warm still from the sea - so much of this picture is ambiguous - but the man's pride is as clear as his crown and all the saturated greys grow as gold as fish scales.

The pictures and the crown seem so familiar though I can recall little of the rest of the displays. The museum felt bigger somehow, the city smaller. Perhaps the coach driver stopped here for his lunch after a visit to the slate mines, or you guided the class this way when a trip to the pier was interrupted by rain. I remember you telling the group we must discover an artefact each so we could share what we'd found on the bus back to school, but that journey is a fogged window now. I walk about the other exhibits and try to recall other people's treasures. I drink coffee in the quiet cafe, and, before I leave, I return to the display.

What I found during your lessons, I pressed to myself. Even then I knew. I would have worn you that way if you had let me. I would have taken the moods your wife seemed to suffer like a heavy sky, taken the crude angles you made of your hands and your lips and I would have worn you weightlessly.

I would have worn you like this broken king wore his tin crown.

Cofiwch Dryweryn

He swears he can't remember it swollen so high,
so we balance at his wet window on tall stools
like chess pieces, calculating the river's rise
and counting down to when its banks will break. All rules
revised, we start to drum and pound upon the glass:
ten, nine, eight, seven, six, five, four, three, hysterically
we chant, daring the day to
deny our trespass,
but the fields and farms we've forged into our grid city
withstand. We descend from our nests to
the classroom,
stills of subdued Treweryn are on the board now:
its graveyards underwater, a church spire that is
lifting its head at low tide, families dredged from their homes
as water urges in at the speed of life. *How
are we elevated by the sinking of villages?*

The Moon as a Drone

You are walking home across that bridge,
the rods banging against your wet legs.
You stop to find the places down here
that you'd fished all day and one of you says
it's those you lose that you most remember
or something like that.
One of you points out
how the tree crowns are wary of each other
on the river islands below, all mustard yellow,
before shy leaves drop. You're trading dialects
skerries aits cays islets ayots keys holms.
and clouds course the water.
You are dropping something - paper, lint –
and thinking about the men roped together
that climbed the rail last week and fell,
hitting the pier structure or the rocks below.
Your silence is falling from that same height,
and washing up at my feet.
Along the riverbank
two women are taking turns to pilot their drone –
a homing pigeon writing messages on the wing.
Its bird's eye will view swans as single feathers,
waders as floating seed and distance will grind
a rocky shore to fine sand.
Like the spores below fern fronds
a lecturer will say when the film is viewed
or yeast cells growing in petri-dishes:
All concentration is drawn to the islands
instead of the river's swell. Even the moon
is distracted by itself in water.
I approach the undertow
where the water eddies before the bridge

But, waist high in the anonymous dark, I stop,
look down: there are so many stars carried
upon the river's surface it seems like the sky
is breaking. I slip the stones from my pockets.

Harbour of Grace
Catherine McNamara

Frances catches up with a woman in a suit on a Sydney footpath. Adrienne is now a barrister who lives with a teenage son in a flat on Rushcutters Bay. Frances knows she's had death threats; that she put a man behind bars who threw his girlfriend over a high-rise balcony. The woman on the footpath turns around, halts. She recognises Frances. Years back, on a high school lawn in a faded grey tunic, Adrienne had bandy legs and a monkey jaw full of teeth. Even then she was a leader, she bore others to their fates.

There are no greetings. Adrienne has ignored three emails Frances sent from the other side of the world.

'She won't see you. She's doesn't want anyone to see her.' Adrienne turns and marches on. She murmurs a sentence which includes the word *Stop*.

Frances thinks her frame looks smaller than when they were young, but her *regard* is just as ballsy. Now that she has been away Frances has learnt languages, so words like that come to her before anything in English can cross her brain. She is certain Adrienne is wearing lenses to highlight the green flecks in her eyes, and that her lovers have been tall, wide-shouldered men – swimming types – whose bodies have provided warm concaves. She is sure there will be a large dog in her apartment, a walker who passes twice a day.

Frances has resorted to stopping Adrienne in the street because she knows Adrienne has the will to ignore her forever. All she wants is news of Adrienne's younger sister Erin, who has disappeared into the suburbs, or is submerged in some hamlet along the coast. Erin had been Frances' double for the whole arc of youth, their souls or what they knew of them had been sewn together, their minds a limpid collective. It was Frances who had obeyed the restless twinge that would see her married and settled in Paris, while Erin stayed behind here, marrying a Sydneysider soon after.

Sixteen years ago, in fusty Darlinghurst which lies not far to the east, these two couples became acquainted for the first time. Frances – eight months' pregnant – had flown out from Paris with her French husband. She watched broad, burly Alain shake hands with Erin and Toby at their terrace door onto the street. Erin's husband – Toby – was far more graceful and splendid than the photos showed, leaning into Frances' face so she smelt his pale hair and retracted slightly. Inside, Alain was given a glass for his can of beer and Toby shook out peanuts into a bowl, while in the kitchenette the women embraced, sniffling and tracing cheeks and laughing. Erin's hands travelled endlessly over Frances' swollen belly. This was the baby conceived on holidays in Sicily, that she had brought home to deliver.

But later there'd been a turning point, a dark discourse. Toby was an anti-abortion campaigner and it soon rattled through his talk. He took pamphlets from a drawer, telling them about a demonstration they'd been to – a huge rally downtown – his voice hardening as he said abortion was *illegal*, it was *murderous*.

There'd been no reason to but Frances had felt charged with some sort of parallel crime. Could she have aborted this child, had she wished? Of course she could have, and would have if she and Alain had decided that way. She had waited for Toby to ease up or make amends, or for Erin's forehead to crinkle and her eyes to start rolling. But *no*, Erin stared at her new husband with a face Frances had never seen that was softened, afflicted. Toby continued ranting about burning salt solutions that peeled away the baby's skin, of scraping tools and dismemberment.

Frances watched Erin's face, as it sank in that her best friend had married a man she would only ever find repellent. Toby was a plumber and after a couple of beers he started talking about *lebbos* and *chinks*. He said he'd worked in poofters' houses in the Eastern Suburbs, where he once found three men at it in a bed. This had made Erin laugh and laugh into her cupped hand and Frances remembered thinking she looked like a ferret.

*

The day after Frances spoke to Adrienne she goes to lunch with Lucas, an old university friend. She tells Lucas that she stopped Adrienne in Phillip Street, up by the courts, where she knew she would be going back to work after lunch. She says that Adrienne stormed off without telling her where Erin was living.

Lucas' eyebrows lift. They are tangled middle-aged men's eyebrows that, because he has a robust marriage, he doesn't have to trim. Lucas has two daughters who are the same age as Frances' girls, and he knows she has lost custody after a battle that ended last month. He's concerned, he knows he's still allowed to tell her that. She can see he's uncertain what to say next: whether to blame Alain for his affair, or ask her how the hell she let the courts steal her kids away. Frances wouldn't have had an answer. Just that her behaviour had gone crazy for a while, and she had been shown up as unfit by Alain's lawyers. She *had* been unfit. She'd spent a month – it was a condition after the incident in the street – at a clinic along the banks of the Seine. But she doesn't tell Lucas about this. While she was at the clinic the person she thought of most was her childhood friend Erin, recalling their conversations under the telegraph pole halfway between their two homes, or the night when Toby's anti-abortion rant should have made Frances shake Erin down on the spot; or the way she wrote to Erin so rigidly two years after that, as her toddler staggered on Alain's Persian rugs, announcing their friendship had to end because she found Toby's views offensive. Months after the letter had been sent Lucas who was more elastic told Frances that Erin had found out she was infertile (he used the word 'sterile') and was living down the coast, with or without Toby he didn't know.

Frances had never contacted her again. She let Erin live on in some shabby fibro town. Her girls grew older. It wasn't until that month at the clinic – her marriage concluded – that her mind was unfastened and the emblems of her life resurfaced. Then Erin had come back to her, the smell of Erin's skin, the streetlight on her fair hair and cheeks, her half-lit eyes and the wafting summer wind in the dark; and Frances realised the eager permeation of their sisterhood still resided in her body.

Back at home in Paris, with Alain gone and the custody case ahead, she wrote to Lucas asking him to look up Erin again, desperate to contact her. But Erin had burrowed down somewhere and he didn't have any luck. Lucas said Erin now had a history of mental illness between her escape to the south coast and when he had last heard of her. There had been IVF treatment, joblessness, a failed attempt to adopt an Indonesian child; her divorce from Toby who had fathered numerous kids, and someone had said she was living on welfare out of Sydney.

Lucas' eyebrows settle again and he's getting ready to ask Frances about Erin's big sister Adrienne, whom he knew at university and whom he has certainly read about in the newspapers. He affords Adrienne respect because she is a fine-looking woman in a world of jowls and suits, who puts killers and rapists behind bars. Straight out of uni Lucas married Sarah, a quiet athletic blonde who coaches netball.

'So you saw Adrienne?' he asks. 'How was she? How did she look?'

Frances tells Lucas that Adrienne is smaller than she remembered, but she still packs a punch. Curvy and compact with wavy russet hair. Her face has set wider, as some women's do, but she has the same exploratory eyes and diffidence, heightened by all those years in court. Frances, wondering what effect this might have upon Lucas – and how he might now classify herself – adds that Adrienne looked horny, unmated.

He lets out a laugh she recalls from way back. She reckons she's given him enough, something to bring back to his mates at the office, or for Sarah listening to him from the kitchen, her own radar set off. Frances asks him if he's heard any news about Erin.

Lucas says, 'I ran into her brother in a pub in Mosman. They don't want to talk about her. The only thing he said was that Erin is ashamed. Doesn't want anyone to see her. He said she's up in the Blue Mountains living on junk food. She's lost half her teeth and has matted hair down to her waist.'

He looks at her. 'That prick she married. That Toby guy. He ruined her. Just leave it, Frances. It's not your business anymore.'

So many years ago they had been a dancing trio at university,

Lucas and Erin and Frances. But Frances could never decide whether she wanted to be Lucas' girlfriend or not. Neither could Erin. He was goofy and ape-ish around them, and sex never happened. They were just kids studying for exams and backpacking in Asia and working the pubs, but then Lucas had swum up to the frontline of his gender and worked in city offices and become employable, where Erin and Frances had let love steer their lives. Decades on he could afford to be overweight, double the slim figure he used to be, with tangled eyebrows. His daughters were in private schools and they lived in a lavish house on stilts at Balmoral, overlooking the beach. And here was Frances whose mother had slipped two hundred dollars into her purse this morning.

Lucas has ordered a large Coke with his food. Says he has to stay awake at work. He is designing what he explains is a giant hinge for a naval vessel stationed in the harbour. It's inconceivable to her. Lucas is part of the world of men that wheels ahead the nation, while Frances could sit in a corner relishing a novel and no one would expect any more of her.

'Why don't you just order a coffee?' Frances says.

He shakes his head. 'Not into that stuff. Sarah won't let me near it.'

*

This time, Frances has flown back to Sydney without Alain or her daughters so she is sleeping in her old bedroom, across the hall from where her mother listens to the radio to fall asleep. After midnight, Frances closes the door and sits at her desk, under the same fluorescent study lamp that buzzed over her homework when she was a kid. She is tussling with her age on a dating site, ticking boxes on her profile. Very quickly – it's like entering a heated pool – she starts chatting with guys. There is one who is a widower, so she thinks that's safely removed from subterfuge. She ends up chatting with him into the dawn.

On Friday night they arrange to meet at a noisy inner-west pub. Frances pushes open a door, wearing espadrilles and a cotton sundress. Her date is parked at the bar looking out for her.

Immediately, she searches for vestiges of wife-death on his shoulders or an aura of mourning. But there is nothing, nothing unsteady. So far. In looks, there is a reasonable equality, and this soothes Frances. Rob is a children's entertainer which means a clown. She knows he works in hospitals and schools (initially he said he was a 'performer') and after one beer it's her turn to supply a less reticent portrait of herself. She's already told him she's been living in Paris for two decades, that she's just divorced. There was a custody battle which was lost. She reads his face as she half-shouts in the deafening pub, sometimes directly into the curves of his ear. She realises she sounds jostled, unbridled, *vécue*. She doesn't like talking about Europe, she wants to hear about Sydney, about local politics, about the places where he works, the sick kids, the satisfaction; this way he becomes human to her. When the pub closes Frances follows the children's entertainer down an Annandale street, tripping up gutters, pushing past him into his front room where she gloriously pulls off her cotton dress and brings all the aching out of her. They lie on his couch – she tells him she doesn't do bedrooms, seeing him spring up – and for a long while she is lost in the flux of their bodies, until a cry of hers cracks open her mind and she sees Alain at work in Paris in the wake of time behind them – there's ten hours' difference now – and Alain's lover on a moped downstairs, waiting for him to climb on and press against her back.

The woman is so ordinary-looking in her white helmet and navy pants, her flat shoes planted on the road.

Frances' eyes water. She is in both places and the fucking hurts now. He vaults over her and all she can see is Alain's denuded lover and her ex-husband's convulsed clutching.

As he comes Frances asks him to slap her and his face goes awry.

He pulls off and she hoists up sitting, walks naked down the hall to the bathroom, pisses wretchedly. Ten minutes later Frances is apologising and explaining she is clueless as to where that came from, though she knows he can tell she's asked for it before. The guy – Rob – touches her cheek, says he was shocked but might have done it if he'd known her better. It's a bold, eye-to-eye conversation between adults; she realises it's the apex of their intimacy. They hug each other but the words that come afterwards feel soundless, spoken underwater. They say, *Sure, that was great. Let's meet again.* He tastes of dry mouth and calls her a cab.

*

Frances drives her mother's car across the Bridge and all the way to Camp Cove, a harbour beach where she once frolicked with Alain in the shallows, a mythical place she needs to revisit. Today, she has a hangover from drinking with a neighbour last night. Will has remained in their street for most of his adult life, looking after his father now that his mother has died. He is nerdy, unchanged from high school. Walking home, Frances had parted the shrubs between their two houses and stared into the burnt brown sky, reminded that the spirit of this continent had been mutilated and broken, and its inhabitants like Will had been relieved of these crimes. Her ex-husband Alain had called it a pop culture, marvelling at barefoot white guys in supermarkets and enclaves of pumped-up lawfulness, the parrots carking in the trees. Alain said Frances would have gone mad here. Then, she had felt the gratitude of recognition, for it had seemed built into her narrative that she would be drawn away by some adoring ally, whom she had found. But now this spurning of her culture translates into a feeling of being rectified, or salvaged.

The beach is a long way past the city centre just short of South Head, one of three bastions enclosing the blue belly of the harbour from the beating wall of the Pacific. Frances parks in front of a smoky weatherboard house behind a wooden fence, an arpeggio of jasmine releasing scent. These are million-dollar properties, no longer the workers' cottages whose occupants trudged uphill from the poor man's ferry stop. Frances looks askance through the open front door, down the hallway to where a woman lies on a daybed at the other end of the house, engraved by light. She feels a slow translucent envy and takes her time gathering her things, saving this motif for later.

On the beach she watches people, travellers and rich folk from the Eastern Suburbs. She listens to a pair of young Spanish women with tawny saturated bodies, ankles in green water. She understands their small talk about the cities they have left behind. Next to Frances a sunburnt gay guy is doing a crossword, briefs pushed into his arse crack, buttocks hairy and full.

She strips down and stretches out on her towel. She lights a cigarette, wondering if it's okay to smoke in this law-abiding town, or whether she will be pulled up if she goes topless or naked. Frances is coming from two decades of Mediterranean summers and loves to be nude on the sand, nude in water. Her boobs are dying to be sun-swept. She unties her top, pushes her bikini bottom down until it just screens her labia. The smoke in her lungs and sun coursing on her skin make her feel more vital than she has in months. This is the first time in four years that she has been back home. The first time since she was childless that she has been here by herself. Her body feels unmoored, dangling. She won't see her daughters for any length of time until the European summer when they finish school, and she is not sure if she misses them. Surely she does, she must. She is already wondering if parenthood is as tapering and finite as childhood. She no longer feels selfless. Frances looks at the concave between her hips – like French women she has never thickened there – but instead of pregnancy she remembers being a teenager, gleaming baby oil on her belly and thighs, beach towels on prickly lawns, her best friend Erin's body plumper than hers, always whiter, her diets. Weirdly, she never saw Erin naked. Never. Not in all those years of fitness camps and swimming carnivals and borrowed clothes and sleepovers. There was something puritan in all of their families, especially their mothers who were virgins when they married, who guarded their pallor and their violet midriffs.

*

She writes another email to Adrienne. A week has passed since the episode in Phillip Street near the courts. The email begins politely. Frances apologises for chasing after her in the street, but says she would like to take this chance to explain. After a few lines she pauses. Realises she still feels inferior to Adrienne, who will always be a few years ahead of her in high school. She starts up again, feels clumsy to be describing the motion of her life with labels like divorce and custody. She recklessly introduces Alain's name, his betrayal and her month at the clinic (she is indecisive here because this marks her as a freak). Finally, at her most earnest, she plunges. Frances writes that she is at a junction in her life and she wants to reconnect with Erin, whatever Erin has been through, but with respect for what might suit Erin, as she knows it's been hard. She tells Adrienne she doesn't think this is unreasonable.

Please. Please tell me where she is.

Then she thanks her, glances over the torrent above, wishes her well and presses 'send'.

Adrienne emails back within the minute saying she will file a harassment claim if Frances writes again or comes within fifty metres of her on the street.

*

She carries a chilled wine bottle onto the back veranda when her mother goes to bed. She pours herself a fraction of a glass, not the full bowl they serve in bars here, and sits on a rattan chair at the table. Her belly is itchy. It's sea lice from the harbour. She brings her laptop outside, knows she won't be seeing Rob-the-children's-entertainer again. That evening, her history had been written all over her, within and without. Frances goes online to check if he's logged on, and of course he is. Instantly she feels grumpy and callous.

It's not too late so she calls Lucas. She wants to tell him she's decided she is going to look for Erin, that she's going to drive up to the Blue Mountains where her brother said she was living. If that doesn't work she'll drive down the south coast. Someone will have heard of her. She doesn't care about Adrienne's legal threats. Frances wants to tell Lucas she can't stand it any longer, she *has* to see Erin before she leaves Sydney in less than a month. Lucas doesn't answer his cell phone and he hasn't given her his house number. She emails him, but deletes the words she sees streaming down the page. Lucas found an excuse not to have lunch with her last week. Frances suspects his wife Sarah has laid down new laws.

Why had she and Erin married so early when there was absolutely no need? How to explain this premature consecration to equally juvenile men, when these should have been carnal, bondless years? In the suburbs, they had grown up knowing they were cringing fictions, that life and art and history occurred beyond their continent, far away from their hungry talks in the dark. This was what they had ceaselessly spoken about – saving money and travelling and finding real boyfriends and *getting out of here* – which is why it hurt when Erin, eight months into Frances' trip to Europe, said she would no longer be joining Frances in London. She said she'd met this guy and it was serious; she said she loved him! Eventually it came out that he was a local plumber.

Frances had felt shocked. So overruled, so unredeemed for her.

She recalls the vile evening she and Alain had met tall, militant Toby. Frances remembers reading an anti-abortion leaflet, a hand resting on her belly where her daughter swam in her salty cocoon; Alain's perplexed comments on the drive home. After Sophie's birth, letters between Frances and Erin had paused, but when they resumed neither of them spoke of the battle cries voiced that night. Frances had never asked Erin what she was doing with a bigot and racist. She wrote aromatic vignettes about her child and her life in Paris. Erin replied with Sydney talk and her hopes of being pregnant by the following summer.

Two years later there had been another trip to Sydney, yet it wasn't until they were days away from their flight back to Paris that Frances arranged to meet Erin. She'd put it off, reluctant to see her. She remembers leaving Sophie and Alain in a park. Driving west along Parramatta Road where the city was angrier, more metallic and blistering, out to the shopping mall where Erin now worked. She remembers Erin throwing off her apron behind the counter, and being gathered within her broad yellowy arms that smelt of yeast and sugar.

You look different! God, you're beaming! They'd found a bench in the arcade, between two old Lebanese men like bookends, and hugged. Erin wanted to hear all of Sophie's milestones. She swore she was coming to Europe to see them one day, but right now she and Toby were living in a place at Randwick and Toby was out of work. Erin said he'd had a throat infection, he was tired of Sydney and wanted to move down the south coast. She rambled on about her sister Adrienne having a spoilt child with another lawyer and more money in the bank than good sense.

Frances looked at her flushed cheeks and saw there were gaps where she took breaths, little dips or slurs, as though this were a reprieve and it had to be milked. She sensed it would have caused pain so she didn't tell Erin she was four months gone with her second child – that was what the beaming was about. She wanted to put her hand on Erin's arm and say, *What are you doing here? Get away from this. From him.* But she didn't. She looked at her raw open pores and her eyebrows plucked so thin, and saw the real Erin standing behind them, stark and beaten. She was relieved when Erin jumped as she checked her watch and moaned that there was no time to walk her to the escalator. Frances couldn't wait to get away from her yeasty smell.

Before the year's end, by which time Frances' belly rolled with feisty Eveline and their Parisian life had resumed comfortably, Toby was caught up in a gang bashing in the rough outer western suburbs of Sydney. A Vietnamese guy was hit with a pipe and his skull fractured, Lucas wrote to her. Toby was charged but got off on a good behaviour bond as it was his first offence. Frances never asked him if Adrienne had helped him out in court, and Lucas left it open.

That was the day Frances sat down at her desk in Paris and composed the short, toneless letter to Erin that called their friendship off.

*

A few nights later Frances cancels her dating profile and begins to look at two-bedroom apartments in quartiers bordering her old neighbourhood in Paris. There will be no more love. Not the love she had felt for Alain. There will never again be the time for two unmarked adults to be thrown together, and in middle age to look back over the frieze of their common history. Her life lies squandered at her feet, a skinned carcass from the woods, neck snapped and paws threaded with wire. He had not protected her as promised. In bed her muscles clench and she feels the extrication of her love taking place, across her limbs and through her organs; she awakes shivering with sunburn and this feels solar. Her sex rages and she wishes she had deceived him all the times she could have, when she had not.

In the daytime she heads back to Camp Cove beach. She feels a pull towards this place. It is snobby in the way that only Sydney can be. There are no voluptuous structures or regal heritage, just the cloth of the trespassed land, and these uncontrived outposts that trill with beauty. Only in Sydney can a cottage where children with typhoid or diphtheria were shovelled down close to the sandstone, become a millionaire's palace made of wood. Today Frances has decided that the drive was too far and she is sitting on the deck of the Watsons Bay ferry. Alain calls her, his voice leaning over time into the day he is yet to live. With those first syllables she knows he is visualising the young couple they once were wandering the sub-tropical city, but she also knows that these recollections are being reframed for the woman he now loves, who awaits fresh minutiae from his past.

When she resists the invasion of this phone call – they had agreed – Alain protests that it was necessary. *C'était absolument nécessaire, Frances, cette fois-ci.* One of their daughters has fallen from her moped onto the road, struck by a car door opening. Eveline's cheekbone is bruised and there is a hairline fracture, the bruising has travelled down one side of her face.

After the call Frances moves under the canopy where she weeps.

Probably, there was a final time they had coupled but it hasn't been flagged in her mind. Her desire for him had grown stringent and debased. If he'd have told her to get on her knees or pleasure another man in front of him, she would have. For the last months this possibility changed the texture of their interactions, but not their course. There is always a no man's land – ventured into, pitted – between the annihilation of one couple and the manifestation of the next. Hearing Alain's voice, she remembers this monstrous territory and these moments dashed against the rocks, how a cavernous oblivion had been made available to her but at the back of his eyes she would see a panel of guilt, and he would go off naked to retrieve his phone. Frances knew that even more mournful texts were exchanged afterwards, she had read them.

There was the incident in the street with one of her daughters present, white-faced. Frances had been certain it was Alain's lover on the moped parked there, waiting for him under the apartment; she had grown so deranged as the weeks advanced. Frances had lunged at this innocent woman, almost knocked her onto the road. She had been arrested. In court her mental health had been shown as torn up, explosive. She paid a fine and had been obliged to consign herself to the clinic. That is when she was told she would possibly lose custody of the girls.

She will never tell Lucas any of this. Only Erin, should she find her. She knows she has come to Sydney to see Erin, to stand in front of Erin and speak of this.

Frances arrives at the beach and sits down, crosses her legs on the sand. She rolls a cigarette. She undresses, throwing aside her bikini top and exhaling, tanned now. She tries to imagine Erin's fruitless undulating body: the skin stretched and marbled, the acne mounds in her cheeks and the muttering that will come from her as she sits in a shady garden, hand in a packet of sweets. There will be cicadas drilling the air and currawongs warbling, steely arrowheads dropping down from the trees. Perhaps Adrienne will be threatening on the phone already, or striding out of a white car in a printed dress.

Frances will hear Erin's unfazed laughter.

They say that the Nenet population wash but once a year; they wear reindeer skin coats and hoods lined with the fur of blue foxes. These warm migrating people emit no body odour and know less of the stars than the northbound deer guiding them. Every clan has a sacred reindeer which must not be slaughtered until it can neither stand or walk.

On Seeing His Shoes
Niamh MacCabe

On Seeing His Shoes

She reads her son like a dog-eared book
Her hands running blind over ribs
Three rent, the bone edges jutting
Clear through his pearled casing

She cups his head, lifting skull as chalice
From the stainless steel table
His body laid out, laid out as if
As if this is, this is yet worth seeing

Her fingers tip his frayed eyelids
Tip the tags around his broken neck
Tip the breastbone, split like a tattered stem
Tip the signet ring sunk into his skin

And the wedding shoes she bought for him last year
Patent black leather with silver-tipped laces
A scrawled HELP! ME! still legible on the soles
Why do these spent things remain flawless?

After Words
John Lavin

This fifth anniversary issue arrives a little later than planned and I would like to begin by thanking our contributors and readers for their patience during this most difficult of years. It is very much appreciated.

2020. Our fifth anniversary year. Ah yes, *2020*. A 'widening gyre', falconer-no-longer-in-touch-with-the-falcon-kind-of-affair if ever there was one. A literal *plague year* for the love of God. If the title of this issue appears to allude to one of Bowie's more apocalyptic tracks then, yes, *of course*: it most certainly does. Who knows where we will be in another five years? Because the world of Bowie's 'Five Years'; with its certainty of doom, with its weeping newscasters and frenzied attacks on children; appears to be more or less here already. Perhaps, God willing, in another five years' time we will all be at a conventional literary launch, drinking terrible wine and celebrating ten years of this publication. In the meantime, one lyric from the opening track on *Ziggy Stardust* can't help but resonate with me – even more so than the one about the earth dying – and I dare say it may resonate with you too, dear readers: *'My brain hurts a lot'*.

*

2020 began ordinarily enough. True, my partner and I had recently become first time parents and for us, at least, there was nothing ordinary about that – nevertheless day-to-day-life carried on in its usual manner. True, we were newly governed by one of the central villains of Fintan O'Toole's incisive and brilliant, *Heroic Failure: Brexit and The Politics of Pain*; a man that had infamously eaten his wife's round of NHS toast after she had given birth to their child. (Having newly become a father myself, I was aware of just how egregious such an act actually was.) And yes, America appeared to be entering some kind of deadly Fall of the Roman Empire meets *Dr Strangelove* endgame; but at least I could still take Aldous, our son, to meet his Gran at the now defunct Cardiff Carluccio's and down a sneaky Negroni or two, while she sang old Irish nursery rhymes to him. True, there were whispers of a new SARS-like virus but we didn't worry about that because it would only affect Asia, and maybe mainland Europe too – but never, no definitely *not* the UK.

For us, it all changed in the final week of February. And it all changed especially suddenly. My father, who had been living with dementia for close on ten years, (an agonising period during which nothing had *ever* happened suddenly but only slowly and inexorably), had acquired a cough and a fever and said that he felt like he was going to die. I wasn't worried at first as Dad had presented many of his ailments in recent years in a similarly dramatic fashion. But my mother thought it was different this time and when I arrived at my parent's house it was immediately obvious that he wasn't well. His cough was alarmingly loud but at the same time terribly hoarse and clearly in need of a break. However, the cough, as they say, was *persistent*. It never let up. It was a cold February night and Dad was given oxygen before being strapped onto a stretcher and carried out to an ambulance which remained steadfastly parked outside my parents' house for two hours, while the local hospitals argued over who would take him in (i.e. neither had room for him.) When we finally reached the A&E at Llandough Hospital we were told that there had been an error and that it was actually the Heath we would need to go to.

This time we actually waited in late night A&E for a while, until the increasingly sheepish ambulance crew came back and informed us that there had been another mistake and we would need to go back to Llandough. By this time it was midnight and the jolting journey in the by now overly familiar ambulance was painfully cold for both of my parents. Once back at Llandough, the argument between the two hospitals and the ambulance crew appeared to continue, while we waited in a corridor with my father still strapped onto a stretcher, the aggression that sometimes came with his condition beginning to bubble to the surface.

It may be a cliché to say that nothing can ever really prepare you for pivotal life events but it is certainly true. The inimitable qualities of our lives far outweigh the universality of events. Nothing had prepared me for the ordeal that my partner would have to go through in order to bring our lovely son into the world, just six months previously, and nothing could have prepared me for the shadow-long corridor that constituted the short stay ward that my father finally found himself on at two-thirty in the morning. A young doctor, whose bearded, easy-going face took on a slightly nightmarish appearance in the torchlight, enquired breezily whether we would like my father to be resuscitated if the circumstances arose. '*Of course*', I said, assuming that this was obvious but the doctor's perplexed expression told another story and the following day we were informed that it was not in fact within our power to decide this.

My father was moved to a geriatric respiratory ward unused to dealing with dementia cases and seven unmoored days and nights were to follow, listening to the elderly men around us wheeze and gasp for air. Late at night, I would walk down the deserted corridors to use the loo or the instant coffee machine and marvel at how eerie and devoid of comfort the building seemed once the majority of the staff had gone home. If a building retains something of all that has happened within its walls then a hospital must retain something of the pain and death that has haunted its structure. The low volume 90s chart music emanating from the deserted hospital radio booth near the coffee machine added a kind of budget horror effect, like an opening scene in some ill-advised Welsh remake of *The Shining*.

On the seventh night, or the eighth morning, my father died. It was still early in March and my mother and I were lucky in that sense, as we were able to be with him. We were both on either side of the bed, holding his hand. 'Don't leave us. We need you,' I said to Dad and he gripped my hand with what felt like his usual strength, even as his body began to wind down, the morphine that he had just been given easing the passage of his soul. He was beyond words by that point but he could still feel our nearness. We were in a place *after* words, and for a few moments, it felt like we were all three of us there, in a space between worlds, neither part of one thing nor another.

After*wards*, I couldn't really function. I couldn't question the nurses, I couldn't properly comfort my mother. No, I simply couldn't function. I was in a place beyond words where there is no comfort.

*

But in time words return and words not only have the power to give us comfort but the power to give us strength and empathy and of course, *pleasure*. It was with all of these factors in mind but perhaps primarily with pleasure, that I began putting this anniversary issue together what seems like a lifetime ago now: *at the beginning of the year*. I had the desire to create an abundant trove of short stories, poems and criticism that readers will come back to again and again for many years. Indeed, more than any other issue

314

of The Lonely Crowd to date, this really is a book and not a magazine. It is, I believe, a collection of uniform excellence, and one which, hopefully shows the distance we have travelled in five years; from a fledgling publication with inevitable highs and lows, to a publication where every piece of work has within it the power to inform and astound. When I read back the pieces in this issue now, I do find that I am by turns offered comfort, strength, empathy and above all else, pleasure. The pleasure of excellence, yes. But also the pleasure of being in the company of another person's mind, working at full tilt to convey something important to me and to you; to the reader.

I had originally imagined that this piece would be an introduction in which I talked about my initial vision for this publication five years ago. About how I had wanted to foster a home for the short story in Wales. About how I wanted the magazine to promote new Welsh writing but always be international in its reach. And so on and so forth. But this year has not really been like that. I have had other priorities. And it has made me realise that my vision for this magazine has primarily always been for it to give pleasure. For it to be an abundance of riches. I do hope that you have found that to be the case in this anniversary issue.

About the Authors

Craig Austin is a London- based writer and arts critic, and is an Associate Editor at Wales Arts Review, as well as a Director of Literature Wales. He cites his primary influences as the 84/85 Miners' Strike and Roxy Music.

Elizabeth Baines' new novel, *Astral Travel*, is published by Salt. Her short stories have been published widely, and two collections, *Balancing on the Edge of the World* and *Used to Be*, are available from Salt along with two other novels, *The Birth Machine* and *Too Many Magpies.*

Cath Barton is an English writer who lives in South Wales. She won the New Welsh Writing AmeriCymru Prize for the Novella 2017 for *The Plankton Collector*, now published by New Welsh Review under their Rarebyte imprint. Her second novella, *In the Sweep of the Bay*, will be published in November 2020 by Louise Walters Books.

M. W. Bewick grew up on the edge of the Lake District and now lives in rural Essex. His second collection of poetry, *Pomes Flixus*, is out now. His poems have appeared in journals including *Under the Radar, The Mechanics' Institute Review, Envoi*, and *The Stinging Fly*, as well as anthologies including *The Cottongrass Appreciation Society* (Maytree Press) and *Tempest* (Patrician Press). He is co-founder and editor at independent publisher and art project Dunlin Press. *The Orphaned Spaces*, a collaboration with his wife, the artist Ella Johnston, was published in 2018.

Mark Blayney won the Somerset Maugham Award for *Two kinds of silence*. His third story collection *Doppelgangers* and poetry *Loud music* *makes you drive faster* are available from Parthian. He was an inaugural Hay Festival Writer at Work, won a Wales Media Award for his journalism and has been longlisted for the National Poetry Competition. He lives in Cardiff.

Justine Bothwick grew up in Kent and Hampshire, and studied in London. She is a graduate of the Manchester Writing School's Creative Writing MA programme and has short stories published in Fictive Dream, Virtual Zine, Confingo Magazine, and forthcoming with Nightjar Press. Her work was highly commended in the Bath Short Story Award 2020. Her debut novel – *In the Mirror, a Peacock Danced* – will be published with Agora Books in 2021. She lives and teaches in Rome, Italy.

Sue Burge is a freelance creative writing and film studies tutor based in North Norfolk. Her first collection *In the Kingdom of Shadows (Live Canon)* and debut pamphlet *Lumière (Hedgehog Poetry Press)* were published in 2018 and her second pamphlet, *The Saltwater Diaries (Hedgehog Poetry Press)*, in September 2020.

Hisham Bustani is an award-winning Jordanian author of five collections of short fiction and poetry. Hisham's fiction and poetry have been translated into many languages, with English-language translations appearing in prestigious journals, including The Kenyon Review, Black Warrior Review, The Poetry Review, Modern Poetry in Translation, World Literature Today, and The Los Angeles Review of Books Quarterly. His fiction has been collected in The Best Asian Short Stories, The Ordinary Chaos of Being Human: Tales from Many Muslim Worlds, The Radiance of the Short Story: Fiction From Around the Globe, among other anthologies. In 2013, the U.K.-based cultural webzine The Culture Trip listed him as one of Jordan's top six contemporary writers. His book The Perception of Meaning (Syracuse University Press, 2015) won the University of Arkansas Arabic Translation Award. Hisham is the Arabic fiction editor of the Amherst College-based literary review The Common, and the recipient of the

Rockefeller Foundation's Bellagio Fellowship for Artists and Writers for 2017.

Aoife Casby's short fiction has been published in The Dublin Review, The Stinging Fly, Banshee, 'Noir by Noir-West' (Arlen House), Ropes, The Cúirt Annual, Whispers and Shouts, West47, Criterion, The Cork Literary Review, Divas anthology (Arlen House). She was the winner of The Doolin Short Story Prize 2017 and has been long listed for the Seán Ó Faoláin Short Story Award and the Fish Short Story Prize. She has been awarded literature bursaries from the Irish Arts Council and Galway County Council. She is completing a PhD at Goldsmith's University, London.

Fergus Cronin is a native of Dublin. He has had a variety of occupations ranging from water engineering to theatre. In 2004 he moved to north Connemara in Galway. He now divides his time between Dublin and the West. He completed an MPhil degree in Creative Writing at the Oscar Wilde Centre in TCD in 2014. His stories have been published in *Surge*, a Brandon Books collection of new writing from Ireland, in *The Old Art of Lying*, (an anthology of work from the Oscar Wilde Centre), the Manchester Review and the Irish Times.

Tony Curtis is Emeritus Professor of Poetry at the University of South Wales where he ran the Writing M..Phil. He has several current projects including the editing and production for an anthology to support the Ty Hafan children's hospice charity – *Where the Birds Sing our Names*; also the tour of his talk on the Second World War "Poets, Pacifists, Painters and my Parents: Wales and the Second World War" which he is presenting at the north American Welsh Societies Conference in Philadelphia in September 2019 and later at the National Library of Wales and the National Museum of Wales.

Gerald Dawe's new poetry collection, *The Last Peacock* is published in autumn by The Gallery Press. *In Another World: Van Morrison and Belfast* was published by Merrion Press in 2017; a sequel *Looking through You:*

Northern Chronicles will appear from Merrion next year.

Glyn Edwards' first collection *Vertebrae* is published by the Lonely Press. He has co-edited 'Cheval', the annual Parthian anthology of the Terry Hetherington Award for Welsh young writers, and been Guest Poetry Editor for the Lonely Crowd. Glyn has been the poet in residence at the Chester Literature Festival and the Dylan Thomas' Boathouse, and has had writing published by Verve Press and The Guardian. Glyn's poetry has featured in a Poetry Jukebox installation, used as libretto in Manchester, and has been translated into Welsh and Greek. Glyn has an MA in Creative Writing (Poetry) from MMU and he works as a teacher in North Wales.

Thoraya El-Rayyes is a writer, literary translator and political sociologist based between London and Amman. Her English language translations of contemporary Arabic literature have won several awards, and have appeared in publications including The Kenyon Review, Black Warrior Review, and World Literature Today.

Martina Evans grew up in County Cork and trained in Dublin as a radiographer before moving to London in 1988. She is the author of eleven books of poetry and prose, including *Now We Can Talk Openly About Men.*

P.C. Evans is an Amsterdam-based Welsh poet, writer and literary translator.
His latest collection is the pamphlet *Cadaver Dog Cantos* (KFS, 2017). His next collection, *Grand Larcenies* will be published by Carcanet in 2021.

Mike Fox's stories have appeared in journals in Britain, Ireland, America, Australia and Singapore. His story *Breath* (Fictive Dream), and *Blurred Edges* (Lunate Fiction), gained Pushcart Prize nomination. His story *The Homing Instinct* (Confingo), was included in *Best British Short Stories 2018* (Salt). His story *The Fun Police* (Fictive Dream) was listed in Best British and Irish Flash Fiction (BIFFY50) 2019-2020. His story, *The Violet Eye*, was published by Nightjar Press as a limited-edition chapbook.

Jonathan Gibbs is the author of *Randall* (Galley Beggar Press) and *The Large Door* (Boiler House). His short stories have been anthologised in *Best British Short Stories* 2014 and 2015, and shortlisted for the inaugural White Review Short Story Prize, and he curates the online short story project A Personal Anthology, in which a weekly guest picks and introduces a dozen favourite stories. He teaches creative writing at City, University of London.

Angela Graham is a Welsh-speaking film maker and writer from Belfast. Her poetry has appeared in *The North, The Honest Ulsterman, Poetry Wales, The Ogham Stone, The Open Ear, The Bangor Literary Journal, The Interpreter's House, CAP 2020 Anthology* and elsewhere. Her short story 'Above It All' is in #10 of *The Lonely Crowd*. Her story collection *A City Burning,* completed with a Bursary from Literature Wales, is due from Seren Books this autumn. She has written a novel on the politics of language in Northern Ireland and is currently doing a poetry and prose project there on Place and Displacement. For both of these she gratefully acknowledges the support of the National Lottery through the Arts Council of Northern Ireland.

John Goodby is Professor of Arts and Culture at Sheffield Hallam University. He is a poet, critic, and translator, and an authority on Dylan Thomas, whose *Collected Poems* he edited in 2014. His poetry books include *Illennium* (Shearsman, 2010) and *The No Breath* (Red Ceilings, 2017), and he has published translations of Soleiman Adel Guemar (with Tom Cheesman), Heine, Pasolini and Reverdy. With Lyndon Davies he ran the Hay Poetry Jamborees 2009-12 and edited the anthology *The Edge of Necessary: innovative Welsh poetry 1966-2018* (Aquifer, 2018). His edition of the lost fifth notebook of Dylan Thomas, edited with Ade Osbourne, has just been published by Bloomsbury.

Jackie Gorman is from the Irish midlands and her first collection *The Wounded Stork* was published by The Onslaught Press, UK in May

2019. In 2017, she won the Listowel Writers' Week Single Poem Award and was commended in the Bord Gais Energy Irish Book Awards Poem of the Year Award. She has recently completed a Masters in Poetry Studies at Dublin City University and has had work published in Poetry Ireland Review, The Lonely Crowd and The Honest Ulsterman among other journals in the past.

Lisa Harding is an actress, playwright and writer. Short stories have been widely published and anthologised in the Dublin Review and Kevin Barry's Winter Papers, among others. Her first novel, *Harvesting* was chosen as an Irish Times book club of the month in 2018, was awarded the Kate O'Brien Award and shortlisted for best newcomer at the Irish Book Awards and the Kerry group Irish Novel of the Year award. Her second novel, Bright Burning things is to be published by Bloomsbury in March 21 and Harper Collins US in 2022. She is currently writing the screen adaptation for *Harvesting* in development with the BFI and working on her third novel.

Jake Hawkey was born in London, studied Fine Art at the University of Westminster and MA Poetry at the Seamus Heaney Centre, Queen's University Belfast. His poems have been published by Live Canon and The Honest Ulsterman. Jake was the inaugural intern at The River Mill Writers' Retreat, Co. Down and is currently a poetry PhD candidate at Queen's.

Claire Hennessy is a writer, editor and creative writing facilitator from Dublin.

Lauren Mackenzie was born in Sydney, lives in Dublin, and has an MA in Creative Writing from UCD. She was shortlisted for the 2018 Cuirt New Writing Prize and Hennessy New Irish Writing. She has been published in *The Irish Times, The Moth, Banshee, The Honest Ulsterman* and *Skylight 47*. Last year she was awarded Literature and Travel bursaries by the Arts Council of Ireland for a collection of linked short stories called *That Sky That Sky*.

Niamh MacCabe is an award-winning writer and visual artist, with experience as collaborator and director on many multi-disciplinary art projects. She is published in over forty literary journals and anthologies in Ireland, the U.K., and the U.S. She lives with her sons in rural Leitrim, Ireland.

Eamon McGuinness is from Dublin, Ireland. His fiction has appeared in The Stinging Fly. He has won the Michael McLaverty, Wild Atlantic Words and Maria Edgeworth short story competitions. He holds an M.A in Creative Writing from University College Dublin.

Catherine McNamara grew up in Sydney, ran away to Paris at twenty-one to write, and ended up in West Africa running an art gallery and bar. She is the author of the short story collections *The Cartography of Others* and *Pelt and Other Stories*, and her flash fiction collection *Love Stories for Hectic People* will be published in February 2021. Catherine lives in Italy and loves shoes, West African art, classical piano, hiking.

Laura Morris is an English teacher, living in Caerphilly. She has an MA in Creative Writing from the University of Wales, Bangor.

Mary Morrissy is the author of three novels, *Mother of Pearl*, *The Pretender* and *The Rising of Bella Casey* and two collections of stories, *A Lazy Eye*, and most recently, *Prosperity Drive*. Her work has won her the Hennessy Prize and a Lannan Foundation Award. She has just completed a speculative novel, *Penelope Unbound*, about Nora Barnacle.
    A member of Aosdána, Ireland's academy of artists, she is a journalist and teacher of creative writing and was until recently the Associate Director of Creative Writing at University College Cork. She now offers literary mentoring online, see The Deadline Desk on https://marymorrissy.com/

Fiona O'Connor is a former Hennessy Short Story Award Prize winner. She contributes to *The Irish Times* Books Section, writes features for *Byline Times* and *The Morning Star*. Her stories have been included in anthologies: *The Stinging Fly, Fiction International, Crannog, Honest Ulsterman, The Wrong Quarterly* and *The Lonely Crowd*. She lectures in Psychology at the University of Westminster, London.

Nuala O'Connor lives in Co. Galway, Ireland. Her forthcoming fifth novel, *NORA*, is about Nora Barnacle, wife and muse to James Joyce. Her new chapbook of historical flash fiction, *Birdie*, is just published by Arlen House. Nuala is editor at flash e-zine *Splonk*.

Fiona O'Rourke lives and writes in Dublin, Larne, and Wexford. Her stories have been included in the Fish Anthology, Francis MacManus, Troquel Revista de Letras, The Broken Spiral, Spontaneity, Sonder, Shaped By The Sea, and her debut novel was a joint winner at the Irish Writers Centre Novel Fair 2016. She holds the M.Phil. in Creative Writing from Trinity College Dublin

Stephen Payne is Professor (Emeritus) at the University of Bath. He lives with his family in Penarth, South Glamorgan. His pamphlet *The Probabilities of Balance*, was published by Smiths Knoll in 2010. His first full collection, *Pattern Beyond Chance*, was published in 2015, by Happen*Stance* Press, and shortlisted for Wales Book of the Year.

Marcella Prince grew up in Wisconsin. Her poems appear in *The Tangerine* and *The Open Ear* and others. She is a 2019 winner of the Ireland Chair of Poetry Student award and is currently studying at Queen's University Belfast for a PhD with a focus on Midwestern-American poetry.

Tracey Rhys' first pamphlet, *Teaching a Bird to Sing* (Green Bottle Press, 2016) was longlisted for the Michael Marks Award in 2017. Her poetry has been exhibited at The Senedd and has been integrated into two stage plays for Winterlight/Company of Sirens. Examples of her work can be found in Planet, New Welsh Review, The Lonely Crowd, the anthologies *Poems from the Borders* (Seren) and *Bloody Amazing!* (Yaffle Press).

Ethel Rohan was raised in Dublin and lives in San Francisco. 'Unwanted' is included in her forthcoming collection *In the Event of Contact* (May, 2021) which won the 2019 Dzanc Short Story Collection Prize.

Deirdre Shanahan published a collection of stories, *Carrying Fire and Water*, with Splice Books in 2020. Her first novel, *Caravan of he Lost and Left Behind*, came out from Bluemoose Books in 2019. Her work was included in *The Best of British Short Stories* 2017 from Salt. She has been awarded a bursary from Arts Council England, won an Eric Gregory Award from the Society of Authors and held a residency at the Heinrich Boll Cottage, Ireland.

Matthew M. C. Smith is a Welsh poet. He was nominated for 'Best of the Net' by Icefloe Press in 2020. He is published in Finished Creatures, barren Magazine, Anti-Heroin Chic and Fly on the Wall Press. Matthew is the editor of Black Bough poetry and edited 'Deep Time' 1 and 2 in 2020.

Richard Smyth is a writer and critic. His work appears regularly in the *Guardian*, the *Times Literary Supplement* and the *New Statesman*, and he is the author of the non-fiction books *A Sweet, Wild Note* (Elliott & Thompson, 2017) and *An Indifference of Birds* (Uniformbooks, 2020). His novel *The Woodcock* was published by Fairlight Books in May 2020.

Breda Spaight's debut chapbook *The Untimely Death of My Mother's Hens* is published by Southword Editions, in their New Irish Voices series. She is the 2020 winner of the Doolin Poetry Prize. Her poems have appeared in *Poetry Ireland Review, Southword, Ambit, Aesthetica, The Stinging Fly*, and others. She holds an M.Phil in creative writing, Trinity College, Dublin.

Laura Wainwright is from Newport, Wales. Her poems have been published in a range of magazines, journals and anthologies. She has been shortlisted in the Bridport Prize poetry competition twice and awarded a Literature Wales Writer's bursary in 2020 for her poetry. She is also the author of the literary-critical book, *New Territories in Modernism: Anglophone Welsh Writing 1930-1949* (University of Wales Press, 2018).

About the Editor

John Lavin has a doctorate from the University of Wales, Trinity Saint David, as well as an MA in Creative Writing from Cardiff University. The former Fiction Editor of Wales Arts Review, he edited their short story anthology, *A Fiction Map of Wales*, as well as their acclaimed online series, *Story: Retold*. His criticism has appeared in The Irish Times, Wales Arts Review, The Lampeter Review, The Cardiff Review and The Welsh Agenda.